MAKE ME DREAM

THE SAGE CREEK SERIES - BOOK ONE

DILLON BANCROFT

This book is a work of fiction. Names, characters, businesses, organizations, places, events, and incidents either are the product of the author's imagination or are used fictitiously. Any resemblance to actual persons, living or dead, events, or locales is entirely coincidental.

For information contact:

Dillon Bancroft

PO Box 1181

Wimauma, FL 33598

http://www.dillonbancroft.com

Book and cover design by © The Pretty Little Design Co.

Editing by: Amy Briggs, Briggs Consulting, LLC.

Ebook ISBN: 978-1-7369012-2-9

Paperback ISBN: 978-1-7369012-3-6

First Edition: January 2022

10 9 8 7 6 5 4 3 2 1

To my sisters. I see you. I hear you. I stand with you.

LOOKING TO CONNECT?

Do you want to stay in the know and receive behind the scenes musings, deleted scenes, and upcoming project updates? Make sure to sign up for my newsletter and follow me on social media!

Email: dillon@dillonbancroft.com

LinkTree: https://linktr.ee/dillon.bancroft

Website: www.dillonbancroft.com

Bancroft Boulevard Facebook Group: https://www.facebook.com/groups/bancroftblvd

AUTHOR'S NOTE

While Make Me Dream is a contemporary romance, Aria has suffered a horrifying past in an abusive relationship in which she speaks about with a therapist, and with Derek. Because of this, I urge you not to read this book if domestic violence and graphic violence is triggering for you.

For a list of triggers, please visit the list in its entirety at www.dillonbancroft.com/mmd-trigger-warnings

PROLOGUE

DEREK

The night is clear and brisk. A blanket of stars shines brightly in the desert while I exhale nicotine into the air. It's a nasty habit, I know, but when you're in the midst of a shady kidnapping of the man who killed your sister-from-another-mister, people tend to be more understanding.

And by people, I mean my brothers.

In the eyes of the United States, I'm an only child, but when you join the military, bonds are formed. Most of the time, those bonds are stronger than the ones you have with your own blood. Which is why I'm about to help kill a man and destroy the evidence.

We're not bad people. The person who's about to be wailing into the night is a bad person. Johnathan Rockwell. The seller of innocent women and children.

The door to the shack slams closed, and a familiar presence stands beside me. I hand him a cigarette and my lighter which he takes gratefully and lights up beside me.

"Are you ready for this, Barnes?"

Logan Barnes, one of my "brothers" is the victim in all of this. He knows what he has to do even though he knows it won't bring the love of his life back.

"Ready as I'll ever be," he murmurs. The cloudy smoke he exhales into the air is the nerves leaving his body. The law didn't serve justice for Heidi but we sure will. "Novak has an eye on the area. Once that shack is up in flames, nobody will come looking."

The door slams again, and another bulky figure joins our posse. Nate Olson trudges toward us.

"Archer's getting ready to wake him up. Almost done?"

Showing Olson the nub I have left, I put it out on my boot and shove the butt in my pocket, leaving no evidence of our involvement. Barnes takes one more drag and does the same.

"Are you all right, brother?" Olson asks.

"If someone dropped Eve dead on your doorstep, would you be all right?" Logan demands.

The tension in the air is thick. The peace that flitted in the air is now gone and hostility takes over. This is hard.

Life is one of those precious things. The whole point is to live a good one and be a decent human being. But when someone you love's life is stripped away without any warning, the need to exact revenge permeates every aspect of your being. For Barnes, it's the only thing that's kept him going for this long.

Heidi has been dead a year. We've been on the hunt for Rockwell for two. And now, that waste of life is sitting bound to a chair inside a one room shack, unconscious, and about to face the longest night of his life.

"Come on, man. Don't bring her into this," Olson pleads.

Barnes shrugs indifferently and shoulder barges Olson on the way back into the shack.

"You good, Hawthorn?" Olson asks.

"All aces, buddy. Shall we begin?"

A smirk crosses Olson's lips and he tilts his head towards the door. I follow him into the dimly lit shack where Johnathan Rockwell sits, slumped, and his head lolling to the side. It's a crowded room with all of us inside. Archer, Novak, Delgado, Barnes, Olson, and myself…plus Rockwell.

Joey Archer opens a small vile of ammonia and places it under Rockwell's nose. Jolting slightly, he looks around the room, until his eyes land on Barnes.

"How the *fuck* did you find me?!" he demands.

"You're not as slick as you think you are," Tanner Novak answers nonchalantly, a Cheshire smile beaming at the sick bastard before us. "Took me a while to figure out where you were hiding, but I found you. I leaked *all* of your data to the world, so your prissy parents will know how much of a disappointment you were, and now, so will the rest of the world."

Rockwell's swollen eyes widen.

"Why do *you* even care? She wasn't yours, she was *his,"* he snaps, looking at Barnes.

"Because she was our sister, you stupid waste of life!" Archer shouts, punching his right eye.

Rockwell scans the room for a weak link, for an ally. He won't get one. What he's done is too painful.

"She was nice and tight. I got to have her one last time before I ended her." He wheezes when he laughs, gasping for air that won't be there for him when this is all over. Without even a single beat, Barnes cocks the handgun in his hand and fires a shot right through Rockwell's right thigh. His screams echo through the shack.

I get pleasure knowing nobody will hear him.

"You are a *child,"* Barnes seethes. "She tried to see the best in you, but you couldn't take no for an answer. Have you ever been told 'no' before, Johnny? Did it hurt your fragile ego when she agreed to marry me?"

Rockwell growls and tries to break his ropes.

"She was *promised* to me!"

"And yet, she said yes to me." Barnes smirks.

"My people will be looking for me."

His empty threats are laughable. We're the shadows in the night. Invisible to cameras and the guards we drugged.

"I doubt it," Barns retorts.

"If you're going to kill me, then do it already!" he screams.

"Buddy, we're just getting started," Archer says, the leader of the pack, inching dangerously closer to him. "You tortured and killed our sister. We're not letting you off so easily." Plunging his blade into Rockwell's other thigh, his screams once again fill the shack.

My turn.

"This is Bubba."

I cringe at Archer's nickname for me. He knows I hate it, but we're not giving away our identities. "Bubba's a vet, and, he's going to fix you up." His weary eyes meet mine, but there is no hope. I'm keeping him alive long enough to inflict maximum pain.

"In the service, I was a SARC, but you won't know what that is," I announce, grabbing my kit and opening a package of sterile gauze. I slam it down on the open wound while he growls in pain. "You see, SARC stands for Special Amphibious Reconnaissance Corpsman. I can dumb it down for you if you'd like."

"Fuck *off*!"

"It basically means I can save your life. I can take you away from the brink of death and have you walking within a day." *Lie.* "But you took something of ours. So, this is what I'm going to do. I'm going to keep bringing you back into the land of the living until Barnes has had enough. The sun comes up in four hours. By that time, you'll be dead and then we're going to set the place on fire. The whole world is going to be looking for you, but they'll never find you." I stitch up the knife wound, but I don't bother numbing him up.

Every prick of my needle has him squirming and screaming. I wish he'd stop only because the blood is getting in my way.

It won't matter, anyway. It'll reopen again, and I'll restitch it just so they can reopen the wound.

"I will find your family," he seethes. "What I did to Heidi will be child's play compared to what I'll do to your bitch!"

Smirking, I tug the stitching so tight his hoarse scream echoes again. "Then it's a good thing I'm single and ready to mingle, buddy."

The door of the shack flies open, and the man who could end us with one keystroke enters with narrowed eyes and balled fists. His salt and pepper hair is only cosmetic, because even though he's over sixty, he's a force to be reckoned with. Stephen McKenzie is more fatal than we are all put together.

He storms through the shack and pushes Rockwell's chair back, so the chair is only standing on two legs and his hair is barely an inch away from the roaring fire behind him. His hand clamps tightly around his throat while Rockwell screams at him to stop, along with more choice words.

"You're going to tell me everything you know about Charles Franklin Dodge III."

Recognition crosses Rockwell's prim features. His dark eyes finally lighten. And whether he's laughing out of hysteria, or if he finds this fucking hilarious, it's all unsettling.

"He has one of yours, doesn't he?"

1

ARIA

If there's anything I learned about being the youngest of three children, it was to be light on my feet. While my sister was constantly getting caught for *trying* to sneak out, I learned from her mistakes. I knew which stairs were creaky, and which floorboards upstairs would groan under my weight.

I knew the window in the hallway next to my brother's room was silent when you opened it—probably because he fixed it up so he could sneak girls into his room without our parents ever catching on.

So I would know when to walk on eggshells in this vast, sterile, and luxurious apartment while my *warden* works silently on the island in our kitchen, to avoid the beating of my life.

That's what happened last night.

He took a phone call in the bedroom. I didn't know he was on the phone. I was telling him dinner was ready. I interrupted *the* phone call to the whale of a client his family has been trying to lock down for years.

He held me against the stove while the burners singed the skin on my back.

I can't see the burns. Even using a mirror, I can't look at them. It sends a wave of bile up my throat—that I let it get this bad. I allowed him to push me in a corner and strip my freedom away.

He says he loves me. Then he says I'm disgusting and useless. I'm the biggest disappointment to him, yet he won't let me go.

Why won't he let me go?

"Does your face hurt?" His baritone voice breaks through the silence of the room. I'm afraid to answer. I'm afraid *not* to answer.

"No." My clipped answer forces his blond head to snap up and glare at me with his icy, cutting eyes at the insubordinance.

It happens so fast I don't think it fully registers in my mind. It's like a record scratch or a car accident happening in real time.

The barstool scrapes against the marble floors and his long strides reach me before I can even dart the other way. His large hand wraps around my throat and he pins me against the refrigerator.

This is a typical Friday.

I *hate* when he works from home.

"Are you forgetting something?"

"Sir," I add quickly. "No, sir. I'm sorry." As much as I try to sound sincere, I can't. I'm sick of this.

I've been praying for death for months. Living with Charles Franklin Dodge III was supposed to be a fairy tale. I was supposed to be whisked away to a man who loved me, farm girl blood and all. Instead, I was bamboozled into a solitary life. A life where I have to wonder if today's the day he snuffs my life out like the rest of the women he got close to.

"Was last night not lesson enough?"

I gasp for air, but I can't get enough of it. Black dots swirl in my vision as the grip on my airway gets tighter. I beat against his forearm to no avail.

"I-I'm s-s-sorry—"

"Enough with the apologies!" He cocks his fist back and punches me directly in the bruised eye from yesterday. He releases his grip and I slump to the floor, coughing and gagging. "I don't like hurting you, Aria. Why do you make me hurt you?"

I don't make you do anything, jackass.

The front door is busted open, and suddenly dozens of men in black swarm the apartment. Silver handcuffs are slapped around Charlie's wrists.

"What is the meaning of this?" he shouts. One agent reads him his Miranda rights. Other agents start processing the scene. Meanwhile, I'm left in the middle of the kitchen like chopped liver.

"Charles Dodge, you are under arrest for embezzlement, extortion, domestic battery..." the agent's voice trails off as Charlie is walked out of the apartment.

"Are you okay?" A figure sinks down next to me and carefully takes my face in his hands, looking for any signs of cuts.

"Just dandy," I reply darkly. The man I've only met twice, Agent O, stares at me with concern. If I wasn't swearing off relationships forever, I'd probably make a pass at him. He's pretty. Sandy blonde hair styled smart, Disney Princess green eyes, and a jaw that could crack a nut. Charlie was pretty too. I've learned my lesson. Romance and relationships are not in the cards for me.

"You should see a doctor before we leave."

Over my dead body.

"Absolutely not. The faster we get on the road, the better chance I have at surviving." When I've finally caught my breath, I shakily stand up. My legs feel like Jell-O. Agent O steadies me by placing his hands on my shoulders.

"Are you sure? Maybe we should talk about going into witness protection again—"

"Are you a trust fund baby, Agent O? Is your family wealthy beyond belief? Is this god forsaken city in your family's pockets?"

He sighs in impatience. "No. I'm not."

"Charlie is. All it takes is one fat stack of cash and someone swings to the other team. I need to go home." *If they'll even have me.*

I haven't spoken to my family in over a year. My daddy warned me about Charlie, but I knew better.

Agents and crime scene techs swarm my home. Someone seizes the laptop he was working on, and more enter our bedroom to find God knows what.

"Let's step outside at least. You don't need to watch this."

But I *want* to. I want to watch Charlie fry for everything he's ever done.

Regardless, I grab the suitcase I packed while Charlie was sleeping last night from the entryway closet and follow Agent O into the crowded hallway. Our neighbors watch from beyond the yellow tape, gossiping about what's happening.

Screw them! They've heard my pleas for help for a year and did nothing. No cops called, no good Samaritan knocking down the door.

"You're sure he didn't delete anything?" Olson asks.

"Pretty sure. He didn't waste any time getting up when I defied him."

All the evidence is on the laptop. He squeezes my shoulder in reassurance.

"This is the last time you'll see him before the trial. You've got a brand new lease on life, Aria. You can put this behind you."

I meet his eyes and frown.

"I can't put this behind me," I murmur. "When I close my eyes, I see him. I feel him crushing my throat, holding me against the stove. Forcing me to..." *pleasure him.* I take a deep breath. "You don't know him like I do. You don't know *them* like I do. I'm living on borrowed time. Charlie and his father will make me pay for this."

My heart still hammers in my chest when we step off the elevator and make our way into the crowded street where the paparazzi snap pictures and bark questions at me. My gaze instinctually looks up to the windows surrounding me for snipers...something Charlie's threatened me with for the last year.

Agent O helps me into the front seat of the black SUV and shuts the door behind me.

"You've got me," he says, settling into the driver's seat. "I've been hunting this family since I joined the bureau. I'm not resting until the Dodges are behind bars. I'll protect you; I promise."

Promises, promises.

It's a thirteen hour drive from Chicago to Sage Creek. Agent O and I avoid sit down restaurants at all costs. Lucky for me, he loaded up on snacks and drinks before they raided the apartment. My stomach swirls with nausea and hunger by the time we make it into Sage Creek. We're forty minutes from home. Forty minutes to find out if my parents are going to tell me to fuck right off and fend for myself.

"So, tell me about home. Who lives there?" he asks as we drive through the heart of downtown.

"My mother and father - Steve and Betty Lou, though you should address them as Mr. and Mrs. McKenzie. Then there's my older brother Chris, and my older sister Annie. We live on four hundred acres, so we have at least fifty people who board their horses with us."

"Anyone I should be briefed on?"

Someone from Sage Creek? No. We're a small town, and even though I don't have the best reputation, they still wouldn't sell me out. Unless we're talking about the Parkers.

"No, I don't think so. You could probably ask my dad about a contact list."

Adrenaline pumps through my veins as we turn onto the country road that brings us to the middle of the property—fifteen miles from town.

"Anyone else living on the property?"

"No, not for a while. It's just the five of us."

"We'll have a meeting with your whole family, but I want to talk to you about what to expect. Are you up for it?"

Unfortunately, yes. I'm essentially moving from one warden to the next.

"Sure." I rest my forehead on the cool glass of the window and watch the rolling hills race past me.

"This is going to get invasive, Aria. I apologize in advance, but there isn't anything we can do about it. Charlie has already been bailed out and under strict instruction not to contact you. Regardless, we're tracing your calls and text messages. I'm going to become your shadow. If you're going into town, I won't be far behind."

"K."

He heaves an exasperated sigh.

"This is serious."

It doesn't matter. He'll find me either way.

"I know."

He presses his lips in a hard line and drums his fingers on the steering wheel.

The driveway to the main house comes into view fifteen minutes later. The mile long driveway brings back so many memories. I brought Charlie down this road. He didn't appreciate it the same way I did. He begged me to turn around as soon as the paved road transformed into a gravel road. It was the beginning of what was to come. He wasn't abusive then. But the day after...

Momma's truck sits in the driveway. Agent O parks next to it and throws the SUV in park. We stare at my childhood house. He's probably thinking he won't see civilization for months. For me, well, I don't know what lies beyond the front door.

"There's always witness protection," he says teasingly. I crack a small smile and roll my eyes.

"Let's go."

He grabs my suitcase and I lead him to the front door. I hesitantly ring the doorbell. I'm not just going to walk in. I would scare the shit out of them, and they might shoot me.

The door swings open, revealing the most beautiful sight in the world. My sister, my opposite in looks and personality, stands just inches in front of me. So close to throwing my arms around her, yet so far because I cut her out of my life.

Her eyes sweep over Agent O, and then fall on me.

"Peanut?" Her bottom lip wobbles and pulls me into the biggest hug I've ever had. She sobs into my hair. "Oh my God. I thought we lost you. What happened to you?" My own tears soak the sleeve of her shirt.

"I'm so sorry," I sob. I spent a year away, wishing I'd never left. That I could take it all back and stay put. I've hurt more people than myself it turns out.

"No, don't be sorry. Holy shit. I've missed you so much." She pulls away and stares deep into my eyes. Her eyes are Momma's; kind, forgiving, and happy.

"It's a long story. Um. This is Agent O. He needs to talk to everyone."

Annie freezes.

"Oh...okay. Can you stay for dinner Agent O?"

He nods and flashes her a flirty smile. "Sure."

Annie steps aside to let us in.

Time has stood still in this house. It's like I'd never left. The family room is still plastered with pictures of all of us—including our honorary brother Jay, and my best friend—*if she still is my best friend*—Jackie.

I've disappointed so many people in a short period of time. Annie leads us into the kitchen where Momma is doing dishes at the sink. My heart pulses in my ears. Will she have me? Will I be able to hug my momma again?

"Who was at the door, sweet pea?"

Tears fill my eyes at my momma's voice. For the last year, I've craved to hear her voice, to tell me everything is going to be okay.

Pot roast wafts through the air, making my already nauseous stomach growl. Momma places her wash rag behind the faucet and slowly turns around.

Her eyes immediately water. I should've put on some makeup before I left. I should've been more considerate. What mother wants to see her child like this?

"Baby?" Her voice cracks. She approaches me timidly, her warm, wet hands cradling my face, gently tracing my bruise. It's like she's trying to make absolutely sure I'm me.

"Hi, Momma."

She cries out and throws her arms around me. "I'm so sorry, Momma. I'm so sorry."

"I know, baby. You have nothing to be sorry for. Do you know how much I love you?"

Look at you! Your parents are so disgusted by you too! Do you honestly think they're going to take you back after you ignored your father?

I banish Charlie's voice from my mind as my mother strokes my hair. Annie, tired of being left out joins our embrace. We're a sobbing mess.

"Who is this?" Momma asks.

I back up and turn to Agent O.

"This is Agent O with the FBI. It's a long story, Momma. We'll talk about it over dinner." Where I can watch my father tear me apart. "Where's Daddy?"

"Finishing up evening feed with your brother..." I'd love for my father's first reaction to be with just me. I've suffered through enough humiliation already.

"I'm going to go find him."

"Baby, please, wait for him to come inside. I just got you back. Let me love on you a little bit longer."

The thing is, she knows Daddy as well as I do. I ignored him when he begged me to leave Charlie. This won't be a warm welcome. This might be the beginning of World War III.

"I have to get this out of the way, Momma. The anticipation is killing me."

Annie shifts uncomfortably. "Let me come with you."

"I need to do this alone." I glance to Agent O to drive my point home. *"Alone."*

"Aria, we talked about this," he warns.

"It's my dad and my brother down there. There are no threats." I don't give him any time to protest. I give him a confident smile and storm through the house and out the front door, down the cobblestone path.

My flip flops crunch the grass with each hurried step. It'll be more fuel to the fire when I meet him face to face. He'll berate me for wearing open toed shoes to the barn, but I've lived here all my life and I know how to get around a horse without them stepping on me.

The old me would've welcomed the darkness, but now...there are too many monsters.

I cross through our makeshift neighborhood, which consists of four houses. I avoid the house my father built for me to stay in, because there are too many horrible memories surrounding it. Shoving my hands in the pockets of my jeans, I hurry down the grassy hill and head toward the only barn that's lit up.

I hope I catch him before he heads up to the house.

Horses in the field ignore me and graze without paying me any mind. Barn number three, the barn exclusively housing our horses is the only barn with the lights on. When I step into the empty breezeway, my heart aches at what I left behind.

I thought I knew it all. But *they* don't judge.

A hoof pawing impatiently against the concrete grabs my attention. I pick up the pace and find my best gal on the crossties.

"Hi, gorgeous." I creep closer to her and rest my head on hers. "I missed you." My mare is sassy. Everyone else calls her a psycho, but I know better. She's the best horse around, and she has character.

Her soft mane slips through my fingers. She relaxes at my touch and leans against me.

"I'm sorry for leaving."

"You can't be here without a waiver." The voice from behind me sends me a mile in the air. I spin to face the unfamiliar voice behind me.

Intense, cutting, icy blue eyes stare angrily at me, like *I* did something wrong. But then he sees what everyone else sees.

"Did you run away from somewhere? Do you need to call the police?"

I slowly back up to create as much space as I can between us.

"I already talked to the police."

He doesn't need to know about the FBI agent who is up the hill.

He has this Prince Eric thing about him, just less…nice. His wavy black hair is disheveled, like someone was running their fingers through it minutes ago. He doesn't smile though, I think if he did, it would be terrifying.

"And?"

Well excuse the fuck out of you!

"It's taken care of."

He sighs and places his bag in the lawn chair next to Coley. My skin crawls as he looks me up and down.

"Have you ever been to a barn before?" he asks condescendingly.

He doesn't know who I am. Which can either be a curse or a blessing.

"Let me give you your first lesson. You can't wear fucking flip flops. See these?" He picks up Coley's foot and traces the front of her hoof. "All she'd have to do is take one step and she'd break your toes."

Thank you for mansplaining that to me, jerk.

Yet, my eyebrow arches as high as it'll go—the *only* trait I inherited from my mother.

"Go up to the main house. Ask for Betty Lou. She can get you set up with whatever you need. If you want to come back down here, you need to sign a waiver and wear some boots."

My silence fuels his anger. I don't care. He doesn't scare me. I'm not here for him anyway. And I'm not moving just because he told me to. I'm past that life now. This is my new beginning—for however long it might last.

"Okay, you're not going to listen. Cool. Steve should be here any minute. He can take care of you. Stay out of the way. This one is a psycho."

Anger pools in my belly. All women have to be psycho, eh?

"She's not a psycho. She's misunderstood."

He chuckles poisonously and starts tracing the planes of her back.

"She's a psycho. I know plenty of mares like this. This one kicked out a whole panel of fencing because the golf cart with her food on it wasn't moving fast enough."

That's my girl.

"Doesn't make her psycho."

"You're right. It doesn't. But almost killing a rodeo clown does."

It was an accident and not her fault!

"Clear that pasture out before anyone else figures out there's no fencing. We'll fix it tomorrow."

My body locks at the sound of my father's voice at the other end of the barn. The grouch watches me with a smirk. He thinks I'm gonna get it.

He isn't wrong.

Chris and Daddy talk to each other so intensely they don't even notice me standing here. Daddy stops in front of Coley and talks to the grouch and points at me.

It's a weird thing. My father and I have this telepathic way of communication. Not literally, but the way he's looking at me now, I know I'm in for a world of hurt.

"Holy shit, Peanut! What the hell did he do to you?" Without a beat,

Chris shoves the lead rope into my father's hands and envelopes me in a tight hug.

My burns singe at the contact, causing my eyes to water.

"I'm sorry." It doesn't matter how many times I say it. It won't ever be enough. "I'm so sorry."

"Aria." My father's voice is like a spell. It breaks Chris off me so quickly it's like he wasn't even there. He hands the lead rope back to Chris and steps toward me. I shrink under his angry stare. I wrap my arms around my father before he can lay into me in front of everyone.

"I'm so sorry, Daddy."

"How long?"

Slowly backing up, I can't seem to find my words. Chris stares at Daddy like he's crazy, like he has no idea what he's talking about.

"A year."

His hazel eyes, the ones only I inherited, fill with rage, and then glance at the grouch behind him. Who is this guy?

"And you escaped? Just like that?"

"No...I contacted the FBI. There was already an investigation opened. I was able to give them evidence and they arrested him this morning—"

"And when he makes bail?" His voice steadily rises higher. He's pissed. He's more pissed I'm bringing danger to his front door. He already made bail.

"Look, there's an FBI agent up at the house. He wants to talk to all of you, but he's going to be around for a while."

"What is it I always told you and your sister? *If you want to be strong, learn how to fight alone.*"

Which is why he took us shooting every weekend. He pawned it off as female empowerment. Maybe it was. It obviously didn't work for me.

"You relied on that *ass* to take care of you, and yet he beat you to hell, now you're relying on the *fucking* FBI to clean up your mess!"

I swallow my tears. I refuse to cry in front of him. Doesn't he realize I *already* am beating myself up for all of this? His stupid quote has been running through my mind since Charlie decided he'd take corrective punishment into his own hands!

"I'm sorry, okay?" Like always, it's the wrong thing to say.

"It's time to sink or swim, kid. You've already squandered away your second chance at life. Don't squander your third." He angrily storms out of the barn, leaving me with my brother and the grouch.

"He doesn't mean it," Chris says softly. I love my idiot brother. The class clown, the heart breaker. But he's wrong.

"Yeah he does." I sink to the ground and pull my legs up to my chest. What Daddy doesn't know is my third chance at life is already squandered. The FBI will do everything they can, but the Dodge name holds more weight. They'll come in the dead of night and slit my throat and call it an accident. The whole world will believe him. I won't get the chance to live.

2

DEREK

Michelle collapses on top of me as I finish inside her. She pants, our sweaty bodies spent. She rolls over and pulls the comforter around her and turns on her side. She's gorgeous. She could be on the cover of *Vogue* or something, but I wish she would leave. I *need* to be alone.

Maybe I'm supposed to feel something, but I just…*don't.* I stare at the ceiling fan, wishing she would get the hint. I'm not subtle. My friends tell me I'm too direct and it hurts the feelings of the many.

I don't care.

Life's too short to play games and get up in arms about a simple miscommunication. Michelle knows what we're doing. No feelings, no attachments, and she shags ass when my daughter spends the weekend with me.

It's simple. Nobody gets confused, and Zoey doesn't get attached to a woman who won't love her.

"That was amazing," she sighs. I can't muster a single sound. I'm starving. I'd rather be eating dinner right now. "Derek?"

"Hmm?"

"I wanted to talk to you about something."

I spoke too soon. I reluctantly sit up and wait for her to drop *the* bomb.

"So, we've been doing this for a few months now..."

"Please don't beat around the bush. Come out and say it."

She drops her gaze. I wonder if she is going to regret the next words that fall out of her mouth. I know I will.

"I, um...I know we said no attachments, but, I have real feelings for you. Like, butterflies in the gut, sick whenever I see you around town..."

This is where I get stuck. I've been labeled a heart breaker, Sage Creek's very own playboy. Those were the words of the town gossip, Bethany Hunt anyway. This is why I *must* be too direct. Feelings fuck everything up.

"Stop."

She freezes, her eyes watering. Great. Now I have to kick her out of my house, and she'll cry all the way home.

"You're a nice girl, Michelle, but I was serious when I told you I don't have any room in my life for attachments. I can't do feelings. I *won't* do feelings."

"That's bullshit." She stands up and gathers her clothes. "You told me about Zoey and Emily."

"It was a mistake. I'm sorry, honestly. But I'm not a guy you can change. I'm never going to want anything more."

She rips the alarm clock out of the wall and chucks it in my direction. It smashes to pieces once it hits my closet door and shatters on the floor.

"You're thirty-six years old, Derek!" Her voice breaks. Did I miss the signs of her falling? Why didn't I end this sooner?

"Is the marriage thing what you're looking for? I already told you I can't do that."

"Shut up!" she shrieks, looking for more ammo. "Emily wasn't the love of your life, so what! Not all women are toxic like her!"

"Do you honestly think my preference on how I want to be with women is because Emily left me?" I stride closer to her and steady her hands, so she won't throw anything else at me. "I don't give a shit about Emily. I care about Zoey!"

Michelle stills at my confession.

This isn't Earth shattering news. My daughter will always come first. Always. I'm not going to spend my time with a woman who will pretend to love my daughter until the dotted line is signed. I can't do that to Zoey.

"A woman can love you *and* your daughter, Derek. It doesn't have to be one or the other."

Yes it does. In this town, yes. It absolutely does.

"It's not happening."

Sighing she drops her clothes on the bed and looks me in the eye.

My phone vibrates on my nightstand. I could kiss Stephen McKenzie for bailing me out.

"Hey, Steve."

"Coley broke out of the front pasture. Took out a whole panel of fencing. You think you can take a look at her?"

"Yeah. I'll be right there." I hang up and reach for my underwear on the floor. Michelle angrily crosses her arms and huffs.

"We're having a conversation. You can't leave in the middle of it!"

"This wasn't ever up for discussion!"

She scoffs and whips her clothes on at the speed of life.

"Lose my number, Derek. Don't seek me out. Don't call me, text me, talk about me. I never want to see you again!"

I give her a five minute head start before I start my trek to the barn.

What is it about the women in this town? Their mothers play matchmaker and practically pimp out their daughters any chance they get. There's nothing special about me. I'm a veterinarian. I work on animals because they don't talk back.

I'm a divorced man in the midst of an ugly custody battle for my ten year old daughter with my bitch of an ex-wife.

What woman in her right mind would *want* to get in the middle of a shitshow? If I'm not giving Zoey my full one hundred percent, then what's the point? My truck is parked out at the barn. Before I head inside, I grab my bag from the front seat.

Barn number three is the only barn lit up. I enter the barn from the middle breezeway and find Coley on the crossties with some chick hanging off her face.

"You can't be here without a waiver." I don't mean for it to come out as a bark, but it does.

She jumps and clutches at her chest.

Familiar hazel eyes stare back at me in pure, unadulterated fear. Who wanders to the middle of nowhere and hangs on a horse she doesn't know?

I study her face. *Damn.* Her left eye is nearly swollen shut. Dark bruises cover her face. I'm certain her right cheekbone is fractured. She stands flush against the stall behind her, creating as much space between us.

"Did you run away from somewhere? Do you need to call the police?" I don't like surprises. And I definitely don't appreciate the unwelcome danger that will inevitably show up here at any given moment.

She nervously glances down the aisle. "I already called the police." Great. Perfect. Now go away.

"And?"

"It's taken care of."

Plopping my bag down on the lawn chair next to Coley, I reluctantly stare down the beast before me. I've got my work cut out for me.

The women of this town are branded with a special kind of crazy.

I should've known when I married Emily.

The woman catalogs my every move, watching me like I'm some sort of predator.

If her face wasn't beat to hell, I bet she'd be a knockout. She wears a black T-shirt, and while it doesn't show anything *extra,* it's stretched out over her full breasts. The *Black Sabbath* lettering is cracked and worn. Denim covers her slim hips and her long legs and her feet—

Who the hell wears flip flops to a *barn?*

"Have you ever been to a barn before?" She doesn't answer, yet a hint of amusement touches her split lips. People like this ask to get hurt. They show no regard to simple safety measures and then sue like we didn't warn them. "Let me give you your first lesson; you can't wear *fucking* flip flops. See these?" I pick up Coley's leg and trace the front of her hoof. "All she'd have to do is take one step and she'd break your toes."

Her left eyebrow arches high.

Why does that look so familiar? Whatever. I don't have time for this. Betty Lou can take care of her better than I could anyway.

"Go up to the main house. Ask for Betty Lou. She can get you set up with everything you need. If you want to come back down here, you need to sign a waiver and wear some boots."

She stands stock still and watches me with contempt. I'm obviously not a nice guy. I'd never hurt her like she's been hurt, but I'm not nice. I'm not the guy people seek to cry about their sorry lives.

But does she *have* to stand there staring at me like I'm a big idiot?

"Okay, you're not going to listen. Cool. Steve should be here any minute. He can take care of you. Stay out of the way. This one is a psycho."

She furrows her brows when I turn around and start checking for any injuries on her back. This is Aria McKenzie's horse. She's the only McKenzie I haven't met. And while she's traipsing around Chicago and dating some rich guy, her horse is getting hurt. Steve doesn't want to admit it, but he hopes she comes back. So I'll make sure her horse is all right, because he changed my life for the better.

"She's not a psycho. She's misunderstood."

A chuckle escapes my lips. What does she know about Coley the psycho mare? This horse has been my ultimate cock block due to her Houdini acts.

"She's a psycho. I know plenty of mares like this. This one kicked out a whole panel of fencing because the golf cart with her food on it wasn't moving fast enough." The corners of her mouth quirk as I find the wound with the splinters sticking out of it on her back leg.

I heard once on a barrel race Aria was doing, Coley almost ran down a rodeo clown in the chute. That constitutes as psycho, right?

"You're right. It doesn't. But almost killing a rodeo clown does."

"Clear that pasture out before anyone else figures out there's no fencing. We'll fix it tomorrow." I breathe a sigh of relief when Steve's voice enters the barn. The woman locks her spine straight. The pulse in her neck ramps up and her chest rises and falls rapidly.

"Hey, she just walked in. Wouldn't give me any info." Steve turns and glances at the woman, doing a double take.

"Holy shit, Peanut! What the hell did he do to you?" Chris throws the lead rope into Steve's hands and envelopes the woman named "Peanut" in a tight hug.

"I'm sorry," she sobs. "I'm so sorry." Her eyes bore into Steve's, like they can communicate with just a glance.

"Aria."

Chris drops his embrace quickly and takes a reflexive step back.

Aria? *That's* Aria McKenzie?

She steps urgently forward, wrapping her arms around Steve's torso. "I'm so sorry, Daddy."

She looks *nothing* like her brother and sister.

"How long?"

"A year."

Steve stares at his daughter for a long beat before turning to me. He's going to fuck up the rich guy, and he's going to ask for my help.

"And you escaped? Just like that?"

"No…I contacted the FBI. There was already an investigation open. I was able to give them evidence and they arrested him this morning—

"And when he makes bail?"

Steve is an easy going guy. Not much gets him going. But I also know the secret life he hides from his family. It's a little unsettling seeing him go off on his abused and battered daughter.

He was afraid of never seeing her again. I'm afraid he's digging his hole deeper. If he keeps this up, she'll probably run.

"Look, there's an FBI agent up at the house. He wants to talk to all of you, but he's going to be around for a while."

"What is it I always told you and your sister? *If you want to be strong, learn how to fight alone.*"

The silence is deafening. Chris groans.

"You relied on that *ass* to take care of you, and yet, he beat you to hell. Now you're relying on the *fucking* FBI to clean up your mess!"

Aria's hazel eyes water, but the tears never fall. I wish he'd stop yelling at her.

If Zoey ever got herself in a situation like this, this isn't the approach I'd be taking.

"I'm sorry, okay?" she snaps. But it's the wrong thing to say, the wrong tone. Rage builds in Steve's stature. He balls his fists angrily and holds a staring contest with his daughter who doesn't allow him to walk all over her.

How'd she get into this situation anyway? Why didn't she leave sooner?

"It's time to sink or swim, kid. You've already squandered your second chance at life. Don't squander your third." She doesn't get another word in, because he's already storming through the barn, angrily latching open stalls.

Third chance at life? How does one get more than one?

"He doesn't mean it," Chris says softly. I've become obsolete. This isn't my fight. The FBI is involved, and I get the funny feeling danger is going to be knocking down my front door.

"Yeah, he does," she replies softly.

Chris offers her his hand and pulls her up.

"Let's go up to the house. At least you got that out of the way." Chris glances at me, and then to Aria. "Oh, Peanut, this is Dr. Derek Hawthorn. He's living in Jo's old house."

Aria's watery gaze meets mine. It wasn't nice to meet me, I know. I screwed the pooch on this one. I berated the boss's daughter, but in my defense, I didn't know who she was.

Aria sighs and starts towards the house.

"Chris, she needs a doctor. Her cheekbone looks fractured. If it's affecting her breathing, she'll need surgery."

He shrugs in reply and kicks a small piece of gravel across the barn.

"Yeah, we'll get her to one." He shoves his hands in his pockets. "Aria... she's not usually so cold..."

Abuse will do that to a person.

"She'll come around." All the women do. I probably won't explore that avenue with her. Too bad. I bet she's a bombshell.

After Coley's leg is dressed and bandaged, I put her away for the night and head home. All traces of Michelle are gone. The clothes she's strategically left over the last few weeks are off the sofa and out of my dresser drawers.

I breathe a sigh of relief. Fucking hallelujah!

Dinner is nothing spectacular. Two eggs, over easy. Toast. Bacon.

Zoey's not here, so I only need to eat to fuel. I take my dinner outside on the front porch swing and revel in the quiet.

I hadn't heard of Sage Creek until I met Emily. This is her hometown, and when she left, the only way I'd get to be with my daughter is if I moved here too. It's grown on me. The McKenzies are good people. Betty Lou and Annie have babysat for me multiple times and treat Zoey like she's one of them. They're…family.

Three figures make their way down the paved road of our makeshift neighborhood and ascend up the wooden stairs of the empty house. The porch light flicks on and the Agent's eyes meet mine.

Well, isn't this interesting.

They disappear into the house, and I finish my dinner. The girls, Annie and Aria, leave about ten minutes later and disappear into Annie's house. The front door to the empty house opens and he starts my way.

I grin as the agent approaches with a grimace.

"Well, well, well. How deep did Steve lay into you?"

Olson scoffs.

"He didn't, but I'm waiting for him to get down here and rip me a new one." Nate Olson, one of my "brothers" has been a part of the FBI since he got out of the Marine Corps. I didn't realize this was his case.

"Why didn't you say anything?"

"Because it's a federal investigation, Bubba. You're my brother and I love you, but I'm not losing my job because it's Steve's daughter who's caught in the middle and you're his bitch."

I punch his shoulder with a smirk.

"I'm not his bitch. I have a good deal here, and I'll help him out any time he needs it."

Nate groans and sinks onto the porch steps.

"What's going on, Nate? Why are you here?"

"She refused witness protection." He rolls his head so he's looking into my eyes. "Aria has been an integral part of this case. I've been on the Dodges since I started, and she voluntarily handed over evidence. She wants to bury the guy, and I don't blame her. He and Rockwell are cut from the same cloth."

This has me sitting up straighter.

"What kind of crimes are we talking?"

"I'm not going there. I can't tell you everything. I'm her witness protection until he's put behind bars."

"How long do you anticipate that being?"

He shrugs. "Could be months. Could be years."

What about his girlfriend, Evangeline?

"What does Eve think about all of this?"

He frowns and turns away from me.

"The Dodges are dangerous people, Bubba. I did what I had to do to make sure Eve is safe."

"You broke up with her?"

"Worse. I told her I was cheating on her."

I catch a silhouette storming down the paved road. Steve is here for the four-one-one.

"Why? Couldn't you have told her the truth?"

"She can't have any hope. I can't have her missing me and calling me to shoot the shit. I can't take a random weekend to visit her, because then, Aria would be vulnerable. I won't make Eve a target."

"You have five seconds to explain why you failed to mention you're the agent on the damn Dodge case."

Where did Steve come from? And why didn't I hear him approach?

Nate pulls himself up and creates space between them.

Nate tells him everything he told me.

"I wanted her to enter witness protection, Steve, but she refused. This is the first place he'll go looking. I'm not leaving here until they're dealt with."

"What did you do when he was beating the shit out of her?"

Nate's face falls.

"I couldn't do anything. If I were to bust in there when she first came to me, she'd be dead. She insisted on staying until the warrants were signed."

Steve broods in silence while glaring at Nate.

"I'm here to keep an eye on her. It would help if I had an extra set of eyes." He looks directly at me. I can't shut him down in front of Steve, but damn it! I don't want to be in the Dodges' scope, either! I have a daughter to worry about.

"If you do your job right, you shouldn't need an extra set of eyes," I quip.

Nate rolls his eyes and turns to Steve.

"I'm sorry I didn't tell you. You know the rules, man. I wasn't going to let him kill her."

"If she's not okay, Olson, it's *your* ass."

3

ARIA

"Charlie, where are we going?"

His vice like grip on my wrist is cutting off my circulation. I've learned not to resist, because it makes everything worse. I can't match his long strides as he pulls me through the rough terrain of the forest. We're hours outside the city.

"Stop walking so slow and shut the fuck up!" The only light is from the full moon and it's useless. Poison ivy is known to be around, but I can't see a damn thing. Foliage and brush scratch my arms.

"Charlie, please. I'm sorry. I didn't know you were on the phone—

He stops in his tracks and his hand cracks against my cheek.

"I'm not telling you again. Shut. The. Fuck. Up."

He's back to yanking me through the woods.

Is this the end? Will he finally put me out of my misery?

We reach a point in the woods, and he finally puts his phone away.

"Look around you, Aria."

There isn't much to see. Darkness, mostly. I can make out a few trees. Otherwise, I don't know what I'm looking at.

"Do you remember when we talked about expectations?" Unfortunately, yes, I do. That was the night we came back home from meeting my parents. He pinned

me to the wall and yelled at me so loud, the ringing in my ears lasted for a full twenty-four hours.

To avoid another beating of a lifetime, I nod. "Yes sir. I remember." He smirks.

"This is a graveyard, Buttercup." My heart races. It's time. He's going to kill me, and I'll never get to apologize to my parents. A rustling a few paces ahead of Charlie attunes the rest of my senses.

It's sticky out. Muggy. Sweat beads in my hairline when he releases my arm.

I could make a run for it now.

That would be stupid. I don't know where I am and he'll hunt me down. The only way he'll let me go is if I'm dead.

"Come on. I want to show you something." It's not like he gives me much of a choice. He yanks my arm again and slingshots me ahead of him.

My heart drops into my stomach when there isn't any ground left to walk on. There's a hole two inches from the tips of my shoes. Charlie shoves me in, turns the flashlight on his phone on, and tosses it in with me. The bright LED light lights up the hole I'm in.

He ignores my screams.

I'm not in here alone.

I'm with a decomposing corpse who is wearing the same dress his stepmother was wearing the night she disappeared.

"Charlie! Please—I'm sorry!" Oh my God! He's going to bury me alive! "I love you so much, I'm sorry! It won't ever happen again!" He snickers and crouches down and smirks.

"She wasn't a good listener either." It's difficult not to disturb her body. Her bones crunch under my two inch heels. I reach for Charlie, but all he does is laugh. "Let's review expectations again, shall we?"

"Charlie please!*"*

He leans over, steadying himself at the edge of the hole with his left hand and grabs a fistful of my hair from the crown of my head. He laughs when I cry out.

"List the rules, Aria."

"Be quiet. Only speak when spoken to. Keep a clean house. No interrupting. Always appear to be busy."

"I'm adding a new one to the list. Learn your lesson the hard way." He releases my hair and stands straight. He throws in a water bottle. "I'll be back in the morning."

"Charlie!"

"PEANUT? ARIA! WAKE UP!"

I wake with a jolt. Why didn't the alarm go off? Oh no…

I race out of bed and run straight into the wall and sink to the floor. That's not supposed to be there… The sunlight filters through the big picture window, helping me adjust to the bedroom I spent the night in.

Annie crouches beside me and frowns.

"What happened?"

It was a dream.

"Bad dream."

She frowns.

"Are you all right?"

I scoff and rest my head against the wall while I try to catch my breath. No. I'm not. But I play the cards I've been dealt, right?

"I'm sorry. I didn't mean to wake you up."

Annie sinks next to me and pulls my head to her shoulder.

"Was it about Charlie?"

I'm not sharing that part of my life with her. It isn't fair to her.

"Yeah."

"I'm sorry I didn't try to find you, Peanut. I wanted to, but you stopped taking my calls. I thought you were mad at me."

I close my eyes in frustration. *I'm* the one who has to apologize. He forbade me from ever talking to my family again. If she came looking, it would've been my death sentence.

"No, I'm the one who's sorry. I shouldn't have left here with him."

"You're here now. You can start over…"

I'm here, yes. Yet my father can't stand being in the same room with me, I have an FBI agent living in the house my father built for me until the trial is completed, and some guy is living in Jo and Jay's old house.

There's too much uncertainty. Too many things in the air.

When I close my eyes, I'm with Charlie's stepmother. The beetles are crawling over my skin, the maggots are moving in her eye sockets. I *still* smell the putrid scent of her decomposing body.

It sends a wave of nausea through me. I can't hold it.

I race to the bathroom and empty the contents of my stomach into the toilet. It isn't long until I feel my hair being pulled out of my face, though the damage is already done.

"Get it all out," Annie says softly.

I'm grateful she's here. But all the while, I feel so damn guilty for bringing my bullshit home. I'm putting my entire family in danger.

Finally, when I stop retching, I lie flat on the tile floor. It's the only comfort I can find in this state.

"Are you up for some food? I can make you some scrambled eggs…?"

The thought of my sister cooking for me sends me back to the toilet. There's nothing left to vomit, but my stomach hasn't gotten the memo.

"I can scramble some eggs. You don't have to be a jerk about it." She giggles for good measure.

Annie's alarm chimes and the front door shuts, rattling Annie's mirror on her dresser.

"That's probably Momma. Clean up and then come to the kitchen." She saunters out, her sandy blonde hair whipping behind her.

I manage to get off the floor, but I grip the sink like a life raft. I squeeze toothpaste onto my finger since I'm too lazy to root around for my toothbrush in my suitcase and rub it all over my teeth to get the taste out of my mouth.

Trudging down the hall, I hear Momma and Annie talking in hushed whispers. Another reason I didn't want to come home. I don't want to be the black sheep. I don't want to be the target of whispers and gossip. Especially when it comes to my own family.

"Good morning, baby. Take a seat. I made you some eggs."

Annie rolls her eyes and grabs a premade smoothie out of the fridge.

"It's insulting when you barge in here and cook my food. I know how to cook."

Momma purses her lips, ignoring her and smiling at me.

"You started cooking?" I ask with a hint of a teasing smile.

"Hilarious. I can cook eggs."

"And yet, you still turn up for dinner," Momma teases.

Annie scoffs and shovels eggs into her mouth.

"Can you eat quick Peanut? We have a doctor appointment in town."

Of *course* she set up my doctor appointment. Betty Lou is predictable —meaning she knew I'd never go so now she's going to cart my ass across town and make sure I speak to a professional.

"Doctor appointment?"

"I called Dr. Grigg after you left last night and he said he could fit you in."

Dr. Grigg, my childhood doctor with the horrible bedside manner.

Awesome.

"Momma…"

"Sweetheart, when was the last time you went to the doctor?"

A real doctor? One who wasn't paid off by the Dodge's to keep their traps shut?

"I don't know. It's been a while."

"Don't take this the wrong way, but your face looks horrible."

Cool.

That's something *every* girl wants to hear about herself from her momma. I mean, I know I didn't exactly escape Chicago looking like a Victoria's Secret model.

"Keep diggin' your hole, Momma," Annie teases.

"Oh, hush. Baby, you don't need to endure the aftermath of this alone. Let me help. Let me hold your hand."

She's going to lose her shit when she sees me with no clothes.

"Does Daddy know you're doing this?"

Momma smirks and washes the pan she used to make the eggs.

"Let me worry about your dad. Eat."

I reluctantly take a forkful, expecting my stomach to rebel, but once I swallow, I'm suddenly relieved. The ache is fading.

"And don't worry about Agent Olson. I already told him where you were going."

"Is he coming with us?" God, I hope not. I don't need him seeing me naked too.

"No, he said he's still working the case. He has eyes on the Dodges. Besides, Derek's office is across the street. He can keep an eye on things."

I arch an eyebrow.

"The jerk who lives in Jo's house? Who is he, anyway? And what happened to Dr. Karver?"

Annie giggles. "He's not bad. You probably caught him when he was in a bad mood."

"Dr. Karver passed away a few months ago. Before he died, he signed the practice over to Derek," Momma adds. "He's sweet."

A poisonous laugh escapes my lips.

"Regardless, he's family." Momma gives me a pointed stare, silently demanding I play nice. That's all well and good, but I don't think *he* knows how to.

"And he gets around." Annie grins, wriggling her eyebrows suggestively.

Even more reason to stay away. The front door opens, and heavy footsteps cross the hardwood floors.

"Good mornin', Momma," Chris says, striding into the kitchen and pecking her on the cheek.

"Good mornin', baby. Sorry, no more breakfast here, but I've got some sandwiches in the freezer at home if you're interested."

Pouting, he plops down next to Annie and gently nudges her with his elbow.

They laugh easily, and suddenly I'm a stranger here.

I don't belong. I should've gone into witness protection. At least then I could live with the memories of a happy family.

"I'm gonna shower." I leave my family as they chat like nothing has changed. But *everything* has.

THE WAITING room of Dr. Grigg's office is freezing and sterile. The women who surround me, women who *love* to talk shit about me *in* church, stare at me in bewilderment. Has Aria McKenzie *finally* driven a man so crazy, he had no choice, but to beat the shit out of her?

Momma sits next to me, leafing through a magazine, paying the old biddies no mind. Several reached for their phones as soon as they saw us walk through the door, to text the entire town.

"McKenzie, Aria?"

Momma pats my knee and hoists herself up. I follow closely behind, trying my best not to look anyone in the eye.

I'm brought into an exam room where all of the invasive processes are done. They measure my height and weight, the nurse tsks at my being underweight, and then I hand over a cup of my urine. Which reminds me, I need to drink more water.

I'm instructed to strip and put on a paper gown. I keep my back hidden from my mother while oh so gracefully tying the back as tight as it will cinch.

Dr. Grigg enters the room timidly five minutes later, shooting my mother a concerned glance, and then to me, obviously uncomfortable.

"Mrs. McKenzie, good to see you as always. Would you mind stepping out for a few minutes?"

Momma's spine locks straight. He's only had a brief glance of me. Is he going to kick me out because I scared the old bags up front?

"Um, it's okay. Momma can stay."

Hesitantly, he lowers himself into the swivel chair and rolls closer to me.

When I was a kid, he was gruff and rude. Now, he's gentle, kind even.

"Aria, can you tell me when your last menstrual cycle was?"

"I've been under a lot of stress. I haven't had my period in months."

He nods and jots something on his clipboard.

"Have you been feeling nauseous? More tired than usual? Tenderness in the breasts?"

What the hell is he getting at?

"Nauseous, yes, but that's been a part of my daily life for..."

Oh.

Shit.

This isn't happening!

"We tested your urine. Aria, you're pregnant."

My world that's already fragile, shatters. The jagged pieces fall all around me, splintering on the ground. There's a Dodge inside of me.

"That's impossible. I'm on birth control. I've never missed a day."

"Well, the pill is only ninety-one percent effective..." He talks of statistics and date of conception. All I hear is Charlie Brown's teacher yammering on.

I've no tears left to cry.

It's another nail in the coffin, another way Charlie has ruined my life.

"I'd like to examine the injuries on your back—"

"Momma, can you step out, please?"

Her watery, denim blue eyes meet mine.

"Sweetheart..."

"I don't want you to see this. Please. I'll get you when I'm done."

She gathers her purse and tearfully walks out.

Dr. Grigg unties my gown and starts the exam. He measures each burn and assesses the damage. He measures the long, deep scars from Charlie's "sexy time accessories" as he liked to call them.

Charlie believed I deserved it. If anyone around town caught wind of this, they'd think I deserved it too.

"I'm prescribing some ointments. It looks like you did a good job of keeping them clean. Do you have someone to apply them for you?"

No. But I'll figure it out.

"Yeah, I'll be fine."

He ties up my gown and crosses in front of me. "Lie back. I'm going to X-Ray your face. I'm concerned about your cheekbone. Do you have any problems breathing?"

"No. I haven't noticed anything."

Lie.

"This won't hurt the baby at all. I'm going to place this lead apron over your chest. Just relax, and I'll be right back." He lowers me to where I'm completely horizontal. He moves some machinery over my face and exits the room.

What am I going to do? How will this affect the trial?

A wave of nausea washes over me, but I refuse to vomit. I'm *not* pregnant. I can't be.

Clicks and shutters sound off in the room and Dr. Grigg re-enters with Momma.

"The good news is, your cheekbone isn't fractured, just bruised. The swelling will go down over the next few weeks. Here are your prescriptions…"

My dad is going to kill me if Charlie doesn't kill me first.

"Let's go, sweetheart."

I redress once Dr. Grigg leaves and follow my mom outside.

It's not like her to be this quiet. If we don't talk about it, it can't be real, right?

Momma pulls out of the parking lot and drives down Western Boulevard. She pulls into another parking lot and throws the truck into park.

"What's this?"

"Were you in the same appointment with me? This is Dr. Cash's office."

"Who?"

"The obstetrician Dr. Grigg recommended. He was able to get you in with her right away…"

Shit.

Shit.

Shit.

This is real. This is happening.

My eyes water. This can't be happening.

"Baby…"

"I'm sorry I came home."

She unbuckles my seatbelt and pulls me closer to her.

"I'm fucking everything up. I can't win! I'm sorry I fell for him—"

"Stop it, Aria. It has been my greatest blessing you came back to us. This is terrifying, I know, but we'll get through it."

I sob on her shoulder, and she kisses my head through the curtain of my hair.

"I don't mean to embarrass you. I don't know what I was thinking. I thought he loved me. He said he loved me."

"You're not embarrassing me, honey. He's out of your life now. I won't let him get near you."

I squeeze my eyes shut. That's what I'm afraid of! She *would* do anything in her power to stop Charlie. But I don't want her to die because of a stupid decision I made!

"Come now. Let's go in. Dr. Cash already assured Dr. Grigg the office was empty."

I don't bother fixing my face. There's nothing to fix. My appearance is horrible no matter what I do.

The office is just as freezing as Dr. Grigg's. Except this office is decorated in pictures of happy families. A gallery wall of people I recognize, people I grew up with, hold their bundles of joy and grin at the sleeping baby, not paying any attention to the camera.

I'm twenty-six. Maybe there was a time I thought I'd have children, but that image was shattered after I brought Charlie home to meet my parents. In fact, it was the night we finally made it back to our apartment in Chicago I had the thought. He was angry about the stories the women at church told about me. Mixed with the fact I didn't start unpacking the second we walked in the door, and you've got yourself a terrifying scenario of a man you thought you knew, beating the ever living crap out of you.

I couldn't bring a child into that chaos.

What about now?

I don't want to think about this. I don't want to be forced into a decision I'm not ready for.

"What do you think about these?" Momma asks, appearing beside me.

"They seem happy," I respond, shrugging with indifference. I hate them. I hate that they get to enjoy this moment and I'm stuck wondering what the fuck to do.

My mother is a devout Christian. This doctor is going to talk to me about my options, abortion being one of them. It'll break her heart.

But what about mine?

"Aria?" The nurse calls me from the door to the back. Momma gives my hand a reassuring squeeze. I can't do this without her.

It's the same spiel. They take my height and weight, make me pee in a cup, and send me off to a quiet room in the back of the damn building with a pat on my ass.

"Sweetheart, what are you thinking?"

I lean back on the exam chair and shift my gaze to the ceiling.

Different colored baby footprints brighten up the ceiling tiles. It makes my stomach churn.

"This isn't happening."

"I heard a saying once mothers don't feel like mothers until they hear the heartbeat of their baby."

"Don't put that on me, Momma," I plead. I can't picture myself as a mother. I'm barely keeping myself alive.

"Whatever you decide to do, we'll support your no matter what. Even if you decide to..."

The fact she can't even say it makes me want to break into hysterics.

"You can't even say it."

"Abort." It sounds so dirty coming from her. "This is traumatic. I'm not here to judge you. I'm here to make sure you're safe and that you feel heard."

I don't deserve her.

A light tap on the door makes the both of us sit a little straighter. A woman in a white lab coat enters the room, her chocolate hair in a high pony. She looks mid-thirties, and...kind, which isn't the norm around these parts.

"Hi Aria, Mrs. McKenzie, I'm Dr. Cash. It's so nice to meet you."

I shake her cold hand and try to return her smile.

"I spoke with Dr. Grigg a few minutes ago and I have your chart. Now, tell me about what's going on?"

"Um...I don't know; I just found out I'm pregnant."

"Do you know the last date of your menstrual cycle?"

"No...Like I told Dr. Grigg, I've been under a lot of stress. I haven't had a period in months."

"She was in an abusive relationship," Momma chimes in. It's embarrassing to hear it out loud. I wish I could cover my face in shame and pretend the last two years of my life weren't such a big farce.

"Abusive, how?"

"Physically...emotionally...verbally...*sexually.*"

Momma cringes while Dr. Cash's face falls.

"I know you received this news a few minutes ago, do you know what direction you're leaning towards?"

No! I have no idea! Can't she just make the decision for me?

"Um...what exactly are my options?"

"There's adoption. You can have it either open or closed. You can keep the baby, if you feel like you can handle it. Or there's abortion." The silence in the room is deafening. "In the state of Virginia, it's legal to have an abortion in cases of rape or incest. I'm not trying to be insensitive, Aria, but do you feel like this is a case of rape?"

Can it be considered rape if you were in a relationship? I let it happen...I mean, I let it happen so I could live.

"Why don't we start the exam? We can see how far along you are and then we can continue the conversation."

She rolls the ultrasound cart over and has me pull up my shirt. She squirts the frigid jelly on my stomach and places the wand on my belly.

I can't bear to watch this. I don't want to see it. I don't want to see the *gift* Charlie left for me.

A whooshing sound fills the room, forcing my eyes to fly open. It's difficult to decipher the black, gray, and white that fills the screen. But there is one white kidney bean shape.

"Is that it?"

Dr. Cash nods and continues measuring the bean.

"I'd say you're about nine weeks along. Would you like to bring home pictures?"

The little feet on the ceiling tiles carry me out of this room. How many people come in here hoping to hear good news? This isn't a blessing. It's an ugly curse. All of my past transgressions are coming back to bite me in the ass.

Maybe Bethany Hunt was right about me. Maybe I *was* asking for it.

"You have some time to make a decision. I can hold onto these, if you'd like. I'll leave them up at the front desk for when you make a decision."

"Will it turn out like him?" She raises a quizzical brow, silently asking for elaboration. "Is...is behavior genetic? Will this kid come out wanting to destroy everyone in its path?"

Momma sniffles.

"This child is half you, Aria," Dr. Cash says gently. "This baby will be surrounded by kind people—people who go out of their way to *help* other people. You have the power to shape this child's life."

Until Charlie kills me.

"Can I still ride?"

A small smile twitches at her lips.

"I highly discourage it. But you can ride horses all the way up to twelve weeks. Summer is coming up, so make sure to keep hydrated. I'd stay inside during the day unless you're going to the pool or something. Regardless of your decision, take your prenatals."

Shoot me.

"Around eighteen weeks of pregnancy, we can do an amniocentesis. It checks for any genetic abnormalities. With the trauma you've endured, I'd recommend it. Do you have any questions for me?"

Shaking my head, she cleans up the jelly and crosses the room to wash her hands.

"Any time you have questions, call me. I wrote my personal cell on the back. I know this is scary, Aria, but I'm here for you every step of the way." I take the business card she offers me and shove it into my back pocket.

"I'll make your next appointment," Momma whispers and steps out into the hallway.

4

ARIA

9 weeks pregnant...

COMING out of Dr. Cash's office feels like a dream. Or in my case, a nightmare. Stepping foot onto the sidewalk, the ground moves beneath my feet. I suppose the Earth isn't really quaking, but it feels like it.

This new information is like a ticking time bomb, ready to explode at the slightest prod. The easiest thing to do would be to run away. Literally. Run until I'm out of breath and in the next town over.

When Daddy gets a load of this, it'll end any sort of attachment toward me. I'll be that creepy has-been begging for shelter.

"Running isn't going to take you away from this, baby. Get in. Let's get lunch."

Of course, I don't have to say anything out loud for Momma to know exactly what I'm thinking.

I settle in the truck, allowing the cool air to blast in my face while we drive across the street to Rhonda's, a dining staple in Sage Creek.

I feel like I'm walking a green mile. When I enter the black and white checkered tiled room, every patron would stare me up and down, and *know* exactly what I've been up to.

Momma pulls my door open and stares at me expectantly. I'm rooted to the spot, but Betty Lou McKenzie is assertive and if I wait any longer to get lunch, she'll lose her head.

Rhonda's is packed to the brim with the lunch rush. I keep my eyes and head down while everyone and their brother greet Momma jovially, eyeing me suspiciously, when Nicole finally shows us to our booth.

It's the person already waiting for us in our booth that sends a shock right through me. Jackie. My best friend. My ride or die.

Her plump pink lips form a wide smile, and she shoots out of the booth to throw her arms around me and crushes me into her. Her chestnut hair tickles my nose, her citrus scent reminding me of better days when I crashed at her house and staying up all night.

"Oh, Peanut. I've missed you so much," she breathes into my ear.

"I've missed you too."

Momma grins like she's had this all planned out from the start. We take our seats and open the menu.

I already know what I'm getting.

"I can't believe you're here! When Annie called me last night, I was ready to jump in the car and head straight to you, but she said that wouldn't be wise."

She was right.

"Annie called you?"

"We've sort of been keeping in touch when we stopped hearing from you. She wanted to let me know you were home. And safe."

Safe. For now.

Swallowing the lump in my throat, I hesitantly ask Nicole for a glass of water and the greasiest fries she has to offer.

Another figure approaches the table, and slides right in next to Momma, a wide, shit-eating grin on her face. Annie.

"How'd the appointments go?" she asks, bubbly.

Here it goes.

The biggest scandal in family history.

"I'm pregnant."

Annie and Jackie freeze. I'm sorry to drop it like that, but how else can I delicately tell them? The thing I need from them most at this moment is to show me a little compassion, even if they don't mean it.

"Aria, Sweetheart, maybe right now isn't the right time..."

There won't be a right time. No matter what way you cut it, this is the lemon in everyone's mouths.

"Pregnant," Annie breathes in disbelief.

"Nine weeks along, apparently."

Momma frowns. The chances of the other patrons overhearing isn't likely, since the place is buzzing loudly already.

"Is it Charlie's?"

A laugh escapes me. But there's nothing funny about this.

"Yes. And I don't plan on telling him."

"With good reason," Annie sighs.

"What are you going to do?" Jackie asks.

There's the million dollar question. I've been presented with three options. Every single one of them makes me sick to my stomach.

"I don't know," I reply honestly. "My options suck, and I don't have a ton of time to figure it out."

"Abortion is off the table, right?" asks Annie. Her comment surprises me. I thought she'd be on the side of pro-choice.

"Is it?" Jackie asks, turning to me. "You can do whatever you want, Peanut. This is hard...you don't have to keep that reminder if it's going to cause you anguish."

Annie grimaces, and Momma watches us like a tennis match.

"I don't know," I repeat, exasperation leaking out of me.

"I know I don't have a say in this, but come on, Aria. You can't just kill someone who shares fifty percent of your DNA—"

"We are not shaming her if she needs to," Momma growls.

Annie shrinks and turns to me, lips pursed, and pain in her eyes.

"Of course I'd support you no matter what you chose," she says quietly. "But I think you should give it some thought before you make any hasty decisions."

"Could you do it?" I ask quietly. "Could you keep a child you didn't want, that was forced upon you by a man who beat you senseless? I don't know what I want to do yet, but I won't let any of you make me feel bad about what choices I make."

Because I've made my bed and I'm ready to lay in it.

"I guess it depended," Annie replies cautiously.

"On what?"

"The situation."

Scoffing, I suck down my water until there's nothing left. It's so easy to put yourself in a hypothetical situation. In a perfect world, you can say you'll keep the child. Because in a perfect world, you can push those thoughts of your attacker away, almost like he didn't even exist. My reality proves otherwise. Even when I close my eyes, I find him staring at me, undressing me with his piercing blue eyes.

"What about adoption?" Jackie asks, getting off the abortion talk.

"All it would take is a bribe. He'd find out where the kid was sent to and hand over a fat stack of cash. The child would be taken so fast, and the pattern will continue."

I won't subject a child to his way of life. I refuse to let Charlie teach our son how to degrade and humiliate women. I wouldn't subject our daughter to a lifetime of abuse and unwanted attention from her father and his cronies.

"So then the next option would be to keep it," Annie deduces.

And if I choose to raise this child to be a functioning member of society, equipped with good manners and a constant need to help other people—where does that leave me?

Dead, most likely.

"I don't want to talk about this anymore," I murmur, shifting in my seat.

"So we won't," Momma assures me, slyly giving Annie a warning glare.

While the conversation moves past my transgressions, my mind wanders back to the apartment and a conversation Charlie and I had before the abuse started.

If we were going to get married, he'd only want one child. A son. He'd hire the best tutors and send him to the most expensive schools. He'd speak at least four languages and marry someone of equal status.

But now that I think of it, I wasn't a part of those plans.

Shock ripples through me. Would he have had me killed once the baby was born? Or would I have lived the rest of my life locked and chained in his bedroom—to be the punching bag he needed to let off steam.

You got out.

Yeah. I know. But did I? Because from where I'm sitting, I still have to make it out of hell. And now I have a miniature Charlie to watch out for too.

It takes me a moment to realize my mother and sister are no longer in the booth across from us. Was I *so* checked out I didn't see them leave?

"They went to the bathroom. They'll be right back," Jackie reassures me. We marinate in the silence for a moment. But it isn't long until she asks the question everyone else asks. "Why didn't you reach out to me?"

"He stole my phone. I wasn't allowed to contact anybody."

"And nobody came looking…" her voice trails off. She's right. *Nobody* came looking.

"He's not going to let me go, Jackie. He's going to find me and end me."

Her bright blue eyes are muted and grow to the size of saucers.

"Surely not with the FBI hanging around…"

"They're scary people. Some of the charges were embezzlement and extortion. It wouldn't surprise me if he had people in the FBI keeping an eye on things."

I'm certain he does. Otherwise, how else would he have gotten away from every law he's ever broken?

Money is a powerful tool. It either enriches you or consumes you. And when it comes to Charlie Dodge, he's well past being consumed.

5

ARIA

9 weeks pregnant…

MOMMA TALKED to my second mom, Jo, and was kind enough to send me a list of therapists around town, but to my surprise—*not*—there is only one woman. As annoying as it is that there aren't enough women in this town, it makes my decision much easier.

Dr. Lindsay Nelson. She came highly recommended from Jo, and even Momma had good things to say about her.

To say I'm not looking forward to this is a severe understatement. Had it not been for Momma showing up and forcing me to get dressed, I probably would've stayed in bed all day.

It sounds lovely.

But it also sounds fruitless.

Her office conveniently sits right next to Dr. Cash's. Which means it faces the whole town and everybody will know I'm a crazy person when I step foot out of this car.

Cowards never win. So I move my ass.

The office is quiet and smells of lavender. I wonder if it's intentional, for some sort of forced aromatherapy, or if Dr. Nelson actually likes the smell of it. For me, it's overpowering. It makes my throat close and my heart hammer in my chest.

Or it's the anxiety.

April, the perky receptionist with the platinum blonde hair styled sleek and loose around her shoulders, greets me with a warm, genuine smile. Something outlandish for these parts.

"You must be Aria. It's so nice to meet you." She pulls out a clipboard and a pen with an oversized fake flower tied to the top of it and hands it over. "Just fill these out to the best of your knowledge, and when you're done, Dr. Nelson will see you."

She brings me over to a white leather love seat and brings me a mug of tea I absolutely didn't ask for. She gives me a reassuring smile and saunters back to her desk.

It must be a crime to be *that* cheerful. It needs to be. Nobody is *ever* that happy.

Five minutes later, Dr. Nelson appears in the hallway, calling my name. She's pretty. And I'd say around the same age as Chris. Her chocolate hair is pin straight, and it compliments her olive skin. She wears a simple gray dress which hugs her curves and slim hips.

I follow her down the hallway to her office decked out in leather furniture and a huge desk that takes up most of the room. I seat myself on the sofa, hands clasped in my lap as I take in my surroundings. Pictures of her paddleboarding, with what I can only assume are her parents and brother stand proudly on bookshelves. Her credentials are displayed neatly.

"Why don't you tell me about yourself and why you're here?"

I blink in surprise, like this is some philosophical question. God, I don't know. Read my paperwork, maybe?

"I don't know what to say...Obviously, I just got out of an abusive relationship. Everyone around me thinks this is a good idea, to talk to someone, but I don't."

"Hm. Why is that do you think?"

Because I don't need to unload my baggage on somebody else.

"I don't know. It's nobody else's business."

She nods and sets the clipboard down, folding her legs underneath her in the chair across from me.

"So then…why are you here?"

I'm taken aback. Why *am I* here?

"Um…"

"Therapy can be scary. Especially when you're coming out of a dangerous situation. Did he make threats to you if you ever told anyone what was happening behind closed doors?"

Yes.

"Well…I don't think it mattered much because he kept me inside all day every day."

"But he made the threats?"

I hesitantly nod, waiting for the ceiling tiles to open up to a swarm of armed men, gunning me down for opening my trap.

"Tell me about him."

My throat closes like he's got me by the throat again. I see his hostile eyes glaring at me, the heat from the stove warning me to shut the fuck up now before I inflict any more damage.

"I don't want to talk about him," I snap.

"Aria, do you have any thoughts of hurting yourself?"

My wild gaze meets hers.

"Is that appropriate?"

"It's my job. When some women get out of these relationships, the little voice in their head becomes their abuser. They constantly tell themselves they're not worthy. They're disgusting. You get the picture. Most of these women end their lives because they think it's the easier path. So tell me. Do you want to hurt yourself?"

I laugh poisonously. "What do you know about these women, Dr. Nelson? Do you have any idea how terrifying it is for me to even sit here? If this was me a week ago, I'd be dead."

"I was one of those women," she replies simply. She shrugs sadly as my face falls in realization. "I was married to my college boyfriend. One day he was nice, one day he told me if I didn't marry him, he'd kill me and everyone I'd ever loved."

"But—"

"I thought suicide was my only way out. So yeah, I tried. But I failed. I was able to confide in a nurse and they quietly moved me to a different hospital. There they contacted my parents and I moved here to Sage Creek. He signed divorce papers, but it doesn't stop me from constantly looking over my shoulder. I may not know what *you* went through. Hell, it might not even be the same. But I went through my own version of hell, and I truly want to help."

I blink away the tears as I try to find my footing.

"I was going to kill myself. Before the FBI got involved. Before I knew I was pregnant. If the FBI didn't come along, I'd be dead. *Because* it was the easier option."

She nods, picking the clipboard back up and jotting her notes.

I'm crazy, I know this. I know I should be locked away in a loony bin somewhere. Hell, it might be safer for everyone at this point.

"And what about now?"

"I don't want to take my life. For however short lived it is, I want to live the rest of my life in peace." *Unlikely.*

"Good. Well then, let's get started, shall we?"

6

ARIA

9 weeks pregnant...

ON FRIDAY, Momma forces my hand. She calls a family dinner, one where the *entire* family is invited. And when I say *entire,* I mean Jo is coming over too. If JJ weren't in North Carolina, he'd be here too.

Jo has been Momma's best friend since they were kids, and ironically, she was my first taste of domestic violence. She's the reason I should've seen the signs in Charlie way before he started beating me.

And now, I'll have to confess my sins in front of her, disappointing my second mother.

"Hey, you have a minute?" Agent Olson's voice suddenly fills the room.

I glance at Agent O through the full length mirror.

"Sure."

He takes my invitation and sits at the foot of Annie's bed.

"How are you feeling?"

I haven't told him yet.

And I don't plan on telling him until somebody forces my hand.

"Okay, I guess. I won't be running any marathons any time soon."

A smirk tugs at his hard lips.

"Is the house to your liking?" I ask.

He shrugs. "It's a mansion compared to what I'm used to."

I arch an eyebrow for further explanation.

"I've spent a lot of time overseas."

"I didn't think your time in the FBI brought you overseas. You never mentioned it."

"It didn't. But the Marine Corps did."

Ah. I should've sensed that earlier. I suppose he has the build, the weird sense of humor when he's trying to lighten the mood. Just like JJ.

Clearing his throat, he folds his hands on his knees and meets my eyes through the mirror. "A team was dispatched to the coordinates you provided, the West Chicago Prairie Forest Preserve. Every inch of those woods were scoured and there were no bodies found."

My stomach churns.

"That doesn't surprise me."

"The soil is being tested to see if there's any evidence of decomposition, but my team isn't optimistic. Do you think he would move the bodies anywhere else?"

I'm sure they did. They own properties out the wazoo. There are a ton of places those bodies could've been moved to. But I don't necessarily see Charlie going through all that trouble—especially when he thought he was above the law.

I know the truth of all of their skeletons. But their empire won't truly be dismantled until both Dodges are dead.

"Has he tried to make contact?" I ask warily, though I think I already know the answer.

Agent O knits his eyebrows, pondering if he wants to tell me the truth or not. "Yes. He's called a few times."

I drop his gaze in the mirror and cross the room, lowering myself onto Annie's desk chair.

"How many is a few?"

He shrugs.

"Let's say he was worried about you in the beginning, but then changed his tune when he put two and two together."

I can't picture Charlie caring to check on me, or ever worrying about me. It's not in his nature. He's a cold, unfeeling...monster.

"The more he calls, the more fodder for the case. It shows he's trying to silence you."

He'll silence me, all right.

"Even though we've got him, I still want you to be vigilant. Study your surroundings. If something doesn't seem right, call me."

He's always my first call. When Agent O slipped me the burner phone that first encounter at the grocery store, he was my only connection to the outside world. I'd met tons of corrupt intelligence agents before because of Charlie. Late night visits, cash being handed under the table, but when it comes to Agent O, something in my gut screams at me to trust him.

If I've learned anything throughout this whole ordeal, it's to trust my gut.

"You look nice. Are you going somewhere?" he asks.

I wear a loose dress, and I'm aware of the scarring on my arms. I just hope my family doesn't see it.

"Thank you, and no, not really. Just to my parents' house for dinner." *To drop the biggest bomb in my arsenal.* "Can I ask you a personal question?"

Amusement plays in his green eyes.

"You can ask, but I might not answer."

Worth a shot.

"Are you...what are you leaving behind for all of this?"

His face falls.

"I had a girlfriend, but once the case started gaining some traction, I broke it off with her." He offers a kind smile, but his eyes aren't smiling back. I know pain. And he's in a world of it. "I don't want you to think I left her because of you, but I broke it off with her because I didn't want her anywhere near this. It was safer to make her think I did something horrible to the point where she wouldn't want to be with me."

He sighs when I gasp. "In this industry, it's best practice to not have any attachments. I love Evangeline, but I would have left her at some point for this job."

Is that supposed to make me feel better?

It's sad, but...I get it.

"I should get going. Did you need anything else?" I ask grabbing the flip flops my father abhors and slide them on. *Leave me alone. I'm pregnant.*

"No, thank you. I'll give you an update when I have one. In the meantime, maybe you can relax?"

A laugh escapes my lips. *Right. Fat chance.*

I pass by him to go meet Annie in the kitchen who's dressed in tight skinny jeans and a Sage Creek High 4-H Club T-shirt. She types furiously at the keyboard, trying to finish those last few words on her next article before her deadline tomorrow night.

"SORRY FOR THE WAIT. Are you ready?"

She glances up at me and gives me a pained grin.

"I'm ready. Are you?"

Nope.

"Yeah, let's get this over with."

Agent O walks us out, but then heads back to my house, while Annie and I start in the opposite direction towards the main house. Dr. Hawthorn sits out on his front porch, smoking his cigarette, and stares into my soul. His intense stare makes me squirm,

He'd be so much hotter if he weren't scowling all the time.

I Pull my gaze away from him, and take two steps to catch up to Annie. From four acres away, Jo's old Ford comes into view in the driveway.

Showtime.

"It's all going to be okay. Keep your chin up."

It's not going to be okay.

Nothing about this is okay.

She snakes an arm around my waist and pulls me into a side hug. "You keep frowning, you're gonna get wrinkles."

Rolling my eyes, I retort, "As long as *that's* what Bethany Hunt is going to be gossiping about, bring on the crow's feet."

Annie giggles.

We reach the front door and let ourselves in. Chris gives us "the look" when we step into the formal living room. Bickering from my mother and father can be heard from the family room.

Jo, with her short strawberry blonde hair and mischievous green eyes meanders in from the kitchen and beams when we come into eye shot,.

"Honestly, Stephen, I'm not asking a lot!" Momma shouts from the kitchen.

"Darlin', yes you are! I'm not dressing up and driving all the way up to New York for a dumb play!" Daddy exclaims.

"I told your Momma I scored tickets to *Hamilton* for the both of them." Jo shifts her gaze, and her once gleeful grin turns into something melancholy. "Hi, Sweet Pea." She closes the distance between us and wraps me in a tight hug.

"Hi, Jo." She kisses my cheek and takes a few steps back, holding my shoulders, her eyes sweeping over my visible injuries. "I'm sorry."

"Baby, whatever for?" Annie and Chris take their cue to referee the fight in the family room, leaving me alone with my other momma.

"I should've known. There were so many signs and I ignored them..."

"You know what I love about you?" When I don't answer, she leads me over to her seat and lowers me down, taking residence in the armchair next to me. "You have always been the one to see the best in people, even when they didn't deserve it. Hell, I've seen you try to be civil with Brandy Hunt and Mia Parker when they openly bullied you in front of the entire town."

Scoffing, I glance away. "And yet, the whole town thinks I had it coming. Once this gets out about *him,* they'll think the same thing."

"We know who you are, Aria. Nobody deserves to be abused." Her warm hand caresses my cheek, over the swelling in my cheek. I close my eyes at the gentle caress, grateful I have somebody else on my side. "It's not your fault. It's his."

Hold onto that feeling for the bomb I'm about to drop.

"Daddy begged me to leave him."

Jo sucks in a deep breath, almost like she already knew.

"The night before we left when we came to visit...Daddy asked to talk to me alone. He told me to stay here and not leave with him."

He told me Charlie was off. He was rude, inconsiderate, and something about him made Daddy's skin crawl.

"He's so angry," I whisper.

"I don't think that has anything to do with you, sweetheart."

"How can it not?" My eyes well up with tears. "I've been the kid that has never done anything right. I've disappointed him more than I've made him proud." *And he's about to be even more disappointed after tonight.*

"I don't believe that. He *is* proud of you. Baby, you left home at eighteen to one of the scariest cities in the country. You got your degree all on your own, graduated at the top of your class, and made moves to forge your own path. We're all proud of you, baby."

"I fell in love with my boss," I whisper and Jo's brows furrow. She knows this path of self-destruction I'm heading down—possibly better than I do. "I let him talk me out of working. My student loans are defaulting, and my degree has been collecting dust—"

"People make mistakes." I stare at her blankly. "You're not Jesus Christ, baby. You're Aria McKenzie. You're not perfect, and that's okay. The most important thing is to learn from your mistakes." The corners of her mouth quirk into a smile.

"What if I ruined everything?"

"I can positively tell you, you didn't. Your daddy is stubborn. He's worried about you...he almost lost you."

Again.

"Aria, your momma needs help in the kitchen," Daddy jeers from the doorway.

I weakly smile at Jo and dart into the kitchen to avoid any more stern and disappointed glances from my father.

Momma races around the kitchen like she's preparing dinner for the pope. Annie and Chris set the table.

"Momma?"

"Take the meat to the table, baby. Chris, sweetheart, I need you to reach the gravy boat in the cabinet above the stove."

My stomach swirls with hunger and nausea. I've learned I need to be full one hundred percent of the time to avoid hurling my guts up. But not all foods do the trick.

I grab the plate of prime rib and carefully maneuver around the island to avoid Chris's rushing around.

"Come to the table, y'all. We're ready," Momma announces.

I'm not.

Chris takes the seat next to mine and grins. I envy his ignorance. Daddy says grace and we dig in.

"Did you hear Brandy Hunt got another DUI?" Jo asks. Momma gapes and hides her gleeful smile.

"I did. It shut Bethany up for a few days. Then she started spreading rumors about Michelle Delaney."

Jo laughs so easily behind her hand.

Daddy chews and pretends this conversation isn't happening. Annie listens closely, but it's obvious her mind is somewhere else. She continues to check her phone every five minutes. Chris gently nudges me under the table.

"Are you doing okay, Peanut?"

I nod, avoiding my father's gaze.

"Can you promise me something?" I whisper.

"Anything."

"Don't get angry."

He stills while Momma and Jo gossip about the other women in town. Daddy watches us with an intense glare.

"Angry about what?" Chris asks quietly.

"You're on my side, right?"

"Of course I'm on your side. But..."

"No buts. I need you to be on my side."

He sighs.

"You owe me."

Believe me, I know.

"What's going on?" Daddy demands, a hush falling over the table.

"Aria," Momma warns. She wants to enjoy the meal she worked so hard to prepare.

"Can we talk after dinner?" I plead.

"After dinner," Momma insists, glaring at Daddy. He purses his lips and sets his fork and knife down.

"Now," he objects.

"I worked hard on this dinner, Stephen. Stop bullying my baby and eat your food."

The tension was thick when Annie and I arrived, but now, I'm sure you can cut it with a spoon.

"So you're all aware, I'll be going to Canada for two weeks next month," Annie announces, changing the subject. "Would you mind taking over my lessons while I'm gone?" She's asking me, but I haven't done anything like that in years. When my name is mentioned, people tend to walk the other way.

But for the sake of changing the subject, I murmur, "Sure."

"Where in Canada are you going?" Jo asks. My eyes are glued to my plate, but Daddy's stare penetrates my skull, as if he's searching for some telepathic sign of the bomb I'm about to drop on him.

Daddy doesn't like surprises.

"Quebec City. Then when I get back, they're expecting a four thousand word article for the time spent there."

"Do you speak any French?" Jo asks.

"Voulez-vous coucher avec moi, ce soir?"

Jo giggles maniacally and Momma and Daddy both glare at Annie.

"Absolutely not," Momma growls.

"Don't you have a boyfriend?" Chris gripes.

"I do. And when Tom asked and I said the same thing, he laughed."

"When are we going to meet this guy, anyway?" Daddy asks.

She shrugs so nonchalant and flashes a mischievous grin at Jo.

"I don't know. When the time is right."

"How long's it been, two years?" Chris asks.

Annie glares and rolls her eyes.

"Don't worry about it. I know what I'm doing."

I can't help but feel that was an unintentional jab at me, but I don't miss the way Momma and Daddy's gazes shift to me.

"What about you, Christopher? Are you finished sleeping around?" Annie teases.

"Oh, he is not!" Momma shouts.

Chris is the first born, and a total Momma's boy, and he can do no wrong in Momma's eyes. According to her, he's a respectable man who is saving himself for marriage.

"You should see the line of women who sneak out of his house at two in the morning!" Annie exclaims.

Chris's face pales as Momma turns slowly and angrily towards him.

"What?" She asks in disbelief.

"I'm a red-blooded, healthy, American male, Momma."

Oh, God.

Jo stifles her giggles, as does Annie.

But sure as shit, it's not Chris Daddy is glaring at.

"I'm pregnant."

A hush falls over the table. Momma and Annie are the only ones who know. They both shift their worried gazes to Daddy, anticipating what his next move is. Jo and Chris stare at me in shock, with Chris squeezing my hand under the table.

"Pregnant?" Jo murmurs in disbelief.

"I'm nine weeks along." I yearn for the laughter and fun gossip that flew around the table just minutes ago. My heart squeezes and my stomach churns with everyone's devastated stares.

"Does…does Charlie know?" Chris asks.

"No. And neither does Agent O. I don't want this anywhere on the reports—"

"What's your plan, Aria?" Daddy demands.

My sad shrug enrages him further. He picks up his plate and stands up. He can't even stand to be in the same room as me. He slams his plate on the tile floor, the plate exploding on impact, food covering the floor. Terrified gasps fill the room, none of them coming from me.

"I don't know what I'm doing yet—"

"How is this even a conversation?" he bellows.

Chris stands up as Daddy strides closer to me, blocking his access to me.

"Daddy, please..." I plead with tears streaming down my face. I promised myself I wasn't going to cry, but here I am.

"He will *kill* you—"

"Stephen, you do not get to bully her!" Momma shrieks.

"Are you going to put another one of *him* into the world?"

Chris swiftly guides me out of my seat and leads me through the house and out onto the front porch. I don't even realize I've been holding my breath this entire time.

"Breathe," his soothing voice coos.

I can't catch my breath. As fast as I suck in for a breath, the faster it escapes me. The screen door opens and closes. Suddenly, Annie's on my left, and Jo crouches in front of me with her hands on my legs.

"Geez, some warning next time," Chris grumbles.

"I'm sorry," I whimper.

"Breathe, baby," Jo coos.

When I was still in the thick of living with Charlie, I was able to find a meditation channel on the TV since the only phone I had was a flip phone with only his number programmed into it. I try to reach for those grounding tools I learned, but they're so far out of reach. The tears destroy my breathing.

"It's going to be all right, sweet pea. We're going to help you."

"I told you I was the disappointment," I murmur. Jo removes my hands from my face and gives me a reassuring smile.

"It seems scary right now, but it's going to take some time for him to come around. Give him some time."

7

DEREK

In true McKenzie fashion, the entire town gathers on the property for a barbeque. The townspeople park in the front pasture and mingle in the tents setup close by while pigging out on free food and juicy gossip.

I don't usually attend these things. I've learned these events are more of a mating ritual for the women either trying to hook their daughters up with me or trying to hook up with me themselves.

It's exhausting.

The only reason why I've come is for Nate because I'm worried about him.

He's been living in Aria's house for a month, working tirelessly on this case. When I visited him this morning, his eyes were bloodshot, and he hadn't showered in days. I'm not exactly proud of this, but I brewed a pot of decaf and spiked his coffee with melatonin. He passed out on the sofa thirty minutes later and I'm at this barbeque – keeping an eye on his charge.

People all around greet me warmly, with few exceptions.. Michelle glares at me from a table full of women I had…relations with. Did they start a fan club? I half expect Emily, my ex, to show up at some point, leaving Zoey at home with a babysitter, but she's more likely to avoid me like the plague.

I avoid Bethany Hunt and her daughter Brandy by weaving in and out of groups of people, while I make my way to the back tents where all three McKenzies are. Chris mans the grill, Annie chatters on with a dreamy look in her eyes and an expressive smile, while Aria watches and listens with a hesitant smile.

"Derek, hey!" Annie greets as I approach.

Aria's untrusting eyes sweep me up and down, as if looking for some sign of danger. I flash Annie a grin and plop down in the chair next to the grill where Chris is.

"Hey, yourself. How are you?"

She gives a careless shrug and tosses me a beer from the cooler underneath Aria's feet.

"Can't complain. I'm surprised to see you."

"I can't turn down a free meal." My gaze shifts to Aria. She wears a black, long sleeved shirt that doesn't expose any skin or cling to her frame in any way. A sheen of sweat coats her forehead, and she chews nervously on the inside of her cheek.

The last time I saw her, she was hardly recognizable. But now, she looks...normal. Pretty, even.

Her hair is styled in loose waves, framing her oval, porcelain face. She pulls her jean clad legs up to her chest and pretends she doesn't feel my gaze.

"Will Zoey be coming today?" Chris asks without looking my way.

"I doubt it. If you don't mind, I'll probably be hiding out with you guys tonight."

Annie giggles. "Who are you avoiding this time? Michelle?"

Yes.

"I'm not avoiding anyone."

"You're a horrible liar," Chris teases.

Rolling my eyes, I glance back to the raven haired beauty who stares blankly ahead to the horizon.

"Peanut, are you all right?" Annie asks cautiously.

Blinking, she turns to Annie and nods. "I'm fine." She licks her lips and pastes on her best fake smile. She's an easy one to read. How long has she had to act like everything was all right?

She's uncomfortable, and avoiding the public. She doesn't want to be here as much as I don't want to be here. She fidgets with her fingers the longer we lock eyes, so to give her some peace of mind, I glance away, looking for anything out of place.

"Can you help me carry these over there?" Chris asks Annie. Without any hesitation, Annie grabs a tray, walking away with Chris, leaving me alone with the youngest McKenzie.

"I think we may have got off on the wrong foot," I announce softly.

She avoids looking me in the eye, but a small smile tugs at her lips.

"Maybe," she replies timidly. "I'm sure you had something else on your mind."

Yeah, the woman who is getting ready to get up and storm over here to rip me a new one.

Banishing the thought out of my mind, I squirm in the awkwardness of the moment. She doesn't want to talk to me. But there's something so... magnetic about her. Like she has no expectations about me. She's not trying to throw herself at me.

"Are you happy to be home?"

"It's complicated," she replies monotonously. She turns her head to face me, and finally, I get a good gander at her undamaged eyes. They're hazel, with flecks of green sprinkled throughout. "I miss the food scene of Chicago. But I guess nothing beats being home." She shudders and finds a spot on the floor to stare at.

"Can I ask you a personal question?"

She freezes, and the microscopic bit of progress we made diminishes.

"Probably not."

"How'd you get the nickname?" I'm asking her anyway. I have a good rapport with all the McKenzies on the property. I'm not messing that up because of one bad day.

Relief washes over her, and she nervously laughs.

"I was premature. *Peanut* is what the NICU nurses called me until my parents could tell them my name. Since then, it stuck." She drops her legs to the cooler and grips the table, her features softening.

Her gaze sweeps me up and down, as if she's forcing herself to look at me. When her eyes finally settle on mine, she loses the courage she tried to build and finds a new spot on the ground to stare at.

"You're not from around here, are you?" she asks with an air of caution.

"No. I'm originally from Charleston but found my way out here after I got out of the Navy."

I hate small talk. Wouldn't it be great when you meet a person, you could magically jump three years into the friendship and avoid talking about the shit that doesn't matter?

"Here… to the middle of nowhere," she murmurs.

"It's not bad. I enjoy the quiet. People have to give some thought to drive all the way out here if they want to see me." It gets me out of the public eye, and grants me the anonymity I crave.

"People like Michelle Delaney?"

What?

Michelle storms this way, her eyes narrowed, and her plump lips pursed.

Fuck.

"Yeah…people like her."

Aria stifles a giggle when Michelle stops in front of me.

"Derek."

"Michelle."

"What are you doing here? You never show your face at these things."

I catch Aria's gleeful smirk from behind Michelle.

"I live here."

She raises a perfectly sculpted, chocolate brow, daring me to tell her I'm on the prowl for a new conquest.

"I thought I told you to never seek me out—"

"You came over here," I state firmly, standing up and narrowing my eyes. "I've been getting to know Aria."

Michelle turns in surprise to see Aria sitting on the table, giving her a weary finger wave.

"Aria McKenzie," she states in disbelief.

"Hi Michelle," Aria greets politely.

"You've got to be kidding," she pouts. "You're that desperate? You're seeking *her* out?"

A poisonous laugh escapes Aria's lips. "That would be the end of the world, wouldn't it?" Aria asks, hopping off the table and straightening out her pant legs. "Fear not, Michelle. I'm securely off the market, most likely for the rest of my life. I'm going to have to insist y'all stop using me as your scapegoat when the men around here see right through your bullshit." She turns to me. "Enjoy your night, Dr. Hawthorn."

Her hips sway as she walks away. I wish I were going with her—even if it meant indulging the small talk.

Michelle's hand pinches my cheeks together and forces my head to face her. I continue watching even the slightest movements and etching it into my brain, just in case Nate starts asking.

"Hey!" Michelle shouts.

Gripping her wrist, I remove her hand from my face.

"You told me to lose your number. I lost it, okay? We had fun. Leave it."

"You can't pursue her," she warns as I attempt to walk away, her delicate hand encircling my wrist. "She's a homewrecker. You love your daughter *that* much? Aria will destroy your life."

I rip my arm from her grasp and glower, "Let me remind you, we were *nothing.* Who I see is none of your business. If you ever bring my daughter into this again, it'll be the last thing you'll ever do. Do. Not. Cross. Me."

She shrinks back and wrings her hands together.

"Oh, hey Michelle!" Annie greets as she walks up behind her. With a pathetic sniffle, she turns on her heel and storms away. Good. Annie's gaze burns into my skull. "What was that all about?"

She forgot her place.

"Couldn't take no for an answer."

Shrugging, she places a new, unused, foil pan next to the grill and takes over Aria's place on the table.

"Where's Peanut?"

"She walked away."

She arches an eyebrow, just like her mother.

"What did you say to her?"

That's the kicker, isn't it? I'm mean and gruff, so *I must be* the one who pissed her off.

"I didn't say anything. Michelle was the one running her mouth."

Annie purses her lips and scans the crowd.

I immediately find Aria sitting with Jackie and her mom. Her mouth moves while she stares at the table. It's the most I've ever seen her speak.

"I'm going to mingle," I announce, even if it's a lie. I'm going to be a creep and stay close to the McKenzie who wants nothing to do with me. It's for her own safety.

She has nothing to worry about. These people couldn't hurt a fly.

I head in her general direction and get stopped by Brandy Hunt a few feet away from Aria. I was *almost* in the clear.

"Hey, Derek," she greets seductively. Her platinum blonde hair hangs loose around her bare shoulders in a top scandalous by this crowd's standards.

"Hey yourself."

She grins and giggles. *This* is why I don't attend these things. There is no such thing as being left alone, no matter how much I want to be left alone.

"You look good tonight." She moves closer to me, our bodies almost touching. She tilts her head up, exposing her long neck and wears a smirk.

This kind of behavior would have gotten to me a year ago, but now…

"Thank you."

"Do you want to get out of here?"

Her strong, floral perfume fills my senses. She'd be easy. She'd get rid of the edge.

It doesn't matter. Because the car speeding down the driveway has me pulled out of this trance. Aria scrambles out of her seat, freezing in place for a beat before tearing down the pasture.

I sidestep Brandy and dial Nate.

"You're an asshole, Bubba—"

"Bogie. Black town car speeding down the driveway. She's heading that way."

"Shit," Nate curses under his breath. "Catch up to her and put her on the phone." I run to Aria, her eyes watering and transfixed on the car.

I push the phone into her hand in which she glares at me. She puts it up to her ear while we close the distance between us and the car.

"Okay," she says softly, handing the phone back to me.

"I'm not going to get there in time. Put the phone in your pocket and on speaker. I'm recording the call."

Without another word, I do just that. I stand behind her, the shield in case shit goes down. It's amazing how still she stands, statuesque.

The driver parks the car in front of the main house and exits the car. He glares at Aria and opens the door behind him.

A slender, bare, leg is the only thing I see when the door is opened. The figure pushes herself out of the car. She's thin and trying for the whole fifties pin up model vibe. Her blonde hair is pulled back so tight it gives her a face lift. She wears a revealing red dress her tits are nearly spilling out of.

She removes the giant sunglasses off her face and holds them loosely in her hands. Her scowl is enough to know her disapproval of the woman who stands before me.

"You've made your point, dear. Charlie's sorry. He got carried away. Come home so we can move on."

"He didn't get *carried away,*" Aria glowers. "You get carried away when you eat too many fun-sized candy bars at Halloween. He shoved me into a *grave* and promised me he would pick me up in the morning and then didn't show up until late the next night."

What the fuck?

"You love him, Aria. He loves you. It's time to put these ridiculous accusations behind us and move on."

I half expect Aria to fold. Women like her always return to their abuser. So when she stands tall and squares her shoulders, I'm surprised of what comes out of her mouth.

"I'm not going back. I'm not recanting my statements either. You should take this opportunity to run."

The woman scoffs, finally noticing my presence.

"Is this what you're worried about? We all need someone on the side that's how you survive this. If you come back *home* with me, I won't tell them about him."

She thinks I'm her boyfriend.

The thought should terrify me, but it doesn't. I want this bitch off the property.

Aria hesitantly turns towards me and narrows her eyes. "No, he's not my boyfriend. I only met him a month ago. He's our family's vet." She turns back to the woman and sighs. "What do *your* parents think about this arrangement you have with Charles? What do they think of the bruises?"

Her lips thin and she tightens the grips her sunglasses so that you can hear the plastic buckling under the pressure.

"Enough. I'm giving you five minutes to get what you need and then we're going home."

"I'm not leaving with you." Her voice is constant and firm. "I stopped loving Charlie a long time ago. He doesn't love me, just like Charles doesn't love you. We're chess pieces, the pawns for optics. I've been trying to escape him for a year, and he hasn't let me go. I want to be left alone, Charlotte. I want Charlie to leave me alone."

"They're not going to accept no for an answer," she snaps.

Aria simply shrugs as if she doesn't care.

"If I return empty handed, it's the end of *my* life."

"Then don't go home."

The driver approaches the woman, *Charlotte,* and whispers something in her ear.

"Wouldn't the two of you be happier if you didn't have the Dodges standing in the way of your chance of happiness?"

"What do you know about that?" she demands.

"I'm an observer. I've seen you sneaking around."

Charlotte swallows nervously.

"You should leave. Or stay. Do whatever you need to do. But I'm not going back and I'm not recanting my statements. But, if you feel like you want to stay, I can make some arrangements."

"Don't expect to survive this," Charlotte's voice drops.

It was a threat, and I have it all on tape. Why is Aria extending a hand when this woman is threatening her? People like them have resources. They'll hire hitmen and have them do their dirty work. Why isn't Aria shaking in her boots?

Charlotte turns on her heel and is let back into the car. When the car is safely out of the driveway, Aria turns to me with fire in her eyes.

"What are you doing?" Her voice raises an octave. Those hazel eyes fire with intensity with a promise to verbally grab me by the balls and castrate me.

And we were getting along so well.

"Agent Olson couldn't get here in time. I was trying to help—"

"You're involved now, don't you get it?"

Dozens of eyes watch us. Whispers flit amongst the tents.

She swallows nervously, tears welling up in her eyes. "I have it handled, okay? So maybe next time you should mind your own fucking business." She storms off toward the neighborhood, ignoring all the stares coming from the hungry townspeople.

She's mad at me?

I recorded that woman threatening her!

"I don't understand why you're mad at me. I was just trying to help—"

"I bet that's how you get all the girls, huh? You're the knight in shining armor coming to their rescue. *I* don't need rescuing, Dr. Hawthorn. My days are numbered, and I've come to peace with it. I don't need your dumbass on my conscience too."

What the actual fuck?

I race after her, desperate for her to understand I'm nobody's knight in shining armor. I can get any woman if I so much as winked her way.

"If I wanted a good time with a woman, all I have to do is ask. I don't play games, Aria. I've never needed them."

"Well bully for you!" We march in the direction of the houses while everyone watches this unfold. "If you're trying to get in my pants, I can confidently tell you it's not going to happen. I don't need you to help me in any way, shape, or form."

"Your stupid FBI agent told me to keep the call going so he could record it!"

She stops and glares.

"It doesn't matter! Do you know anything about the Dodges, Dr. Hawthorn? Because I do. They're exterminators. You inserted yourself when it wasn't welcome and now your life is going to be on my conscience."

"I don't know anything about them, no. But if they want to try to threaten my life, let them. They're not the only ones with friends in high places."

She stills.

"Stop following me. Go whore yourself out to any of the women who are at this stupid barbeque, because I'm. Not. Interested."

She breaks into a sprint toward the house where Nate is staying.

What the hell just happened?

8

ARIA

13 weeks pregnant...

"He was following orders from me," Agent O reasons, tapping furiously on his laptop, typing up the report to send to his superiors.

"I was serious when I told you I didn't want anyone else getting involved. I don't know this guy, Olson. I don't know what his family is like—if he even has one—or if he has someone he likes. Sage Creek might be a biased town when it comes to the women, but this is my home, and I don't want to see anything bad happen to anyone because of a stupid decision *I* made."

Relaxing his fingers, he swivels on the chair and gives me a reassuring smile.

Fuck him for being so nonchalant!

"Have you seen him? I'm sure he could hold his own."

Rolling my eyes, I plop down on the sofa and glare at him.

"It doesn't matter."

"Aria, I know you don't see it this way, but this is a win. We caught her threatening your life on tape. The evidence is stacking up against them."

"You are seriously underestimating them."

"I know he manipulated you into fearing the power he and his family hold, but it's not as much as you think."

"How long have you been on the case?" I already know the answer. He's been with the Bureau since he started years ago.

He grimaces and flips me the bird, obviously not impressed with me calling him out.

"Regardless, Dr. Hawthorn is an ally. I looked into him myself. He's a great second set of eyes."

I lean back on the couch and wish I would've stayed home.

"What did you mean when you said your days were numbered?"

I don't intend on coming out of this alive.

"Nothing. I'm going down to the barn. My dad will want to know what happened."

I'm sure he watched the whole damn thing unravel, but I need five minutes alone without someone fawning over me.

My wish for the rest of my days is to be left the fuck alone.

The barbeque is still in full swing when I hop off the front porch steps. Nobody will miss me, and honestly, I'd have it no other way. I pass Dr. Hawthorn's house without a second glance.

The golf cart stacked with feed buckets and hay race past me to the back barns with Chris at the wheel. I've missed evening feed by a hair.

The horses in barn number three are eating furiously by the time I arrive. I stroll to the feed room, grateful I'll have ten minutes to myself.

I can't believe Charlotte drove all the way out here. Did she honestly think I'd return to Chicago with her?

Unless…

She knew I wouldn't go back with her.

Was she scoping the place out? And to do it with hundreds of people around as witnesses…

Oh fuck. This is worse than I thought it was.

My chest tightens as I pace the length of the feed room. I knew they'd kill me, but I thought they'd drag it out as a new form of torture.

What about Olson's girlfriend? If they come in the dead of the night and kill us all, she'll never know the truth of why he left her.

God! I didn't want to get other people involved. It would've been better for me to die. This would've been a lot better for everyone involved if I were killed.

My legs buckle from under me, crashing to the ground. I gasp for air like I'm submerged in water. Why can't I breathe?

"You have to take a deep breath." A child's voice rings through the chaos. She's cute, like ten or eleven years old. She crouches next to me, her mousy brown hair falling into her freckled face. She has a bright smile, one with only one missing tooth, and bright, curious, blue eyes. "What are five things you can see?" the child asks.

Is this death? Is this the child inside of me trying to comfort me? Is this some trick of reality where my kid is trying to get me to get a grip?

"What?"

"What are five things you can see?"

I glance around the room while my heart hammers in my ears. "Um, the trashcans, hay, you..."

"Two more. You've got this."

What the hell?

"Gizmo and the whiteboard."

The child grins.

"Good job! What are four things you can touch?"

My hands instinctually find the concrete, the stone cool and rough against my palms.

"The ground, the clothes against my skin..." I reach up and grab her hand. She squeezes my hand and grins. "Your hand, and the tears on my face."

She sits down across from me and kneads my hands with her slender fingers.

"What are three things you can hear?"

My racing heart slows as I close my eyes and listen to my surroundings. "The fans, William banging his feed buck against the stall wall, and Gizmo's purring."

"Good. Keep your eyes closed if it helps. What are two things you can smell?"

I inhale slowly. Swirls of hay and sweet feed fill my nose.

"Hay and sweet feed."

"And one thing you can taste?"

The sweet barbeque sauce still lingers in my mouth from the pulled pork sandwich Chris insisted I eat for quality assurance.

"Barbeque sauce."

Her fingers continue to knead my hands.

"I have anxiety attacks too," she says quietly. "This is a trick my dad taught me."

I open my eyes to her smiling face.

"You're good at this."

She shrugs.

"Sometimes you have to be." She sighs. "I was looking for my dad, but he isn't here. I should probably get back to the party before my mom sounds the alarm."

Whoever's kid this is, is lucky. I hope *I* can be that lucky.

"Thank you for coming to my rescue. You can tell your dad his trick worked."

She scrambles up when the feed room door opens, revealing Dr. Hawthorn.

"Oh, hey, Dad. I was looking for you."

Oh, God. He procreated?

"Hi, gorgeous. I've missed you."

She wraps her arms around his torso and his intense, yet gentle gaze bores a hole through my skull. It's weird to see him gentle like this, especially how we just entertained the town with a screaming match.

"Your trick worked, by the way."

He quirks an eyebrow. I can't help but notice the love pouring out of his embrace and the adoration in his eyes for her.

"Which trick?"

"The senses."

I pick myself up off the ground and dust myself off.

"She found me in here. I didn't know she was your daughter," I offer softly.

"No worries. Zoey's friendly. You wouldn't hurt her, right?"

My gaze locks on his and a victorious smile spreads across his lips.

So arrogant.

"No, of course not."

"Would you like to get a sandwich with us?" Zoey asks.

"Um…"

"I find it better to eat once you calm down. Anxiety takes a lot out of you."

I hate that she's so adorable and she's rational for her age.

"You don't have to talk to us if you don't want to," Derek adds. "I don't know how you could ignore this face."

Zoey's toothy grin brings a smile to my face, and her cheerful giggle reminds me there is life outside these barns.

"I don't know if I'll be good company."

Zoey shrugs. "Dad can be grouchy sometimes, but I don't think he can help it. I can sit with you, and we can ignore him."

A nervous laugh escapes my lips. So I'm not the only one whose noticed Dr. Hawthorn is a little intimidating.

"Hey now. I haven't seen you in two weeks. What if *I* want to catch up?"

"Fine, but you have a five minute limit."

I find myself agreeing. Dr. Hawthorn and I walk in silence while Zoey chatters on about how school is almost over, and she gets to spend the summer here with her father. Hundreds of eyes watch our approach. I'm not even surprised about the rumor mill churning at this completely innocent exchange, but what can you do?

We proceed through the buffet line and find Chris and Annie off to the side, eating quietly while Annie scrolls through her phone.

"Miss Annie!"

Annie glances up at Zoey's exclamation and a megawatt smile lights up her face.

"Zoey! Hi, sweet pea! I've missed the heck out of you!"

She sets her plate down next to Annie, and I occupy the seat next to

Chris. I need someone looking out for me. Who better than my idiot brother?

"I missed you too! Hi Uncle Chris!"

I choke on the uncle and clear my throat as Zoey wraps her arms around my brother.

Why didn't anyone ever mention this guy? His daughter became a part of our family and I'm the odd one out.

"Hey, gorgeous! I'm so glad you came to visit."

Zoey takes her seat next to Annie and starts in on her brisket sandwich.

I meet Dr. Hawthorn's curious gaze as he bites into his sandwich. Annie and Chris question Zoey about school. There's a weird silence now we're the two outcasts.

"Are you going to yell at me again?" he asks.

"The night is still young," I counter with a hint of amusement.

"I'm not a threat to you, I promise," his voice drops a few decibels, not gaining the attention of Zoey and my siblings.

"Maybe. But I don't know for sure."

Sighing he plops his sandwich on the plate.

"Can we start over?" he asks sincerely.

For what? I'm not particularly interesting. I'll be inside more than half the time, and we don't owe each other anything.

"Hi. I'm Dr. Derek Hawthorn, but my friends call me Derek."

He holds his hand out for me to shake, but the thought of him touching me makes me want to puke. My ears ring at the prospect, and I stare at his outstretched hand, with what I'm sure the other people at this table would call disgust.

The table grows quiet, and my brother and sister watch the exchange. Zoey watches me with excitement—like I'm a new fixture in her life.

Keep the peace.

"Nice to meet you, Dr. Hawthorn. I'm Aria McKenzie." And that's all he's getting. I reluctantly grasp his hand in a firm handshake. His large hand practically covers mine. He's firm, yet gentle. He flashes a boyish grin while my brother and sister breathe a sigh of relief.

"Derek," he reiterates. "My name is Derek."

His name is Dr. Hawthorn. I'm not getting close to him, so I'm going to insist I stay formal.

"So does that make you Uncle Chris and Miss Annie's sister?" Zoey asks, vibrating with excitement.

"She's our baby sister," Annie replies for me.

"Do you ride too?" Zoey implores.

"I used to. Not so much anymore." I turn my head to Derek and narrow my eyes. "It wasn't Coley's fault for almost killing a rodeo clown. It was Liam Parker, and he was being an asshole. He jumped behind her while we were in the chute and Coley was understandably spooked."

Dr. Hawthorn smirks, earning groans from my brother.

"Oh, you called Coley a psycho, didn't you?" Annie asks with a laugh. "Big mistake."

"I call them like I see them."

Cue eye roll.

"Don't listen to him. He doesn't like to admit it, but he's a big softy." Zoey leans closer to me and drops her voice into a whisper. "He still likes to cuddle with me before I fall asleep."

Dr. Hawthorn's face pales and gently sits her back in her seat.

"Okay, that's enough. Eat your food or you'll waste away to nothing."

She mischievously giggles and flashes me a Cheshire smile.

Zoey is adorable. She's smart as a whip and when she's finished and the other three take over the conversation, she pulls a paperback out of her backpack.

"What are you reading?" My voice speeds off without asking permission from my brain. Zoey peeks up and lifts the book so I can see the front cover.

"*Holes*," she replies easily, dogearing her place and quickly closing it. "My teacher wants to show the movie in class, but I think I want to read the book first before I see the movie."

"That's a great book. Have you read *Harry Potter* yet?"

She scoffs.

"I read the first one, but Mom says I read too fast and a trip to the bookstore is wasted on me because I read them within a day."

I don't miss the angry tic in Dr. Hawthorn's jaw and the way he flinches when he hears her reading is being muted.

"What did you think?"

She sets the book down and taps her bottom lip as she ponders my question.

"I think the story is brilliant. It would be awesome to attend a school like *Hogwarts*..." She dreamily sighs. "I like fantasy, but I like how J.K. Rowling also gives the story more than one genre. I love mystery books too."

She's a gal after my own heart. She reminds me so much of me when I was her age. I worked in the barn because it was my job. But books...they brought me to new places while I tried to forge my own path.

"You'd like a school like that, eh? What about me? Wouldn't you miss me?" Dr. Hawthorn teases.

She giggles at her father and scrunches her nose when their gazes meet. I adore how she can be her authentic self around her father.

My heart aches in sadness. My father and I used to be the same way. I hung the moon. And he was the one who collected the stars.

"I could come home for Christmas."

Dr. Hawthorn sighs. "Only Christmas? That's not enough time."

Zoey rolls her eyes.

"Maybe over the summer I could read the rest of them? The movies are played everywhere but I don't want to see them until I read all the books first."

Without my permission, my tears well up in my eyes. Flashes of my childhood, hanging out with my dad, him showing me how to use the riding lawn mower appear before me. It's like I don't even know him anymore. I just want him to love me.

Where is he?

I scan the area for him and find him at the grill starting the cleanup. He hasn't talked to me since my pregnancy announcement. He can barely even look at me. Other than the occasional glare, I'm barely in his line of vision anymore.

"Peanut? Are you all right?"

I ignore Annie and get out of my seat. I stride quickly to the grill as Daddy brushes all the crap off of it.

"Daddy?"

He places the brush on the table and reluctantly turns around. If he were anyone else, this would scare me. His intense glare and generally intimidating stance would send anyone far away from him.

But I'm not.

As much as he doesn't like to admit it, we're eerily similar.

He's hurt. I'm the root of it, I know. Before I even made it into the world, I nearly killed my mother and myself on the way out. Growing up, I garnered too much attention even if I didn't search for it. And now... well, I'm disappointment after disappointment.

"I love you."

Nothing changes. He still stares at me like I'm an idiot.

"I'm sorry I didn't listen to you when you first asked me to leave him. I..." Sniffling, I wipe away the tears. "I don't mean to keep fucking everything up and I'm trying hard not to embarrass you, but I'm scared."

There. I said it.

His shoulders relax, but his face is as stony as ever.

"I can't give the kid up." His jaw tics in annoyance. I'm treading dangerous waters, but this is *my* choice. "Like you couldn't give me up."

"Aria, there's a big difference—"

"I know. But you were the one who convinced Momma not to terminate the pregnancy even when the odds were stacked against me. I can't give this baby up even though I *hate* its father. I'll do whatever I need to do. I can open up more lessons in the riding school, I can find a job somewhere in town—I'll pull my weight."

For however long I'm still breathing.

"This isn't some horse you can leave with your parents while you skip town for a decade."

My leaving will constantly be thrown in my face.

"I know."

He sighs.

"Did you resent me, Daddy? When I spent all those months in the NICU before I came home, did you resent me?"

"That's not fair."

"Somewhere deep inside I know you do. It's why you get so angry at me when things I do don't go your way."

"Aria," he warns.

"All I ever wanted to do was forge my own path. Chris is a teacher, Annie's a travel writer, and then there was me. Nobody had any high hopes for me."

"That's quite enough of that."

"What was your big dream for me, Daddy?" I should stop challenging him like this. But how am I supposed to move on with this festering between us? "Anyway, I wanted you to be the first to know what I was thinking. You made it quite clear you don't like being the last in the know."

Resigned, I turn on my heel, but I don't return to our table.

Right now, I need a quiet place to cry while my father wraps his head around being a grandfather to a kid none of us wanted.

9

DEREK

After the party breaks up, I help with cleanup and placing all the tables and folding chairs back in the shed behind the main house. Now all that's left to do is trudge back to my empty house and chain smoke my last pack of cigarettes.

Aria stormed off two hours ago. We were getting somewhere. Zoey wanted to talk to her more about the books she was reading. All it took for her to crumble is one conversation with her father.

It obviously didn't end well, but it's none of my business.

When I reach the porch, the light flicks on. I freeze, listening for any signs of intruders. When I turn my head, I find Steve swaying slowly in my porch swing.

"I'm leaving for a while."

I'm not even the least bit surprised.

"Where are you going?"

He stands up and stretches.

"Chicago."

Yep. There it is.

"Steve…don't do this."

"Don't tell Nate. I'm going to put the fear of God into this asshole. He ruined her life. I told Betty Lou and the kids I'm going to New York to visit family. Don't let them think otherwise."

I wince at the notion of Steve's thinking his daughter's life is over. She's young, and she has so much more life to live. And yet again, here I am, stuck in the middle.

But this time, I don't feel so aggravated by it.

They say kids can sense the best in people. I've never seen Zoey light up like she did around Aria. If she can befriend my kid, then we can be friends.

"Call me if you need any help. I can possibly get Archer and Novak to be on alert should you get arrested."

Steve smirks.

"They'd love the hell out of that, wouldn't they?"

"They would thoroughly enjoy it."

Steve grins and starts down the porch steps.

"Keep an eye out for her, okay? She's vulnerable."

"Yeah. No problem." I doubt she'll tell me *anything.* I'm the big bad wolf. And she's...I don't know... Some mystery water alien whose about to get boiled.

10

ARIA

14 weeks pregnant...

DADDY LEFT to visit family in New York *without* his family. While he's gone, I pick up the slack. Chris tends to harvesting while Annie and I handle the horses and steer. Dr. Hawthorn helps with feed times, especially since he's overseeing our new rescue horse's care plan.

For the last week, I've been up at the ass crack of dawn, thrown my guts up, and gotten to work. From the hours of eleven to four, I'm stuck inside until the temperature drops a few degrees.

Annie left for Canada this morning. Momma helped with the stalls along with Zoey and Dr. Hawthorn, and Chris said he'd help me with evening feed.

Ever since Charlotte turned up last week, I'm terrified to be alone. I'm hyperaware of my surroundings. It's like I'm waiting for a Dodge hitman to storm through the barn Bonnie and Clyde style and packing me full of bullets.

"Can I help you with anything?" Zoey's voice appears in the doorway of the feed room.

Glancing at my new best friend, I grin and shake my head.

"Thanks. I'm just about done. You can help me drop feed in a little bit."

She gives me an enthusiastic nod and grabs her copy of *Holes* off the ledge and drops down on a bale of hay and loses herself in the pages.

The sultry sounds of Blondie fill the feed room from the new phone my mom picked up for me after the barbeque. Zoey crosses her legs and taps her foot to the beat. I sing under my breath while I replace the lids on all the trash cans.

"Ladies," Dr. Hawthorn greets, strolling into the room and dropping down next to Zoey. "Why don't the two of you start feeding the horses in the barns and I'll start on the horses in the pasture?"

Grateful for the easier task, we agree and start feeding down the line while Dr. Hawthorn loads up the golf cart and starts feeding the horses in the pastures. Once we're done, Zoey brings me back all the buckets and continues reading while I set up morning feed.

My back aches. My stomach growls with such ferocity, Zoey glances up and giggles. The low hum of the golf cart approaches the feed room. I continue fixing up morning feed while Dr. Hawthorn finishes up the closing duties.

"Everything is off in all barns. Are you almost done?"

No. Because going home to an empty house means all of my bad memories can line up and play ahead of me like a drive-in movie theater.

"You can head up if you want. I'm finishing up."

I can't get myself to go back to Annie's house, but I don't necessarily want to spend the evening with my mother talking future plans for the baby either. Although, she seems to be the *only* person in the family who is excited about it.

"Zo, why don't you head home and start getting cleaned up for dinner?"

Without looking up from her book, Zoey hops off the bale of hay and reads her way out of the room.

I avoid Dr. Hawthorn's hard gaze. Maybe he's like Dad and he can see right through my bullshit too.

I swept the feed room an hour ago. But I do it again, because what else am I going to do?

"I think this is as clean as it's going to get. Unless you're going to mop the concrete."

Straightening up and leaning the broom against the wall, I turn to face him and his stupid, charming half-grin.

"That's not a bad idea."

He steps in front of me as I try to escape him. My heart thunders in my chest at his proximity, yet he makes no moves to touch me. Will this always be terrifying? Will the prospect of a man's touch drive me to the brink of insanity, no matter how innocent it is?

"Is there a reason why you're terrified to go home?"

Ugh.

I'd love it if everyone could stop thinking they know me so well. Who the fuck is this guy, anyway? He's known me all of two seconds.

"I'm not afraid to go home."

He snorts. Yes, this must be *hilarious.* I hate that my sleeve bears my entire heart. People like him, like Daddy, can tell exactly what I'm thinking without me having to say anything. It's an invasion of privacy.

"Then come on. I'm starving. I can walk you to the front door."

I squeeze my eyes shut in frustration.

"I'm a big girl. I don't need you to babysit me."

"Can I ask you a serious question?"

I sigh extra hard for special effect cross my arms across my chest and arch my eyebrow, Betty Lou style.

"One question. Make it count."

His throaty chuckle has my stomach flip-flopping. He's beautiful when he isn't angry at the world.

"Is what happened to you the reason why you're so closed off, or has it always been you against the world?"

I blink. Once. Twice. A third time.

"You don't have to answer if you don't want to."

"Why do you think that?"

"Just a few things I've observed since I came here."

I hate his victorious smirk.

And his stupid chin dimple.

"Fine. I'll bite. What things?"

"The first: your dad told you not to squander your third chance at life." When I don't respond, he sinks to the ground, waiting for me to expand. "What happened to your first two chances? And do you have a death wish?"

Despite my defiance towards him, a laugh escapes me.

"I suppose the first two chances don't matter much. When my mom was pregnant with me, the doctors told her it wouldn't be a viable pregnancy. My mom went into preterm labor and I nearly killed the both of us coming out."

My dad isn't a religious man, but when he talks about that time, he's not ashamed to admit he hit his knees and prayed to any God out there who was listening.

"And your second?"

Sighing, I occupy Zoey's old seat.

"I moved to Chicago against my parents' wishes. I mean, you see the lengths they've gone through to keep us here. They built four houses as a bribe to keep us here. Someone has to take over the farm." I shrug and drop my gaze to the small line of ants crawling around me. "I have a reputation here, Dr. Hawthorn—"

"Derek."

"Dr. Hawthorn," I reiterate firmly. "I couldn't wait to get out. Can you imagine living in a place where everyone roots to see you fail? I couldn't. I wanted to get out of here as fast as I could. I wanted to prove to everyone I wasn't this...*whore* they all portrayed me as. I applied and was accepted to Northwestern, got my degree and started a prestigious job at Dodge Enterprises." My stomach somersaults at those memories. Charlie wasn't always a monster. Or perhaps he was, he was good at stashing it away. "He was my boss."

I'm past the point of crying about it. Now, I'm angry. At him. At myself. At the people around me who knew what was happening behind closed doors and didn't say a damn thing about it.

"Anyway, obviously, you saw me when I came home, you see Agent Olson around...I'm sure you can put two and two together."

"I'm sorry that happened to you. You couldn't have known."

I scoff and shake my head. I could've known. I *should've* known. The signs were there.

"What are the other things you observed?"

"The incident with Michelle." Derek muses.

This time, my smile is genuine. There's nothing greater than getting under the skin of the women who slut shamed me from the beginning. I quite enjoyed it.

"She's not the first to call me a slut, and she won't be the last."

"I don't think that was the word she used."

I shrug again. *Potato, po-tah-toe.*

"It was implied."

"When that woman showed up. You stormed over there without backup."

"Yeah, well, I didn't want the whole world knowing what was going on with me. The faster I got her off the property, the faster everyone would stop talking about it."

Who am I kidding? This is Sage Creek. It's been a week and I can guarantee people are *still* talking about it.

"Charlie's sixth stepmother," I murmur. The woman I'd eventually become had Agent Olson not tracked me down at the grocery store. "Charlie's stepmother."

"If I hadn't chased after you, would you have gone with her?"

"No." It comes out firm, confident, even. The only way Charlie is getting out of my life is *when* he kills me. But until then, I'm content with living the rest of my life out here. He nods slowly and rips apart a few strands of hay. "So to answer your question, yes, I suppose it's always been me against the world."

"Isn't that lonely?"

In all honesty, yes. It's soul crushing. But I play the hand I've been dealt.

The way he watches me feels like an autopsy. He's trying to surgically remove all of my secrets, probably because he wants to ruin my life.

"Tell me about you, Dr. Hawthorn." I deflect, "I told you my life story, you tell me yours." He stretches his legs out and finds my eyes.

"I joined the Navy right out of high school. I was in an all Marine unit who went on special forces missions. And that's all the detail I can get into."

I raise my eyebrows. "That's only one part of your life. Obviously, you wound up here, had a daughter..."

"Emily Richardson. Do you know her?"

"No." It doesn't sound familiar.

"She attended college in North Carolina. We met at one of those local bars around campus. We got married, because it's something you do in the military. We got along until I deployed, and then after, things progressively got worse for us. She lost interest in me, but then got spiteful, like it was all my fault. I was going to enlist for a third term, but then she got pregnant."

A small smile twitches at the corners of his mouth.

"Kids weren't a part of our plan. But she knew if she got pregnant, I'd get out. She thought her pregnancy would get me to stay with her, and she was right. I'd never leave my kid." He sighs. "But it didn't change the fact she didn't love me anymore, which was fine by me because I had Zoey. We stayed together for a while, but there comes a point where it's toxic for kids to see their parents unhappy. Emily partied a lot, started hanging with the wrong crowd. My weekends with Zoey turned into weeks. One time even a month. At that point, I figured if this is how it's going to be, I may as well petition for full custody. When she caught wind of it, all hell broke loose."

Zoey's toothy grin comes to mind. My heart aches for her being pulled in two different directions. It's obvious she adores her father, and he adores her too. But for a mother to abandon her child for a month...

Which is why I can't kill the jellybean inside of me.

"I try to make the time I have with her fun. I'll indulge her in all the books she wants to read and make her favorite foods because I know for sure her mother doesn't do that for her."

His talk of fatherly love makes me miss my dad. My parents have a fairytale romance, but if they would have divorced back then, I'm sure my dad would be exactly like Dr. Hawthorn - thick as thieves from day one.

"I know you're scared, and you don't trust anyone around you, but I don't think hiding out in the barn all night is any safer."

All of the air deflates from my lungs as I let out a shaky laugh.

"You know nothing. All of these horses would go to war for me."

"You made it out the other side, Aria."

When I lift my gaze to meet his, I feel like I'm being punched in the gut. Not because he's hurting me, but because he's seeing past the brick wall I've built over the years. And little does he know, he's taken out the first brick. The one in the middle you can sort of see through.

"Did I?" My question hangs in the air like rotten garlic. "I'm never going to be the same. I know I haven't been a ray of sunshine, but I'm not mean."

A fond smile stretches across his lips.

"I didn't think you were mean. Defensive, maybe. People say rash things out of fear."

My mind flits back to my dad. Is he afraid I've fucked everything up so badly he feels he has to escape before I bring this family's downfall after me? He loves me, I know this. But at what point will he throw in the towel? Where's the line?

"You said you were off the market for the rest of your life..."

Yes. It's best for everyone involved. It's for everyone's safety.

"I meant it."

His melancholy grimace brings the slightest twinge to my heart. One I want to banish away forever.

"Can I ask why?"

Chewing on my bottom lip, I sit up a bit straighter, and force myself to look him in the eye. "I've done my time and I'm *exhausted.* The only person I need to give the life they deserve is myself." *Even if there's not a ton of time left.*

"I can respect that," he says softly.

"What about you, Dr. Hawthorn? Why are you whoring yourself out to the flocks of women around town when you can settle down and raise a family?" I ask with a teasing smile.

His stare grips me in a tight squeeze. Pain and wariness cling to his features. It's then I can appreciate the strength his aura holds. He's confident, but there isn't any cruelty, not like when I first got here. I admire the freckles sprinkled on his face and the way his wavy hair falls into his line of vision. He's handsome. He has his pick of anyone around town, and with a happy-go-lucky kid like Zoey, he should be looking to complete his life.

"Like you, I've done my time."

I grimace. What a lame excuse!

"And besides, I have a family. I have Zoey. I have my brothers. That's all I need."

So he scratches the itch when it arrives?

"Isn't *that* lonely?"

Chuckling, he pulls himself to his feet and offers his hand to help me up. I reluctantly place my hand in his and grip it tight as he pulls me up. It's not so disgusting to me anymore. Maybe a little bit. But his hands don't promise punishment. They promise help. My back sings in pain at the position I've been sitting in for the last fifteen minutes.

"I'm not a man of romance. When my needs arise, I satisfy them."

Scoffing, I dust the dirt off my pants.

"And once again, I'm going to have to insist you call me Derek."

I follow him out of the feed room, shutting off the light and locking up. *Derek—suppose we're there now—*stands behind me at a respectable distance. Unlike before, there's no animosity between us.

"If you're scared to go home, you're more than welcome to have dinner with Zoey and me. But I'm sure you'd rather hang out with your mom or your brother. Regardless, I can walk you to where you want to be."

We're silent for a beat, having a staring contest we're the only ones privy to.

"Do you want to be my friend, Derek?"

A slow smile spreads across his full lips. There's no challenge in his eyes, or any hidden meanings. Friendship is all we're equipped to offer each other. And I think I'm okay with it.

"I'm friends with the other McKenzies. It would be weird if we weren't friends too."

"Okay."

"Okay," he replies. "So…dinner?"

"Thanks, but I think I'm gonna keep my momma company. Thanks for offering to escort me, but I think I can make it on my own."

"I'll see you tomorrow then." We set off on our separate ways, but my stomach churns at the change in atmosphere.

11

DEREK

Zoey and I enjoy breakfast for dinner and then spend an hour watching *Wheel of Fortune and Jeopardy!* before she turns in for the night. While I load up the dishwasher, my mind wanders to the raven-haired beauty who runs into danger as if it's an old friend.

The rumor mill around here is to be taken with a grain of salt. Women like the Hunts or Deborah Baker tell stories of Aria getting around with the guys around town.

The woman I spoke to tonight—without ripping my head off this time — is kind. She's pensive and intuitive. Maybe that's who she was trained to be when she was with the likes of Charlie Dodge and it's stuck.

But there's a nagging in my gut that tells me otherwise.

I know the McKenzies. They're hardworking people who stay out of the gossip. Annie is free-spirited and the kindest person I've met besides her mother. Chris has become my little brother, despite his perpetual bad mood and denial about inheriting the farm.

Jay Parker, the honorary McKenzie is one of my closest friends. He's stationed at Camp Lejeune, and still, when he returns home, we pick up right where we left off like there's no time passed between us.

Steve. Well, he's a different story. He's my commander. My friend. A force to be reckoned with. But seeing him with Zoey, with Annie and Chris, I know he's kind.

I'm a girl dad. I understand how angry he was when his baby came home looking like she'd been pushed through a meat grinder.

Knowing what I know about the McKenzies, I *know* Aria isn't the person Sage Creek has painted her to be. And knowing I love the McKenzies for adopting my daughter and I into their family, the least I can do is keep an eye out for their "wild child."

My front door swings open, and as I look over my shoulder from the sink, I see Nate stroll in and drops himself on a barstool and sigh.

"Dude."

"What's yours is mine, buddy," Nate teases.

"Do you want some pancakes?"

Nate scrunches his nose and shakes his head.

"Thanks, I've already eaten."

"To what do I owe the pleasure?"

Sighing, he reaches for the bowl of leftover blueberries on the kitchen bar, popping a few in his mouth.

"She's pretty."

My lips thin at the implication.

"Nate."

"I'm here to remind you what's at stake. And I'm *begging* you to be professional. She's the lynchpin in my case and if you fuck it up for me..."

"I won't fuck it up. We're just friends. That's it."

"She's a good person, that's all I'm saying. I've gotten to know her. She has fire even though she's suppressing it. You have no idea the horrors she's lived through. She helped me get the Dodges. I want to help her by giving her a second shot at life."

Third.

"I need her to live. But I don't want her to get hurt."

"Agent Olson?" Zoey's timid voice echoes down the hallway.

"It's okay, Zo. Nobody else is here."

She breaks into a grin and races over to Nate, throwing her arms around him.

"Hi, Uncle Nate. I missed you."

"I missed you too, gorgeous. I come bearing gifts too." He reaches into his back pocket, taking out a rolled up paperback of *Heartland* and handing it off to Zoey who wrinkles her nose in disapproval at the state of the paperback.

"Heartland?"

"Someone in town told me this was a great series."

She grins.

"I should be angry at you for rolling it up."

"Zoey," I warn.

"Thank you," she replies gleefully. "So…I have to call you Agent Olson around Miss Aria?"

Nate frowns. "For a little while."

"Is she in trouble?"

Nate has always been good about keeping a lid on his job around Zoey. He loves her. So when she asks, I know he'll respect the boundaries I've put in place to not bring shit home.

"I'm keeping her safe," he replies cautiously. "She's one of the good guys, Zo."

She considers his words and drops her gaze to the book.

"I like her. She's nice."

Nate smirks and wraps her in a tight hug.

She lifts her gaze to Nate and grins.

"Where's Eve?"

Nate's smile immediately wanes.

"Zoey, it's time for bed, sweetheart. Say goodnight."

Frowning, she wraps her arms around Nate's neck and plants a small kiss on his cheek. She races back to her room, her light flicking on. She'll be up for hours reading her books, and I don't have the heart to shut the light off on her.

I'm not a mind reader, but our life together has been content. With the exception of Emily constantly trying to pit us against each other, our life is drama free. Zoey doesn't ask me about getting married again. In fact, we've fallen into a stable routine and my flavors of the night don't get brought up.

The secret is she doesn't know about them.

If I'm being honest, that's the point.

Nate turns to me and sighs bringing me out of my thoughts.

"She's not a one night stand kind of girl, Derek. She's been through enough."

I throw my hands up in the air in frustration.

"Dude! You guys are the ones who think I can't keep it in my pants. I can exercise self-control, jackass. Besides, she already told me she's off the market for good."

It should pacify him, but it doesn't.

How close have they gotten? He knows her predicament because of his job, but do they shoot the shit like Nate and I do?

"Your track record isn't great, forgive me." He slides off the barstool and stretches. "This has to be kept on the downlow. If the bureau finds out about our connection, this is going to look too fishy."

"I can keep my trap shut, don't you worry."

He glares at my indifference

"Just…be careful. Stay vigilant. And keep an eye on her if I'm not around."

I want to know Aria McKenzie. I'll help keep her safe for her parents' sake, and I suppose for Nate's.

It won't ever happen for us. I'm not looking for someone for Zoey to call mom and Aria isn't looking for another man to boss her around. On paper, it's a perfect reason to never be together, but I can't for the life of me get her shy smile and those magnetic hazel eyes out of my head.

12

ARIA

16 weeks pregnant...

Sage Creek is one of those places you can find *anything* in. To promote tourism, we have chain restaurants out the wazoo, along with the mom and pop shops people come here for. The shopping is great—that is, if you don't mind airing your business out to the town if you're going to leave the next day anyway.

I mind.

And yet, I agree to take Olson out into the world, rather than our farm so he can eat something he didn't cook for once—regardless of the rumor mill.

Our waitress is a teenager who would rather be on her phone than giving customer service. It's a distraction I welcome.

He orders a bacon burger; I stick with a patty melt and tense up once she leaves to put our orders in. I'm eager to hear about the case. I *want* to know when I can bury him in the trial. So far, I've only head the investigation is ongoing.

Maybe the evidence I passed along wasn't enough to convict him.

Or, and most likely, they're hard at work paying off everyone who crosses their path.

He smiles politely, passing me a straw to put in my sweet tea.

"You've been keeping busy?" he asks, trying to break up the tension swirling in the air.

"Yeah, I guess. I don't mind helping out around the farm. Gives my mind something else to focus on."

"Has Charlie reached out to you?"

His name sucks the pleasantries right up. It's sickening. He's the killjoy who lurks around even when he physically can't be around.

"I'm not sure. You have my phone."

He grimaces in annoyance, crumpling the straw paper into an accordion.

"What about Charlotte? Has she tried to make contact since she showed up?"

"No letters, no calls to either house, and she hasn't shown up since."

He lays his hands flat on the table, seemingly wanting to reach out and comfort me, but thinks better of it.

Good. As long as we can blast the memo of me not wanting to be touched, I can live the rest of my life in peace.

"How are *you* doing?"

My stomach gurgles with nausea. It's the first time somebody has asked me how I was doing and was genuinely curious. My family tries to make me move on by not talking about Charlie. Jo has called Annie's house every day to check in and asks about my progress with therapy.

I still dream of him.

At night, I force myself to stay awake as long as I possibly can until the sleep takes me. Where I think I can escape to happier memories of my childhood, but instead wind up his stepmother's grave, or with Charlie's hand tight around my throat, pressing me up against the front door while he shoves his hand in my panties and scratches his way into my vagina.

"I'm fine."

Olson scoffs. "Aria."

"I don't know. What do you want me to say?"

His steely exterior softens as I banish unwelcome tears away.

"Be honest with me."

"How can I be anything but terrified?"

"He's locked up on house arrest."

Scoffing, I push my drink to the middle of the table and lean back into the booth. I can't bother to meet his gaze. House arrest is a small hurdle and knowing Charlie he will somehow find a way around it.

Why is it when a woman goes through the worst kind of trauma, everyone expects her to move on and repress those memories?

Don't you think I would if I could?

"*They* are. But what about their associates?"

Olson isn't one to wear his emotions on his sleeve, but when he furrows his brow and drops his gaze as he loses himself in thought, I *know* he has the same suspicions I do.

At least I'm not crazy.

"I'd be naïve to think I'm safe with you. You can't be awake twenty-four hours, seven days a week. My family can't either. So where does that leave me?"

When he doesn't answer, the pit of dread consumes me. I already know I'm a sitting duck. A dead woman walking. If Charlie finds out I'm pregnant, it buys me time. Which makes it so detrimental he never finds out. I'd rather die with this child inside me where he won't ever get to him, than give birth, have him kill me, and steal my child and have the cycle continue. I refuse.

"You're right. I can't be up twenty-four-seven. *But,* I have rigged up all the houses on the property and they'll alert me should anyone intrude. Your sister told me she had a gun in her nightstand. Do you know how to use it?"

I roll my eyes. We're farmers. *Of course* I know how to use a gun.

"Yes."

"Prove it."

He isn't serious, is he?

"What?"

"There's a gun range around here, right?"

There will be a ton of eyes there. Men who want to whip their dicks around to show they know more than I do. Men who will condescendingly put their hands on my waist to show me the right way to stand.

The thought of hands has me heading for the hills. I'll take my chances with the outdated knowledge of pointing and shooting from when I was a kid.

But…he's right. It would be helpful to have a refresher. Just in case Charlie gets brave and tries to steal me under the veil of nightfall.

"Aria?"

"We have a vacant pasture. We could shoot there."

Our food is placed in front of us, and suddenly, I'm not hungry anymore. The jellybean inside of me demands food, however, if I take one bite, I'll vomit all over this table.

"Okay. I can get it set up. Do you have targets?"

Shrugging, and reluctantly shoving a fry in my mouth, I answer with a full mouth, "Bales of hay?"

He thinks to himself.

"I know a guy. I'll get us some targets and we'll practice today. You don't leave until I know you won't miss."

My tongue feels like sandpaper. The food in my mouth tastes like ash. Growing up, Daddy was the one to teach all of us how to use and clean a gun. We never thought we'd have to use it.

Now…there's a real possibility I could take someone's life away before they take mine. It gives me a strange sense of peace and debilitating fear all at the same time.

Charlie had a gun. He liked to torture me with Russian Roulette. Whenever he deemed me disobedient or in the way, he'd take it from the safe, plaster me against the wall and place the barrel in my mouth.

He pulled the trigger, only to reveal he never loaded the damn thing.

I *always* prayed for death.

AFTER LUNCH, Olson drops me off at Annie's house while he gathers the things we need for target practice. I feel weird walking around my sister's house, digging through her belongings when she isn't here. But alas, I find the *Sig Sauer* at the bottom of the drawer—with the safety off.

Oh, Annie.

I scoff, quickly flipping the safety on, carrying the cold metal in my hands carefully down the hall. A part of me is miffed it was lying so carelessly at the bottom of the drawer. People get killed all the time because of negligence. I love my sister, but holy crap.

What the hell am I supposed to do with this, anyway? I have no holster, and only God knows what Annie did with the case it came with.

I set it on the counter and text my mother that my *babysitter* and I will be shooting in the pasture, not to be alarmed.

Who the hell am I kidding? She's going to be alarmed regardless.

My phone buzzes in my back pocket. Every time the damn thing goes off, my body automatically locks up. That niggling fear in the back of my mind, nagging me to pick up the phone because there are consequences if I don't comply.

Which is why shooting is so fucking important right now.

"Hey, Peanut! How's everything going?"

I smile at Annie's voice. I miss my sister, and I'm also insanely jealous she gets to spend time in Canada while I can't leave the damn country.

"I'm good. How is Canada?"

"So much poutine," she groans and giggles. "It's beautiful here. I'm putting my French to use."

"I thought you only knew the one phrase."

She laughs again. I can picture her in the middle of a cobblestone street, smiling like the weight of the world isn't on her shoulders, her blonde hair flowing with the wind. I wish I were her. Just for a day.

"Well, that's true. But the magazine sent a translator with me. She's cool, I guess. She thinks my accent is embarrassing."

I hop up on the bar stool.

"Is there something you needed?"

I want to take back the words before they even left my mouth. I'm an idiot.

"Geez, Louise, I was calling you because I miss you."

Right. Because people can *miss you without getting possessive.*

"I'm sorry. I miss you too. I'm having a crappy day."

Annie hums while she tries to find the right words.

"Do you want to talk about it?"

Absolutely not.

"Thanks, but no. I'm meeting Olson in a little bit. We're shooting in the front pasture so I should probably wrap this up."

She sighs.

"Peanut, please don't shut me out. I just got you back." Shutting her out keeps her safe, no matter how much I miss her.

"I won't, I promise. I'll call you tonight before I go to bed."

"No. FaceTime me. I want to see your face."

Not likely.

I wrap up the call, shove the phone back into my pocket and step out onto the front porch. I crash onto her porch swing, carelessly tossing the gun on the cushion next to me.

We're in April, and it's starting to heat up. The gentle breeze brings me balance, while the silence brings me fear. There's nothing amiss here.

It's equally a relief and disconcerting.

Dr. Hawthorn's truck starts down the driveway. I get a brief glimpse of him through the driver's side window while he talks angrily on the phone. This angry demeanor is something I've only seen once: that one time when we first met.

Although I found his little outburst comical, I don't want to be on the receiving end of his wrath.

He gets out of the truck and slams the door.

"You're being unreasonable!" It's the only sentence he shouts until he closes himself inside of his house.

Olson steps outside my house, his holster on his belt and closes the distance to Dr. Hawthorn's house, knocking on the door.

Is this the guy he was talking about?

He answers the door, a scowl on his face. They talk for a minute, and then they disappear into the house together.

I curl my legs under me and allow the wind to gently move the swing. I wonder how Charlie is doing with house arrest. How many people has he bullied? Will the board still keep him on when he's under so much scrutiny? Are their stocks plummeting?

I hope so. What I wouldn't give to be a fly on the wall as they plead for his sorry life.

Were they surprised to find out I was the one who took a wrecking ball to their reputation? Did they even suspect I was working against them from the second Charlie laid a hand on me?

I may not have been able to escape right away, or get law enforcement involved, but I made plans. Olson was the one who learned my patterns and found me at the grocery store while I was shopping.

He's my savior. The freer of chains. His girlfriend—ex-girlfriend—must be so proud.

"You ready?" I straighten up at Olson's voice. It takes me a few seconds to register Dr. Hawthorn's ornery glare.

"Um, yeah. I'm ready." I grab the gun off the cushion which makes both men leap a few paces back. "Calm down. I'm not flagging you and the safety's on."

Olson strides over and takes the piece out of my hand, inspecting it.

"Don't you have a case for it?" Dr. Hawthorn asks, inspecting it right after Olson does.

"It's not mine. It's Annie's. Mine's stashed away in my dad's closet." And there was no way I was going to waltz into my parents' house demanding a gun. It wouldn't end well.

Dr. Hawthorn's dark eyebrow arches in the most Betty Lou way.

"Be glad you weren't the one who fished it out of her nightstand. The safety wasn't even on."

Olson groans and Dr. Hawthorn scowls.

"Well, let's go. Derek's allowing us to use his targets."

I instantly freeze.

He's coming?

Olson looks at me expectantly, silently urging me on, because I'm the one holding the whole party up.

"Do you have any objections?"

I reluctantly shake my head, but I do. I have so many objections. The first one is the neighbor with the adorable daughter who has been watching me with…*strange* eyes. Strange, but exhilarating in a weird way.

I hop in the back of Dr. Hawthorn's truck and move the stack of books I assume are Zoey's over a few inches.

A smile spreads on my lips. I love that she reads. As Dr. Hawthorn drives, I peek through the stack, impressed with the selection she chose. It warms my heart *Heartland* is the first book on top. The next time she's over, I'll have to bring her the next book in the series. I find her copy of *Holes,* a kid version of *Pride and Prejudice,* and a tattered copy of *Because of Winn Dixie.*

Dr. Hawthorn's gaze meets mine in the rearview mirror, his brows furrowed, annoyance etched in his steely gaze. I drop his gaze when my stomach churns. The open fields race past me while he drives erratically through the back pasture. He opens the gate without assistance, and slams the car door when he gets back in.

The truck is silent. Olson gives him a sidelong glance, wondering if we made a big mistake by inviting him along. Spoiler alert: we *absolutely* made a big mistake inviting him.

When we reach our desired area, Dr. Hawthorn hops out and starts setting up the targets. I bring the small box of ammo with me to the folding table Olson sets up. Dr. Hawthorn sets up six bales of hay, two per stack, creating a small barrier so we have something to rest our guns on.

"Aria?"

I turn my head to Olson as he stares at me like I am the craziest person on Earth.

Maybe I am.

"Are you listening to me? Is the gun clean?"

Sure.

I didn't exactly check, but I'd love to get this show on the road.

"Mmhm."

Without a word, Dr. Hawthorn strolls behind me, taking the gun out of my hand and disassembling it, inspecting every inch of the weapon. Once he's satisfied, he assembles it and places it in my hand.

What the hell is wrong with him? And why is he taking it out on me?

"It's fine," he grumbles, grabbing his gun out of his holster and carrying it out to our setup.

Rolling his eyes, Olson turns to me and places a hand on my shoulder. "When is it okay to put your finger on the trigger?"

"Only when you're ready to kill someone," I mumble back, turning away from him and walking to the setup, just as Dr. Hawthorn empties his magazine. I drop to the ground, throwing my arms over my head.

"Hawthorn! What the hell, man!"

My cheeks burn when Olson helps me up. I brush the grass off of me while Dr. Hawthorn inserts a new clip, misery in his stance.

"What?"

"Give us some warning!"

"Fine! I'm emptying another magazine!"

This time, I'm ready for it. Olson slaps some ear protectors over my ears and only the muffled sounds of the *pop, pop, pop* can be heard. Casings cover the ground. He doesn't show any signs of slowing down. Olson growls something at him, and then the earmuffs are yanked off.

"Ignore him. You were right. Where are you going to aim?"

"The chest. It's a bigger target."

"Right."

And if it's Charlie wielding the gun, I shoot to kill. I don't give him the opportunity to get back up.

"If you're pulling the trigger, you're prepared to kill someone." Daddy's words echo through my head.

I swallow my nerves and turn the safety off. I line up the shot, cock the gun, and nearly shit my pants when Olson stands so close to me and then tells me to relax.

There's no relaxing in this position.

This isn't going to relieve any stress.

"Breathe," he says softly. "Don't lock your arms."

The target is blurry, but only because it's so far away. I focus on the chest and finally gain the bravery to place my index finger in the trigger well, curling it around the trigger, and squeezing.

The bang makes my ears ring. My arms immediately shake. The gun is taken out of my hands and laid on the hay.

"You did good."

I blink at Olson's words. It doesn't *feel* good. In fact, it feels the opposite.

"But that was only one shot. Remember what I said? We're staying here until I'm confident you can't miss."

"Yeah, I remember."

"You're strong, Aria. Remember that."

I'm *not* strong. I'm lucky.

We're here for fifteen minutes before I run out of ammo. I don't have to worry much about it, because Dr. Hawthorn brought ammo that could last him three years, so I switch out for his gun.

He remains quiet. He watches on with narrowed eyes and quiet confidence. Anger exudes off his body.

Olson's phone interrupts the lesson and he tells me to continue and takes the call in Dr. Hawthorn's truck.

I ready the next shot, grateful I'm finally left alone to think.

"Are you right-handed?"

I jump at Dr. Hawthorn's voice behind me, accidentally firing off a shot.

"God! You have to announce yourself!"

He chuckles, the first time a smile cracks his hard exterior.

"Yes, I'm right-handed."

"Which is your dominant eye?"

What does that even mean?

I appreciate how his features soften. Shooting a gun is one thing. Shooting a gun while someone watches you, while he scrutinizes your every move is...*terrifying*. It's like I'm on display all over again, waiting for him to jump in my face and yell at me Drill Instructor style.

"Which eye do you close when you shoot?"

My right eye closes. "Why does that matter?"

"This is going to feel weird, but try pulling the trigger with your left hand."

I change my hand placement and stand with my feet hip width apart. He steps closer to me but respects my bubble. He doesn't move to touch or correct me.

"Breathe through it. You'll pass out if you hold your breath."

I grip it tight, and squeeze the trigger, my eyes closing involuntarily. I miss the target by a foot.

"It didn't work."

"When you closed your eyes, you moved your arms."

Looks like I'll be the first one murdered. He motions for me to get back in stance. He moves behind me.

"I'm going to touch your elbows, okay? I won't touch anything else."

My body immediately tenses at his touch. I let out a gasp as soon as the anxiety ebbs. At least he told me what he was doing. My skin isn't crawling and begging me to shower his touch off.

"When you have someone in your sights, don't hesitate. Don't close your eyes. If that fucker is standing over you with a gun in your face, you shoot to kill. You watch him die at your hands with no remorse." He helps line me up and releases my elbows.

If Charlie is standing over me with a gun in my face, I don't want to be the one who doesn't have the upper hand. If he dies at my hands, I want to watch the life drain from his eyes. I want to be the one he fears. And most importantly, I want to be the one who takes everything away from him, just like he did to me.

"Get out of your head, Aria." His voice is gentle and smooth, not like how it was twenty minutes ago. I lick my lips and squeeze the trigger, my eyes remaining open. "I'll grab the target. Stay here."

He moves so smoothly. And I can't help but ogle the swirling tribal tattoos on his right arm. He grins as he jogs back, showing me the hole through the target's chest. Relief rushes over me. Maybe I *can* kill him if the need ever arises.

"Hey, I need to get back. My team has a lead."

My face falls. I've only had one successful shot.

"No worries. Take the truck. I'll stay here with Aria, and I'll let you know how it goes after. We'll clean up tomorrow."

"Aria? Are you okay with this?" Olson asks.

"Um…yeah. It's fine. I don't think I'll stay much longer."

He eyes us both suspiciously. He won't leave me if I'm not comfortable.

"Honestly, Olson, it's fine. I'll be okay."

He frowns, and then narrows his eyes at Dr. Hawthorn.

"Not a scratch, asshole. I mean it."

Dr. Hawthorn waves him off dismissively and retreats to the bales of hay. I wave goodbye to Olson and follow Dr. Hawthorn back to the makeshift stand.

"How do you feel?" he asks, keeping his eyes on the prize.

"Fine."

He scoffs.

"You need to get better at lying." I regret not going back home with Olson. "That last shot was great. Let's keep it going. Evening feed is in two hours and we're not leaving until you can group."

What are the odds of me using this thing, anyway?

"Is this how you get all the ladies?"

Chuckling, he grabs hold of my elbows, steadying my stance, but keeping a respectable distance.

"There isn't this much talking with the ladies."

I smirk and pull the trigger. "Good. Do it again."

And we do. I use two entire boxes of ammo, and by the time we're finished, I can group my shots with ease, though I'm still a little shaky holding the damn thing.

"We'll pick it back up tomorrow."

I raise my eyebrows.

"Excuse me?"

He picks up all the shell casings and rounds up the other garbage around us.

"You want to be ready, don't you? Sure, you can group, but what if he doesn't show up for another six months? You're not going to do shit if you don't practice."

I freeze on the spot. "What if I had things to do?" *Like sit in front of Annie's TV all day so I can watch all of Netflix's catalog.*

He smirks and straightens.

"What do you have going on, Ace?"

Absolutely not a goddamned thing.

When I don't answer, he chuckles. "Move your plans around. This is important."

I flick the safety on the gun and place it carefully on the bales of hay as I help get the rest of the garbage.

He emptied three magazines on anger alone. I saw his target. A few of those shots went into the same holes. What could get him so angry he felt the need to shoot something?

"Did it make you feel better?"

I don't dare make eye contact with him. Was that too personal?

"Did it scare you?" His question takes me off guard.

Charlie lived for my fear. My dad doesn't mean to scare me, but he doesn't coddle me, either.

When it comes to my family, I was always the afterthought. Maybe not on purpose, but I wasn't one to speak up. That was for Chris and Annie—the planned children.

"No."

"Is there a reason you feel you need to lie to me?"

I hate how he can read me like an open book.

"I'm not lying."

He shrugs and shoves the garbage in a plastic bag.

"You hit the ground, Ace. You were scared."

"You caught me off guard! What psycho empties a magazine with *no* warning? Who has *that* much anger bubbling inside of them?"

His boyish grin melts the animosity I have towards him. Yeah, I hit the ground, but I thought he was shooting at an intruder.

I exhale a cleansing breath and sink to the ground, allowing my head to rest on the bales of hay behind me.

"You'll get used to it."

I fucking hope not.

"I doubt it." I lace my fingers through the soft grass, close my eyes, and take a deep breath. I'm grounding myself to the moment.

A gun isn't being shoved in my mouth.

And the man sitting next to me isn't making any sudden movements.

Progress.

"Do you ever get out of your head?"

"It's safe there."

He chuckles.

"Safe is boring."

Safe is...safe. Safe means not saying the wrong thing and facing the consequences. Being safe is playing my cards close to my chest. There's only one person who will fight for you, and that's yourself. I'm enjoying whatever time I have left with my family—despite the fact they're livid with me. They still love me regardless, even if my dad has a shitty way of showing it.

It's like he realizes he says the wrong thing, because he shifts his body so he's facing me.

"I didn't mean it like that."

"If Olson didn't track me down at the grocery store, I'd still be a slave to Charlie."

He frowns and opens his mouth to say something, but I'm too quick.

"Safe is what kept me alive."

"Survival is one thing, Ace, but what are you planning to do once all of this is over? You're in a good position now. You can reinvent yourself...be the person you always saw yourself as being."

How easy.

Why didn't I think of that?

Let me just repress all of the memories of him beating me within an inch of my life, or burning me until my ear piercing screams filled the top floor of our apartment building.

"Why is it everyone wants me to just bounce back like nothing ever happened?" I leap up and grab Annie's empty gun and start for our houses, his heavy footsteps behind me, the plastic bag rustling in his hands. "Am I supposed to forget he shoved me in a grave with his dead stepmother for a full twenty-four hours before coming back to get me? Or how he shoved an unloaded gun in my mouth and pulled the trigger because he got pleasure from watching me squirm?"

"That's not what I'm saying, Aria."

"Then what is it? Because I guaran-fucking-tee my mother is sitting at the kitchen table, working her rolodex to see what other idiot she can stick me with so I can stop embarrassing the family—"

"Do you honestly believe that? I know your mother, and she genuinely cares about all of you. And saying that about her is insulting. You went through something horrific, but I think you're the only one who thinks you're a burden."

I laugh poisonously.

"My dad couldn't get away from me fast enough. You're new around here, so I don't expect you to understand how our dynamic works."

The way he freezes sends a shiver down my spine. Does he know more than what he's letting on? Does he know what my dad is really up to?

"You don't know me, Dr. Hawthorn, and I'd appreciate it if you would stop pretending like we're friends."

"Oh, great. So we're back to the formal business, then? Okay, *Ms. McKenzie,* what I was trying to say is your family is bending over backwards to give you a sense of normalcy. You obviously don't want to be pitied, or treated any differently than your siblings, then what the fuck do you expect everyone to do?"

Tears prick my eyes. He thinks he knows, but he doesn't. I stop in my tracks. His footsteps sound from behind, and then his boots slide into my line of vision on the ground. He sighs.

"Fuck, Ace, I wasn't trying to make you cry."

"Don't take it personally. It doesn't take much nowadays."

His fingers twitch, wanting to reach out and give me a reassuring squeeze, or whatever, but he respects the bubble. I wish he'd respect the bubble to not fucking talk to me either.

"I had a shitty day and I'm taking it out on everyone around me."

What, possibly, could have gone so wrong in his life to warrant a shitty day?

"I'm not going to pretend to know what horrors you faced while you were with him. But you're doing yourself a disservice by closing yourself off to everyone around you. That's how he wins."

That's how he wins.

He already fucking won. Everyone around me doesn't know how to act around me. He isn't involved in my day to day anymore, but still, I'm acting like he still has a say.

My phone vibrates in my back pocket. I reach back and glance at the caller ID. My hands shake at the 312 area code.

"Aria?"

"I have to go. Don't follow me." I storm past him, but he's hot on my heels.

"We're going in the same direction. I can't *not* follow you!"

"Then wait. Wait until I get all the way inside and then go home. Momma will help with evening feed." *Probably.*

Just when I thought he's gone, he finds some way to make sure I comply.

13

DEREK

Aria doesn't show up for morning feed, so Chris and I are stuck doing morning chores. I can't wait for Annie to get back. I have a job I like, and I don't exactly have all the time in the world to pick up her slack.

Feeding is a mundane task. It doesn't take me any more brain power however, it eats into my running time. I don't consider myself a gym rat, but I like to stay fit. I get exercise from feeding, but not at the same rate I'd get at the gym.

As my mind clears, I'm haunted by a certain McKenzie. I hope she's all right. I hope I didn't screw up all our progress by putting in my two cents.

I think I pushed too far. I should've shut my mouth when I made her cry. Fuck. I don't like being *that* guy. I don't get off on tears or watching a broken woman crumble into the ground. That's not who I am.

But it shouldn't matter. She's made it crystal clear she doesn't want to hear from me. So why do I keep trying to force my time on her? Her sense of humor is like mine, dark and dry. Her presence brings some kind of… calm to me. Which is ridiculous because she's anything but calm. She's a bundle of high-strung nerves that will erupt into chaos at the slightest prod.

But I keep going back for more.

Regardless of how she feels about me, I'm still taking her back to the pasture to shoot today. It's essential she can shoot an intruder. If her family is going to bat for her, she needs to learn to go to bat for herself.

If this danger she unintentionally brought home with her affects the rest of us, then *everyone* needs to know how to defend themselves.

Topping off the last water bucket, I catch sight of Emily's car speeding down my driveway. She's not done picking fights with me.

Cool.

I take my sweet time and let her stew on my front porch while I wind up the hose and sweep down the barn. I walk at a glacial pace to my front door, to find her standing at my front door with her arms crossed and annoyance etched in her tan and doe like features.

It's nice to know where my child support is going. It funds her tanning habit while Zoey has to beg for new books to read.

Emily's blonde hair is in a low pony, her eyebrows furrowed, and her glare is hidden by her ridiculously large sunglasses. She wears a black and white striped dress on heels she can barely walk in.

I hope her feet hurt.

"Go away, Em."

"You don't get to hang up on me, Derek."

I open the door and allow her entry. Off come the sunglasses as her gaze sweeps over my minimalist living room, huffing in disapproval.

"I do when you're being ridiculous."

"It's a good opportunity. I'd be an idiot to pass it up!"

An opportunity that takes Zoey to California while Emily gets to live her best life. Anger surges through my veins just by her presence. I've given *everything* I have to her to be able to have a relationship with my daughter and she thinks she can pull the rug out from under us.

"I'm not from Sage Creek, Emily. I moved here because you purposely got pregnant to spite me. I've nearly killed myself getting everything you've required or asked for in order for me to have a relationship with Zoey. I'm not letting you take her when she has a life here."

She purses her pouty lips and it's now I see her eyes watering. I'm not relenting, and I'm sure as *hell* not going to let her take my kid away from me.

"I'm putting my foot down. You can take the job if you want to, but you're leaving Zoey with me if that's the case."

"God, was there ever a time you cared about me?"

Is she fucking serious?

"I *married* you!"

"Oh, what for!" she shouts, pushing past me and settling on the couch. "You picked me up at a bar and it was only supposed to be one night!"

"Am I high? Am I tripping balls right now? Do you not remember the conversation from that night? How I bared my mother fucking soul to you while I spooned you? Are you fucking serious, Emily? I've done *everything* in my power to give you everything you ever wanted. *You* were the one who stopped taking your birth control out of spite. Now I'm the one who wants to step up for our kid and your first instinct is to turn tail all the way to California for a job you're not even sure you'll like."

"You can't keep our daughter here, Derek. This town keeps you hostage forever. I want her to have a real chance in the real world—"

"You're the one who came back! Don't pretend you're doing this for her! Have you even asked her if this is what she wants?"

She turns sheepish and drops my gaze. It's answer enough. Of course she didn't. Why would she?

"You'd get the summers with her. Winter break, Thanksgiving—Easter, if that's what you want—"

"You know what, I think it's time for you to leave because I cannot be civil with you. If you want to talk about this further, then get in touch with my lawyer because I will not let Zoey go without a fight. And I'll win. I promise you." I turn on my heel and storm into the kitchen. I make a travel cup of coffee so I have something to do with my hands before I explode at the fact she's still here.

"We don't need to get the lawyers involved," she says quietly, entering the kitchen.

"I don't have energy to play your games, Em. I'm done. I'm serious. Contact my lawyer and we'll start getting the ball rolling."

Taking her defeat, she trudges out the door. I'm not able to expel the breath I've been holding until I hear her car back out of the driveway. I make a mental note to get in contact with Logan to clue him in, since the bastard's my lawyer.

Before leaving the house, I grab my gun and a few boxes of ammo and head over to Aria's house.

I'm no ray of sunshine. Hell, even my friends tell me I'm miserable to be around sometimes. This is important. I don't mind being the bad guy if that's what makes her safe. And besides, It gives me an excuse to hang out with her even if it's for an hour. And for that hour, she's safe.

I knock on her door, dumping my gun and ammo on the side table, just in case she thinks I'm going to shoot the place up.

"Derek! What are you doing here?" Jackie appears behind me, her arms full of grocery bags and duffle bag.

"I could ask you the same thing…" Jackie O'Brien is my only friend outside the McKenzies in this town. She's my assistant, yes, but I particularly enjoy the bond we've formed. She was never a flavor of the night, though I suppose at one time, she was *somebody's* flavor of the night. One who lives on this property.

The door opens and the sight before me scares the shit out of me.

Her dark hair is tied up in a bun, but it doesn't matter. It's falling out. Her skin has a greenish tinge. She drowns in the heavy gray sweater and sweatpants. Even her feet are covered.

"Are you okay?" The words tumble out of my mouth, but I already know the answer. She's not okay. She's…sick.

"Peachy. What are you doing here?" She steps aside for Jackie to come in, but immediately blocks the door with her body.

"I wanted to take you shooting again."

She scoffs and leans up against the doorframe. "I'd like to. But later. When I'm not knocking on death's door."

I raise an eyebrow. "Please don't take this the wrong way, but you look like hell."

She gives me a thin-lipped smile, totally sarcastic.

"And you look like you need a shower. Don't throw stones at glass houses."

I sigh impatiently. One of these days, the two of us are going to be friends. But I don't think today is the day.

"You use fear as a crutch, Ace."

"Are we going to fight again? Because what I'm fixin' to do is projectile vomit all over you if so."

A grin breaks through my defenses. She doesn't mean harm, I don't think. She's just not feeling well.

"Can I help you with anything?"

"No. I have Jackie. And if you see Olson around, tell him I'm not up to visitors today."

"Anything else?" I ask through gritted teeth.

"Yeah, kick rocks."

"Aria, I'm sorry for last night."

It's almost like she hasn't heard that phrase before. Her bottom lip trembles, her eyes go glassy.

"I'm not trying to be a dick. I'm trying to help."

She wraps her hand around the doorknob as she considers my peace offering.

"You were right," she says softly. "I don't know how to act around everyone else. Which I guess rubbed off on everyone else and now they don't know how to act around me." She lifts her gaze to mine, offering a small smile. "You said you wanted to be friends, right?"

"You agreed to that. I'm your friend so I'm allowed to throw it back in your face."

One single "ha" escapes her mouth.

"Right. I'm feeling like absolute shit right now, but I should be better after I eat. Would you like to come in? Jackie's making soup and I'm binging *Community*."

I should turn tail and spend the rest of my weekend at a distance. But I don't. I accept her invitation and follow her into the living room.

Jackie makes herself at home by washing the vegetables she's using and situating herself at the island in the kitchen. She narrows her eyes at me while she watches me sink into the big, green, ugly sofa next to Aria.

Aria bundles up under two blankets and folds her legs under her, resting her head on the arm of the sofa.

I've only ever been in Annie's house once. Jay and Chris invited me over and Annie insisted on cooking—which we *all* regretted a few hours later. Without Annie's presence, which I assume Aria finds comfort in, I struggle to figure out the McKenzie lying next to me.

Annie takes after her mother in style. It's that trendy farmhouse style with giant clocks and shabby milk jugs. I'm pretty sure the trend started on this property. This stuff looks ancient, like it could've originated from the McKenzies who once lived here.

I don't see Aria as a trend follower. I guess that's what I'm trying to reconcile. I don't know this woman from Adam. I don't know what her style is like, or whether she's always this abrasive.

Jackie clears her throat and motions for me to meet her in the kitchen.

"Can I help you with anything?" I ask.

She shrugs absentmindedly, her attention being driven away by a naked Joel McHale. Fine. I trudge into the kitchen and reach for the stock pot Jackie points out for me to grab.

"What are you doing?" she whispers.

"You asked me to get this down for you…"

"No, idiot. What are you doing *here?*"

"Were we not in on the same conversation? She invited me."

"Derek, you're my friend, but you're also my boss and I have to say, I *really* want to hit you right now."

I reflexively take a step back.

"Why?"

"She's not like your Michelles or Brandys. She just got out of an abusive relationship. She doesn't need you around to confuse her even more."

"I can hear you," Aria's tired voice carries through the small, open floorplan.

She pulls the blankets off and shuffles into the kitchen, wrapping her arm around her best friend.

"I'm not confused in the slightest. Dr. Hawthorn is a friend, and it won't ever be more than that." She grins at me. But what is this sinking feeling in my stomach?

Jackie narrows her eyes.

"Are you sure, babe? Because I can kick him out right now. He'll try to fire me, but he knows he can't run the practice without me."

She's right. I would have filed for bankruptcy if Jackie hadn't stayed.

There's something special about this Aria McKenzie that turns everyone around her into the biggest, baddest, guard dog.

"I'm sure." She offers a hesitant smile while Jackie sends me a warning glare. Don't worry. This woman is off limits. I've received my threats and can take it like a man.

Probably.

I'd be lying if this didn't pose a challenge for me. However, I'm coming to the realization that being one of those guard dogs for *her*, has me craving her presence. Aria sighs and grabs a water bottle from the fridge and flounces back to the sofa.

"You have nothing to worry about. I promise." Jackie purses her lips and chops a carrot.

"I know I have nothing to worry about. Because you're a smart guy. You know what would happen if you crossed me." She points the knife at me, a sinister smile soon following.

Yeah. I got it.

I find my way back to the sofa and focus my attention to the TV.

"Can I ask you something kind of personal?" Her voice is strained, like she's been yelling all night. She dares not to look me in the eye, however, something about how still she holds her head on the arm of the sofa tells me she *wants* to see my reaction.

"You can ask. I might not answer."

Her parroted words force a smile.

"What made you change your mind? I mean, when you said kids weren't a part of your plan with your ex-wife…what changed?"

My mind flashes to the moment Zoey was born. She looked like an angry potato, but once I held her, my heart changed.

She wasn't a burden.

She's the sole person I'd go to war for in a heartbeat.

Emily's hormones crashed hard once Zoey was out. We stayed for days longer than necessary because they weren't bonding. Which I guess looking back on it, it was the precursor to their relationship together. They can't stand one another, even still.

I stayed up and did the feedings while Emily slept. Holding Zoey in my arms, I made silent promises to her that no matter what, she would be the center of my universe. She could count on me for always being there.

I miss her.

"She was mine." Her hazel eyes blink and water. "I held her in my arms, and I knew she was going to change me for the better." I shrug because it's the simplest truth. "When it comes to the people I love, I'm flexible. I'd do anything for Zoey or my brothers."

I'd do anything Steve McKenzie asked me to because he's my commander. He pulled me out of the darkest pit in my life and gave me a place to call my own. He's taken my child into his family and treats her as if she were blood.

She nods quietly, fidgeting with her fingers.

Why the sudden interest? She hasn't made any point to get to know me and now she's asking something so profound?

"So...you're sick?"

"It's a bug. Like I said, I'll feel better once I eat." She stretches and sits up, turning off the TV. "I don't want to be a sitting duck. Contrary to what my father believes, I'm not a complete waste of life." I involuntarily flinch at the harshness of her words. "Charlie will find me. He and his father will make sure I don't get a future, but...I think I want to live whatever life I have left."

Is she asking for help?

"What are you asking me, Ace?"

"I'm not entirely popular around these parts, and I'm okay with it."

"I'm not hearing a question." I give her a teasing smile, which makes her green cheeks redden.

"I want to shoot more. I want a schedule where I can practice."

Not where I thought where this was going...

"Are you asking me for help?"

A nervous giggle escapes her.

"I didn't want to overstep. You don't know me well enough, yet...I know I'm not the easiest person to get along with."

Jesus Christ. She thinks she's a burden.

"I'll help you."

Immediately, her whole face lights up. It's nice to see her smile after seeing her angry and distraught.

"I'd like that a lot," she replies bashfully, her cheeks flushing in approval.

14

ARIA

17 weeks pregnant...

My EYES FLY open for some strange reason. It's pitch black, and while I scan the room to see if anything is out of place, I come up empty. Jackie slumbers next to me in the fetal position. I sit up and reach for the bedside lamp when I hear it. A shuffle. A rustle against the chair under the window.

"Don't."

One spoken syllable. One voice I was assured I'd ever hear again, shatters my illusion of security. An FBI agent who promised me nobody would get through his security systems is proven wrong.

"Don't turn the light on, Buttercup. You don't want to wake your friend."

Instinctually, I glance at Jackie, and place my hand on her back so I know she's still breathing.

Sweat beads in my hairline, my breathing runs a race against itself, not able to catch up. I reach for the gun in my nightstand, but I freeze when I feel his body next to mine. My hand is picked up and moved back to my person, and the drawer of the nightstand is slammed closed.

"That would be a mistake."

This can't be happening. I've been too careful. I haven't picked up any of his calls.

"There's an FBI agent in the house next door, Charlie. The property is quiet. If I so much as scream, he'll be over here faster than you can choke me to death." It's a hollow threat. The house is only one story, and my house isn't close enough for them to hear me scream. It'll alert Jackie at the most, but what could she do?

"Yes. Agent Nathan Olson. I noticed him around quite a bit, but I couldn't put my finger on why *he* took an interest in *you.*" My heart pounds in my ear as adrenaline fills my veins. I could jump over Jackie and make a run for it, but I don't think I'd make it far.

I'm trapped. And I'm going out the same way I knew I would—at the hands of Charlie Dodge—literally.

"But you won't scream, will you, Aria? You know better." *Now.* I know better *now.* Unfortunately for him, I have too much fight in me. I want to live. I *need* to live.

When I don't say anything, he steps closer to me, fisting his hand in my hair, forcing me to meet his terrifying icy eyes.

"You've been busy, sweetheart, haven't you? Telling fibs to the government, hiding the *real* truth. Did you tell Agent Olson about the guard you killed when you tried to escape the first time?"

My mouth dries at his words. I did. I told Olson, but he told me not to worry about it. He would handle it.

"Come home, Buttercup. I miss you."

He misses his punching bag.

"I *am* home, Charlie. And as soon as you walk out the door, I'm calling Agent Olson and I will tell him every single one of your hideouts."

"Do it. I *dare* you." His icy hand grips around my throat, and his stale and hot breath washes over my face. What awaits me if I do? Why is he so confident being here when he's breaking the protection order?

I reach for my phone, but he takes it away and sets it gently on the nightstand.

"You would do it, wouldn't you? Did you forget how much I love you?" he asks quietly.

"You never loved me." It comes out as a whisper. *You never loved me.* It repeats in my head like a mantra. I was a pawn. I was a challenge. I was the eager twenty-two year old woman, fresh out of college, eager to please the big boss.

"You reminded me so many times I wasn't good enough. I was never going to make it. That's not love, Charlie. I refuse to let you make me think otherwise."

"It'll be different this time. You have my word. If you come home with me right now, it will be different. You'll have an allowance. You can come and go as you please. You'll have your own room. I won't touch you."

The exhausted side of me begs me to leave with him. Why worry about this kid when you know the Dodges will take care of it?

I'm exhausted. But I'm not stupid. The only person who can ensure I have a good life is me. I may not have the Dodge money, and my family might not be so impressed with me at the moment, but I have too much drive to be under anyone's thumb ever again.

I don't need Charlie anymore. I don't need my mother and father to clean up my mess.

I can do this.

"Go home, Charlie. I'm not going with you."

"You'll regret this."

I'm certain he's right. Maybe I will.

MY ALARM SHRIEKS. It's still dark outside and my phone is still plugged in. Jackie stretches and cracks her eyes open.

"Good morning, Peanut. Sleep good?'

No. No I did not.

I don't answer her, too terrified to hear what comes out of my mouth. I gather my outfit and change in the bathroom. My head is pounding and when I close my eyes, I feel his stale breath on my neck, waiting to literally devour me.

"Aria? Babe? What's wrong?"

"N-nothing. I'm fine. Go back to sleep. I'm going to help Chris feed and then I'll be back."

When I open the bathroom door, Jackie stands in front of me, worry etched in her exhausted features.

"Talk to me. What's going on?"

"Just a bad dream." My nightmare brought to life. I tie my hair into a tight bun. "I'll be back."

She calls after me, but I don't waste a minute. Was I dreaming? Or was Charlie in my bedroom last night?

I knock furiously on my—*Olson's*— front door. Much to my dismay, the house is silent. Eerie even.

"Hey, Ace. Are you okay?"

"I need to speak with Agent Olson." Now. Yesterday.

"Agent Olson is asleep. But you can talk to me. I'd be happy to help—"

"No, thank you. I need to speak with Agent Olson. Right now."

Derek tenses beside me. I'm terrified to look at him. At least he's here. If things go sideways, he can drive me over the border or something.

The door is locked when I try turning the knob, but what surprises me even more, and quite frankly makes my stomach churn, is Derek pulling out his keys and sinking his key in the lock.

Who gave him a key?

It's not important. Not now.

The sounds I make like an elephant dancing, racing up the stairs, would wake up anybody in the immediate vicinity. But Olson is a heavy sleeper. And I don't think that settles my nerves any.

I rip open the master bedroom door and close the both of us inside, afraid of who might follow us in here.

Olson lies in the middle of the bed, hugging the pillow next to him, and snoring. Loudly.

"Lights, lights, lights, bitch," Derek snaps, turning on the light. Olson stills and cracks an eye open.

"If you wanted to cuddle, Bubba, all you had to do was call."

Who's Bubba?

"We have company. Wake up." Nate grumbles and sits up. His bare chest, sculpted in hard lines, strong pecs stare back at me. I knew he was ripped but I mean…hello, Agent Olson. "Put some clothes on." Olson's eyes land on me, and with a small insurgence of purpose, he pulls on the shirt next to him.

"To what do I owe the pleasure? And why are you here at the ass crack of dawn?"

Derek defers to me, eyeing me carefully. It's then I realize he's not even wearing shoes.

"Aria? Did something happen?"

I swallow the lump of tears in my throat. Derek has me sit on the office chair behind the desk while I try to find my words. Olson jumps out of bed, throwing on a pair of sweats and grumbles out of pure exhaustion.

While Nate gets dressed, I breathe, trying to collect my nerves.

I'm not entirely confident it was a dream. It was so…real. I could smell his expensive cologne and feel the force of his hand in my hair.

We follow Olson downstairs where he readies a pot of coffee.

"Are you all right?" Derek asks softly so Nate can't hear.

Far from it.

"I think Charlie was here."

He scans the property through the window, looking for any signs of distress. He surprises me by breaking his rule of not touching me. Can he tell I'm on the brink of losing my damn mind?

I surprise myself by not flinching away. His calloused hands aren't rough and demanding, rather gentle and protective.

"What's going on?" Nate asks quietly, dropping himself at the head of the table. He urges us to sit down, to spill our guts. I press my hands together so I stop shaking.

"I think Charlie was here last night." Derek narrows his eyes at Olson, like he's trying to communicate telepathically.

"Aria…are you sure?" Olson asks, with the hint of doubt lacing his words.

"No." I lift my eyes to meet his gaze. "I don't know if what I saw was real. You tell me; he's donning an ankle bracelet, but I don't know for sure."

He sighs. "Okay. I can check the feed for you. But I promise you, he's locked up." He reaches for his cell phone, finds a name and taps on it, putting it on speaker.

"You're a fucking dick, Olson! What the fuck is wrong with you? Do you know what fucking time it is?" The voice on the other end gets everyone in the room to smirk.

"Good morning, Tanner. That was a lot of F bombs. Be decent. We have ladies present."

He grumbles unintelligibly while the rustling of sheets on the other end sounds clumsy and hurried.

"Good. Now I assume you and Eve are back together so she can stop harassing me every day."

Olson shifts uncomfortably, glancing at Derek and frowning.

"No, not Eve. I'm with Aria McKenzie and Dr. Hawthorn."

The silence on the other end is deafening.

"She's been calling you?" Olson asks sadly.

"Olson," Derek growls.

"What do you need, Nate? Why are you calling me so fucking early?"

"How do you feel about breaking into video feed without alerting the FBI?"

Tanner sniggers on the other end. Keys on the keyboard clack loudly over the phone.

"That sounds like a fun fucking time. Where am I breaking into?"

"The video feed from Annabelle McKenzie's room."

The silence is back. It holds so much uncertainty, so much fear.

"He's going to get me killed," Tanner mutters. "What am I looking for, exactly?"

"I need you to look over the last eight hours of footage. Did somebody enter the room?"

"Give me fifteen. I'll call you back." Olson hangs up and reaches for my hand, giving it a reassuring squeeze.

"Tanner is the best in his field. He'll look over the feed."

"Will he be able to tell if the feed was tampered with?" I'm not putting anything past Charlie.

Nate weakly smiles. "Yes. He's trained to find anything that doesn't belong. There's a reason I didn't ask my team at the FBI."

This should make me feel better, but there is something deeply planted inside my brain where I now have to question *everything.* My sanity included. This is a new level of torture.

"We can at least get morning feed going and then we can listen to Tanner's findings together," Derek announces.

I'm glad he's here. It's been so long since somebody's been on my side. I walk with him down to the barn and start setting up feed while he loads everything onto the golf cart. I clamor onto the passenger seat and he drives. The monotony of feeding and driving takes my mind off of the chaos for the briefest of moments.

Chris arrives fifteen minutes after we set off to feed and starts feeding in the other barns.

"Have you talked to someone?" Derek asks when we reach the farthest paddock.

"I've talked to a lot of people since I got home."

He snorts.

"I mean to a therapist." I don't need to see a therapist to tell me what I already know. I'm broken beyond repair. The only way I'll move on from the abuse is when he ends my life.

"Yes. And I don't want to talk about it."

He sighs dramatically and climbs back into the driver's seat.

"Why is that?" he asks softly. "You're away from the people who would brush you under the rug. I believe you, Aria. I believe when you say he made your life a living hell."

Tears burn my eyes. All I ever wanted was for *someone* in that damn apartment building to give a damn about what was happening in the penthouse. I wanted someone to come to my rescue because all of my movements were scrutinized. Because my access to help was taken away from me.

And now, this *guy* is telling me I'm not crazy. What I went through was real.

"And then what?" I croak. "I tell you about the horrible things he did to me, and then what?"

"You move on. You grow from it. You put it behind you."

It's never simple. Trauma lives with you your entire existence, whether you like it or not. The scars on my back, which I'll *never* show another human being, are constant reminders I was less than human to a man who was supposed to love me. That I wasn't worth the extra care and concern, I drove somebody so crazy the only release he could get was to mutilate my body.

"I'm not trying to make light of what you went through, Ace, but he's on lockdown and you're not. You have your life back. And maybe you can't return to what it was like before you moved to Chicago, but you hold the power to blaze the trail of the person you want to be. Hiding away, becoming a spinster—that's how he wins."

My bottom lip wobbles.

"I'm scared," I whimper. "Every time I close my eyes, I'm back in the grave. Or he's slamming my head against the wall and none of our neighbors call the police."

"I'm sorry," he murmurs. "You're home now. And we'll *all* go to bat for you."

I wish I could believe him. My father had to escape Sage Creek to get away from me. Annie's in Canada until tomorrow, and my mom and Chris don't know how to act around me. And Derek...

I refuse to give him more than a passing glance.

We drive back to the barn and Olson waves us over.

"I can confidently say the feed was tampered with. Their feed has been spliced and put on a loop. You wouldn't have been alerted to it. Not without me." Tanner's voice filters through the speaker.

I feel like a bucket of ice has been spilled down my back. What I saw was real. I *know* it.

"And you're sure?" Olson asks.

"I'm positive. I can keep an eye on it if you'd like. I can set up alerts for any movement in the room."

Olson meets my gaze, waiting for my approval.

There are so many eyes already. Do I want to add another pair to the audience?

"I'll let you know. Thanks, buddy." Olson ends the call. "Are you all right?"

There's one thing I've found comforting about Agent Olson: he's never made me feel like an idiot.

He's the only one who's ever believed me about Charlie.

"No…I don't think I am."

"I'm going to call the Chicago team and see what's going on. Everything is going to be okay."

Yeah. So they say.

15

DEREK

The appointments at the office are keeping me sane. Exhausted, but sane. Bethany Hunt is the one client who comes in multiple times a week, trying to pimp out her daughter, and for some odd reason, she's not getting tired of my indifference. Even when I'm firm with her, she laughs it off and comes back in the next day.

This town is weird.

Once Bethany is gone, I meander out to the front where Jackie is typing furiously on her computer. The empty waiting room is a sight for sore eyes. I lock the door and flip the open sign to closed and settle into the seat across from Jackie.

"Do we have anyone else on the docket for today?"

"Nope. Bethany was the last." She stops typing and grins. "Hard day, Derek? You look beat."

"Has she always been this pushy? How many times can I politely decline her offer to date her daughter?"

Jackie snorts. "That's your problem. You're being too polite. You have to be blunt."

Being too direct with the women I sleep with ensures the

message of no attachments is loud and clear. Being polite to the likes of Bethany Hunt, the town gossip is different. Everyone hates her. But everyone still *listens* to her. I may be the only vet in town, but I'm not risking my business because I want to tell Bethany Hunt to get bent.

"Do you have anything going on tonight?" I ask.

"No. My mom is moving to Seattle in a few weeks with her new beau, so I'm hanging out with her as much as I can before she leaves." She smiles sadly.

"Hey, it's an excuse to get out of this sleepy town for a week. You should use more of your vacation days."

She snorts in reply.

"I'm serious!"

"Yeah? And who is going to run things while I'm gone? You?" She smirks victoriously.

While it's true, I can't run this practice without her, she deserves a vacation. I'd happily give her as long as she needed.

"I'm not just a pretty face, Jackie. I can hold my own."

Rolling her eyes, she scoots back in her chair. "Are you letting me off early? Because I could shut down right now and be in my pj's in twenty minutes."

"Yeah, that's fine. I was going to grab a late lunch at Rhonda's and head home."

And run until my legs fall off.

I don't have to tell her twice. She directs her attention to her computer, clicks in a few places and shoots up out of her chair.

"I'm leaving before you change your mind. Have a good night. I'll catch you in the morning." Jackie locks up her desk and strolls out a few minutes later.

WHEN I PULL into the driveway, I'm surprised to find Aria on my porch swing. She still insists on wearing the long sleeves. Not an inch of skin is showing.

"Hey," I greet cautiously, climbing the porch steps and dropping my bag beside the bench.

"Hey," she replies.

"What are you doing here?"

She shrugs and drums her fingers on the wood.

"You said I should talk to someone."

I nod.

"So you went to see your shrink?"

She shakes her head. "Are you busy? I wanted to go for a walk, but Olson won't let me out of his sight. I have a funny feeling he'll stay away if you come with me."

Yes. Absolutely.

"Sure. Let me change and I'll be right out."

"I'll text him."

I race inside and call Nate.

"She wants me to go on a walk with her."

"Why?"

"It sounds like she wants to talk. She was waiting for me when I got home."

Nate sighs. "Fine. Keep your eyes peeled, okay? Keep an eye on your surroundings and keep your phone on. Encourage her to talk to me if it has anything to do with the case."

"Relax. It's going to be fine."

After I end the call, I change into a shirt and basketball shorts, the total opposite of what she wears. I lock up behind me and shove my phone in my pocket. She stands up and starts down the steps. I follow her quiet lead, wondering what she wants to talk about.

We walk through the front pasture, about two miles into the property until we reach a shallow creek. She sits down on the bank and takes off her socks and shoes, dipping her feet into the icy water.

I follow suit, waiting for her to make the first move.

"Do you ever wonder what your life would've been like if you hadn't joined the Navy?"

"No. It was always something I wanted to do. It was always supposed to be my path. I don't regret joining."

She smiles and trains her eyes on the flowing water.

"I liked living in Chicago. Before Charlie, I mean. I felt like I had so many opportunities…all I had to do was keep my head down and focus."

"What did you major in?"

"English." She laughs. "I could've been anything."

"You still can."

She smirks and shrugs.

"Maybe."

"What did you see yourself doing, Ace?"

"I don't know. I knew I wanted to be successful. I wanted to prove to my parents I could live a life outside of farming." She sighs, tossing a stone into the water. "I did. Right out of college, I was able to secure a good paying job and a decent apartment. Sure, I had to eat Ramen a few times a week, but I had a space all my own. No strings attached."

And then Dodge came along.

"I made a mistake going after Charlie."

It sounds to me like she didn't have much of a choice in the matter. Once he had his sights set on her, it didn't matter what she wanted.

"Maybe I'm going to come off sounding desperate, but back then, all I wanted was to be loved. I knew my parents loved me, and so did my brother and sister. But I mean, I wanted to feel the love of somebody else…that romantic kind of love."

I can relate. That's what Emily was for. Everyone around me was getting married, and I was the odd one out.

"That's not desperate, Ace. It's human nature to want to be loved. It takes a special kind of person to be open to all the pain that comes with it."

She shrugs. "My parents didn't get together right away. It was years after high school before they found each other. Even then, my momma was a free spirit. She was a lot like Annie."

This is the first genuine smile I get out of her.

"When you think of love, is the love between your parents what you envision for yourself?"

She purses her lips in thought. She pulls at the grass next to her, only to let it float from her hands back to the ground.

"No."

I raise my eyebrows in surprise.

"Don't get me wrong, I love the love my parents have together. But I think what I was looking for was my own kind of love." A melancholy smile stretches her lips. "I know it doesn't make sense. But it doesn't matter now. I have myself to work on. There isn't room for love in my life."

Disappointment pangs through my stomach, making an ache I didn't think could happen to a guy like me.

"Working on yourself is admirable. You've been through a lot."

She grins.

"What about you? You blame your lack of a love life on Zoey. What's the real reason?"

A chuckle escapes me. "My ex-wife is threatening to move to California with Zoey. She thought I would concede, but now I'm pressing harder for sole custody."

"I'm sorry," she murmurs. "For both of you. Zoey must be devastated."

"I don't think she knows about it." Em likes to use the element of surprise to dash Zoey's hopes. "Anyway, being married once was enough to ruin the taste of it for me. My system right now scratches the itch for human contact. It doesn't need to move any further."

A teasing smile spreads across her lips. "Are you afraid of another woman hurting you again?"

She's a minx. And she's not going to get the real answer out of me.

I married Emily because it's what I thought I was supposed to do. The divorce option was always on the table in case it didn't work out. As far as her hurting me...I don't think I let her in enough for her to hurt me.

"Not me. I'm more afraid of Zoey getting attached to somebody and then it doesn't work out."

She considers this a moment and nods.

"You're a good dad, Derek."

Her gaze captures me. For the first time since I met her, her gaze isn't haunted by fear or pain. There's something about her delicate features that shows me she's more than a victim. She's free. And she's spending her time with me.

"Thank you."

We reach a comfortable silence. The current of the water relieves the ache in my feet. The gentle breeze tangles in her hair, which bothers her enough to tie it in a ponytail.

"I'm not a mean person," she says quietly. "I...um...I think when you challenge me, I tend to get mean."

"Because you feel threatened?"

She shakes her head. "No. Because you point out the ugly truth and I'm a sore loser." She refuses to meet my gaze. "I don't know what to do about you. You're family to my family, you're my best friend's boss and friend, apparently...but when it comes to me...I don't know where to place you."

I itch to pull her into a hug, but I refrain. We're not there yet.

"I thought we were friends."

That gets a giggle out of her, albeit a nervous one.

"Yeah, we're friends." She sighs. "I missed so much here. There's a chunk of my family's lives I wasn't a part of. It's a little disorienting."

"I didn't take your place, Ace. You have no idea how much they all talked about you while you were away."

She groans. "I can only imagine."

"Nothing bad. They called you the quiet one. The *real* free spirit." I won't tell her what the rest of the town says about her. I'm not here to be cruel. "How did you meet Olson?"

This question takes her by surprise.

"The time I was on lockdown, I learned to be observant. Charlotte was constantly sneaking off with her driver, Charlie used to get hard beating the shit out of me, Dodge Senior liked to watch...stuff like that. But I noticed Olson would watch me when I went to the grocery store. I had a security detail follow me everywhere so I wouldn't run.

"He couldn't approach me in the store without Charlie's goons finding out about it. So I learned sign language. Not all of it. I used to listen to videos as I walked to the store and practiced when I would spot his SUV. I learned enough phrases to discreetly get a message out to him as I passed him. He caught on and left a burner phone in a box of pasta. Then...we came up with a plan together."

"He's a good guy." I know he is. He's my baby brother.

"Yeah, he is. He kept me informed how my family was doing. I couldn't have escaped without him." She weaves her long fingers in the grass. "It took me a while to gather everything Olson needed. I met him twice before he got me out of there, but we spoke on the phone every day."

He's good like that. He took care of Steve's daughter the only way he could. And in doing so, he's going to put away her abuser and make her world a little bit safer.

I shift my gaze to her and study her watching the current in the creek, gently swinging her legs.

Who is the *real* Aria McKenzie?

"What do you do for fun?"

She swings her wild gaze to meet mine.

"Um…I don't know. I used to ride, but it's not an option at the moment."

I want to ask her why, but she continues. "I like to cook, I guess. I read."

"You're not one to hit the town?"

She bursts into a fit of giggles.

"Absolutely not. Not even pre-Charlie was I into that."

Okay, making progress.

"What do you and Jackie do when you hang out?"

"Oh…um TV, usually. Trash TV is a guilty pleasure of ours."

"Would you like to join me for dinner tonight?" It's out before I can stop myself from saying it. I close my eyes in frustration. "I meant as friends. I was going to invite your sister and Chris too."

"That depends. What are you making?"

"I was thinking about going to Rico's. It's this taco bar in town—"

"I know where Rico's is. That was one my haunts when I lived here." She grins. "Sure. As friends, of course. No funny business."

Of course. A woman this broken should be a giant red flag, a hoard of flashing warning lights to stay away from. But I can't. It's important to me she's safe…she has the opportunity to live her third chance at life.

16

ARIA

19 weeks pregnant...

"I MEAN, I'm never going to say no to Rico's, but is there another reason why you want me to come with?" Annie asks as she sets her suitcase on the bed, throwing all the dirty clothes into the hamper. She got back from Canada two hours ago, and I bombarded her the second she got in the door.

"No. He said he was going to invite you and Chris anyway."

Her smile is contagious. Derek Hawthorn is a handsome man. I'm not blind. However, I could always do with more friends. And I'd *love* to stop acting so awkward around him.

Because secretly I find him tantalizing.

"Are you crushing on him?"

I roll my eyes. "I'm not in high school anymore. No, I'm not. He's just my friend. And I already told you I'm forever off the market."

Annie frowns, continuing to empty her suitcase. "I don't like that. Don't let Charlie ruin you for other men."

I want to avoid this part of the conversation. I should've shut my mouth.

"I'm not. But I have other things that require my attention."

Her gaze falls to my abdomen completely disguised by my baggy shirt.

"Have you thought about finding out the sex?"

Nope.

"Um, haven't thought about it yet." *Lie.* "Anyway, it would be cool if you could come tonight. I haven't had Rico's in forever. And now that I don't look like I was mugged in the back of an alley, I wouldn't mind eating out. Under the watchful eye of my favorite sister and my idiot brother."

Annie snorts. "He *is* an idiot." *A lovable idiot.* "Fine. I'll go. Then I want to hear about what's been going on since I've been in Canada."

"When do you have to have your article written?"

She huffs. "I got a lot of it done on the plane. If I spend all day tomorrow finishing it up and then editing, I should be on target." She eyes me up and down with concern. "I'm sorry for leaving you, Peanut. I know you just got here, but I couldn't cancel."

I throw my arms around her and breathe in her floral scent. "You have a life, Annie. I don't expect you to drop everything for me. I managed. Jackie stayed over a few nights. I'm okay."

And it's the first time I somewhat believe it.

She squeezes me and pulls back. "Okay. Give me fifteen and I'll be ready."

Right on cue, the doorbell rings.

"I'll get it."

I shouldn't be this excited. I'm *not*, but I'm excited for Rico's. It's the only place in town with good Mexican food.

Without warning, the door opens, and Chris lets himself in.

"Hey, Peanut."

"Does this mean you're coming to Rico's with me?"

He grins. "As if I'd ever miss an opportunity to go."

"Annie's getting ready. She needs a few minutes."

For a Wednesday night, Rico's is packed. We're led to a table by the window. Olson joins our party in plain clothes. He's still tense, and constantly on the lookout. I sit across from Derek, sandwiched between Olson and Annie. I scour the menu to focus my attention elsewhere. I already know what I'm getting.

"Tell us about Canada," Derek says to Annie with an amused grin.

"It was fun! I learned how to make Ice Wine. And I ate at a lot of places too. The weather was beautiful and much to my surprise, the coffee was better there." She grins widely.

"Where are you going next?" Chris asks.

Annie shrugs. "I have a few things lined up. Malta, Australia, and Bora Bora, but that's closer to the end of the year. The magazine gave me some time to spend at home."

To be with me. The guilt hits me like a freight train.

My phone vibrates in my pocket. Olson narrows his eyes at me when I make no moves to silence it. Yet, the sound brings everyone's attention to it. I don't want to know what else Charlie has to say to me. That last message was enough to scare me into the next lifetime.

The jellybean inside me demands sustenance. Nausea swirls in my belly, and when the waitress stops by with a basket of chips and salsa, I could kiss her.

"What are you doing tomorrow?" Derek asks while Chris, Annie, and Olson all talk amongst themselves.

"I'm giving a lesson tomorrow. But other than that, nothing."

"Would you like to go shooting again?"

Yes. Especially after the scare the other morning, I absolutely want more practice.

"That's not a bad idea," Olson pipes up. "Count me in."

Chris scowls but doesn't voice his concern about his baby sister hanging out with a bunch of guys and shooting guns.

"By the way," Derek chimes, shifting his gaze to Annie, "maybe you should come too. Aria found your gun in your nightstand with the safety off."

Annie scoffs and rolls her eyes. "I highly doubt it. I'm careful."

Chris barks out a laugh. "No you're not!"

"Regardless, it wouldn't be a bad idea. I'd feel better if you at least had a few lessons with us," Olson says. "I know you're busy, but we can book around your schedule."

Annie isn't one who likes guns. She was the one who cried every time Daddy pulled us out into the pasture to shoot. Getting her to do this is going to be like pulling teeth.

"Name the time and the place and I'll show you guys up."

Everyone chuckles.

"I'll be right back." Chris excuses himself.

Chris, the guy who thinks he's so smooth, approaches Eliza North, a local, like she's a deer in headlights. They chat while Annie and I spread out in the booth.

"So, Olson, tell me about yourself," Annie probes, not so innocently.

Derek and Olson share a look, one that tells me there's more to...*this* than either of them is letting on. Does it make me feel better, or worse?

"What do you want to know?"

"Your life story. How you take care of my sister...you know. I'm trying to gauge if I need to kill you now or later."

I face palm my forehead.

"You can't threaten a federal agent," I snap.

"It wasn't a threat!" She grins like a hyena, but she's not as innocent as she likes to pretend to be. Luckily, Olson is tolerant and chuckles.

"I'm from Lancaster, Pennsylvania and joined the Marine Corps right out of high school. I did some things I can't tell another human soul about, but after I retired, I joined the FBI. Your sister found a way to communicate with me when she realized I was watching." He glances at me and offers me a reassuring smile. "We've gotten close over the last few months, haven't we?"

I shrug nonchalantly. Olson has become family to me. I trust him with my life.

"You didn't give up on me." Even when I told him I killed someone in an attempt to escape.

"I still won't." He turns to Annie. "Her safety is important to me, not because she's the lynchpin in this case. In fact, I'm hoping we stay in touch when all of this is over."

When all of this is over. Is this a reality?

"Sure."

He grins and shifts his gaze back to Annie. "I'm capable. I'm trained. I've been to hell and back, and I promise you, the Dodge's won't be an issue for your family when all is said and done."

Except for the baggage I carry.

"Stop interrogating him. He's here to help," I plead with my sister. She grins at me and pulls me close.

"I've missed you so much," she coos. "I'm looking out for you. I want you to be able to live your life without *him* hanging over your head."

Yeah, me too. But I've accepted the fact it's not a possibility.

Olson's attention is taken by his phone. He excuses himself and takes the call outside while Annie sways in her seat to the upbeat, Latin music. Derek's eyes scan the crowd, and then not so casually, out the window to stare at Olson.

My eyes follow his. Olson's brows are furrowed, and he stares at the ground. A vein in his forehead pulses with anger. While he listens to the other person on the phone, his lips press into a hard line.

"That doesn't look good," Derek murmurs so only I can hear him. I can't bring myself to say anything back. "Whatever it is, it's going to be okay. He can handle it."

I turn my gaze to him. It's now where I notice how icy the blues of his eyes are. His face is relaxed, like he believes what comes out of his mouth is fact. He gives me a reassuring smile, and the idiot inside of me longs to push the long hair out of his eyes.

Derek Hawthorn makes me nervous, yet content all at the same time. It's totally inappropriate, I know. I shouldn't be wanting for whatever he's trying to sell me, and now I can't stop thinking about the guy who literally followed me into a crappy situation with Charlotte after only knowing me for like two minutes.

His full lips quirk into a smile, and it takes me a whole minute to realize my sister has vacated her seat and is somewhere else in the restaurant, mingling like the social butterfly she is.

"Please don't take this the wrong way, but you're beautiful."

And there it is. The sucker punch to remind and taunt me of what I can't have.

"Derek…"

"Don't worry. I'm not trying to get into your pants or convince you to drop everything and be with me. I wanted to let you know."

I lick my lips nervously. He thinks I'm beautiful and all the while, I look like I stepped into a burlap sack.

"I'm sure you say that to all the girls."

Shut. The. Fuck. Up!

He smirks and sits up straight.

"Beautiful isn't the word I use." I raise my eyebrows in anticipation for whatever charming bullshit comes out of his mouth next. "When you're trying to set an expectation of no strings attached, you have to create a barrier. Beautiful isn't what you call someone when you're trying to push them away. You call them hot. Or sexy. Pretty."

"So by calling me beautiful, you're not trying to set a barrier to keep me out?"

He leans slightly closer to me, lowering his voice and putting the fear of god into me when my downstairs tingles. "You and me? We're kindred spirits. We don't play games. We keep our eyes on the prize. You don't want to be with anyone. I don't want to be with anyone." He shrugs. "We're friends. That's all it could ever be, right?"

Right.

It has to be like this.

I'd never forgive myself if I brought my bullshit home to Zoey. That isn't fair.

"You're beautiful, Ace. I don't need to beat around the bush, because I know nothing could ever happen between us. But…I feel like you should know. Someone should tell you every day how incredibly beautiful you are."

My cheeks heat, and it's right this very second I wished I put make up on to hide the stupid blush on my cheeks.

"If we're telling the truth here, I think you're dumb."

I love taking him off guard. The way he gapes, like he wasn't expecting me to roast him. But somebody needs to tell *him* he's being an idiot.

"Derek, you're handsome. You're passionate and irrationally hard-headed. The way you treat your daughter...I can only imagine how you'd treat a woman you invested your heart into. Zoey is a strong girl, and if she's anything like me, she'd only want you to be happy. Stop blaming your fear of commitment on her."

He leans forward, like he wants to tell me a secret.

"I appreciate your honesty."

Yeah, right. I'm sure he does.

"Do you think this...fear of giving your heart to someone is going to last forever?"

His question shouldn't surprise me, but I feel the pit in my stomach. The pit that craves love and affection or when it sets the butterflies free.

"Yeah," I whisper hoarsely. "I do."

His smile wanes.

"Okay," he replies softly, the smile never leaving his face. "I'm just double checking."

If I close my eyes, I can picture us. Not *together,* but losing myself in him, even if it was just one night. My hormones are all over the place. And this is the first time in a year I've wanted to *be* with someone.

"Derek..."

I can't say what I want to say. It's too embarrassing. He's beautiful too. So beautiful it's insulting.

"Sorry about that. I had to check in," Olson announces, sliding in next to Derek, saving the day before I said something incredibly stupid.

"Everything all right?" Derek asks.

Olson gives him a hard look and a wince. Derek nods. They've known each other for what, two months, and they already have some telepathic language between them?

I smell fish.

"So, what's good here, Aria? I was eying the tacos, but there are a bunch of other shit on here that looks good."

I clear my throat, to banish the awkwardness, to wake Derek up from staring at me with that stupid, but dreamy look.

"Anything on the menu is good. I always go for the fajitas. The beef comes from our farm."

Olson glances up in surprise.

"Seriously?"

"So does the corn and dairy." I grin. The day Daddy signed the contract with the owners was one of the happiest days of my life. Rico's has been a staple in our family...where we celebrate all the good that comes our way.

"Okay, I'll bite. I'll do the fajitas too."

Chris announces he won't be eating with us, which means he's going home with Eliza and there will be another crying woman on our street tonight.

Annie eventually returns but spends the rest of the evening scrolling through her phone absentmindedly while the three of us shoot the shit.

I catch Derek watching me as the night progresses.

Annie continues to interrogate Olson, and I lose my voice. Not literally, but I can't tell Annie about what he said. There would be so much speculation. A visit from my brother with demands about treating me right.

He's handsome. And I'm sure he'd ruin my life in the best way, but I'm not up to it. I doubt he'd think my *predicament* is attractive. He has his own kid to deal with!

He thinks I'm beautiful. And that's okay. Because he's beautiful too.

17

ARIA

One Month Later

23 weeks pregnant...

I SWORE I wasn't going to see Dr. Nelson again, especially not after the last time. However, my mother knows how to lay on a guilt trip as thick as peanut butter, so I go. I don't know what I can possibly tell this woman that wouldn't get me sent to the loony bin, or worse, back into Charlie's arms, but over the last month, my heart has lightened.

People have stopped asking about Charlie. They've stopped encouraging me to move on and it allows me to be...*me.*

The voice in my head who screams at me not to bury the abuse has won out. I've had too many nightmares and I need to get it off my chest.

I've hemmed and hawed about canceling at the last minute. I even turned around and headed home once. But if I don't *try* to live my life, then I don't deserve to live. Period.

My phone vibrates in the cupholder and when I see the North Carolina area code, my heart skips a beat.

"Jay?"

"Hey, Peanut!"

My eyes water. Jay is my extra brother. The one who always took my side when Annie and Chris were being jerks.

"I'm so happy to hear your voice—"

"I'm so happy to hear *yours.* Peanut, you have no idea how much I wanted to go AWOL and find you…"

I sniffle, guilt washing over me like ice water.

"I'm sorry, JJ. I'm sorry I stayed."

"Don't do that. It wasn't your fault."

"Why didn't I see the signs?" I whisper.

"You're a romantic."

Isn't that the understatement of the century?

"People do stupid things for love, Aria. You were always the one who tried to see past everyone else's ugliness, even when they didn't deserve it."

I wanted him to love me. If anything, I'm more relieved I don't have to look into his icy eyes anymore.

"Everything's a mess. Daddy's gone. He left a month ago because he can't stand the sight of me. And…um…I'm pregnant."

The silence on the other end isn't a surprise. JJ's protective and usually reacts first before asking questions.

"What are you gonna do?"

"I'm keeping it, I guess." It. *It.* I can't form a connection with this jellybean…and I'm not sure I want to.

"You guess?"

"I'm currently in denial. I'm pretending this isn't happening because any other alternative is scary. I'm praying I wake up in the morning and it will all have been a big joke."

"Aria…"

"Isn't this the turn of events? Everyone thought I was going to be the first one to get pregnant, I was the one going to wind up living in sin with a man while he slept around on the side. I guess they were half right."

"Oh, that's enough of that. I hate to burst your bubble, but you're not perfect. Shit happens, Peanut, whether we like it or not. Take it from someone whose been there."

I shudder as the image of JJ's bruised and battered body on our front porch flashes in my head. His father, William Parker was an alcoholic who took out all of his frustrations on Jo and JJ. And that time, JJ almost died.

"All those people who told you that you wouldn't amount to anything has their own skeletons. I can confidently tell you the reason John Hunt left dear old Bethany is because he's gay. Can you imagine *that* getting around town?"

Yeah, but John didn't beat the shit out of her.

"My point is these are the cards you've been dealt. You can either play your hand the best you can, or you can fold and succumb to regret. And let me tell you, folding is a dumb choice. You're a good woman, Peanut. Life is too short to play it safe. Learn from this. Heal from this."

I pull into the office building parking lot in downtown Sage Creek and turn off the car when I reach a parking spot.

"I don't know how to be me again," I say in my smallest voice.

"People reinvent themselves all the time. You're a strong woman. You don't have to be the old you. Be *you.*"

What does that even mean?

How does one be themselves when they don't even like who *they* are?

"I have to take off, JJ. I'm not trying to brush you off, but I just pulled up to my therapist's office..."

"Oh, you're talking to someone? That's great! Okay. I love you, kiddo. I'll call you as soon as I can, okay?"

I disconnect the call after telling him I love him too and begrudgingly trudge into Dr. Nelson's office.

April, the kind and gentle receptionist greets me warmly which is surprising with how I left here the last time...

But until Dr. Nelson is ready, I make myself at home on the love seat in the waiting room.

I stare at the ceiling, wishing it could provide me with all the answers. I *don't* want to talk about what happened with Charlie. It's all over the news, for God's sake! I have to heal, I know. But I've come to terms with what he did.

At least I think so.

"Aria, I'm glad you came back."

I glance up to Dr. Nelson, who wears a smart, pantsuit and a comforting grin.

God, I have to work on my people skills.

I follow her into her office and take a seat on the leather sofa, scanning the room for any ice breaker I can use to distract her from remembering my behavior from the last time. She sits in the chair across from me, folding her legs underneath her and readily posies with a pen in her hand and her yellow legal pad at the ready.

"How are you doing today?"

Small talk.

I *hate* small talk.

"I'm fine, thank you." I clear my throat awkwardly and drop my gaze. "I didn't mean to go off the deep end the last time I was here. I'm sorry... he's a touchy subject."

"I totally understand, and I hold no judgments against you. Grief is a funny thing. It makes us do uncharacteristically weird things."

I wouldn't call it weird. And I wouldn't call it grief, either.

"Grief? Nobody died..."

"A piece of you did," she replies gently. When my body tenses, she softens her stance even more. "It may not feel like it, but you're grieving a relationship you thought had traction. A future. And then it was brutally taken away from you in the most traumatic way, and you almost lost *your* life because of it."

"But I'm still...I..."

What? I survived? But for how much longer?

"What do you think is the hardest thing to reconcile in your head?" she asks.

Everything.

"We have a family friend. Her marriage with her husband was...lethal. He abused her and their son. They came to live with us until she could get back on her feet. But I saw *everything*. Including the red flags." I slowly lift my gaze to hers and hold my breath. "*Why* didn't I see the red flags? Why didn't I run when I *knew* there was something...*off* about him?"

She considers this a moment and places her notebook on the coffee table.

"What would have been the outcome had you not started a relationship with him? I'm talking about still working at his company, but turning him down instead?"

I shudder at the thought.

"I don't know. I suppose I would've been fired. My direct supervisor wasn't impressed with me. So I guess I would have had to turn tail and return home until I figured something else out."

I imagine taking over the riding school so Annie could write full time, Derek would have a helping hand with the rescue barn while he worked in his office.

My heart aches. It sounds lovely...like this was made especially for me.

Fuck.

"I think it's important to think out those scenarios, but not dwell on them. Maybe you would've come home and taken over the family business. But can you honestly tell me you would've been happy?"

No. I probably wouldn't have. I was still admiring the grass on the other side of the fence.

When I don't answer, she leans back in her chair and grins. I hate her. But I love her at the same time. I don't like people making assumptions about my life, but it seems like she's got me pegged.

"I'm not happy now, so what's the difference?"

"Mindset," she replies with a giggle. "What would it take for you to achieve happiness, Aria?"

More than sixteen ounces of caffeine a day for starters.

"I don't know."

She rolls her eyes. "Come on. You do yourself a disservice when you sweep questions like that under the rug. You deserve happiness, Aria. You deserve a full and happy life with the people you love around you and a mind that weighs a little less at night. Tell me what would get you there."

"I guess that's the joke, isn't it? I *don't* deserve a full and happy life. My father can't stand being in the same vicinity as me. I cut everyone down who tries to make an effort with me. I'm not a nice person, Dr. Nelson. I'm everyone's living nightmare."

"Have you ever tried asking those around you how they feel about you?"

A poisonous laugh escapes me.

"Do you honestly think they would look me in the eye and tell me the truth?"

"This is your family we're talking about, Aria. They took you in when you claim they're not happy about your arrival. You're living and sleeping in the same bed as your sister. Your brother follows you around because he thinks you're an expensive vase on the verge of being knocked off a high shelf. I *absolutely* think they would tell you the truth."

She moves forward in her seat, resting her elbows on her knees and steepling her fingers underneath her chin.

"I haven't been in this town long. I've seen how ugly these people can act towards each other. But there is one family who restores my faith in humanity." She gives me a pointed stare. "When I first moved here and was in the process of setting up my practice, your mother was the first one through the front door with a congratulatory vanilla cake with pink icing. Your sister literally beat a man for hitting on me at Rico's and wasn't taking the hint I wasn't interested. Your father and brother bring me fresh eggs every Monday morning just because they felt like it."

My family is probably the only family who would go out of their way to make someone feel welcome.

Hope blooms in my chest that they would extend the same courtesy, even though they already have.

"Why can't I go back to the old me? I miss not caring what other people thought of me. I miss being confident in my own thought process..."

"He manipulated you into thinking you can't trust yourself."

I frown and shift in my seat, ripping apart the tissue in my hand.

"This isn't going to be a one way road into blissful happiness, Aria. You are going to have great days where you feel like you're on top of the world. And because this universe needs balance, you'll experience unbearable days too. But the difference is you have people around you who are going to build you up when you're at your worst. You have a support system who will help you fight off those negative thoughts. And, you have me."

I glance up at her and allow the smile to spread across my cheeks.

"I promise you you're going to have a love/hate relationship with me. I am here for you whenever you need it. I can be the calm in your storm if you need a friendly face. I can be the swift kick in the ass if that's what you need. I refuse to let you fall. We're in this together."

WHEN I GET HOME, I pull into my momma's driveway and enter the house through the garage. Country music plays in the background as she washes the breakfast dishes. She sings along and sways her hips to the music.

"Hi, Momma."

She turns around and sashays over to me, taking my hands in hers and spinning me.

"Hi, baby. How was your appointment?"

"Fine. Have you eaten lunch yet?"

"Not yet, but I was fixin' up some soup. Want to eat with me?"

"Sure. What can I do?"

"Take a seat. It's almost ready."

I trudge over to the dinner table in the kitchen and drop into my seat. Daddy's seat remains annoyingly empty. I miss him, and more than ever, I wish I would've kept my trap shut.

A bowl of baked potato soup is dropped in front of me, and Momma takes a seat with a grin.

"I was wondering when you were going to meander this way. I haven't seen you in days."

"You could come to the barn..."

Momma scoffs and rolls her eyes.

"I did my time. Besides, I have enough to do here."

I spoon the soup into my mouth, the bacon and cheese melting away my nausea.

"Like?"

She gives me a pointed stare.

"Well…Jo and I have started a business of sorts."

Of sorts, eh?

"Selling drugs?"

She giggles and playfully pushes my shoulder.

"No. We're working with the folks from the Live Oak Foundation. We're starting up a state-of-the-art women's shelter here in town. It'll be a multi-county project, but Jo's heading it up. I'm there for moral support."

This has me sitting up a little straighter.

"Do you have a building already?"

She nods enthusiastically. "The old papermill. As we speak, they're gutting the inside and adding in annex buildings. This is going to be big, baby."

Momma, you know exactly what you're doing…

"Right now there are a lot of hoops and red tape to get through, but by the end of the summer, we should be able to accept our first cohort of battered women."

Battered women gives me the heebie jeebies. It sounds so…derogatory.

"What?" Momma asks when she notices my sour face.

"I'm sure there's a better term than *battered women.*"

"I'm sure there is. What do you think we should call them?"

"Women."

Her gaze softens and she reaches out and squeezes my hand.

"Of course."

There's a beat of awkward silence before she speaks again.

"Do you think you would want to get involved with this?"

I don't think that's a great idea.

But…I *want* to help the other women like me out there. I want to give them a safe space and a fresh start. I feel my past will bite us all in the ass.

"I don't know…"

"Think about it. I'm sure Jo would love to have you on. You could do a lot of good with this, baby."

My shot at redemption.

"Yeah…I'll think about it."

I push the small chunks of potatoes in the bowl, struggling to find the right words.

"Momma, can I ask *you* something?"

She nods enthusiastically and pushes her soup bowl back. "Yes, baby. Anything."

"How do you feel about me?"

She stares at me like I asked her how to become an astronaut.

"I love you..."

"No. I mean, I know you love me. But how do you feel about me... being here. Coming back home. My pregnancy. The trial..."

Tension hangs in the air, but for the first time, I don't feel like I'm under any scrutiny.

"I knew you were going to leave after high school, Aria. You didn't exactly make it a secret you didn't want to be here."

Flinching, I fidget under the table with my fingers and drop my gaze.

"I admired you for wanting to forge your own path. I know your daddy can be...intense when it comes to the business. I'll be honest, I was terrified when you brought *him* here. The way he *watched* you was unsettling. We called you every day, sweet pea. I left messages for you every day until your mailbox was full. Your daddy even went to Chicago a few times to see you."

My world stops turning for a beat.

"What do you mean he came to Chicago?"

"He got as far as the revolving door before the doorman called the police on him. If you ask me, I think Charlie had pictures of us given to the staff to send us away."

My eyes itch with unshed tears. They were going to save me.

"You being here is the greatest blessing, baby. I've worried about you for so long, and now I have you right under my nose where I can see you living and breathing." Her gaze trails me down to my belly and a melancholy smile spreads on her face. "I know *this* isn't easy. But I want you to know we want to help you in any way we can. This is our grandbaby...our first grandbaby."

My stomach churns, whether it's the nausea or the constant reminder Charlie took my options away from me, I'm not entirely sure.

"I don't know how to be a mom, Momma. I'm not emotionally equipped to deal with this. I don't even know if we'll get along—"

"None of us do, Aria. Do you think I had everything figured out when Chris came along? It took me a month to figure out how to change his diaper without him peeing on me. Every night for the first month I cried myself to sleep because I thought I was ruining him."

A giggle escapes me.

"You learn from trial and error. And the most important thing is they're happy and healthy. You're going to be a great mom, sweetheart. It takes a lot of work. And besides, you'll have us."

My heart jolts with a sense of warmth. My Momma doesn't resent me for being here. She isn't a liar. She's the most honest person in the world.

"Is Daddy still mad at me?"

She waves me off dismissively.

"He is a crochety old fool. Let me handle him."

That's what I'm afraid of. I don't want him to be beat into submission into caring about me.

After lunch, I drive the truck back down to Annie's before heading to barn number three. When I reach there, I find Zoey sitting on the ground cross legged reading the third book in the *Heartland* series.

"Hey, Zoey. Are you here for the weekend?"

She dogears her page and closes the book before lifting her watery gaze.

"What's wrong?" I crouch on the ground, sitting next to her. It's not until I hear the faint yelling from the rescue barn. Derek and another female voice I don't recognize.

"My mom wants to move to California with me."

Frowning, I wrap my arm around her and pull her close.

"Oh..."

"She's the worst human being on the planet. She doesn't care about me *or* Dad. She always does whatever she wants to do, and I'm stuck wishing for a different life."

My heart squeezes. I've been there.

"What's in California?"

She shrugs and sniffs. "She says it's a job, but I don't care. I like it here and I want to stay."

Derek's voice raises decibels louder, and suddenly the woman's voice gets shaky and shrieky.

"So, what do you think of the *Heartland* series so far?"

She wipes the tears from her eyes and leans her head against the stall door. "I love it. Thanks for letting me borrow your collection. I'll be nice to it, I promise."

"I have no doubts you will. Want to help me groom Coley?"

"Thank you, but I think I'll just watch. I'm in the middle of a good scene and I don't want to put it down yet."

We scramble from our spot on the ground, and I set up my phone to the docking station and put on some rock playlist to drown out the yelling and screaming. While Zoey settles into the lawn chair close by, I get Coley out of her stall and bring her to the cross ties.

This is sort of my routine nowadays. I can't ride anymore because it's dangerous, but the monotony allows my mind to settle. Coley is typically a pasture horse, so she's perpetually dirty. I would give her a bath but I'm not feeling it right now. So I curry-comb and brush out her coat and detangle the knots in her tail. I pick out the compacted dirt in her feet.

When I reach for the fly spray, two figures storm down the aisle of the barn. I brace myself for the rest of the shouting match, but all I'm met with is Derek and Emily approaching Zoey gently.

Emily looks familiar. Her blonde hair is styled chic, just like the Hunts. Maybe they're friends. She glances over her shoulder to me and narrows her eyes. Instead of engaging, I shut my trap and spray Coley down.

"Zo, I know you don't want to leave Sage Creek. But you can't scream at your mom when you don't get your way."

My heart grinds to a halt and instinctively, my gaze moves to Zoey. She glares at her mother while Derek crouches down to meet her eye level.

"I'll run away," Zoey murmurs, her eyes watering and voice cracking. "If you take me to California, I will run away any chance I get. I *don't* want to go with you. Let me stay with Dad."

This is none of my business. But I literally can't leave. I'm trapped.

"You're my baby, Zoey. I want to bring you with me..."

"I don't want to go with you!" Zoey shouts.

Derek clears his throat. "This isn't going anywhere." His clipped tone is directed to his ex-wife. "I told you this would happen."

Emily rolls her eyes.

"Excuse me, but do you have anywhere else you need to be?" Emily demands. I awkwardly glance over to the little pow wow and grimace.

"I'm sorry. I'm landlocked at the moment—"

"Go away!" she shouts.

"Emily, don't talk to her like that."

Now I know I'm not interrupting anything, I slip under the cross ties and make a bee line for the feed room. At least I can hide out there until this shit show hits the road.

I don't like conflict, especially when it involves my little best friend. I want to save her from this, to take her mind off of California.

Fifteen minutes later, a car door slams and the grinding against the gravel towards the exit of the property is heard. I take a deep, cleansing breath, and Derek appears in the feed room.

He leans against the door frame with his hands shoved in his pockets and his lips pressed in a hard line.

"I'm sorry you had to hear all of that. As you can see, she isn't the easiest person to deal with."

"Ah. No problem. Sorry I was eavesdropping." I hop off the bale of hay I made myself comfortable on and head for the door. Derek loosely grabs my wrist before I move any further.

"I don't think we gave you much of a choice."

I gently take my wrist back and shrug.

"No worries, honestly. It was none of my business." I attempt to walk back to Coley again when Derek grabs my wrist again. My heart races a mile a minute at his warm touch. But not necessarily in a bad way. I've gotten used to his touch. It's never out of a malicious place.

"Don't you want to ask what it was all about?"

Yes.

"Honestly, it's your business. I'm sorry Zoey is sad. I tried to get her to help me groom Coley, but she wasn't interested."

"Ace."

I close my eyes at the nickname he uses for me.

"Dr. Hawthorn."

He smirks. "Remember when I said you should talk to someone?"

I roll my eyes and nod. Of course I do.

"And I have been." The smile is wiped clean from his face. "*Her* name is Dr. Nelson and she's a great psychologist. I believe all of my mental health needs are being met."

"And what about your social needs?"

"Well, I had a nice conversation with Zoey when I got here, so…"

He scoffs. "We're supposed to see the International Space Station in our skyline tonight. I was going to take Zoey out on the front steps of our porch tonight…would you like to join us?"

For a man who claims he couldn't ever be with a woman because of the alleged fake love she'd have for his daughter, he sure invites me over to their date nights a lot.

"Sure. But I'm not sure I'll be great company because I'm exhausted. But I'd like to see it."

"Great. We'll see you at ten, then."

18

ARIA

23 weeks pregnant...

At nine forty-five, I slip on a pair of flip flops and head over to Derek's house. They both are already on the front porch steps staring into the sky when I arrive. Zoey beams at my arrival and Derek slyly pats the space next to him for me to sit down.

"I've been researching astronauts since we got in earlier," Zoey informs me. "I know how they eat, how they wash their hair. I even found a YouTube channel where they read books to students!"

"You had a busy afternoon," I reply, creating as much space as I can between Derek and me.

"I did. And then I helped dad make dinner. We had baked ziti. What did you have?"

"Well, Annie can't cook to save her life, so it was up to me tonight. I made some beef stew. It's too hot outside to eat it, but that's what I was craving."

Zoey grins and turns her attention to the sky.

"Hey, Ace," he greets warmly.

"Hi, Dr. Hawthorn."

He chuckles and rolls his eyes. Yep. He sees right through me.

"I'm glad you decided to join us. We don't get to see this often, but there was an alert on the news this morning and I didn't want to miss it."

"Well, thanks for inviting me. I was going to sit in front of the TV tonight binging *Cheers.* This sounds like a lot more fun."

"I think so too. Dad insisted I give the books a rest for tonight."

"Good thing too, right? How often do you get to see the International Space Station?"

Zoey shrugs carelessly and leans up against the banister.

"I don't know. But how often do you get to check books off your bucket list?"

Derek groans.

"We have *vastly* different bucket lists, Zo. My bucket list is pretty empty at the moment."

So is mine.

"Boring!"

The night sky is a sight to behold in this little corner of the property. There aren't any streetlights, save for the two that light our street, so the blanket of stars is vibrant and majestic. In Chicago, I dreamed about these nights. I dreamed of the prospect of coming back home and living in my element.

"What are you thinking about?" Zoey asks.

"Oh, I was thinking how much I missed this sky when I was living in Chicago."

Zoey scrunches her nose.

"Um...it's the same sky everywhere..."

Giggling, I shake my head. "In Chicago, the city is lit up so bright at night you can't see the stars. Even from the balcony I couldn't see one. But here...there's something different about the sky here."

"When we were in Afghanistan, the sky was similar. We were in the desert, so the stars were always on display at night. For some reason, I got a strange comfort out of it."

"Do you miss the Navy?" I ask.

He shrugs. "Sometimes. I miss the camaraderie. I miss how easy it was." At my quizzical brow, he continues, "The military is only hard if you make it hard. They tell you what to do, you do it. You show up for duty. You show up on field days. You deploy with your brothers and sisters and keep them safe. Civilian life, it's hard to find your place. I got lucky and was able to take over for Dr. Karver. But, if I had the choice to go back in right this minute, I wouldn't."

He meets Zoey's wide-eyed gaze and smiles.

"You're my life, kiddo. I don't know what I'd do if I had to be away from you for months on end."

"JJ says the same thing. He's found his calling, I think. It wouldn't surprise me if he was a lifer because of those same reasons."

"Hey, a lot of men do. I know Jay. He's a great marine—a great leader. I know he'll be fine."

I hope so. It doesn't stop me from missing him so much.

"But this is nice. I was lucky to find your family. They gave me a place to live, patients to work on, and a family to depend on."

My mind races to my father and it makes my heart squeeze. I can always count on him, but I think I royally fucked it up this time.

"Yeah...you're not the first person to tell me that today."

"You have a lot on your mind, Ace?"

"A lot," I reply sadly. "I wonder if it'll be like this forever. Will I be plagued by the past? Will I be able to put *this* behind me? On first instinct, my answers are: yes, it will be like this forever. Yes, I will always be plagued by the past, and no, I won't be able to put it behind me."

"I had a brother in the Corps. Not biologically, of course, but after he got out, he suffered from major PTSD. He had the whole nine yards, the night terrors, the intrusive thoughts, insomnia, mild hallucinations...it wasn't an easy transition. In fact, it took him a few years before he started to feel even the littlest bit normal. Don't sell yourself short, Ace. Healing is a part of life, yes, but it isn't a fast process."

I take comfort in the fact that even though our PTSD is different, there isn't a set timeline for everyone. Everyone is different. Every trauma is different.

"Yeah, I suppose you're right. I'm the world's most impatient person. I thought I'd see results by now. I'm an instant gratification kind of girl."

He shrugs thoughtfully.

"Two months ago, you wouldn't have sat on the front porch with us searching for a mysterious space station. I'd call that progress."

"Do you think we could ever visit NASA?" Zoey asks.

"Maybe one day. That would be fun, wouldn't it? We could buy some astronaut ice cream."

Zoey's face lights up and she squeals with delight. Oh to be ten again. I get excited about any form of ice cream too.

"So Miss Aria, you like to cook right? What's your favorite thing to cook?"

"Hmm. I like to cook a lot of things. But I do love making chicken fried rice. It's cheap, it's easy, and it's fast. I don't mean to brag, but mine is better than take out. What about you, Zo? What's your favorite food to cook?"

"I'm not great at cooking, but I *love* to bake. Dad says I make great cheesecake."

Derek grins and closes his eyes in bliss.

"She sure does. But I'm also a sucker for cheesecake. Especially made by my favorite girl."

Zoey grins and giggles.

Derek's phone goes off with the alert tone. We meander off the front porch and wait. Suddenly, we see a streak in the sky, almost like it could be a shooting star. Zoey gasps in pure astonishment and for some odd reason, my eyes well up with tears.

Something so far away, so mysterious can peer down on this planet we live in. And *my* problems must be so insignificant to them.

"Are you crying, Ace?"

"No!" I whimper and turn away.

Chuckling he spins me around and pulls me closer to him. I breathe in his herby scent. His arm snakes around my waist, but his eyes still are trained on the sky. My head rests on his chest while I compose myself. My arm curls around his stomach and I nearly die of embarrassment. I've never seen him without a shirt, but I can tell he doesn't skip the gym. Ever. He's hard. Not *down there*. But like, his stomach is hard.

"That was so cool!" Zoey exclaims.

"It sure was! Holy cow, we're going to need to make this a tradition, eh, Zo?"

"Yes! Can you sign up for alerts? I want to see it again!"

I awkwardly part from him and regain my composure. His gaze follows me with an unreadable expression. Like I've insulted him by stepping away, and longing; like he wants me to come back.

I can't do this.

I just got out of a relationship!

I'm pregnant!

"All right babe, head inside and start getting ready for bed. I'll be in in a minute."

Zoey gives me a hug goodnight and trots up the steps, closing the door behind her.

"Did I make you uncomfortable? I'm sorry. I wasn't thinking. That's my natural response if Zoey's crying—"

"No, you didn't make me uncomfortable. I don't think." I weakly smile. "You surprised me. I wasn't prepared for it."

"There's a thing we learned when Zoey was born. Skin to skin contact. There have been developments in the medical field that hugging or holding hands releases oxytocin which is the cuddle hormone. It helps build bonds and trust."

"Do you do this with all the girls?"

He barks out a laugh and leads me back to the porch.

"No. I don't do cuddling. It's unnecessary, especially because I'm not looking to build bonds. I lost myself for a minute tonight, Ace. I don't typically do things like this. But I was in the moment, and you were crying..."

Oh my god.

"I'm not a crier. I usually have my emotions on lock." Except now I'm pregnant and my hormones have a mind of their own. It's unfair and cruel.

"Creepy space objects will do that."

I laugh. For the first time in forever, I laugh without a care in the world.

"Well, thank you again for inviting me over tonight. It was a lot of fun. Tell Zoey I said goodnight."

I turn to walk away.

"Aria?"

"Hmm?" I ask, stopping without turning around.

Silence greets me. And now I'm wondering if he's being held at gunpoint. I slowly turn around and find him staring at me. Staring at me like I'm the finest steak in the country.

"Goodnight."

Shit.

"Goodnight, Derek. See you tomorrow."

19

DEREK

My fight with Emily could be heard from barns away from where we were. And when Aria McKenzie is literally trapped in the middle of it, I can't help but be embarrassed about my lack of control on my temper. Emily *knows* which buttons to press and she's fucking great at it.

Logan has assured me he thinks he can get me full custody. But this visit from her today has me feeling annoyed and vengeful. She tried to sweeten the pot by giving me every holiday.

The answer is hell no. And I'm not moving to California just because Emily is bored in this town. I already fucking moved here for her.

I wasn't lying when I saw the ISS would be visible on the news. It was the only reprieve from Emily that would distract the both of us. *But*, Aria was in the right place, the right time. I'm fucking pumped she agreed to watch it with us.

I replay the moment I pulled her into me and held her in my arms. I was hyperaware of how her body felt. She didn't even tense up. That alone should have me running as far away from her as possible, but I can't help but *want* to be around her. She's mean and sarcastic. In fact, I don't even know when she's being serious.

At five o'clock, instead of going on my run, I slip into Nate's house for a briefing. When I enter the foyer, a recording is heard from the dining room. A voice I recognize so well now, only with a shaky timber punches me in the gut because she's scared.

"Charlie! Please—I'm sorry! I love you so much, I'm sorry! It won't ever happen again!"

I hear him snicker darkly.

"She wasn't a good listener either. Let's review expectations again, shall we?"

"Charlie, *please!*"

"List the rules, Aria."

When I reach the dining room, Nate quickly pauses the recording and whips his head up to me.

"What was that?" I ask.

"He recorded pushing her into a grave. Tanner was able to recover it from his hard drive."

I occupy the seat next to him.

"He stopped calling this phone," he says, pushing Aria's old iPhone in the middle of the table.

"So he's either dead or lost interest."

"I don't see him losing interest, and he isn't dead. I checked."

"She has a new phone…"

"She would've told me," Nate replies quietly.

I don't know her that well. But something tells me she tells Nate what he needs to know.

"What about the other associates?"

"Everyone we know about has been indicted. Unless Senior has other goons we don't know about. There's only so much the FBI can do."

"That's what we're for," I remind him.

"I already have Tanner running overtime for me. According to him, there isn't anything to write home about."

"Which means there is something more sinister at hand. You think you can get Delgado to do a drive-by?"

And when I say drive-by, I mean he'll slip in while Tanner disables the alarm systems so he can place audio and visual devices so we can get a better view. The problem is, if the FBI finds them, we're in deep shit.

"I'm setting something up with him. Tanner's on stand-by. And I can't leave to babysit them. I can't leave Aria in the open."

"Set it up. I can be Delgado's wingman, that way we can cover more ground. This is Steve's daughter, Nate. We can't let this slip into a blind spot. There are too many innocent lives at stake."

Zoey's, for instance.

Nate grimaces.

"All right. You think you can come back in a few hours? If we're going to do this, we need to do it sooner rather than later."

"Sure. I can come back after morning feed. Is that enough time?"

He nods and focuses on the computer.

"Where's Steve, Bubba?"

"He said he was visiting family in New York."

He glowers, knowing I spew bullshit lies. Again, he's my commander. I do what he asks.

20

ARIA

25 weeks pregnant...

Eric, our farrier, is the only outsider on the property today. Annie was the one who was supposed to be here to supervise, but then she got wrapped up in her article and asked Derek to take over.

Derek is late. And now I'm the one stuck in an awkward game called, "Who can be the quietest?" with a guy I went to kindergarten with. Eric keeps to himself. Always quiet. And me? Well…I definitely don't have anything to say.

Hercules, one of our newer arrivals is on the cross ties while Eric gets acquainted with him. Herc lived with a family who tortured him for five years, and now is too terrified of humans in general. Derek has been working with him and has made a lot of progress, so much so that this is the first time he and Eric are meeting, and he hasn't ripped the cross ties out of the wall yet.

Herc sniffs Eric cautiously, his ears pointed in his direction. They're not doing shoes today. This is more of a trust exercise and non-invasive examination. Herc doesn't dare lower his head, even if it would make him feel better. I feel for him. He went through far more abuse than I did and coming into this environment is a culture shock.

Eric bends over and touches Herc's foot, asking him to lift it up. He stands firm, refusing to do anything. I stand up, not making any sudden movements and reach for the apple cookies in my pocket. I approach him with my palm wide open. He lowers his muzzle, snorting like I'm the most terrifying being in the planet. He inspects the cookie and eventually takes it out of my hand.

It occupies him enough for Eric to get his foot up and check the insides.

"Sorry I'm late," Derek announces from behind me.

"It's okay. We just started. He's being stubborn but I think I won him over with the apple cookies." I turn and greet him with a small smile when Herc nudges me for more cookies. And of course, I oblige. We all need sweetness in our life.

"I can take over if you'd like to head home. It's hot out. You should be drinking some water."

That's what Dr. Cash tells me, but here I am.

"I'll hang around a bit. I'm invested now. I need to know if he's okay."

Derek chuckles as I cross the aisle and sink to the ground. My back aches and my knees are sore. I absolutely should go home and stretch out in bed for a few hours. But home is too far away. This spot on the ground is mighty comfortable. Derek disappears to the middle of the breezeway, grabbing something out of the fridge and walking back this way. He hands me an icy cold bottle of water with a tight lipped, sarcastic smile.

"You'll thank me in the long run."

I doubt it. But this is nice.

He sinks down next to me and we watch Eric work in silence. The fans blow especially hard since this heatwave is unbearable. I wonder when Daddy is coming home so I can spend the days inside like I should be.

"I don't see any abscesses at first glance, so that's a good sign. He could do with a trim, but I don't think that's a good idea at the moment. If it's all right with you, I'd like to introduce him to some of the equipment I'll be using."

"That's good news. Sure thing. Do what you need to do," Derek replies.

"So what do you do with these horses when they're rehabilitated?" Eric asks.

"Depends. Steve will never admit this to the public, but he has a soft spot for them. He usually sends them out to pasture to live out a happy life. Sometimes the riding school will take a few."

My heart plummets into my stomach.

Does he take pity on them because of me?

"What about selling them to other people?"

"Honestly, buddy, it would be an intense vetting process, and I don't mean it would be coming from me."

Eric nods in contemplation.

"You think he'd let me in on this little operation you've got going? I bought a place near the Parkers and I have a substantial amount of land I'm looking to fill up."

"What would be your plan?" I pipe up, genuinely curious.

"Well," he exhales and steps out from under the cross ties to face us. "I'd do something similar. I don't ride at all, but I was looking into opening up some sort of therapy for both people and horses." He sinks to the ground so he's eye level with us. "You remember my sister, Stephanie, right?"

I nod. She's on the autism spectrum and hardly sees the light of day.

"Well, there are a lot of kids like her in the world. I've been doing a ton of research on equine therapy with children with autism. I was thinking this is exactly what this town needs."

"You'd probably do well with women and children from abusive households," I reply.

Actually, that's a great idea. I wonder if Jo thought about that. They could add this service and pair up with Eric. It would be mutually beneficial.

"That's a good one," he says softly.

And suddenly, he's staring at me and seeing what everyone else sees. I shrink into myself and pull my knees up to my chest.

"I can bring it up to Steve if you want me to," Derek offers, trying to steer the conversation back on topic.

And he thinks he isn't a knight in shining armor.

"That would be great. Tell him to call me if he's interested."

Quick and light footsteps echo through the breezeway, and suddenly, Annie appears with a shit eating grin on her face.

"Aria, have I ever told you you're my favorite sibling?"

I groan. "Remind me."

"You're so pretty and nice. And you're the best barrel racer on the planet."

I grimace.

"What do you want?"

"Can you take over my lesson today? She's super easy. It's Alyssa Aldridge. She's Zoey's age and she's a dream client. Tom is calling and it's the first time I'd be able to talk to him in two weeks."

"Fine, but you owe me. And I don't mean by you cooking me something, either. I'm talking Rico's. Fajitas and chips and salsa. And flautas. And chimichangas."

"You're an expensive date," she grumbles. "Deal. She'll be here in a half hour." Annie disappears as fast as she arrived. Eric announces he's done with Herc after showing him the tools. I lead Herc back to his stall and latch the door closed.

"Can I watch your lesson tonight?" Derek asks.

I turn to face him in horror.

"You want to watch my lesson? I'm not going to be teaching her anything dangerous. It's your basic run of the mill, boring shit."

He shrugs. "I don't care. I want to watch. The word around town is you're a champion barrel racer. I've heard all sorts of things about bridleless runs and killing rodeo clowns."

Ugh.

I hate this town.

"Again, I'm not teaching her anything dangerous. And all of those instances weren't our fault. Brandy Hunt and Ashley Parker have a sick sense of humor and have been trying to murder me since we were kids."

He shrugs nonchalantly and smirks that stupid charming smirk. "But *you'd* be in your element."

ALYSSA ALDRIDGE IS one of the sweetest kids I've ever met. Her parents on the other hand...they're prickly. When they drove up, I pasted on the best smile I could muster and introduced myself. They refused to shake my hand, despite their ten year old daughter, Alyssa did.

She gushed about my previous runs with the National Barrel Horse Association and how many times she's watched my videos.

I end up pulling Old Man Kit out of his stall because I know he's bomb proof and the best horse to give lessons on. I give her simple instructions to see where she's at. She brushes him down with no problems. She even tacks him up with no problems. The only thing I had to help with was getting the bridle on since she's too short to reach over his ears.

Derek helped me move poles onto the rail of the arena earlier. We're working on new things Annie probably hasn't covered with her yet. Derek escorts the Aldridges to the set of bleachers on the far end of the arena so they had a perfect view of what we're doing.

After her warmup, she meets me in the center of the ring.

"Alyssa, do you know what your two point position is?" When she shakes her head, I continue. "Okay, so stand up with your knees in, heels down."

She's shaky at the first point, which is fine because she's not used to it yet.

"Great! That's your first point. Now the second point is leaning forward and extending your arms out towards his ears on his mane."

She folds at the waist and grimaces.

"Perfect. You can sit down. Here's what I want you to do. There are six poles on each side of the arena. In a trot, I want you to be in your two point position while you trot over those poles. Once the last pole is cleared, continue posting."

She sends Kit into a trot. She's a little sloppy on the first set of poles as she tries to keep her knees in. She corrects herself on the next set, nearly acing it until she drops to the seat before she's over the last pole.

I have her change directions and try again. Annie's right. She's a dream. I hardly have to talk to her.

"How does that feel?" I call out to her.

"Weird!"

Giggling, I have her push Kit into a canter, a more natural way for her to feel comfortable in her two point position.

Her smile is contagious. I totally envy her freedom. In fact, when I was her age, you couldn't get me to come home from the barn. I was always riding, grooming, trail riding…

I miss that.

I miss that ignorance to this ugly world.

She soars around the arena three more times before I call her to meet me in the center.

"How do you feel about trying out a barrel pattern?"

Her whole face lights up.

"Can we? That would be so fun!"

"Give me a few minutes. Why don't you walk around the arena a few times so I can move these poles out of the way, and I can fix up these barrels."

I don't pick up the poles, but I do push them through the open holes in the fence. I straighten out the barrels and climb up on the first barrel. Let's see what she knows.

I glance over to the bleachers and find the Aldridges with sour grimaces while Derek glares ahead.

Alyssa trots to the chute and waits for my command.

"All right, Alyssa! Let's start this pattern with a trot. After you round your third barrel, get into your two point!"

She nods in acknowledgement, and she trots out of the chute, her eyes trained on me. Sitting on top of this barrel is a distraction, but it's also a necessary teaching lesson. As she rounds the first barrel, she cuts in too close, the toe of her boot knocking the barrel—and me—over.

"I'm so sorry!" she exclaims.

"Don't worry. I'm okay. This happens sometimes." I dust the sand off my jeans and pick the barrel up. "Tell me what you think you did wrong."

"I got too close to the barrel."

I nod. But there's more.

"When you're running to your first barrel, you need to map your pocket around the barrel. You have to see what the safest distance away from the barrel is so you or your horse don't knock it down. What else?"

She purses her lips and shrugs her shoulders.

"I'm not sure."

"You were looking at me."

She mouths oh and frowns.

"As you're rounding your first barrel, you need to be looking at the second barrel so you can start mapping out your next pocket. If you're looking at the barrel, you'll most likely knock it over. Try again."

She trots over to the chute and resets. She gets a good grip on the reins and takes a deep breath. She pushes Kit into a trot and starts my way. She looks just past me, stepping and leaning into the turn. And when she's halfway around the barrel, her head snaps up and searches for the other barrel. I grin when she completes the pattern, a megawatt smile beaming from her cute cheeks.

"I can't believe I did it! That was so fun!"

"You did a great job! Do you want to try at a canter?"

"Ms. McKenzie!"

I glance up to the bleachers, with Mr. Aldridge standing up with his hands magnifying his voice.

Great.

"Push him into a canter and see how you feel. I'll be right back. I'm going to talk to your parents."

She gives me a head start before she turns around and heads for the chute. When I arrive at the bleachers, The Aldridges are angry. For what? I don't know, but I'm probably going to get an earful now. Derek stands up, his arms crossing his chest and narrowing his eyes at Mr. Aldridge.

"We brought her here to be the best. She can't be the best if she's trotting patterns."

Ugh. And suddenly, *they* know best. Fuck me. What do I know?

"Actually, Annie mentioned Alyssa hasn't attempted a barrel pattern yet. So when we introduce it, we have them trot it first so they can get their bearings. It teaches critical thinking and strategy. Speed comes later."

"We were already weary when Annie called earlier and told us you would be taking over the lesson today. We don't know you, but you bet your ass we asked around about you."

"Find your respect, Brian. *Do not* talk to her like that," Derek growls.

Little does Derek know, I've been sticking up for myself my entire life. Nobody walks all over me.

"Oh, you did? Who did you ask? Let me guess: Bethany Hunt and Deb Baker. Does that sound about right?"

Mr. Aldridge takes a step back and pales.

"I'm sure you've visited our family's website. There is a tab where you can see every single competition we've done. I was NBHA 1-D Champion five consecutive years. That's me knowing exactly what I'm doing. On the other hand, Bethany Hunt and Deb Baker are on a crusade to discredit me —and they have been since I was in kindergarten. They were trying to discredit a *child.* As it turns out, Bethany had a thing for my dad back in the day and he rejected her. Chris and Annie have put her in her place any chance the opportunity arose. But I'm quiet. I'm an observer. And frankly, I didn't care. *I knew* what they were saying about me wasn't true. I've learned to rise above it."

I glance back to Alyssa and grin once she turns the third barrel and gets into her two point.

"If you want to go to the Parker's for lessons from now on, I totally understand. Your daughter is a great listener. I'm sure one day when she starts doing this competitively, she'll blow everyone out of the water. Dr. Hawthorn will help Alyssa untack and rinse Kit down. It was nice to meet you."

I turn on my heel and approach Alyssa who stands in the center of the ring with terrified eyes.

"That was an amazing pattern, Alyssa! You did a great job! Okay, so I think we're done for the day, so why don't you start walking Kit around the arena to cool down. Fifteen laps, okay?"

She nods and opens her mouth to say something but thinks better of it. Inside, my heart squeezes. I was never concerned about my reputation around town, but now it's affecting business, and I'm getting angry.

With anger comes tears—ones I wish would disappear. I hide away in the feed room and kick a bale of hay out of frustration. I bury my face in my hands and sob. Leave it to the motherfucking Hunts to continue cutting me down whenever the opportunity arises.

"Peanut? What's wrong?"

Never in a million years would I be so happy to see my idiot brother, but here I am. I launch myself into his arms and wrap my arms around him, sobbing into his chest.

"Dude, this was supposed to be an easy lesson. Why are you crying?"

I can't bear to answer him, because if I do, he'll take matters into his own hands and rip Alyssa's parents a new one. The Parkers are the worst. They'll break her spirit and teach her bad habits. I don't want that to happen.

"It's been a long day," I murmur.

It's mostly the truth, but not entirely.

"Well, you can skip out on feed tonight if you want to head home early..."

Nope. This is my happy place. My safe space. It's more cathartic if anything.

"Thanks, but I'll stick around." I pull back and wipe the tears from my eyes. Derek appears in the doorway with a hard expression, My face is red and blotchy, no doubt. He was privy to watch what went down with the Aldridges. I wonder what bullshit everybody else in town has said to him about me.

"Are you all right?"

Derek's phone tears through the moment.

"Give me five. I'll be right there."

He smiles apologetically and turns away.

21

DEREK

I land in Chicago near midnight. Steve waits for me at baggage claim with a stony look on his face. I briefed him after I got done with Nate. From what Steve has observed, the two Agents who have been put to babysit him are on his payroll. He and Tanner were able to figure it out together through bank records. *But,* the FBI doesn't have a connection yet. And for them to even *look* into these two, someone higher up needs to take notice. Unfortunately, Nate can't investigate them if he never sees them.

Now the real work begins. Delgado is renting a car under an alias and will be in the front of arrivals to pick us up by the time I'm done meeting with Steve.

"How was your flight?" He asks.

"Fine. How has the hunting been going?"

A sinister smile spreads across his lips.

"It was more observing if anything. And, instead of junior, I was checking out the woman who came to the barbeque. She and I had words."

"Yeah? What happened?"

"I have proof of her messing around with multiple other men, not just the driver. I threatened to expose her if she didn't cooperate. She's told us the number for the burner phone and has told Novak everything he needed to know about the conversations she's overheard. We need to get audio and visual in the apartment. He's nearby scouting the place. He's going to stage a block-wide blackout and he'll disable the backup generator for the apartment building. I hope you've been working on your cardio. He lives in the penthouse. Also, Dodge is meeting with the FBI tonight, so he isn't here."

Great.

"Well, let's get moving, then. The faster we can do this, the faster we can put this behind us."

He gives me a questioning look. I'm here because I need Zoey to be safe, and I can't do that if Aria's demons are coming back to haunt her. We live on the same street.

Who am I kidding? She's...interesting. And I want her to feel like she can relax on her own property.

That's concerning.

Steve and I walk out to the curb and find Delgado parked on the side waiting for us. He's a serious guy. I think I've only seen him smile one time. But he's the best at what he does. He's quick. He's lethal. He's thorough. And at a time like this, we *need* him.

"Bubba," He greets quietly as he gets out of the car and pops the trunk.

"Cabron," I reply, earning me a smirk from him.

"Let's move. Tanner's in position."

THE APARTMENT BUILDING looms above us, taunting us with something we won't ever have. I'm okay with my three bedroom house in the middle of nowhere. At least there, the atmosphere is warm, and there are kind people all around me. As for Dodge, this place is...*cold.*

Delgado parks a block away with the building still in sight.

"And we're going dark in three...two...one..." Tanner's voice crackles over our earpieces when the block goes dark.

Delgado's and my ball caps are thrown on and pulled low over our eyes and we walk staggered to the back door of the apartment building.

"Back door is demagnetized. Be quick."

We slip in through the back and enter the back stairwell. Fourteen fucking flights of stairs. Are you kidding me?

We take them two at a time, huffing and puffing until we reach the top. Delgado cracks the door and peers out, his night vision equipment giving us the advantage.

Sweat beads in my hairline and the back of my neck as the minutes tick by. He gives me a thumbs up and we quietly pass through the door,

It's eerily quiet. And…sterile. Not one thing is out of place. There isn't any light filtering through here. Night vision illuminates our way, seeing how this asshole truly lives. There isn't an ounce of clutter anywhere. A strong scent of citrus cleaner hangs in the air. We scan the room, silently cataloging everything. He'll know if something is amiss.

"All rooms need a/v," Nate's voice chimes in on the earpiece. "He's observant so make sure you hide that shit strategically. Otherwise we're screwed and he'll walk free."

"Understood," Delgado replies for us. He sets the brief case on the kitchen island and opens it. He hands me a handful of devices and assures me he'll do the common areas.

My first stop is the master bedroom. The rage flows through me like a coursing river when my eyes rest on the bed he and Aria shared. How many nights did she cower in the fetal position?

Focus…

There's a perfect spot behind the armoire which would conceal the microphone perfectly. Putting the camera in a light would be too obvious. I've learned something important about Charlie Dodge. He's expecting some kind of foul play. He's constantly looking over his shoulder.

"What side of the bed does he sleep on?" I ask.

"Does it matter?" Tanner replies.

"There's not a ton of space I can put the camera without him noticing. I can put it in an outlet that's not being used, which would be Aria's side…"

"It's the side closest to the bathroom," Nate replies.

"Are you sure?"

"She told me he needed to be close to the bathroom when he slept. He needed a quick space he could hide if anything happened."

Pussy.

"Got it. Thank you." I take a mini screwdriver out of my pocket and take the outlet plate off the wall on Aria's side of the room and position the camera.

"I've got visual, but it isn't great," Tanner announces.

"It's better than nothing. We can't afford for him to find it. Besides, he has a distinctive voice, so audio is the main player here," I reply.

"All right. How many areas do you still have?"

"The guest room and I believe that's it. Delgado, what's your status?"

"I'm done, jack ass. Hurry up."

Asshole.

WE RENDEZVOUS at a diner in the suburbs. Steve buys us a late dinner and smiles for the first time in months. Agnes, our waitress, is taken with him. Always refilling his glass of coke up first and flirting horribly.

He texts Betty Lou he'll be home as soon as he can.

Tanner is one of my best friends. And right now, he looks like absolute crap. His brown hair is disheveled, and it looks like he hasn't slept in days. He asks Agnes for a coke, in which I immediately correct to a water. He glares at me.

"Mind your business, Bubba."

"I could knock you out if you'd like," I offer slyly.

He rolls his eyes.

"You assholes have me up all hours of the night. Need I remind you, you only hired one of me."

"We didn't hire you," Steve quips. "You asked to be a part of the group."

Tanner grumbles under his breath while Steve excuses himself to the restroom.

"So, when are you going to tell Old Man McKenzie you have a thing for his daughter?"

"Fuck," Delgado grumbles under his breath.

"What are you talking about?"

"How was the viewing party for the International Space Station the other night, Bubba? Did you strike out?"

"If you don't shut your mouth by the time Steve comes back, I *will* knock you out. She's my friend. And she's Zoey's new best friend."

He waggles his eyebrows suggestively.

"It's good, Bubba. You're letting someone in. You're giving Zoey a new Mommy."

"You may be my brother, but it's not going to stop me from beating the piss out of you the second we step outside."

He rolls his eyes and waves me off dismissively.

"Are you making a play for her?" Delgado asks.

"No. We're friends, that's it. I told her I didn't want a relationship, and she's already said she's off the market for the rest of her life. There's nothing between us."

Delgado inhales and cocks his head as if to say, 'It's your funeral.'

"You hugged her."

"I hug Eve too."

Immediately, Tanner's face falls.

"She's been calling me a lot," he says sadly.

"Have you talked to her?" I ask.

He shakes his head. "Nate told me not to answer her calls. She's smart. She knows she can play me like a fiddle."

Eve and Tanner were always close. Like a brother and sister relationship. And now Nate has broken up with her without much of an explanation, we're all put in an awkward position.

"I listen to the voicemails. First she was devastated. Now she's angry. She's already threatened to come to my house and force me to talk to her."

"It's a shitty situation," Delgado reasons. "This jobs sucks. It's like they say in the Corps. If the Marine Corps wanted you to have a wife, they'd issue you one. Same rings true for the Bureau. I don't blame him for letting her go. I love her. She's my sister, but I don't think I'd ever get over it if she got killed because of a case."

Steve swings back into the booth.

"I wish I wasn't the one she's threatening. Bubba, has she tried to get in touch with you?"

"No. I think she knows I wouldn't say anything. Do you think she bought Nate's story?"

Tanner scoffs. "Absolutely not. She's knows something's up and she gets angrier with every passing day."

"I don't see him saying goodbye a second time. That was it. He's not going to give up his dream job for her," Delgado says.

We reach an awkward silence, soaking in Nate's situation. When all of this is over and the Dodges are behind bars, we'll help Nate get back on the right track. But for now, all of our lives are at stake.

After we're done eating, Delgado and Tanner take off, leaving Steve and I alone.

"How's she doing?"

"I think she's doing okay. She told off Brian and Nicole Aldridge today, so I guess that's progress."

He puffs his chest with pride and tries to hide his smile.

"Betty Lou said she's been seeing a therapist."

"She's not taking any of this lying down. She's a fighter."

This time, Steve purses his lips and twiddles his thumbs.

"When she was born, I knew there was something about her that would be resilient. She was six weeks early. Nearly killed herself and her mother on the way out. When they brought her to the NICU, Betty Lou immediately went into surgery to repair the internal bleeding, so I had to follow Aria. I expected her to cry or scream or...*something*. She never did."

"She hasn't folded under the pressure of the investigation. You've got to hand it to her, Steve, she was in danger, but she noticed Nate was watching and got a message to him. She made it out alive. I think she's a lot stronger than everyone gives her credit for."

Steve narrows his eyes at me, pondering my words.

"People make mistakes, Steve. And I think if anyone knows that it's her. She's sorry. And she just wants you to love her."

"What exactly is going on between the two of you?" He asks suspiciously.

"Nothing. I overheard her talking to Chris."

He nods and frowns.

"I grabbed some rooms in a motel close to the highway. Let's get some shut eye before our flight leaves in," he checks his watch, "five hours."

Three hours of sleep. Perfect.

22

ARIA

25 weeks pregnant...

It's brutally hot outside. Derek isn't around, and I totally could've gotten away with a form fitting, short sleeved shirt, but I'm not taking any chances. Besides, the long sleeves protect me from the annoying flies. My belly is growing by the day, and it's not like I owe him an explanation, *but,* I feel like this secret I'm keeping close to my chest is the only thing I can control at the moment. Pathetic. I know, but I have to grab control while I can.

Annie is slaving away at her computer. She told me she's trying to stack articles so she can get ready for the Summer Series at the rodeo and not have to worry about work. And while Chris is working the crops with Bernard, Hank, and Jose, I'm stuck alone at the barns.

I'm not complaining. In fact, I prefer it when I have the place to myself.

Olson has been quiet. I visited this morning and made him breakfast because he was working so hard, but he barely exchanged five words with me. JJ used to tell us in the military, no news is good news. But when it comes to Charlie, no news is concerning news. He hasn't blown up my new phone in a week or two. I have a new cache of voicemails I have yet to send Olson, but I feel like if I do that, I lose my independence. He'll take my phone away to analyze, and then we'll be in this perpetual circle of changing my number, only for Charlie to find the new one.

It's Coley's day to get her feet trimmed. Eric is dropping by to do a quick trim, and he'll be on his merry way. Thirty minutes tops.

Eric strolls in with a cigarette hanging lazily in between his lips. He waves and sets his equipment down. We don't exchange pleasantries, because of who are as people. You'd think as old as Coley is, her sass would be toned down by now. Nope. Instead, she throws her head back and forth out of sheer boredom. She demands attention. And apple cookies.

"The doc isn't around, is he?" Eric asks as I make myself comfortable on Zoey's lawn chair.

"No. I'm not sure where he is, actually."

He nods and starts working on Coley without a second glance.

It's a quiet afternoon. I left my phone at Annie's so I could lose myself in mucking stalls. Besides, Momma has made it her mission to call me every half hour to make sure I'm doing okay. I've been itching to call my father, but I'm afraid it'll end up in a shouting match and I'm not entirely up for the fighting.

Eric talks to Coley in a low voice. She listens and lowers her head in relaxation. She's spoiled in the sense that any grooming, whether it's brushing or getting her feet done, she relaxes into it and tucks her sass away for another day.

"What's this scar on her back leg?" Eric asks.

"Oh, that happened a few months ago. She kicked down a whole panel of fencing because the food wasn't coming fast enough."

He chuckles and pats her neck.

"It's looking a lot better. Is she still lame?"

"Not really. She does favor that leg, so I'm not rushing into riding her until she feels one hundred percent on it."

Or, once the baby comes since I'm not allowed to ride anymore.

Fifteen minutes later, Eric's done. He gives me an invoice and encourages me to call the office so I can pay with a credit card and leaves the property.

"Hey."

I turn around to Derek's voice. It's then I see Daddy behind him, watching me with weary and untrusting eyes.

Awesome.

"Hi Daddy. How was your trip?"

"It was fine. What's she doing in here?" He asks, walking closer to Coley and stroking her nose.

"Eric stopped by to trim her feet. You just missed him." He towers over me, avoiding my gaze. I literally looked up to him my entire life. Only this time, he refuses to look me in the eyes. "So who did you see?"

"Some friends from college," he replies nonchalantly.

"Friends from college," I repeat in disbelief. When he doesn't say anything, it only fuels my anger more. "You didn't go to college, Dad. Try again."

He smirks and takes a few steps back.

"I'm home now. Where's your brother?"

"Harvesting." My clipped answer amuses him. I don't know what it is about the men in the family, but they thoroughly enjoy pissing me off.

"I'm going to check in with him." Without another word, he storms off out of the barn and hops into the truck and drives off.

"You were with him, weren't you?" I ask Derek without looking at him.

"It was pure coincidence we got here at the same time."

Right. And my mother is Cameron Diaz.

"Oh?"

"Yep. Had a family emergency I had to take care of."

Mmhm.

"I'm going to get some shut eye. I'm beat."

"I'll bet. Conspiring with my father must be exhausting."

I want to be angry, but his smirk makes me smile.

"It is. I can't keep up. Hey, drink some water. It's fucking hot out here."

I wave him off and watch him walk away. There's something they're keeping from me. And I don't like it one bit.

23

DEREK

I've never skipped a day of running, and I'm not about to let an impromptu trip to Chicago ruin that for me. The porch swing groans under my weight as I lazily reach for my tennis shoes and pull them on.

It's a beautiful day, and while I'm usually working at this time, I have the day off and I need to find my normal before my head runs off with the little minx I left at the barn.

I stand up from the porch swing and stretch, allowing my back and joints to pop before I start my three miles. The back pasture is the perfect place to run. For the most part, the ground is pretty flat, and there aren't any holes I need to worry about. And it's close enough to home that I won't have the women of Sage Creek ogling me as I run or catcalling me to take my shirt off.

Pass.

When I step down the hill, the sound of clumsy and panicked hooves against the concrete grabs my attention. I look to barn number three, and find Coley prancing out of the aisle. Her whinny is panicked. The cross ties have been ripped out of the wall and fly freely, still clipped to her halter.

It's not enough she's escaped. She has to let the whole world know about it. I jog that way, and when she spots me, she gallops towards me, skidding to a stop when she's six feet away, and nervously prancing.

"Hey, you. What's going on?" I reach for her halter, but she turns on a dime and canters back into the barn.

Shit.

Something happened.

I jog into the barn and follow Coley until she skids to a stop. Aria lies on the ground, unconscious. Her face is flushed and red, and what makes my heart pound in my chest is she's not sweating. At all.

"Aria?" I crouch down beside her and roll up her sleeves. I remember the scars from that first day she came back home. Most of them are faded, but they still remain. She's been through hell.

I gently pat her cheek repeatedly, trying to get her to come to.

"Ace? I need you to open your eyes. Can you do that?"

Her eyelids don't even flutter. There's literally no change.

"Shit," I hiss under my breath.

My phone is at the house. Time is of the essence.

"Aria, baby, I need you to open your eyes. We need to get you to a bathtub…"

Nothing.

Okay. This is happening.

I gently scoop her up in my arms. She lies like a ragdoll. Her whole body is dead weight and it's difficult to walk. Coley walks beside us like she's Aria's guard dog. She *has* to make sure Aria's getting taken care of.

I get it, girl. I don't want anything happening to her either.

I walk as fast as I can, stopping a few times to adjust my grip on her. I nearly cry when I reach the hill to the cul-de-sac, but I press through it.

When I reach Annie's house, I don't bother ringing the doorbell. I walk right in, kicking the door open, and call out for Annie.

A chair scrapes against the wood floor, and suddenly, Annie appears in the foyer. Her bluebell eyes widen in horror at the sight of her sister.

"What the hell happened?" she demands, rushing over to us and pressing her palm to Aria's forehead.

"Where's your bathroom? We need to get her under cold water. Now."

She motions for me to follow her.

We storm through the house like a tornado. Annie kicks open the door to her room and leads me to lay Aria on the bed so we can begin undressing.

"Everything has to come off. Panties and bra too. Can you do that?"

Annie's eyes whip to me, scandalized.

"She's suffering from heat fatigue. We need to cool her internal temperature down before there's any damage. Where can I find your thermometer?"

"Medicine cabinet," she murmurs, working on Aria's boots.

I race into the bathroom and turn on the faucet to the bathtub, putting on the coolest temperature. I then search the medicine cabinet and find a rectal thermometer. *It's interesting she has one*. But there's no time to dwell on it. I sterilize it with the bottle of rubbing alcohol in the medicine cabinet.

Racing into the room, Aria still has her bra and shirt on, but her jeans and underwear are off.

"Okay, I need help turning her on her side. I need to get her internal temperature. That will give us the most important information we need."

Annie gently rolls her over and I insert the thermometer, holding my breath. I hope it's not too high. I hope we've caught this in time.

"A hundred and three," Annie murmurs.

"Okay. Shirt and bra off."

I turn away to give her some sense of dignity, not that it will matter. I'm about to see everything anyway.

"She's ready," Annie murmurs.

I scoop her up, her skin burns against me. I lower her into the bathtub and stretch her legs out.

Then I see it.

That's not a food baby.

It's a small baby bump.

Shit!

"Annie, is she pregnant?"

"Yes, but—"

"Call an ambulance. Then call her OB and tell her to meet you at the hospital."

Fuck. Fuck. Fuck.

I've never dealt with heat fatigue in a pregnant woman before. In the Corps., they dropped your pants, stuck the thermometer in your ass, and then carted you away to get treatment. Other friends in the Army told me they treated heat fatigue with linens submerged in ice to get the internal temperature down.

"Aria? Can you hear me?" I plead. I need her to come to. I need to know she's okay.

Her eyelids flutter but remain closed. Progress.

"You're in Annie's house. You're in a cold bath. You passed out at the barn. Do you understand that?"

Her lips move like she's chewing.

Come on, sweet thing. Wake up for me.

"Ambulance is on the way. Dr. Cash is on her way to the hospital and Momma is on her way over. What do you need me to do?"

"We need to lean her forward. Aria, can you bring your knees to your chest?"

She doesn't answer, but her legs draw up to her chest, slowly, and her arms hug them for dear life. I push her hair to the side and grab the cup on the side of the tup, filling it with the cold water and pouring it at the base of her neck. I don't mean to peek, I don't, but her back grabs my attention. And apparently, it grabbed Annie's attention too.

She gasps in horror. Long scars mar her back. I've seen this in movies. At least, this is how Hollywood portrayed the markings slaves were given when they were punished. Long gashes of brown and pink, some still red, raised, and scabbed over. I swallow the lump in my throat. I glance to my left and see Annie in tears.

How does a man destroy a woman to this capacity? I get it now. I get why she wears the baggy, long sleeved shirts. I get why she's been so emotional. I don't understand why she didn't tell anyone. *Me.* Why wouldn't she tell me?

Because you're not really her friend. You're a guy who lives on the property.

But it's more than that now isn't it?. It has to be.

A sob sounds off from the bathtub. Aria is coming to.

"Aria? Can you hear me?" I ask.

"Yes," she whimpers.

"Do you know what year it is?"

"2017."

Good.

"Do you know what day it is?"

"It's Thursday," she replies.

"What's my name?"

"Derek Alexander Hawthorn."

Never in my life has my name sounded so sweet. She's okay. Sort of.

"How are you feeling? Do you think you can lay back now?"

She nods wordlessly.

"Baby? Where are you?" Betty Lou's voice shrieks throughout the house.

"In here!" Annie calls out.

"Do me a favor. Grab a few dark colored washcloths. We can cover her up for when the paramedics get here."

It's a forty minute drive from town to get here. But I imagine she'd be mortified if I saw her naked like this. Annie throws me two dark purple washcloths as she races out the door. Aria leans back in the tub, her pools of hazel swimming with tears. When Annie returns, I cover up her full breasts, and her lower half.

"It's going to be okay," I reassure her. "The ambulance is on the way and Dr. Cash is meeting you at the hospital."

Her bottom lips wobbles and she sobs.

"I'm sorry," she wails.

"Why are you sorry?"

"I didn't want to drink the water. The fridge was too far."

I smirk and chuckle.

"How are you feeling otherwise? Do you feel any pressure? Are you cramping?"

She shrugs. At this point, I'm sure she's in shock.

"Annie? Can you check her underwear? Tell me if you notice any blood."

Aria's eyes fly open and she moves to stand up.

"No, sit down. We need to bring your internal temp down. Relax. We've got it from here."

Betty Lou rushes into the bathroom and nearly pushes me away.

"Baby, what happened?"

Aria can't form coherent sentences. She sobs into Betty Lou's shirt, repeating her apologies. What does this woman have to be sorry for? It's not her fault!

"I need some makeshift ice packs. Three of them to be exact. One each for under her arms, and then one in between her legs. Those are the hottest parts of the body and it'll help with bringing her temp down," I say to Betty Lou.

She pats my face, a silent *thank you*, and rushes out to the kitchen.

"You're lucky Ace. If it wasn't for your psycho horse, I might not have found you in time."

She sobs harder. And that reminds me I didn't put Coley back. She's probably roaming the property with the cross ties still hanging from her halter.

"Did Momma see my back?" she whimpers.

"I don't think so." I won't tell her Annie did.

After ten more minutes with the ice packs and the cold water, she shivers. I shut off the water and allow Betty Lou and Annie to get her dressed and into bed until the paramedics get here. Annie opens the door when Aria is decent and allows me back inside.

I sit on the edge of the bed and examine her pupils.

"Do you remember what happened before you went unconscious? Did you hit your head on anything?"

"I'm not sure," she murmurs.

"Does your head hurt now?"

"A little."

She sits up so we're touching from shoulder to ankle. She leans against me, resting her head on my shoulder.

"What's going to happen to the baby?" she asks in a small voice.

Betty Lou's gaze meets mine in the mirror in the bathroom, and she stops what she's doing and listens.

"We won't know anything until your OB checks you out."

"But in your professional opinion?"

"My professional opinion doesn't matter right now. I'm a doctor for horses and cows. And unfortunately yappy dogs I want nothing to do with. You're none of those. But...I think I found you in enough time."

"I'll never forgive myself if something happens to the baby."

My gut twists in anxiety. It's the perfect excuse to put a highway of distance between us. But my instincts tell me something different. I'd be lying if I said I didn't like her leaning on me. I do. I like it a lot.

Her pouty lips quiver.

"Don't jump to conclusions yet, Ace. It's going to be okay."

Steve and Chris race single file into the room on high alert. They catch sight of Aria and relax, slightly. When Chris sees our position, he immediately scowls.

"Man, you think you know a guy."

I grin and glance over to Steve who narrows his eyes at Aria.

"What happened?" Steve asks.

"She's dehydrated. I found her unconscious in the middle of the barn."

"Aria—"

"Say something mean to my baby, Stephen, I *dare* you." Betty Lou barrels out of the bathroom and squares up against her husband. If this wasn't such a serious moment, it would be funny.

"I wasn't going to say anything!"

"You've been home all of sixty minutes and you're already picking fights. If you have nothing to say, get the fuck out!" My insides freeze. Not once in my life have I ever heard Betty Lou McKenzie drop an 'F' bomb.

Picking his battles, Steve leaves the room as my phone vibrates in my pocket. I excuse myself to the living room and answer it.

"Hey Bubba," Logan greets sadly in my ear.

"Hey Logan. What's going on?"

"We have a court date."

Brakes screech in my head.

"A court date?"

"It turns out Emily and her lawyer want to contest the parenting plan.

This is a full blown custody battle now. Whoever wins, gets Zoey for good."

"What happened?" Nate rushes into the living room, giving the McKenzie's some space.

"Emily's a fucking bitch," I seethe.

"Bubba, focus."

"She's contesting the parenting plan, Nate!" My voice carries into the other room, and suddenly, all of the McKenzie's are watching this.

"We'll talk about this later," he says, lowering his voice. "I'm here for you, Bubba. I am. What happened with Aria? Why is there an ambulance screaming over here?"

"Heat fatigue."

Nate's face falls.

"What's Nate doing there?" Logan's voice shouts from the phone.

"He's here for Aria."

"Who's Aria?"

"Logan, I don't care what you have to do, but there is no fucking way Emily is leaving this god forsaken state with Zoey."

"I'll handle it, okay? She won't."

I hang up with Logan as the paramedics sweep into the room. They take Aria's vitals and ask her a ton of questions. Nate's on his phone with his supervisor.

"She's pregnant and dehydrated. You'll need to start an IV in the bus," I say quietly to the nearest paramedic. Nate's eyes snap to mine, and then to Aria. I give Aria an apologetic grimace.

They wheel her out on the stretcher.

"Thank you for finding her," Betty Lou says quietly approaching me.

"Thank Coley. If it wasn't for her crazy ass, I would've gone on my run."

She nods and shrugs. I *know* she wants to say something more. She wouldn't be Betty Lou if she didn't have the last word.

"Thank you for helping her. And…for understanding."

That she's knocked up?

My stomach churns knowing Dodge left her with a parting gift. Now I understand her line of questioning from when we were first shooting. She wanted to know if it was possible to change her mind.

"Mrs. McKenzie, I know you'd like to escort Aria in the ambulance, but I'm going to have to insist I do. This is for her safety, and I'm erring on the side of caution," Nate announces professionally.

Mark, the paramedic with the dark hair snickers.

"That's not going to fly, man. Do you know who you're talking to?"

Betty Lou glares at Nate and places her hands on her hips.

"I appreciate the concern, Agent, but I'm not leaving my baby again."

"Not to worry Mrs. McKenzie, you're always our exception. Agent what's-your-name, you can ride in the middle."

Nate's face sours.

"Fine."

24

ARIA

25 weeks pregnant...

The cat's out of the bag. And I have nobody to blame but myself. Soon, the entire town will know I was living in sin with a man who had a few screws loose. I should thank Charlie for the parting gift, shouldn't I? He's found a new way to humiliate me and he isn't even around to enjoy the spoils.

The whooshing sound from my uterus fills the room, and Dr. Cash sits at the edge of her seat, her chocolate eyes trained on the screen in front of her with her brow furrowed. There's still a heartbeat. And that's all that matters.

"Amniotic fluid is a little low," she murmurs.

"What does that mean?"

"You're severely dehydrated," she replies, wiping off the jelly from the wand and placing it back in the holder. "I know we talked about the amniocentesis and you weren't sure about it, but I highly recommend it.

Heat fatigue can cause some birth defects, and an amniocentesis can tell us if there's anything we need to prepare for."

I feel like such an idiot. All I had to do was drink water. All I had to do was stay inside. But no. That's not who I am, is it? I have to test the patriarchy whenever I see an opening.

"Okay."

She grasps my hand and squeezes it reassuringly.

"How are you feeling, otherwise? Any cramping? Any pressure?"

"No, and no. I'm feeling...foolish."

Her pitied smile makes me want to look the other way. I'm so sick of seeing it on her and the other people around me. It's my own fault I'm in this predicament. They should be angry. I should be punished.

"It happens, Aria. Everyone makes mistakes. But the baby's okay. You're okay. That's all that matters."

Yeah, screw all the other bullshit that brought me here.

Annie sits in the chair beside my bed, staring off into space, uncharacteristically quiet. Annie always has something to say, even when everyone around her doesn't want to hear it.

When Dr. Cash excuses herself, I turn to Annie and offer a pathetic smile.

"Hey, are you alive over there?" I ask teasingly.

"I'm alive, Aria."

Shit.

"Aria, huh? Not Peanut?"

Her hard expression softens.

"I'm sorry. I'm just upset."

Because I'm an idiot.

"Oh. I'm sorry for—"

"I'm not upset at you, Aria." She sighs and turns to face me. "I'm upset with myself. There were so many times I wanted to go to Chicago and figure out what was going on with you. Believe it or not, you're my best friend."

Of course she is. She's mine too. My traitorous tears stream down my face when my sister can barely look me in the eye. I'm so ashamed. I should've known being with Charlie was going to affect everyone around me.

"Anyway, I kept putting it off because I didn't think you'd want to see me. And now I know you did, and more than anything, you needed help, and I wasn't there for you."

My heart plummets to the fiery depths of my stomach.

"I saw your back. I can't imagine the pure hell he put you through. And it's a constant reminder I need to be better—"

"Stop it," I plead. "It wouldn't have mattered if you came for me. Honestly, it probably would've gotten me killed."

She glances up at me with watery eyes.

"I don't blame you at all. He made me think going home with him meant you guys wouldn't want to talk to me again. And if I had any hope you did...he would have snuffed that right out of me. I don't blame you. Mostly, I blame myself. I ignored the red flags and I'm in here because of that."

"It's not your fault," she murmurs, climbing into bed with me and snuggling against my side. "It's his. He's a sick idiot and he'll get what's coming to him."

I wish she wouldn't get her hopes up.

Besides, once the news I'm with child hits his ears, he'll ensure he's the one holding it when this is all over.

I need to get a grip. This baby is going to live. And he'll be surrounded with the best people in the entire world. Even if Charlie kills me, the baby will be safe with Momma and Daddy.

I hope.

HOURS LATER, when Annie yawns for the hundredth time, I beg her to leave. I'll be fine. And Olson is standing guard. He hasn't spoken to me since I was in the ambulance. I'm sure he's pissed I didn't say anything, but I don't regret keeping this a secret. It was for *our* safety.

A light tap on the door rips my attention from the TV, and Derek cautiously strolls in and occupies Annie's seat.

"Hey Ace. How are you feeling?"

Humiliated.

"Better. Um. Thanks…for what you did."

I'm trying not to remind myself you saw me naked.

"I'm glad I found you. That was scary."

Awkwardness hangs in the air. Sure, the cat's out of the bag, but now there's a giant elephant in the room we both pretend we don't see.

"How's the baby?"

Of course, he's the first one to point it out.

"Amniotic fluid was low. I'm under strict instructions not to go out to the barn for a few days."

He grins. "Is that the doctor's orders, or Betty Lou's?"

Giggling, I reply, "Both."

"Do you know what you're having yet?"

I shake my head, lowering my eyes to my ballooning belly, stroking the bump that will soon make its way into the world. "I'm not sure I want to know yet."

"…Was it planned?" My wild gaze meets his. *No!* "I'm not trying to be rude. You don't have to tell me if you don't want to." He stumbles over his words as he tries to justify his question. "I mean…I know he wasn't… *good…*to you."

"No, it wasn't planned. I've been on the pill forever. Never missed a dose. But…I think he tampered with it somehow." I shrug. "My other options suck, so I'm keeping him."

My whole body shudders at the thought. This baby is a product of rape, and I'm keeping it around because…why?

It's not the baby's fault. He didn't ask to be brought into this world. I can't stick him with a greedy couple who might sell him for a fat stack of cash.

"Are you nervous?"

"Honestly, I haven't given it much thought." And there's the sad and horrible truth. I don't see a future with this baby. "I'd be naïve to think I've seen the last of Charlie, and once he finds out about him, he'll take him away."

Derek leans forward, balancing himself on his forearms and folding his hands together.

"Do you have a death wish, Ace?"

A giggle escapes me. Maybe I do. I absolutely did when I was trapped with Charlie. But now…dare I say there is the smallest glimmer of hope the FBI will catch him and lock him away forever?

"I used to. Now, I'm not so sure."

He reaches out and takes my hand in his.

"I'm glad you're okay. You had me worried there for a second."

Weakly smiling, I sit up and fold my legs underneath me.

"Remember at Rico's how we said this was all it could ever be? Friends, nothing more?"

He nods, his icy eyes searching mine, like I'm going to change my mind. Is he relieved, or horrified?

"I meant it when I said I was off the market forever. I can't trust anyone. And you've been nice and helpful, and I get butterflies when I'm around you, but…I have somebody else to look after. You shouldn't worry after me, Derek. You have your own life to deal with."

I wish my heart didn't ache when his face falls. I wish I could tell him I find his presence calming, and I'm craving his company. But the reality is, I carry baggage four miles long. There's shit I haven't even processed yet.

"Maybe not *everyone,*" he reasons, "But you can trust me. You can trust your family. You can trust Nate."

Which reminds me…

"So, when were you going to tell me you and Agent Olson know each other?"

He chuckles nervously and beckons Olson into the room. His eyes sweep over me to make sure I'm not gushing blood or dying on the spot. And when he realizes Derek is holding my hand, he hesitates.

"He's my brother."

My eyes shift to Olson who grumbles and takes a seat at the foot of my bed.

"When I was overseas in Afghanistan, Nate's unit is where I was assigned. I was in charge of patching them up when they were acting like assholes."

"Shut up, Bubba," Nate stammers. He brings his guilty gaze to mine and ducks his head. "It's my job to encourage you to take witness protection, Aria. I really didn't want you to take it. I *prayed* you'd say you wanted to come home."

"Why didn't you just tell me?"

"Because it's a little unethical," Derek replies for him. They share a hesitant look and frown.

"Derek and I have been through war together. Along with him, I can count on one hand the number of people I trust with my life. He knows my dirty little secrets and I still live to tell the tale. I knew if I brought you home, there would be one more person who could watch out for you."

Part of me feels betrayed. They talked about me behind my back…they made plans without my knowledge.

"Why didn't you tell me you were pregnant? And when did you find out?"

It's my turn to become sheepish. I was afraid of this. I don't want to go into this, but now, the important people know. There's no point in trying to hide it anymore.

"The day after we got back. When I went to my doctor appointment that day, they ran a pregnancy test and whomp there it is." Nate arches an eyebrow, expecting me to continue. "I didn't tell you because I didn't want this piece of news to reach Charlie."

"You think I'd sell you out?"

"No! Of course not! I'm afraid of the FBI selling me out. You have moles, Olson. Tons of them."

"Do you know any names? Anybody I should be looking into?"

"Honestly, start with the agents that are with him now. You should be suspicious of everyone."

"We'll talk when you're discharged. But this isn't over, McKenzie." He grins and squeezes my shoulder as he stands up. "You had me scared. I'm grateful you're okay." I wave him off and turn to Derek.

"You should go too. I heard you on the phone."

He groans. The air changes in the room when it's just the two of us. There's hope—the most dangerous weapon any of us could wield. I'm suddenly aware of his fingers laced with mine.

"Just because you're having a baby doesn't mean we couldn't have fun."

I roll my eyes and choke on a laugh.

"Yeah? And what about after that, Derek? What happens when the baby comes?"

He ponders and wages a silent war in his head. When you meet a man like him, a man who is all about the 'no attachments' life, there is only one person who will change his mind. In his case, it's Zoey. His mind is made up and I'm okay with that. Because my mind is made up too. Eventually, I'll have to leave Sage Creek. Again. I'll have to change my name and hide away while the shit hits the fan here. What matters is the life inside of me. His and mine. Until then, I'll stay put because I'm out of options. But once Charlie pays off a judge, or a jury, the hunt is on. And I don't plan on sticking around to find out what it means for me.

25

DEREK

On Saturday, Aria arrives home. That moment of unhindered honesty we shared in her hospital room is over, and now she's using all of her energy to avoid me. Zoey makes us pancakes for breakfast and flips on some Saturday morning cartoons.

Nate has kept me updated on her progress, but other than that, she's made it clear we need to put some distance between us.

It's fine. I shouldn't have been looking in her direction anyway. But when she entertained the thought of us having fun and asking me what would happen after the baby was born, I wasn't thinking of ghosting her.

I want to help. It's not my kid, but I want to help.

I don't know this woman from Adam. She keeps her secrets close to her chest. She cuts me down when I get too close. And still, I keep coming back because she is the most beautiful woman I've ever laid eyes on.

Essentially, she's right. Nothing more could happen. I'm not putting Zoey's happiness on the back burner just because I want to take Aria McKenzie for a spin.

It's more than that...

"I was thinking about going to the movies today," Zoey announces from the chair she stands on at the stove.

"Oh yeah? Am I invited?"

She giggles and nods. "I'm in the mood for popcorn. Plus, I think I might need you to buy me another booklight because the one I have burned out and I've been reading in the dark. My poor eyes need a break."

Of course.

"You're not supposed to be reading in the dark, Zo. That's how you ruin your eyes."

She shrugs carelessly because we both know she's going to continue reading in the dark. It's a good thing I pay for good insurance.

"Anyway, I was hoping to see *Spider-Man.* It looks good from the trailer, but I've always been curious about how many *Spider-Man* movies there are, and which one is the real one."

She's going to be a genius.

"Do you believe in the multi-verse, Zo?"

She sticks her tongue out in concentration as she flips the pancake in the pan.

"I don't know anyone who has died," she admits, "Alternate realities are cool, no?"

"They're an interesting concept," I agree.

"I don't know. I think it would be unfair to rule anything out."

"You're way beyond your years, babe." I kiss her on the forehead and take over so she can grab a bite to eat.

"Maybe Miss Aria can come with us?"

Hearing Aria's name immediately grabs my attention. When I narrow my eyes at Zoey, she bursts into a fit of giggles.

"I knew you liked her."

Shit.

"It's not like that. She's just my friend."

"Do you like her, like her?"

"We're not having this conversation. Eat."

She exhales impatiently.

"Mom has a new boyfriend."

My racing thoughts come to a screeching halt.

"She does?"

"Mmhm. He lives in California, but you're not supposed to know." I'm going to fucking kill Emily. "She's happy, Dad. Usually she's mean to me, but ever since they started talking on the phone, she's happy all the time."

"And your point is…?"

"My *point* is you should get a girlfriend. Because then you'd be happy."

Have I been pushing my miserable existence into the universe this whole time? I've been trying hard to keep my attachments outside, away from her.

"I *am* happy."

She stuffs fluffy pancakes into her mouth and grins.

"You say that, but I wonder if you're telling the truth. I've read about love, Dad. People are supposed to be together. You're not supposed to stay alone the rest of your life."

I'm happy with being alone. From the window in the kitchen, I catch a ribbon of black hair heading down the hill. She isn't aware I'm watching her. I want to scream at her for being outside when she's supposed to be resting, but her slender frame is dressed in form fitting clothing for once. Her pasty skin reflects the sun shining off of it. *I hope she wore sunscreen.*

A silver glint catches my eye. She holds a purple and silver titanium travel cup in her hand. Good. So she's drinking water.

Zoey's giggle brings me back to Earth, and her mischievous smile tells me she knows I was checking her out. Shit.

26

ARIA

27 weeks pregnant...

I FIND myself more often than not in the kitchen cooking...anything. Since I'm bound to the house, I've literally binged everything I could on the TV shows I used to watch and couldn't find anything to pique my interest.

So, I cook.

Annie can't cook to save her life, so it's solely up to me that she eats at least one well-balanced meal every day so she can continue slaving away at her computer.

And she's...

Where is she?

I wander away from the stove and peek my head out to the dining room. Her laptop is open, and a half-typed Word document remains open, but she isn't here. I slowly pad through the house, checking every room for her.

She...disappeared.

Even the bathrooms are empty.

I walk timidly through the rest of the house, back to the kitchen. I jump when Derek's large frame waits for me near the front door.

His icy eyes sweep over me from head to toe. Not in a predatory way. In fact, my stomach somersaults when a seductive grin spreads across his freckled cheeks.

"Knock much?" I ask with an uncharacteristically breathy voice.

"I knocked. You didn't answer. I was checking in on you."

Nodding, I timidly pass him into the kitchen and stir the soup I've been preparing all day.

"No need to check in on me, Dr. Hawthorn. I'm a big girl. I can take care of myself."

He steps into the kitchen and leans against the island with a cocky smirk.

"Can you?"

There's so much implied behind those words. And when I turn around, my heart races erratically in my chest.

"Yes." I don't trust the shaky reply that escapes me.

"Tell me."

My words get caught in my throat. It's like I've completely forgotten how to form sentences. His eyes question me with gentle insistence. It's then I can't stay quiet. He'll coax it out of me whether I want to or not.

"About what?"

"How do you take care of yourself, Ace? Because I take care of myself too. And when I do, you're tattooed on my eyelids."

I choke on a jagged inhale.

"Tell me," he repeats.

"I-I don't know..."

"When Annie isn't here, when you're alone in bed, or taking a bath, do you think of me?" He closes the gap between us, cradling my face in his large, calloused hands, tracing my bottom lip with his thumb. I melt into his touch as my heart races a marathon. "Don't lie to me, Ace."

I swallow my anxiety and nod.

That's the truth, isn't it? Yes. I think of him. I think of him shirtless and doing manly things like running and moving hay. I think about him in the shower…with me.

"Yes. I think about you."

He grins.

"Tell me," he repeats.

My eyes flutter closed as he presses a kiss on my throat.

"I see you…and me…"

He picks me up so effortlessly and sets me down on the counter. My hands rake through his thick, wavy locks, and his hands grip my waist firmly, but gently.

"Is this okay?" He whispers, fingering the button of my cut offs and popping the button out of the socket.

I nod. Heat pools down below. My skin is on fire as he kisses a trail from my covered breasts down to my clit. His tongue swirls and my head bangs against the counter.

Suddenly, the smoke alarm shrieks as the soup boils over, yet Derek doesn't move.

"Derek…the soup…"

"Leave it," he growls.

Is the shrieking getting louder?

"Aria!"

My eyes snap back to Derek, but it's not his voice.

I glance around me and there's not another soul in this house.

"Aria!"

I push Derek away, earning a wild stare as I close my legs and pull my shorts back on as I try to find the voice.

"Aria!"

MY EYES FLY open with Annie standing above me, gently shaking me. I close my eyes in frustration. I didn't even get to the end. I didn't get the sweet release I've been craving ever since I entered my second trimester.

And lo and behold, I dream about the vet who lives two doors down from me, the man too afraid of commitment, the man with the young daughter who loves *Heartland* as much as I do.

I dream about a man in which nothing could ever blossom into anything more than a friendship.

Shit.

"Peanut? Did you have another bad dream?"

It wasn't bad. It was actually…pleasant.

"I'm sorry. I didn't mean to wake you up."

She giggles. "Don't worry about it. You didn't wake me up. It's ten o'clock."

Realization sets in as I launch myself out of bed. I need to be in town in thirty minutes to meet with Dr. Nelson. I pull on a pair of shorts and a dirty shirt I haven't gotten around to washing yet.

"Where's the fire?" she asks.

"I forgot to set my alarm," I groan. "I have a therapy appointment in thirty minutes."

Annie throws me a pair of socks and runs a brush through my hair while I pull on socks and shoes. I appreciate the sentiment, but I don't have time for sisterly bonding moments right this second.

"Be careful, okay? Do you need me to drive you?"

"No, I should be fine. Olson will escort me there so I should be able to shave a few minutes off my ETA."

I race through the house, grabbing a snack size bag of chips and race out the door with Annie shouting at me to be careful. I meet Nate's gaze across the driveway and put up a hand in surrender.

I peel out of the property, a move that will get me in major trouble with my father when I get back, but I can't deal with it right now. I zone out as I speed down the country road.

This is progress. A few months ago, if I would've been late for this appointment, I would've shut down. I would've made myself physically ill because of the anxiety, for the fear Dr. Nelson would punish me for being even a minute late.

I know she'll understand. She isn't Charlie. She isn't wife number six.

That's what I keep telling myself as I speed through town. Nate honks his horn several times, as a warning to slow down before I get hurt.

Thirty minutes later, I pull into the parking lot of the office and launch myself out of the car. I wave a dismissive hand at Nate and enter the office out of breath.

April grins at me and assures me Dr. Nelson is running behind and will be with me shortly. Nate strolls in and grabs the seat next to me, smirking.

"If I knew you drove like that, we would've taken turns when we left Chicago."

I giggle, knowing that I wouldn't have found that funny a month ago.

Again, progress.

"Sorry. I overslept."

He shrugs and grabs a magazine off the side table.

"I'm glad you're doing this. You actually seem like a fun person."

I roll my eyes and nudge him in the ribs with my elbow.

"You're an asshole."

He shrugs nonchalantly and grins.

Dr. Nelson appears in the doorway and beckons me to follow her. I bid Nate adieu and walk the narrow hallway into Dr. Nelson's office.

For the first time since I was hospitalized, I feel like I can breathe. There's nobody here overanalyzing my every move. I mean, except for Dr. Nelson. But even still, she feels like a friend I'm visiting.

"How are you doing today?"

"Um, it's still too soon to tell. I overslept and came straight here. I haven't even had my stupid sixteen ounces of caffeine yet."

She cracks a smile and curls up on her chair, tucking her feet underneath her.

"So…word on the street is you were hospitalized last week."

I close my eyes in frustration. I wonder what Bethany Hunt's explanation was.

"Ah…yeah. I had heat fatigue."

She raises her eyebrows and expects me to continue.

"I'm not wearing the long sleeves anymore. I figure the whole town probably knows by now I'm pregnant. There's no point in hiding it anymore."

"Hmm," she hums, sitting up straighter. "So you don't mind them seeing the scars on your arms?"

"I mean, of course I mind, but what does that have to do with anything?"

"I thought you wore the baggy clothes because you were hiding the wounds on your arms and legs. But now…you come to your session in a short sleeved T-shirt and shorts. That makes me believe you were only hiding the pregnancy…"

And here's where the shrinking begins.

"I'm just making an observation, here, Aria. I'm not judging you. Do you feel more ashamed of your pregnancy?"

My stomach churns as realization washes over me.

"Um…"

"This is a safe space. Tell me about your pregnancy so far."

She notes my squirming, I'm sure of it. This is the first time I'm talking to someone about the pregnancy.

"Um, well…it wasn't planned."

Why is that the first thing I fire at someone? At my scowl, she softens her features.

"Okay, so it was a surprise."

Surprise. A middle finger. A fuck you, Aria!

"Surprise means something happy. I…" I take a deep breath and meet her gaze. "I don't know if I can be happy about this. I mean, I didn't ask for this. I didn't want to have a child with Charlie, and now…he didn't give me much of a choice."

"Does it make you angry?"

I pause.

Does it?

"I don't know."

She gives me a knowing look. "I think you do."

I fiddle with my fingers and drop my gaze. Charlie was the one who dreamed about kids. One to be exact. But what did I think? I can't even remember…

"I don't think I'm angry. Angry isn't the right word. I'm more…sad."

"Why is that? Are you sad because this wasn't in your plan? Or that it happened with the wrong man?"

"I'm sad I didn't have a choice. Charlie made decisions for me. I don't even know why he kept me around for as long as he did. But…I look around me and I see everyone is happy. And if they aren't happy, they're content. And me? I'm…in limbo. I didn't want a child with Charlie. And when given the choice to either *take care of it* or put him up for adoption, I chose to keep it."

Dr. Nelson nods and writes in her notebook.

"Why couldn't you get an abortion, Aria?"

I shudder at the word.

"Because…I couldn't imagine taking another person's life. Even if they're too young to know what's going on. Whether I like it or not, this baby is a part of me." I let that sink in for a moment. This baby will be born in a few months. He'll live among my family and learn the family business. He'll learn how to rope. My father and brother will teach him how to be a good man.

I don't even know if it's a boy.

Aria Louise McKenzie will live inside of this baby, even if Charles Franklin Dodge III catches up with her.

"I can't…get rid of him. I can't give him away to somebody else and pretend like it didn't happen." I shrug. "I know that's messed up. That keeping this baby around as the reminder of my…*relationship*…with Charlie…it's messed up."

"Do you think you can love this child? Honestly. No judgements. Let's say you go into labor right now. The baby is brought into the universe, and you stare at it for the first time…what do you think your reaction would be?"

I picture it in my mind. I'm in the hospital. The baby is coming and I'm…alone. Doctors encourage me to push. And then…he's out. They clean him up and hand him over to me and…what?

What do I feel?

"I don't know," I admit sheepishly.

"And that's okay," she reminds me. "You're opting to keep this baby, and I *know* it wasn't an easy decision for you. It already shows me you have a deep love for this baby. That all of the bullshit Charlie put you through, through all of the pain and uncertainty, you're choosing to keep this baby with you."

I don't want him to turn out like Charlie. I want him to be good. I want him to treat a woman with love and respect. Or a man, if that's what he *is.*

"What if I'm a bad mom? What if I can't get past it?"

"And that right there is the reason why you won't be a bad mom, Aria. You're already self-aware. And if I were to put my money on the table, I'd bet you're already thinking about that baby's future and what you want for it."

She weakly smiles and gives my hand a reassuring squeeze.

"This is the part where I tell you to lean on the people around you. You were alone when you were with Charlie. But you're not alone *now.* He isn't pulling your strings anymore. He can't tell you what to do. You are your own person, and you have an army of people who would go to bat for you. Me, included." She grins.

"I'm going to be a mom," I whisper.

"Yeah," she giggles.

My stomach fills with butterflies as the prospect starts becoming real. Little kicks from my jellybean to remind me he's still here.

The pit in my stomach…the one from this morning when I realized I was dreaming of Derek.

"I, um…I've been having dreams."

She raises her eyebrows and retracts her hand, pen at the ready.

"Nightmares? Tell me about them."

"Um, no. Not nightmares." I sigh uncomfortably. "They're…sex dreams."

She blinks, as if she didn't hear me correctly.

"They're so vivid. It's like I'm there."

"Oh, well those are normal in pregnancy. Vivid dreams."

"I mean, I've looked on those pregnancy message boards online. Women all over have vivid sex dreams. Some straight women even have encounters with the same sex…" I don't know where I'm going with this. "Mine feel…different."

"Explain."

"They're with someone I know."

"Charlie?"

Definitely not.

"No. Not with him. These dreams are…pleasant."

She nods and sets the notepad down, like this would help me feel better. It doesn't. I feel naked and judged.

"Is it an ex-boyfriend you see yourself with? The mind likes to wander. And since you've gone through some major trauma, it isn't uncommon to think back to someone who wasn't necessarily right for you, but was good to you…"

Oh, god.

"Um, no." I sigh and drop my gaze to the floor. "They've centered around the family vet who lives two doors down from me." I squeeze my eyes shut and die a thousand deaths as my confession sinks in.

"Oh…are you seeing him?"

"No."

"Have you ever dated him?"

"No," I reply even more humiliated. "He um…he's been teaching me how to shoot."

"A gun?"

"Craps," I snap sarcastically. I bury my head in my hands and groan. "Yes, a gun. He's…kind of a dumbass, but he's…*hot.*"

I peek through my fingers to Dr. Nelson grinning.

"He is," she agrees cheekily.

"Oh, god."

"Don't worry about it," she giggles, "I can appreciate his beauty from a distance. I know his reputation and I can assure you I have not touched that."

"I want to die. This is so humiliating."

"Do you want a relationship with him?"

I laugh without humor. "Absolutely not. He's…no. I'm off the market for the rest of my life, and I don't want to be *somebody's* ever again. I barely made it out alive the first time."

"The rest of your life is a long time, Aria."

I finally meet her gaze and grimace.

"That's the point. I have the rest of my life to heal, right? I have the rest of my life to raise a kid and take over the family business. How can I ever trust someone to not beat the hell out of me again? How can I trust a man to love me *and* my kid when the kid is…*Charlie's?"*

"While I agree it takes time to build trust again, I don't agree with you becoming a spinster. We're humans. We're meant to share our lives with however many lovers you want."

I shudder. Nope. Nope. Nope.

"I'm not telling you to jump his bones, because that would be unprofessional. But, I urge you to follow your heart. Even if it's telling you one time is enough. Your hormones are raging, you're feeling better for the first time in months. You're not repulsed when you're dreaming of him. Are you repulsed of him in the daylight hours?"

Ugh.

"…No."

"Then what's holding you back from exploring something new with him?"

"Isn't that unethical? He works for my father. I just got out of a terrible relationship. Isn't there a certain number of months where this would be inappropriate?"

"This is the thing about human behavior. Everyone is different. There's no timeline you need to follow. The *only* thing that matters is how *you're* feeling. If it doesn't feel right? Don't do it. If you find yourself falling into bed with him and you feel, happy, or content…then follow your instincts."

"Obviously my instincts aren't great. That's how I got into this mess."

"Your instincts *are* great. You admitted to me that first time you were going to end your life. But it was your instincts that told you not to. It was your instincts that told you to trust Agent Olson. Your instincts are what got you out. And guess what? You're still alive to tell the tale."

I MAKE myself at home on Annie's front porch when I can't get to sleep. It's late. Like eleven o'clock late. Mosquitos swarm my legs until the citronella candle starts doing it's thing. I lie on the porch swing, gently pushing myself into a rocking motion as I stare ahead of me.

The lights in the house that is technically mine are off, which means Olson has given into his exhaustion for the night. The lights at Momma and Daddy's house are off, and Chris...well, he didn't come home tonight.

I can't help but glance over to Derek's house. The living room light remains on, and it's taking every ounce of willpower inside of me to not cross the path and invite myself into his house.

It's wrong. It's so, so *wrong.*

I haven't even talked to him since I was in the hospital. We've avoided each other like the plague. He saw me naked. He saw my scars. He saw the baby bump. But it doesn't stop my heart from squeezing in my chest.

Dr. Nelson is right. My hormones are raging. I haven't had someone touch me the way a woman deserves to be touched in years. I close my eyes, but every time I do, I see his sculpted chest, the hunger in his eyes. The heat of his touch, the flick of his tongue.

Shit.

I can't live like this.

I quietly pull myself up from the porch swing and step on the hot pavement, the heat warming my bare feet. His wooden steps are sanded and stained a dark wooden color. I pull open the storm door and gently knock on his front door before I change my mind.

My heart hammers in my chest, begging me to turn around and go back home and begging me to stay right here, all at the same time. My stomach aches in anticipation.

And to my horror, the door opens. He stands before me, shirtless. And regardless of what my mind's image of him shirtless, somehow it's even better. Tufts of dark hair trail down the center of his stomach. He wears basketball shorts, and his bare feet are in desperate need of some sun.

"You all right, Ace?"

My eyes meet his, and I swallow the anxiety by closing the gap between us, pressing my lips to his.

And oh, shit. It feels like...*heaven.*

"Aria, wait—"

27

ARIA

27 weeks pregnant...

My heart comes to a screeching stop. Maybe I read him wrong. Maybe he really was trying to get fresh with me because he's one of those guys who enjoys the chase. Holy shit, this was a *bad* idea. What was I thinking?

"I-I'm sorry. I'll just—"

"Wait, where are you going?" He grasps my wrist and spins me around so I'm facing him.

"I'm sorry. I didn't mean to jump you..."

"Are you sure about that, Ace?" He grins which only makes me want to die even more. "I'm not rejecting you. Believe me, I'm *not.* But before this goes any further, I need to know where the line is."

"The line?"

He motions for me to follow him inside, so I do. I follow him into the kitchen, and he offers me a bottle of water which I reluctantly take.

I feel like a love crazed teenager again. Going after a man who is so far out of my league, that wants things I'm not sure I'm equipped to offer him.

"Derek, seriously. I'm sorry. This was stupid of me. I'm too—

"What?" He asks softly. "You're too what, Aria?" His voice is velvety smooth. It washes over me like warm water. He respects my personal space by leaning against the counter and watching me like a hawk.

"Broken. Clueless. Naïve. Sullied—"

"—Intelligent. Beautiful. *Strong.*" He takes a confident step closer to me, lifting my chin to meet his eyes.

He smiles softly, and while my heart threatens to beat a hole out of my chest, he caresses my chin with his thumb.

"To me, Ace, that's what you are, and so much more. You're beautiful. More often than not, I want to run my fingers through this hair." I close my eyes when he raises his hand, not to hurt, but to do just that. My skin erupts in goosebumps from his gentle touch. "Keep your eyes on me," he instructs quietly.

My eyes fly open, watery and emotional.

"You're so much smarter than you give yourself credit for. You found a way to get out, Aria. The whole reason why I'm an asshole around you is because you make me feel inferior. You could probably do my job without going to school for it. And you've stayed away from me for so long, even though I *know* you check me out when you think I'm not looking."

A giggle escapes my lips, and he wipes my tears away.

"So no, baby, I'm not rejecting you. I want to know your limits so I don't scare you away."

That sentence alone should scare the shit out of me.

But here I stand, my face cradled in this behemoth's rough, but gentle hands, heat pooling down below because I *want* him.

"You're not him," I whisper quietly.

He shakes his head. "I'm not him. I promise."

"Don't choke me, please." I blink away more tears.

"I won't."

"Don't call me a bitch either."

"Jesus, Ace, I'm not cruel."

I know. But if I don't express it, then it leaves open endings for miscommunication.

He lifts me up by my waist and sets me down on the counter. His hands rub my thighs as he waits for me to continue.

"I might cry," I warn. Because a man in his right mind doesn't want to have sex with a woman who cries at contact.

"Out of fear?"

When I shake my head, he smiles.

"Okay. We'll move slow."

I swallow the lump in my throat and shakily place my hands on either side of his face. His stubble feels like sandpaper against my hands, and his eyelids are hooded. He's beautiful. Perhaps the most beautiful man I've ever laid eyes on.

"Speak up if something scares you, okay? Say the word and I'll stop."

I nod my acknowledgement as he closes the distance between us, his warm lips pressed against mine.

This is so much better than my dreams.

His kisses are gentle but demanding. His hands hold my hips to keep me steady, and slowly, my legs wrap around his torso, the warmth pressing against his bare stomach.

He reaches for the hem of my shirt and pulls it over my head, my breasts bounce free from the release of my shirt. His eyes widen and sweep over my body. I squeeze my eyes shut. He's staring at the bump.

This was a bad idea.

"Should I have left your shirt on?" he asks softly.

"I'm...insecure about..."

"Don't be," he replies. He kisses the valley between my breasts and my breath explodes from my lips and I tilt my head back. I lean on my forearms as he fumbles with the button of my shorts, gently pushing them down and tracing my slit and rubbing my clit.

Every nerve ending is hyperaware. My nipples harden as the friction builds between his thumb and my panties.

"You're so wet, Ace."

I can't bear to say anything. My wires are crossed. My brain is overstimulated. And this...*man* is saying all the right things. His fingers hook into my panties and pull them down and throws them carelessly on the ground with my shirt. He scoots me up the counter so I'm lying flush against the countertop and places my legs over his shoulders.

His tongue encircles my clit, and a moan I've never heard escapes me.

Holy. Shit.

Is this heaven?

Charlie refused to go down on me. He said it was unsanitary and gross. Derek is a real man. A man who knows exactly how to worship my body.

My fingers tangle in his wavy hair as he laps me up from top to bottom. My skin tingles, and my legs wrap tighter around his head. He reaches out and pinches my right nipple. Gently first, and then harder.

"Derek, I'm going to…"

I can't finish that sentence, because I've already taken off. My soul has left my body, the stomachache I've had for years is dissipating.

I've fallen dead weight.

He grins above me and pulls me into a sitting position.

"I'm sorry. I didn't mean to come in your mouth. I tried to warn you."

He pushes the hair out of my face and tucks it behind my ears.

"Don't ever be sorry for that. You taste amazing. And I got to taste your orgasm. It was *delicious.*"

I giggle nervously as he pulls me off the counter.

"Do you want to go further?" he asks cautiously.

I nod eagerly.

I want Derek Hawthorn to fill me up. I want to feel his skin against mine while I give him his. He kisses my lips, my own taste on my tongue feels erotic and earthy.

"Come on." He laces his fingers with mine and leads me to the master bedroom. He leaves the lights off. I get it. Honestly. I'm pregnant with another man's baby.

He rips his shorts down, his thick, and long erection springs free. I involuntarily gasp. I can't believe this is happening.

The slickness between my thighs begs for penetration, for him to claim me as his. He sits down at the edge of the bed and pulls me onto his lap. The tip of his cock teasing me, begging for entrance.

He slams his lips onto mine, fisting my hair and holding my right leg in place.

"You're so beautiful, Aria."

He says these things, and I can't help but close my eyes. What if he's just saying that? What if he's doing this because I'm a challenge he wants to conquer?

"Get out of your head, Ace. You're so tense. This is supposed to be relaxing."

I nervously giggle, but that turns into me crying out because he's taken my breast in his mouth, suckling, soothing, and nipping at my nipple.

Sweet Jesus.

His hands cup my ass and gently lifts me up, lining me up with his cock. He lowers me slowly, and when I feel him, I hiss. He lies back, allowing me to take control of the situation.

I'm in full control. I determine the pace and when to stop. And it's…*empowering.* I lean forward slightly, lifting myself up and dropping down until I get used to his girth.

Every movement has me begging him for more.

Not once has he told me I'm pathetic, or I'm not doing it right. He reaches out again, rubbing my clit with his thumb.

I nearly crumble on top of him. With his free hand, he holds my hip steady, while he matches every stroke.

He tells me I'm beautiful. He tells me I'm strong. He tells me there's no place he'd rather be right now.

I collapse on top of him and let him take over. He thrusts into me and holds me close to his chest.

"Derek," I plead.

"Say my name, Aria."

"Derek," I whimper.

With one final thrust, he finishes inside of me.

I refuse to look at him, too embarrassed to show my face after the stunt I just pulled. I immediately dismount, and try to move to the bathroom, but his arms wrap around my waist, forcing me to stay put.

"Don't go anywhere. Just lay here a minute."

I give up trying to fight him. I face the wall as he scoots closer to me, gently pulling me against his chest. His legs hike up against my bare ass, my wetness drenching his leg.

"Are you all right?" he asks.

Tears prick my eyes. My voice will give me away, so I nod instead.

"Talk to me, Ace. Are you all right?"

"Yeah," I manage to choke out.

He runs his fingertips the length of my arm and trails them back up. I shudder, but a sense of warmth washes over me. He's taking care of me, just like he promised he would.

Fuck.

"You're an amazing woman, Aria McKenzie."

A watery giggle echoes in the room as he kisses the crown of my head.

"Coconuts," he says softly.

"What?"

"I always wondered what your hair smelled like. I'm finally placing it. Your hair smells like coconuts."

"You're a weird man, Derek Alexander Hawthorn."

He chuckles into my hair and nuzzles into my neck.

"Maybe you're the one who's weird. Everyone I've ever met thinks I'm awesome."

I giggle and roll my eyes. "Yes, I'm sure all the women you meet worship the ground you walk on."

He groans. "I think I've got you figured out, Ace. But I'm going to keep it to myself because I don't want to scare you away."

My stomach churns at the thought of this being more than it is. I love his daughter, but I am not about to put her in danger because I like the way Derek's dick feels inside of me.

"Derek…" I turn around and face him. There's no light in this room. My eyes are adjusting to the dark, I still can't make out his silhouette. Maybe that makes things easier.

"What's on your mind, Aria?"

"I've been having dreams…about…*this.*"

His hand tightens on my hip.

"Seriously?"

"I'm in my second trimester now and—"

"Ah."

Shit.

"I'm sorry. I'd stop them if I could. But I haven't been touched by someone nice in a long time."

His hand finds my face and caresses my cheek.

"I'm not sorry," he murmurs.

"But what I said still stands. This can't be anything."

"No, it can't," he replies, though there's no malice in his tone. "Listen, my whole world revolves around Zoey. And this was…*amazing*…and I want to do this at least a dozen more times before the sun rises, but I can't jump into something with somebody *and* fight through the custody battle."

"I get it," I reply softly running my fingers through his hair. "A relationship is complicated. And I don't think either of us do complicated."

He chuckles.

"But…if you wanted to continue this…no strings attached…"

"That's a complication," I retort.

He holds my ass in his hand gently squeezing and tapping it lightly.

"You are the most beautiful woman I've ever laid eyes on. And that's saying a lot, because when I was in Afghanistan, Ava Reid visited."

I scoff.

"What, you don't believe me? I have pictures."

"That's not what I'm dismissing."

He sighs, his warm breath moving closer. His lips find my forehead and his hand splays out on my lower back.

"Mark my words, if Charlie ever got brave and decided to show his face here, I want you to know I'd be the first person to tear him apart."

I weakly smile.

"You would make some woman insanely happy one day, Derek. Not every woman is like your ex-wife."

He stills at my words.

"And not every woman is like you."

My heart soars at this, but I wish it wouldn't. I'm too smart to get my hopes up. This can't happen.

His constant soothing of my skin puts me half asleep before he speaks again.

"I don't know if I believe in reincarnation, but on the off chance it's real, I hope in my next life, we find each other again. I'd treat you right."

Tears cloud my vision.

Because had I *stayed put,* I could've avoided Charlie altogether. I could've made a play for Derek Hawthorn and proved to him I could love his daughter too. Hell, I already do, damn it.

28

DEREK

"This looks cozy," a voice sounds off from the doorway. When my eyes fly open, I reach for the gun in my nightstand and point it to the intruder in the doorway. "You won't do that, Bubba. Now get up and come into the dining room. We need to talk."

Fuck.

She sleeps like a rock, tangled up in my sheets and her hair covering her face. I grab my sweats and reluctantly sneak out to the dining room to find Nate, severely pissed off with a gun in his hand.

Maybe I shouldn't have left mine.

"You have sixty seconds to tell me what the fuck is going on."

I raise my eyebrows.

"She came over last night and spent the night."

He cocks the gun.

"What the fuck, Nate!?"

"She is not your plaything. She is a woman who is supposed to be healing. You're not supposed to be confusing her because you can't keep it in your pants for five seconds!"

Oh, god.

"Put the gun down, Olson. We can talk like adults."

"Hey assholes!" A voice echoes around the room in speakers I didn't even know existed. "Olson, put the fucking gun down, you idiot. Bubba's your brother. Bubba, that was a dick move."

"Stop calling me that!" I bellow to Tanner's voice. I'm going to kill him for putting cameras in here without my knowledge.

"How many houses have you bugged?" Nate asks.

"I'll tell you when you put the gun down. Otherwise, I'm going to alert Steve, and judging by the beauty in your room, it'll end badly. For both of you."

He keeps digging his hole.

Nate growls and places the gun on the dining room table. And to my horror, Aria appears at the doorway, wearing one of my shirts and a pair of sweatpants three sizes too big for her.

"What the hell?" she murmurs.

"Aria, are you all right?" Nate rushes to her and leads her over to the table, sitting her down.

"I'm fine. What are you doing? And how many other people are here?"

"It's just Nate. Tanner's been watching."

I want to take the words back the second I say them. She grows rigid, and she glares at me.

"What do you mean by *watching?*"

"I didn't watch *that,*" Tanner reasons.

Holy shit. He isn't making this any better.

"Saying you didn't watch *that* means there's something to watch," she snaps.

Tanner stays quiet for a moment.

"Um…I don't know what you want me to say…"

"Tanner, will you fuck off already?" I shout.

"Hey, motherfucker! I just saved your life!" Tanner replies.

"I wasn't going to shoot him!" Nate bellows.

Fuck.

Fuck.

Fuck.

Leave it to these assholes to ruin *everything* for me.

"You were going to shoot him?" she demands from Olson. He looks away sheepishly.

"In a place where there wouldn't be too much damage."

"Oh my god," she grumbles in frustration.

"Hey, Saw? Can you get off now? I need to talk to my children."

Tanner snickers, then suddenly goes quiet. She turns to Nate and glares.

"What's your deal?" She asks.

"Maybe we can do this where he's not around…"

For the love of God.

"I came here on my own fruition." Nate narrows his eyes, like he doesn't believe her. "You see, when women get into their second trimesters, our hormones get wacky. I had to take the edge off."

He pushes away, obviously uncomfortable.

I, on the other hand, turn to her to search for any signs of regret.

"I'm okay. And I'm going back to Annie's." Nate stands in front of the door.

"Why, was he too rough with you?"

She sighs.

"I'm not giving you a play-by-play, Olson. He was fine."

Ouch.

"And you're ruining my buzz by being here."

He frowns.

"Are you sure you're all right? Because I can shoot him and blame it on the job."

Asshole.

"I'm fine. Honestly." She takes a deep breath and glances briefly at me before turning back to Nate. "Now, it would be super if you could go back and do your job so I can do the walk of shame without my entire family witnessing it."

Defeated, Nate glares at me once more before stepping out. I approach her quietly, wrapping my arms around her. Her cheek rests on my right pec, and a content sigh escapes her.

"We go back to the way we were, right?" she asks with a hint of a frown.

"Yeah. No complications for either of us." She nods and leans against the door. "I'll miss you when you walk outside the door, Ace."

She giggles and rolls her eyes.

"I'm not going anywhere. I still live here. And now that I'm not wearing what I used to, I'll be at the barn more often."

It's not enough.

I kiss her gently on the lips. Her arms snake around my neck, pulling me closer to her. Her intoxicating coconut scent fills my senses, making a permanent imprint on my soul.

"It won't be the same."

She sighs and drops her arms.

"No. The chase is over," she admits sadly.

Doesn't she know I don't give a damn about the chase? There's something inside of her…what it is, I don't know. But the one thing I *do* know is we are supposed to be together.

"Don't be a stranger, okay? Just because we did the nasty doesn't mean we can't be friends."

She nods and waves. It's early enough so the whole property isn't awake yet, so I watch her walk to Annie's.

She's beautiful in my clothes. She's beautiful stark naked too.

Aria looks over her shoulder when she opens Annie's door and waves. I wave back and watch her disappear into the dark house.

It's three o'clock in the morning when I crawl back into bed. There's no point of going back to sleep, though I don't think I'd be able to sleep even if I was tired. I pull the pillow she used and hug it tight against me. It smells like coconuts. I'm so grateful for that.

I couldn't sleep a wink when she fell asleep. When my eyes adjusted to the dark, I studied the scars on her back. Some of them are deep. Some of them are still slightly raised, but healing. The fresher scars were healing, to the point if I were to see them in the light, they'd be a light pink color.

Aria McKenzie isn't the first woman to appear at my doorstep unannounced, only to crawl into bed with me moments later. But…she is the most memorable. She doesn't play games. She doesn't like the lines. To hold her in my arms is a gift I don't deserve. But *fuck me* if I don't find myself pining after her.

29

ARIA

27 weeks pregnant...

My eyes crack open when the sunlight streams through the living room. When I got in late last night, I didn't want to have to explain to Annie why I wasn't in bed with her, so I crashed on her ugly green sofa.

I've missed morning feed by hours. And when my vision focuses on the numbers on the cable box, I realize it's ten-thirty.

I'm still traumatized by the first trimester, where I was hugging the toilet for most of the morning. But since then, I've learned to sit up slower, to eat something the second my eyes open.

Even if it's month old chocolate that sits in a crystal bowl in the middle of Annie's coffee table.

"Good morning, Peanut," Annie announces as she grabs an apple from her fruit bowl and drops into the seat at her dining table where her laptop sits open at the ready.

"Good morning," I reply groggily.

"So. What's new?"

I slept with Derek.

"Nothing. Couldn't sleep last night. The couch was more comfortable."

"Mmmmhm," she hums as she types, drowning me out.

"Are you hungry? I can make some pancakes," I reply, desperate to change the subject.

"Pancakes sound good. Are you sure you don't mind? You *did* waltz in at three in the morning. You must be exhausted."

Whomp there it is.

There is no point in keeping secrets in this family.

Her mischievous grin is contagious, and I can't help but smile.

"Okay, so I spent some time on your porch swing last night. I got stuck in the YouTube vortex."

Annie rolls her eyes. Good thing she'll let me pretend like she doesn't know exactly what I did last night.

"Nice clothes," she teases.

Of course, when I look down, I'm wearing Derek's shirt and sweat-pants. I close my eyes in frustration. I was floating on cloud nine when I walked in last night I didn't bother changing.

"Thanks."

I shuffle into the kitchen and search for the pancake mix. When I turn around, she's standing inches away from my face.

"Peanut."

"We're *not* talking about this," I grumble, side stepping her and making my way to the island to mix the ingredients.

"Are you okay?"

I stop for a moment.

I feel fine. For the first time since I came home, I don't feel the doom and gloom that follows me like a dark cloud over my head. I feel…normal.

"I'm okay," I reassure her. When I meet her gaze, she stares at me like she doesn't believe me. "Really, I am. He was nice."

"I'm sure he was. Don't get too attached, Peanut. I'm not trying to rain on your parade, but Derek isn't the type to settle down."

My blood starts simmering with anger. This is like high school all over again. Annie tells me what to do as if I'm a clueless idiot.

"I don't want to be with him."

She furrows her brow and frowns.

"It was just sex. It was a one time thing, and I can confidently say it's not happening ever again. He was there to take the edge off, and that's it." I turn on the stove and turn away from her, glowering at the backsplash while she tries to figure out her next words.

"I'm sorry if I'm overstepping, but—"

"Annabelle," I growl.

The silence is welcome. It gives me a minute to calm my nerves. If this gets back to Daddy or Chris, we're both dead. If it gets back to Momma before Daddy or Chris, she'll be planning a wedding.

"Aria, I'm looking out for you. You just got out of a shitty relationship. You're pregnant with another man's baby—"

"Is there a reason why you keep throwing that aspect in my face?" She takes a timid step back. "Don't you think those thoughts are constantly swarming in my head? I fucked up, okay? Is that what you want to hear?"

"Come on, you know that's not what I meant."

"I am a human being." When those words topple out of my mouth, the weight of them crashes down on me. I lean against the counter and bow my head.

I'm a human being. I have feelings that I feel deeply. I have a heart that has been lonely for too long. And I have a brain that has been manipulated for everyone else's benefit.

"At some point, I need to move on. And I can't do that when you keep talking about Charlie. I'm here for a fresh start. And yeah, maybe I won't ever date again, but I refuse to be shamed for taking the edge off when my hormones are everywhere."

I turn away from her and flip the pancake. Annie storms out of the room, and that's when I know the shit is about to hit the fan.

When the pancakes are done, I take one on the go and quickly change into new clothes before heading down to the barn.

I've opened lessons up for jumping and I have three lessons lined up for the day. Everything is going to start picking up once school is out for the summer, but for now, this is fine.

My phone vibrates in my pocket and out of habit I pick it up.

"Buttercup."

It's like a bucket of ice water is dumped over me. His slimy voice still has that effect. And now I'm kicking myself for not looking at the caller ID.

"Don't hang up. You're going to want to hear what I have to say."

I swallow, unable to form any sentences anyway. I turn to face my house, in case Nate is watching.

"Acknowledge me."

"You aren't supposed to be contacting me, Charlie. This is going straight to the FBI."

"I'm counting on it."

Shit.

"You were hospitalized." When I don't answer, he continues. "Are you all right?"

I wish I had some sort of comeback lined up. But for whatever reason, when it comes to Charlie, I'm powerless. I still turn into that terrified woman from a few months ago.

"Answer me."

Instead, I hang up. He'll only have to do a little more coaxing before I tell him everything. I turn on the do not disturb feature and shove it into my back pocket. I'll deal with it later. And maybe now it's time to take this information to Nate.

When I arrive at barn number two, the place is empty except for its inhabitants. I start turning horses out to the pastures so I can start mucking the stalls. When the barn is empty, I plug my phone into the dock and blast Led Zeppelin to drown out anyone who approaches me.

I need to lose myself, and I can only do that through music since I can't ride. I start on George's stall since it's the farthest away from the entrance.

Two hours later, footsteps walk along the breezeway. I step outside to see who's here and am pleasantly surprised to see Jo. Her face lights up when she spots me and jogs over to me.

"Hey, darlin'. How are you today?"

"I'm fine. What's going on?"

"I was hoping you weren't busy. Do you think you can spare an hour or two and come into town with me?"

I have so many stalls to do, but I think I can spend extra time after lessons to get the rest of it done.

"Sure. I can't take too long. Annie and I got into a fight, so I doubt she's going to show her face down here which means we'll be short staffed."

"No problem. I won't take too much of your time, then. Let's get going."

Jo pulls into the old paper mill off of Western Road and throws her truck in park. Dozens of construction trucks surround the place. They're adding on to the existing building, making it twice as big.

As dumb teenagers, we used to sneak in here at night and mess around. Annie used it as her make out spot since Chris caught on to her shenanigans about using his window to sneak boys in.

But now…this is something else. The bricks are being restored and the front steps are being power washed. She motions for me to follow her to the side entrance.

The place is gutted. The cement floors are clean now, and it looks like they're finally putting up drywall, leaving one side of the building with exposed brick.

"I wanted your opinion on a few things."

"Jo, this is your baby. My opinion doesn't matter."

She waves me off dismissively.

"We're putting in magnetized doors with bullet proof window paneling in the front. Our waiting room won't be huge, because my plan is to not having the women and children waiting for long. Five minutes tops. This is going to be their fresh start, so I want to paint the walls something cheery, but not too obnoxious. Do you understand where I'm going with this?"

Sort of.

"I think so. You want to make it comforting, but not overwhelming."

She nods, chewing nervously on her bottom lip as she silently visualizes it.

I visualize it along with her. I can see a reception area, possibly with a small refrigerator for water bottles and juice boxes for the kids. A bookshelf filled with a variety of books.

"Right," she whispers, almost too quietly.

"You don't want them waiting too long, right? So maybe it would be smart to have a few unassigned empty offices behind the security door so you can get all of their intake information. You could stock them with small refrigerators, a snack cabinet, a white noise machine until they can get their bearings..."

Jo grins.

"Oh, I like that a lot. That's a great idea. Perhaps we can give them ten minutes to breathe before we start intake information. Then they can at least satisfy their hunger, until lunch or dinner, and they can talk to us without their bellies growling."

I nod slowly and we walk deeper into the mill. The addition isn't completed yet, but she tells me it will be a cafeteria, a computer lab, and a library on the bottom floor. The top floors will be residences.

"What do you think about setting up a volunteer program?"

I hesitate, finding the correct words to express my concern.

"They're risky. If it were up to me, I'd make them sign non-disclosure agreements, and everyone would need to be thoroughly vetted." I shrug timidly as I continue. "I know if I had the opportunity to go to a women's shelter, I wouldn't trust anyone at first. I think that's a hurdle we can get out of the way this early in the game. We vet each volunteer, full background checks, NDA's, and training."

Jo smiles mischievously.

"You said we. Multiple times."

I groan.

"Well, it was a thought. You said you wanted my opinion..."

"I want more than that, baby."

My eyes snap to hers.

"Look around you, sweet pea. This is the place that should've been around for you and me. Nobody knows what women like us need. The only ones who do have been through it. I want you to be my partner in this. Help me make this place so the women and children out in the world have a place to start over."

"Jo, I'm not qualified for this. I've been out of work for a year and half. I don't know how to run a women's shelter..."

"And you think *I* do? I'm going off the seat of my pants, baby. I know you're a hard worker. When you get passionate about something, you churn out the best ideas. You get behind it one hundred percent and let me tell you, *everyone* can feel that. Look at the riding school. That was your idea and it's still profitable today."

I stare at her in disbelief.

"I majored in English."

"I have a high school diploma," she retorts and shrugs. "I'm not going to ask you to make a decision right now, but I hope you'll think about it. This is going to be an amazing place. I just know it. You'll get paid—we have grants from The Live Oaks Foundation, so salary isn't an issue."

My head spins as she tells me all of this. I *need* a job. I have to support this baby somehow. And what happens if Jo gets tired of me? What if I don't remember what it's like to work in an office again? I don't even have supervisory experience!

"I don't have experience, Jo. I think I'd end up disappointing you."

She nudges me playfully in the ribs and smirks.

"That's why you have me. I don't know what I'm doing either. But I think we're living, breathing proof there is life after abuse. We'll learn together."

Hope builds in my belly.

"Okay. I'm in."

Jo squeals in delight and throws her arms around me.

"I'm so happy to hear that. You start Monday. You can come over and we'll start building our standard operating procedures. This is going to be *great!*"

When I get back to the barn, all of my stalls are done. Derek and Nate step out of Theo's stall in deep conversation until they notice me standing in the middle of the barn. I smile, showing them I hold no hostility especially after the bullshit they pulled this morning.

"Boys," I greet, closing the distance between us and crashing their party.

"Aria, we need to talk."

My insides shut down one by one. I already think I know. But I'd like to live in ignorance just a moment more.

"Okay..."

"Maybe you should sit down, Ace," Derek cautions.

"Spit it out."

Nate frowns, sharing a concerned glance with Derek, and then turning back to me. "Charlie has escaped house arrest."

I raise my eyebrows, waiting for the "psych!" But it doesn't comes.

"What do you mean he escaped? He's wearing an ankle bracelet. Shouldn't you know exactly where he is?"

Nate shifts his weight to the other foot before speaking again. "The ankle bracelet was tampered with. The signal was offline when the bracelet was removed. He hasn't been seen since the blackout. He didn't take any of his vehicles and the FBI has extensively searched his father's house for him."

Derek was right. I should be sitting.

"He wouldn't have gone to his father's house," I say quietly.

No. He would've come straight here, if he isn't here already. I'd bet this entire farm he took the money from his safe and is living off that while he pays in cash under different aliases.

"We're bringing in other people," Nate assures me, but in reality, it does the opposite.

"The other guys from our unit. Joey, Tanner, and Logan. Delgado already works for the FBI, so he won't be coming, but you can trust those three," Derek says softly.

More babysitters.

More people watching my every move.

"I promise you, Ace, he isn't coming onto the property without one of us knowing about it. This is going to end soon."

"You were right," Nate says, lowering his gaze to mine. "He knows about the baby."

And so, this is how it ends. I get a dream job, and my ex-boyfriend is above the law, already on his way to end my life.

30

DEREK

It takes forty-eight hours for the rest of my brothers to get here. They're aware of the situation, and they know to pretend they don't know Steve. Aria has tuned everyone out, except for Zoey. Zoey seems to be the *only* person Aria can be herself with. And when I turn the corner and find them mucking Coley's stall together, I stop at the door and grin.

"She's putting you to work, eh, Zo?"

Zoey grins.

"I asked if I could help and she said yes."

Aria's gaze remains on the shavings around her, continuing her task as if I'm not here.

"That was nice of you. But I have something to tell you."

Zoey stops what she's doing and leans against the wall.

"Are we going to the bookstore?"

She makes me laugh, and it brings a genuine grin to Aria's face.

"Uncle Joey and Uncle Tanner are here. They're waiting for you at home."

Zoey's face lights up and quickly turns to Aria.

"Is it okay if I say hi? I'll come right back. I promise."

"No worries. I appreciate the help. You don't need my permission. Only come back if you want to, okay? I'm almost done and then I have to get ready for a lesson."

Zoey doesn't have to be told twice. She books it out of the stall and runs towards the house. I enter the stall and pick up Zoey's pitchfork and help Aria with the rest of the stall.

"You don't have to that, you know. I've been mucking stalls since I was old enough to walk."

"I know. But I want to."

She heaves an exasperated sigh. That's right. I'm not going to disappear. We work in silence for a few minutes before she stops and turns to stare at me.

"Derek, what are you doing? Don't you have a real job?"

"I do, but I have company. And they're all being assholes and eating all my food."

She snorts and rolls her eyes.

"That's a rookie mistake, inviting them over. Of course they're going to eat all your food. You should be more like me and be a recluse so you have all the food to yourself."

"Where's the fun in that?"

She rolls her eyes and ignores me.

"In all seriousness, Ace, how are you doing with all of this? I know it's overwhelming—"

"That's putting it mildly," she spits poisonously. "Everyone around me tells me it's okay to trust people I don't know. My sister knows what we did and is treating me like I'm clueless." She sighs. "I'm exhausted. And I knew this day was coming where he would come after me. None of this surprises me, by the way."

"Do you trust me?"

She turns and frowns.

"Derek..."

"It's okay if you don't. But I want to tell you, you can."

She grips the pole of her pitchfork tight and stares at me in disbelief.

"So Annie knows?"

"Yeah. She gave me a ton of shit for it too. We're currently not on speaking terms."

I chuckle and continue my task, giving her enough room to feel comfortable.

"I had fun."

She sighs.

"I did too," she murmurs.

I turn to face her and grin at the longing in her eyes.

"You still feeling put out?"

She rolls her eyes and smiles.

"A little."

I lean my pitchfork against the wall and approach her, cradling her head in my hands. Her eyes show no fear or indifference. In fact, they show me she wants me too.

She stands on her tippy toes and presses her lips to mine, her tongue tapping my bottom lip for entrance.

My tongue dances with hers, her breath tasting like caramel coffee and pancakes. I swallow her sighs and slowly press her against the wall.

"You can't start just to stop," she pleads.

"This is too public. Your dad could walk in any minute and he'll shoot me without blinking."

She giggles and rolls her eyes.

"I thought you were adventurous, Dr. Hawthorn."

"I'm adventurous, McKenzie." I shove my knee in between her legs, her core like molten lava. I kiss her again, threading my fingers through her hair and gently pulling her head up so I have access to her porcelain throat.

I press my lips to her pulse, and she whimpers with desire.

"Please, Derek. You've already opened the flood gates and if you stop I might cry. I'm not above begging."

My erection presses painfully against my zipper at her desired pleas. I pop the button on her shorts and gently push them down.

"This has to be quick," I tell her, though her eyes are closed and a smile spreads across her full, pink lips.

"Do it. I can be quiet."

God, I hope not. Her moans are the heaven my dreams are built on. Her juices coat my index finger. I lick my finger, so I can have a quick taste of her. I want more, but we don't have the time. Her pupils dilate at the act and her pulse nearly beats out of her neck. I pull her panties down and turn her around.

She grips the bars of the stall and arches her back. Her full and curvy ass beckons me to plunge deep inside of her. I pull down my jeans far enough if someone comes down here, I can pretend I was taking a piss.

I tease her with the tip of my cock, coating me in her slickness.

"Derek, I'll murder you if you don't—*oooh....*"

Good God. She's so fucking tight. She grips me like a vice, and it takes me a moment for my vision to stop swirling.

"I love how wet you are for me," I grumble in her ear.

She shudders and her eyes flutter closed.

"Pick up the pace, Derek. I need it hard."

I oblige with conditions. I slow down but plunge into her hard.

She gasps at the sudden pain. She reaches in between her legs and rubs her clit. I bat her hand away and massage her bundle of nerves.

She covers her mouth and moans, which makes my skin erupt in goosebumps. My hips piston faster, searching for the friction we both need. She moans my name and grips the bars tighter.

"You're beautiful," I tell her softly.

She comes undone before I do, her whole body shakes as I finish inside of her. I take a moment and gently kiss her back. Her spine locks straight, which gets her to pull up her panties and shorts too fast.

"God damn it," she whispers.

"What?"

"It was only supposed to be a one time thing, Derek. I can't undress every time you flirt with me."

I grin and peck her on the lips. I can't get enough of her. I need to do this a few more times to get her out of my system and then I can return to what I was doing before she came around.

"I'm sorry."

She scoffs. "No you're not. Seriously. This was the last time."

I think she even knows it isn't possible. She closes her eyes and sighs.

"Okay. This was the last time," I repeat softly.

She frowns. "Somebody always catches feelings in these no-strings-attached arrangements, Derek and I can't get attached to you."

Her words are a dagger to my heart. I shouldn't want more, but I can't help but imagine putting her into the places in my life where Emily should've been. I see her hanging out with my daughter, reading books together and doing barn chores. I see her in my kitchen cooking dinner with me and sleeping in the same bed as me.

The thing is, a guy like me can't be with a girl like her. Not only would her father murder me, but she'll have a baby soon. And that baby isn't a part of me *or* Zoey. I refuse to put Zoey on the back burner.

And if for some god forsaken reason I don't win full custody, I don't want Zoey thinking I replaced her. I won't do it. The raven haired succubus is the essence of every thought, every dream. Shit. I'm in so much trouble.

AT MIDNIGHT, when the whole street goes dark, the boys and Steve congregate at Aria's house. We take over the dining room table with Nate's paperwork splayed out for everyone to see. Delgado's on speaker phone, calling in from a burner phone so he can't be tracked.

Steve walks circles around the table while Tanner sets up his three laptops. Logan brings coffee to the table that sits untouched.

"What do we know?" Steve finally breaks the silence.

"There are suspicions the blackout was staged. The elevators were not in service, so the agents downstairs couldn't get upstairs in time. The agents stationed at the front door were knocked out cold," Delgado reports from his end. He isn't even on the case, but from where he is, he's getting a lot of the gossip.

"Affirmative. Agents Willow and Triste. They're fairly new. This was their first shift on the Dodge case so I don't believe they have been corrupted as of yet. What I find interesting is the seasoned agents weren't posted outside the front door. That leads me to believe they were in on it."

"Are those two being investigated?" Logan asks.

"Yes. I got word from my supervisor they are being interrogated as we speak."

"Do we have any idea where he'd potentially go?" Steve demands.

"Aria told me he wouldn't try his father's house. His first stop would be here," I reply, glancing to Tanner to see if he can start a search in the area.

"He'll be using an alias. Any ideas?" Steve asks.

"Rockwell gave up two," Tanner replies, starting up his computers and finally taking a seat.

"So far, I haven't been alerted those aliases have been used anywhere. But I would imagine he'll be using a new one. I'll have a ton of CCTV footage to sift through. I'll see if there was any recording with traffic cameras when he left Chicago, but don't get hopeful. Since the whole city was on a blackout, I doubt we'll find his exit."

"Is his father still in Chicago?"

"He is in interrogation with Agent Wilkes. Charlotte Dodge is at the bureau, currently in the waiting area. Phones have been confiscated and one of the FBI Technical Analysts is currently looking through call and text logs."

They wouldn't have used their phones. They're smart, but not smarter than us.

"Let me know if they find anything," Steve barks.

Tanner mock salutes, even though Steve was talking to Nate. Tanner has his hands in everything. How he hasn't been caught by the CIA yet is beyond me, but I trust him to have our backs.

"What about footage from the bugs we put in his apartment?"

"We know he has a burner. Image quality isn't great since he keeps the curtains closed all day every day and uses the TV as his only light source. I assume he knows about the bugs. I can't pull a make or model from the phone. Nate, do you know if your goons collected another phone in evidence?"

Nate shakes his head. "He wouldn't have left it for anybody to find. He would've brought it with him." Nate's computer emits an alert. "A warrant has just been signed for search of Senior's house. They might uncover something there, but I make no promises."

"She said he'd come here, right?" Logan asks. When nobody answers, he turns to Tanner, deep in thought. "How many vacant properties are in town *and* within a five mile radius of the city's limits? Steve, how many people do you know would take cash only?"

My mind flits to the Parkers. They're shady as fuck, and they have tons of properties they rent out to the public with not so much as a credit check.

"Check out the Parkers. They have at least thirty rental properties around town, and I don't think they would mind the cash," I reply.

Tanner uses his sneaky tech ninja skills to access the IRS, pulling all of their property information.

"I'm printing out a list. Since the two of you live here, go through every single one of them and highlight the ones you *know* are occupied. We'll work our way in and start a search on the ones outside of town."

"Hold on," Delgado says.

We're all quiet when we hear voices on his end. I can't make any of them out, but we all wait with bated breath.

"They're sending Senior home," Delgado warns.

"What the fuck? Why?" Nate demands.

"He couldn't confirm anything. He wasn't around the penthouse all day. Phone records have been pulled and according to them, he hasn't tried to make contact with junior."

My stomach sinks when I realize Aria's greatest fear is coming to light. Zoey sleeps in the house next door to this one, with trouble a hair away. I don't like this. I don't like danger close to my daughter. But I *especially* don't like danger coming to Aria.

31

ARIA

28 weeks pregnant...

Jo and I spend the morning writing our standard operating procedures when Nate, Derek, and three other dudes interrupt our process. Derek, usually upbeat, sarcastic, and with a glint of mischief in his eyes, is now serious and angry. Nate is uncharacteristically stoic and stiff.

Jo takes her cue and leaves, leaving me with a group of men that should terrify me. Maybe if they appeared two months ago, I'd be shaking in my boots. Now, they're a nuisance. My new wardens.

"Hey, Aria. Do you have a minute?"

I nod, slinking back into my shell where I'm safe.

"These are the rest of our brothers. This is Joey," he points to the tall one, the one who looks exactly like Archie from the comics, with his short, buzzed, blond hair, and bright blue eyes. His muscles have muscles. I'd suggest a looser fitting shirt since he's about to rip out of this one, but he's watching over me. So I'll keep my mouth shut.

"Logan," he points to the other guy…the shorter one, but not by much.

His chestnut brown hair is shaggy and disheveled. It hangs in his eyes and compliments the just as shaggy beard that looks like he hasn't shaved in years. His chocolate eyes, however, tell his whole story.

He's experienced loss. Don't ask me how I know that, but I can tell. He doesn't smile, but he doesn't appear to be angry being here either. Exhaustion has set into his hard features in the form of heavy bags under his eyes and the slouch of his posture. He doesn't care. But he cares about Derek and Nate.

"And this is Tanner."

The famous Tanner. The one who watched Derek and I bump uglies. He's...different than the others. Where the others are bulky and muscular, Tanner is lean and toned. He wears an amused smile, like he can't ever take anything seriously. I don't know why, but I feel like the two of us could be the best of friends. As long as he doesn't bring up the other night.

"Delgado works for the bureau too, so it would raise eyebrows if he came down here. Anyway, I thought it might be best if you got to know everyone because they'll be on watch until Charlie is caught."

My eyes scan the men hesitantly and they rest on Derek. He offers me a reassuring smile before returning to his stoic nature.

"Okay, so what does this mean for me?"

Nate sighs and straightens. "It means you can't leave anyone's sight. It means even going to the barns, your doctor appointments, the store...you need to have someone with you."

More babysitters. I don't think I'll even be allowed to use the bathroom by myself.

"It's not a death sentence, Ace, we're just taking extra precautions." Derek's smooth voice rumbles.

"You might think that," I reply, standing up, shoving the chair back under the table. "I've moved from one warden to the other. I'm used to this."

"Aria, it's not like that," Nate reasons.

"Maybe not. But you're asking me to trust three other men I *don't know.*" I glance to the others and grimace. "No offense. You could be the pope and I'd still keep you at a distance."

"She's fun," Tanner quips to Derek. Derek glowers at him and Tanner shrinks back.

"Anyway, I've started a new job. The building isn't complete yet, but Jo will be a regular here. So, probably don't harass her much." I sidestep the boys and head into the kitchen and yank open the fridge and hide behind the door for a moment's peace.

"Ace..."

I close my eyes in frustration.

"What."

"You're moody."

I white knuckle the refrigerator door handle tight as I restore my full height and narrow my eyes.

"And you're nosy."

He places his hand over mine, blocking my view from the others.

"This won't be forever."

"It will certainly feel like it," I retort.

"Do you remember what you said a few weeks ago? That it was inevitable for fuckface to find you?"

I nod reluctantly. I still feel it in my bones. I thought I could hold off until the baby was born, but it was dumb of me to think otherwise. If Charlie is anything, he's predictable.

"Maybe he will. But maybe when he finds you, he finds us instead."

"It doesn't change the fact I didn't want anyone to get involved," I snap, slamming the fridge closed. "How many of you have kids? Wives?"

The boys stand stock still. Joey narrows his eyes at me, like I asked how much he weighed. Logan's stony face literally does nothing, and Tanner just snickers.

But fuck me running, none of them pipe up.

"We're here because we want to be here," Derek says gently behind me.

"So it's just you, then? You have Zoey."

He nods, which sends my stomach into a knotted mess.

"Then get out while you can, Derek. Because if anything happens to her because of me, I'll never forgive you. I'll never forgive myself."

The front door opens and Annie stares blankly at the men in front of her, and then to me. Fight be damned, when she sees me crying, she rushes over to me and glares at Derek.

"I'm going to put my sister back to bed, and when I come back, the rest of you are going to tell me what the fuck is going on." She snaps her head to Nate and glowers. "Strike one."

Nate groans, and suddenly, I'm being swept away into the bedroom.

"I'm sorry I went crazy on you," I whimper when she climbs into bed with me.

"No, I'm sorry for jumping to conclusions. That was shitty of me." She weakly smiles and adjusts her head on the pillow. "What's going on, Peanut? Do you want me to kick all of those guys out?"

"I don't think it'll matter. They're here to babysit me. I'm not allowed out of anyone's sight until Charlie is caught."

"What do you mean caught?" she demands.

And so I tell her. I tell her the hell I've been through since she's been staying at Momma and Daddy's house while we silently fought.

Charlie is on the hunt. And sooner or later, he'll find me and finish what he started.

"So...who are *they?*" she asks, referring to Nate's men.

"They're from Nate and Derek's unit when they were in Afghanistan. Nate says they're the only ones he can trust not to be corrupt, so yeah... they'll be around."

Annie frowns.

"Okay. Give me a few minutes. I'll kick them out and we can spend the day watching TV."

"That sounds fun, but I don't want to be cooped up inside. I'd rather do stalls."

Annie grins.

"Well then, you can do all of mine."

A FEW HOURS LATER, once I'm certain Derek's at work, I head down to the barn where Tanner is waiting for me. I try not to acknowledge him, but when he greets me, I have no option *but* to be polite.

"So…how long have you been a cowgirl?"

I roll my eyes and scoff.

"I'm not a cowgirl. I'm a farmer." Sort of.

I move Tippy out of his stall, turn him out into the paddock a few feet outside barn number four and pull a wheelbarrow up to the front of the stall. I grab the pitchfork and start mucking out the stall.

"Okay, so how long have you been a farmer?"

"Since day one," I reply easily. He hangs back, watching the ground and occasionally scrolling and typing on his phone. "So…you're a marine?"

He smirks. "Once upon a time, yes. I did my four years and was ready to get the fuck out, but then Bubba convinced me to stay." He shrugs casually. "It was fun while it lasted. But now…"

His voice trails off and stares at his phone.

"Now, what?"

"Hm?"

Whatever.

"Hey, I'm sorry about the other night. I didn't mean to embarrass you. But I saw one brother trying to shoot the other and that doesn't sit well with me. I had to intervene before Nate did something he'd regret."

My stomach sinks, leaving me in that air of blissful ignorance, spending the night tangled up in Derek Hawthorn.

"You watched us?"

He shakes his head slowly.

"As soon as the doorbell rang and I saw you jump him, I turned the feed off."

My cheeks heat, and I turn away. I refuse to let this stranger watch me blush.

"But eventually you turned it back on…"

"Yeah, I did. Because I might live two states away, and I miss my brother like crazy, though if you tell him I said that I'd deny it, but we've been through a lot. All of us. And sometimes when our demons pay me a visit, I get paranoid and keep an eye on everyone. It's how I'm assured that everyone is safe."

I get it. Thankfully, there weren't any children involved when I was with Charlie. Because if there were, I probably wouldn't have left. And if we did get rescued earlier on, I'd probably never leave their rooms.

Trauma has a funny way of keeping you on your toes.

"I don't think he knew you had his place bugged."

Tanner snorts and shoves his phone back into his pocket.

"That's fine. He knows now. And…I don't think he'll mind. It's comforting knowing there's more than one pair of eyes that are keeping an eye on Zoey. I don't know if you've noticed, but we'd do *anything* for her."

Yeah, so would I. Which is why I'm so angry at her father for being so careless.

"She's special," I reply softly. "She's my little best friend and I only get to see her a handful of times." I shrug, leaning the pitchfork against the wall and approaching him timidly. "I don't know what you've assumed at this point, but this thing with me and Derek…it was a one time thing. It won't happen again."

The hollowness in my stomach is back. Nothing can happen. I have to keep reminding myself about that. For Zoey's sake.

"Bubba isn't the type who settles down. I mean, he did with Emily, because you're supposed to get married young when you're in the military, just for everything to go to shit." His crooked smile makes me want to love him. Not like a woman loves a man. But like a sister loves a brother. Or a gay best friend. "I've seen the long line of women he keeps at arm's length. But you're different."

Don't give me hope.

I don't want it.

"I don't want to be different," I whine. "It can't ever happen, Tanner. So please don't try to play match maker."

He snickers.

"Okay, fine. I won't. On the condition you behave."

I arch my eyebrow.

Excuse me?

"I don't mean to scold you like a child, but you *did* walk down here on your own after Nate told you to be with someone."

"Charlie wouldn't strike in broad daylight."

"*He* won't."

But his associates might.

Fuck.

"Anyway, Logan and Joey are grumpy fucks. Logan has a reason to, so maybe don't press him on it. But Joey? I'm almost positive he's still a virgin and *that's* why he's so miserable. But they're good people. We'll look out for you and we promise not to invade your space too much. We're here to help. Plus, I think my brother has the hots for you."

I glare at him while he cackles away, leaping back a safe distance.

"Is he giving you any trouble?" Nate's voice sounds from where Tanner was just standing.

"No, he just likes the sound of his own voice."

Nate snickers and punches Tanner in the arm.

"Tell me something I don't know." He grins at Tanner as he starts walking the length of the aisle, giving us a minute alone. "I'm sorry about this morning. I wasn't trying to overwhelm you."

But you did.

"I don't like people in my space, Olson."

"I know," he replies gently. "But like Bubba said, it won't be like this forever. We'll get him, that I promise you."

Maybe.

Or maybe Charlie will get *all of us.*

"I'm trying to survive as long as I can. I'm not used to relying on other people. I can't depend on anyone because every time I have, I've been burned, literally, in the end."

"If you think he's getting out of this alive, I'll save you the agony, Aria. If my gun is pointed in his direction, I'm shooting to kill. I can sleep perfectly fine at night knowing I exterminated someone like him from the Earth."

I could too.

"And...you can depend on us. I can't say too much. But we know what we're doing. Charlie isn't the only person we've dealt with."

His words have deeper meaning, and yet, I hang on every word. Who else has he had to kill?

"Well, enjoy the rest of your day. Tanner will be around probably until Bubba gets back."

Oh great. And then I have the rest of the evening to ignore Derek.

After my two lessons, Chris appears in the barn and helps me set up evening feed. He's unusually quiet. He ignores Tanner and when Annie gets to the barn, she ignores him too. Between the three of us, we could run this whole place without any input from Daddy.

Speaking of, he shows up as we're loading up the hay in the second golf cart. He hasn't even looked in my direction, but he chats with Tanner in low tones so we can't hear him. But damn it, I'd *love* to know what he thinks about all this.

They finish up their conversation and Daddy approaches me quietly, not showing any signs of anger like he has the last couple of weeks.

"Let's take a walk."

I raise my eyebrows.

"A walk?"

"That's what I said. Move it."

I glance back at Annie, and she shrugs.

What could he possibly want?

We walk in silence out of the barn and to the farthest pasture, about a mile away from the barns. We hit a patch of woods and I freeze. My mind flits to that night where Charlie dragged me through the woods with nothing but the flashlight on his phone and pushed me into his former stepmother's grave. I smell her decaying flesh. I feel the tiny legs of beetles crawling all over me.

I can't walk through there.

My body won't let me.

Daddy stops and waits, watching me like I'm a crazy person.

"When you were three, you ran away from home because Annie got to go to school and you couldn't yet."

My father isn't a sentimental person. He's one of those people who throws children's artwork away simply because it's cluttering up a space. He hates reminiscing.

I'm not sure where he's going with this. And I *know* I'm not going into those woods.

"You waited until your mother wasn't watching and you made a break for it. It didn't take long for your mother to call in the cavalry and before I knew it, the whole town skipped work to come and help us find you."

Oh, I bet he *loved* that.

"Your favorite place in the whole world was the barn. I was certain I'd find you there, but even then, you were unpredictable. You were always an observer. And you knew how to exploit that."

Ugh.

"I saddled up and started looking for you around here. About an hour and a half tearing the place apart, I had a hunch you'd be hiding in the woods. I'm not sure why, because you were always afraid to come over here. In my gut, I knew I'd find you. And sure enough, you found Chris and Jay's treehouse and were coloring on the floorboards with crayons."

Why don't I remember this? I know I avoided this patch of woods, but I don't ever remember running away from home.

"You were probably furious with me."

He smirks.

"I think I was more impressed a three year old could bring a whole town to its knees just because she wasn't allowed to go to school."

He takes a step into the woods and beckons me to follow him, but I *can't.* It's broad daylight. The sun will shine through the trees and my father will be with me. But doesn't take away the flashes of Charlie's step-mother's rotting corpse, or the awful smell I had to deal with for hours on end.

"I'm your father, Aria. I'm not going to hurt you. I want to show you something, and then we can come right out."

My body shakes as I take a timid step forward.

There are no bodies here.

Charlie isn't here.

My father isn't going to leave me here.

"I can't," I whimper. "I'm sorry, Daddy, but I can't go in there."

"Because of the grave?"

My head snaps up, and my wild gaze locks on his. How does he know about that? I shouldn't be surprised. When it comes to my father, he has a way of knowing everything.

I nod, quietly. He ponders this a moment and holds out his hand for me to grab onto. I reluctantly reach for it and gasp when he squeezes my hand tight and leads me forward.

The sunlight filters through the trees, and when we step under the canopy of shade, the heat of the day cools a few degrees. It's an overgrown mess of ivy-cover trees, and giant, moss covered rocks.

I can't imagine coming here on my own as a toddler. What could this place offer me, anyway?

Soon enough, the treehouse comes into view, and we climb up. Like he said, faded crayon drawings cover the floorboards. My name is sloppily written, and the scribbles cover every inch of wood.

"I asked why you chose this place, and do you remember what you said?" When I shake my head, he smiles. Like a real, genuine, face lit up smile. "You said you didn't know."

A watery laugh escapes me. That sounds like me.

"But we colored as you told me about what you were drawing. You told me you wanted to go to school, and it wasn't fair the other kids got to go and you couldn't. You were mad at your mother for refusing to put you in day care...You always had this unbridled passion to learn. Whether it was horses or tending to the crop...even cooking. You *loved* to learn."

What does this have to do with anything? And why did he have to drag me all the way out here to show me this?

"When you told us you were accepted to Northwestern, I asked you why you wanted to go there. Do you remember what your reply was?"

"I don't, but if I had to come up with a guess, it was probably because I wanted to get away and forge my own path."

He grins and shakes his head.

"You said you didn't know."

I groan.

"I had an idea of why I wanted to," I reply sheepishly. I put a lot of research into going there.

"There's something I've learned about you, Peanut, and that's you don't take any shit from anyone, even when you don't know what you're doing." He leans against the wall of the treehouse and smiles. "It's something I've always admired about you."

I scoff. "Don't bullshit a bullshitter, Daddy. It's the one thing you *hate* about me."

He considers this a moment. "There's nothing I hate about you, Aria Louise. Some of the things you do certainly piss me off more than anything, but I could never hate you."

"Even when I almost killed mom coming out?"

He presses his lips in a hard line and scowls at me.

"I've never hated you. And it wasn't your fault you came early."

I scoff and lean my head back.

"You know, ever since I could remember, I didn't care about impressing everyone. That's why when the Hunts were making me out to be a dirty slut or the Parkers sabotaging my equipment when it was my turn to run at the rodeo, I never said anything. I didn't care. I didn't give a rat's ass what they thought about me. But for some odd reason, you're the only one I care about impressing."

His eyes narrow.

"Chris was *always* the golden boy. He can't do any wrong and he was the one who was going to inherit the place. Then there was Annie who is so fucking bubbly and quick witted. She always knew how to charm people and get everyone on her side. And then there was me."

"There's no point in comparing—"

"There is, Daddy." A poisonous laugh escapes me. "From the moment I was born, I was a fuck up. I came too early and almost killed Momma in the process. I ran away from home because you guys refused to put me in a day care. In school, I wasn't charming like Chris or Annie, which made everyone pick on me because I was quiet and weird." The tears fill my eyes. This hasn't bothered me like this before. "Chris and Annie went to college an hour away from home, and they came right back. I went to college four states away and had an inappropriate relationship with my boss. Who later manipulated me into moving in with him and beat me within an inch of my life whenever he saw fit. And now? I'm pregnant."

I sob into my hands as my father watches me uncomfortably.

"My options, *suck*. I don't think I could kill something that lives inside of me. And I can't give it up to some family we don't know. That wouldn't be fair. And it wouldn't matter what I chose because people judge me anyway. Hell, *you* judge me for keeping it."

"Aria, I don't judge you."

"Yes you do. I'm not perfect like Chris and Annie. I can't charm the town like they can. I'm an embarrassment. It's the whole reason I've covered up and wore baggy clothes to hide the baby bump I find no point in hiding anymore. I'm tired, Daddy. I'm tired of being the one who makes one bad move after the other. It doesn't matter how much I *try*, or try to think what you would do, because I always choose wrong."

My sobs take over me, now. I wish I was closer to town so I could bother Dr. Nelson, because I'm sure this whole meltdown would buy her a nice long vacation in Hawaii.

"I was upset when you told me you were going to keep the baby," he admits softly. "But it was mostly because I was scared you'd go back to him."

Ha! That would be the day.

"I've made plenty of mistakes, Peanut. A lot of them. Mistakes your mother has helped me cover up and will take to her grave. My biggest mistake *and* regret, is not giving you enough credit. You found a way to get out, and you did it by yourself."

Because that's who I've relied on.

"I'm sorry for being hard on you. Honestly. Your mother tells me I have a knack for pushing people away. I'd like to say I could change, but…"

He won't.

"Anyway, your brother and sister don't want to inherit the farm."

Shocker.

"So, now I'm asking you. When I die, would you like to take over Sage Creek Acres?"

"This feels like a bribe."

He chuckles. "I'm afraid I wouldn't be giving you much in return. This is a beast to run. If I didn't have the three of you, I probably would've sold a long time ago. It's been in the family a long time…I don't necessarily want to give it to some schmuck off the street. I'd rather it went to somebody in the family."

"I just got into a partnership with Jo. I don't think I'll have the time to do what you do."

"But you and Derek would—"

You've got to be *fucking* kidding me!

"There's no me and Derek, dad. How did you even know about that?"

He smirks.

Derek has a big mouth.

"I can't believe he told you," I murmur, the rage boiling in my blood.

"He didn't tell me. I saw you walking out of his house way too fucking early a few days ago."

Oh, god!

"This isn't happening. Please do not breathe a word of this to Momma. It was a one time—" *two time* "—thing. It won't ever happen again, and I don't want to talk about this with you."

He shrugs.

"You've done worse."

32

DEREK

Quitting smoking is the pits, but Logan told me it would look better in front of a judge if I was making the effort. But after the last few days, I need a break. I need a moment of nicotine corrupting my insides.

The boys are staying in Aria's house so they can make the switching out easier. Tanner is spending the night on Annie's couch since it's his night to keep watch. I have Zoey for the weekend, and she's tucked away, sleeping.

The raven haired beauty across the way is in my every waking thought. I'm not sure whether I'm disappointed or impressed she *still* hasn't trusted me and hasn't come back over again.

My heart leaps when her front door opens, and she notices me and starts this way. She's light on her feet, almost like she's a dancer. Her small baby bump gets bigger by the day, now looking like she's pregnant.

"Dr. Hawthorn," she greets with a teasing smile.

"Aria," I greet back, scooting over so she can sit with me. I quickly put out the cigarette and push the table with the ash tray with my foot so she doesn't have to breathe it in. "To what do I owe the pleasure?"

She shrugs nonchalant and rests her head on my shoulder.

"Couldn't sleep."

"What's on your mind, Ace?"

"Everything." Her voice is small.

"Wanna talk about it?"

"Charlie's been contacting me. I accidentally answered a few weeks ago."

My muscles go rigid. Why didn't she say anything?

"Did you tell Nate?"

She shakes her head and sighs. "No, I didn't. I was afraid he'd take my phone again."

Going without a lifeline for so long is understandable. Once you get it back, you don't take it for granted.

"I'll have Tanner pull the phone records. What did he say when you answered?"

"Nothing of substance. He wanted me to acknowledge him, and I threatened to turn it over to the FBI and he said he was counting on it. I hung up after that. I didn't want to hear anymore."

Regardless, letting us know ahead of time puts us two steps closer to figuring out what he's planning.

"My dad asked if I wanted to inherit the farm. He insinuated you and I could run it with no problems."

I sit up stock straight.

"What?"

"He apparently saw me doing the walk of shame the other night."

And he hasn't killed me yet?

"What'd you say?"

"I turned him down. When the time comes, we'll figure it out. I'll probably quit Jo's place and take this over since I already know Chris and Annie want nothing to do with it."

"But they help out every day…"

She snickers. "I know. But I don't think they want the full responsibility falling to them." She sighs and not so subtly sniffs me, turning her nose up when she smells the smoke on my clothes.

"And what about you?" I ask.

"I figure both Chris and Annie are going to have their own families one day. Jay will too. I don't have any romantic entanglements in my future. It makes sense."

My heart from sinks into the pit of my stomach with an audible and painstaking 'thud.'

I'm falling for her, and she hasn't even told me her middle name. I'll make Tanner tell me. But I'm desperate to get off the subject. I want happy times with her while I can get them, especially when it feels like a war is coming my way.

"If you didn't attend school for English, what would you have done, Ace?"

Her smile is dazzling. The way her eyes crinkle when her smile reaches her eyes is sexy. And I'm not even mad she's leaning on me because I could smell her hair all day.

"I don't know." That makes her giggle. "I've heard it isn't wise to dwell on the 'what-if's.' So…honestly, I don't know."

I can respect that. Asking what-if is a dangerous game. It takes out of the now. It takes you away from what you have around you.

What if I didn't marry Emily?

Simple. Then I wouldn't have Zoey.

I have zero regrets with how my life turned out.

"If you didn't have Zoey, would you have stayed in the Navy?"

Yes.

"Probably. I was used to it, and it gave me the perfect avenue to travel the world."

"Sometimes I wonder what would've happened if I didn't go to Chicago for school. When I was trapped with Charlie, I used to wonder what my life would've been like had I followed Chris and Annie to the college they went to. Would I have taken over the farm already? Would I have been stuck in a loveless marriage with Chadwick Hilton?"

God, I hope not. He's a tool.

"Maybe our paths would've crossed sooner."

"Maybe. But I doubt you would've looked my way."

"I don't think so. You're *stunning*. I *definitely* would've looked."

She rolls her eyes. "Thank you for saying that, but I'm going to agree to disagree. I don't consider myself a person with a ton of strength and courage. Everyone around me tells me that's exactly who I am. I'll admit, my time in Chicago has only added to my cynicism and 'strength and courage.' I think my confidence in being alone for the rest of my life attracts you."

Ouch.

"You think I'm in it for the chase?"

She shrugs, keeping her eyes ahead of her. "Yeah." She turns to me and grins. "Look around you, Derek. Every time you step outside this front door, the women of Sage Creek fawn over you. They flag you down in the middle of the street to help them with their poor, sick, animals because you're the only guy in town who wasn't born and raised here. They love your dumb chin dimple and the way your eyes shine when they land on something they like. It doesn't hurt that sometimes you're nice. Other times you turn them away which only makes them come back for more."

"Wow."

She giggles again and it's music to my ears. I shouldn't feel this naked, but I do. She's found me out.

"Hey, I call them like I see them. You like the chase, Dr. Hawthorn. I posed a challenge to you and now you can't get off my ass."

"What can I say? You have a nice ass."

Her melodic giggle has me longing to press my lips onto her porcelain throat.

"There's usually some give and take during a chase. You want nothing to do with me," I tease.

"I jumped you that one night."

"That doesn't count. You're hormonal and you needed a release. I was the closest guy around who isn't related to you or in charge of your case."

Her careless shrug shouldn't hurt so much.

"And what if I gave up the chase?"

I meet her curious gaze and arch an eyebrow.

"Are we having this conversation, Aria?"

"It's hypothetical, of course. But let's say, hypothetically, yes. Maybe I want a little of what you're selling No attachments. A few more weeks of feeling great, both of our needs get met, and once the baby arrives, we go back to our lives."

It's tempting. Especially since I can't get her out of my head.

"Hypothetically speaking, yeah. I like the way that sounds."

She smirks. "And honestly?"

"Yeah. I'd want that. And what about you, Ace? Is that what you want?"

She nods slowly, contemplating the proposal.

"Yeah."

She nervously lifts her gaze to mine, her waning smile threatening to turn into a frown. I won't let her cry. She's cried enough—and I'm not going to be the reason for it. Not when I have the power to make her feel like the queen she is.

"For so long, I've seen passion in two people. They drove each other crazy, but when all was said and done, their love stood the test of time, and distance. And sometimes some terrifying situations that threatened to tear them apart."

"Your parents?"

She nods. "I didn't hang the moon and the stars in the sky. I'm not the easiest person to get along with, I know that. But just once, I want to be touched by a man who isn't looking to ruin my life. I want to feel like I'm *wanted,* to feel like there's a part of me that's worth redeeming."

"I wish you could see yourself the way I see you," I whisper gently. Her bottom lip trembles when I tilt her head to meet my gaze—to really *see* me. "In my eyes, Ace, you've hung the moon and the stars. The way you are around Zoey...*nobody* has ever gotten that close to her. Not even Annie.

"When I tell you I *want* you, it takes every morsel of my willpower not to maul you in the middle of the barn because you're the most beautiful woman I've ever seen and I want to take up a little of your time."

"Derek," she whimpers.

"Maybe this is inappropriate. Maybe it's too soon for you to be looking my way. But *I know* that when I'm around you, when you show me that microscopic glimpse of what you keep behind that stony exterior, I can't stop wanting to break my own rules."

"This is a complication, Derek," her voice cracks.

"Just a little fun, Ace. I'll do whatever you want me to do. If you're thinking this is all one sided on your end, I promise you it's not. I don't spit lines. I don't play games."

"I'm not…experienced," she murmurs. "Before Charlie, I was only ever with one other person. They were both…vanilla."

"Vanilla, hm? And what is it you're looking for, exactly?"

Her cheeks flush and she drops her gaze, toeing the concrete with her flip flop. Her hair curtains her face, a natural shield against me.

"I don't know."

"Yes you do."

She licks her plump lips nervously, slowly inching away from me. I reinforce my arm around her waist and tilt her chin up. Her pupils dilate in the way they did when she came over to my house that night.

Why so shy, now?

"Tell me."

She sighs.

"I want to forget who I am."

A slow smile spreads across my lips.

"Forgetting who you are isn't what you're looking for."

She sighs and drops her gaze, my finger falling to my lap.

"I want a taste of what you and I could have been."

Her eyes water slightly. It takes a lot of guts to be vulnerable with a guy you barely know, let alone a no strings attached deal.

She wants to be treated like the queen she is.

"You *are* beautiful. You don't even realize it, do you?"

Her Adam's apple bobs nervously.

"I promise you, the time we have together, before the…baby…gets here, you'll be treated like a woman. I'll worship your body the way your idiot ex-boyfriends should have because *you* are a work of art."

A few tears escape from the corners of her eyes. I pull her onto my lap so she's straddling me and push her long hair behind her ears.

"I bet you say that to all the girls."

I chuckle and shake my head.

"There's a first time for everything, Aria. Fortunately for *us*, we can treat it as such."

I crash my lips into hers, the warmth of her sweet breath filling my senses. I don't give a shit if the whole world is watching right now. I want her to know at this moment, she's the only one on my mind.

I pick her up, her legs locking around my waist and bring her inside. I pray Zoey doesn't peek her head out because she's curious. I don't want to have to explain that this isn't what she thinks it is.

Aria's cool fingers thread in my hair as she gently nibbles on my bottom lip. My hands palm her ass as I pray to the spaghetti monster in the sky I can find my way to the bedroom without having to put her down.

I'd die if I have to.

I clumsily walk down the hall, feeling around for my doorknob. And when I reach for the correct one, the cool air from my bedroom sends a shiver down her spine. I flip on the light which is like a douse of cold water. She doesn't want it on, but *damn,* I want to see her in all her glory.

Silently obliging, I flip it back off and crash into her, gently backing her up to the bed. She dips below me and yanks my basketball shorts down along with my briefs. My breath gets caught on my throat as she strokes me, her hands working me.

She licks her lips and takes me into her mouth.

She's velvety smooth, her tongue is heaven dipped in sin. She takes me to the back of her throat and gags.

"Holy shit," I groan.

Her lips curl around my dick, and she licks me down my shaft.

Good god, I can see the light!

I push her head down further, and she gags again, her throat contracting around the tip.

"Oh god," I groan. "Stop. Or this is going to get embarrassing, real quick." I gently push her on the bed and kneel. I peel off her sleep shorts, the scandalous lacy panties I *hope* were just for me.

Her legs naturally fall open. I'm starving for her. I want to taste her release. I want her legs to lock around my head and threaten to suffocate me. Because if this is the way I die, I'd be fucking happy with that.

She shudders when I lap her up. She's sweet like honey, and already her pussy pulses in my mouth. It begs for penetration.

And what am I, if not a gentleman?

I start off with one finger inside of her, gently stroking her.

Her breathing is ragged, and she covers her mouth with her hand.

"Don't cover your mouth Aria, I want to hear you cry for me." Ensuring her hand leaves her face, I insert another digit, bringing her on the brink of ecstasy. I bury my face in her pussy, inhaling her sweet scent, devouring everything she has to offer me. My fingers pump harder, and her cries get louder.

I remove my fingers and lap up her orgasm, greedily taking everything for myself. She scoots back on the bed while I hover over her, crashing my lips to hers.

"Please, Derek," she whispers.

"What do you want, baby? Tell me what you want."

"You," she whimpers.

"You have me. What do you want me to do?"

"Fuck me," she groans. "Fuck me so I can forget."

"Open your eyes, baby. Look at me."

My cock throbs with anticipation. But we're not fucking to forget. We're fucking to create new memories. Because once whatever this is, is over, I'll replay these moments in my head when I crawl back to fucking the women of this god forsaken town.

Her hazel eyes lock onto mine, welling up with tears.

"I don't want you to forget this," I whisper.

She nods and pulls me closer. I kiss her lips, her cheek, her long, delicate throat, her collarbone. I slowly enter her and watch the stress disappear from her face. Like...contentment. Like this is exactly right for *her.*

And it is.

This is all for her.

I make it a point not to talk during sex.

But I want to hear her voice. I need to know if she's okay.

I move inside of her, her walls already contracting around me, squeezing me for dear life.

I move faster, basking in every stroke until she detonates around me. I explode in her and thank the gods I was the one around when she needed a release. That one was all for me.

33

ARIA

29 weeks pregnant...

Derek Hawthorn isn't human. He's some super freak with a perfect penis and insanely healthy sex drive. I wish I didn't crave his touch, but I can't fucking stay away. He's a siren, one I wish I could ignore. But here I am, laying wrapped up in his arms while he strokes my hair.

This is exactly what I *need*. It's the perfect remedy to all the hell Charlie put me through. To have a man worship my body like I was the one who created beer...or football.

"Is there something about the dark that makes it easier for you?" He asks.

I'm on cloud nine. I'm walking on sunshine. I'm the mellowest of the mellow. And if he would've asked me tomorrow, I would've been offended. But right now? I'm...content. I feel like a woman.

"I haven't shown my back to anyone before. And I guess I'm a little insecure about the...bump."

I feel his lips curve into a smile on my back. He moves my hair away from my back. His finger lightly trails the lines of scars, soothing the damage Charlie inflicted.

"I saw your back. The day I rescued you."

I snort. He rescued me, all right. Got a free show out of it too.

"I don't want to remember that."

He presses a gentle kiss into my spine, gently squeezing my hip.

"Scars don't make you ugly. And if I'm being honest, you wear pregnancy beautifully. You glow."

"That's called sweat. And it's because I work outside all day every day."

His breath explodes on my back, tickling my sensitive skin.

"Do compliments make you uncomfortable?"

I wish he'd stop reading me like an open book.

"People don't compliment other people without an ulterior motive."

"I've showed you all my cards, Ace. I'm an unlovable buffoon who seduced you into a no strings attached deal."

I snort.

"I think it was I who seduced *you.*"

"Yeah," he sighs. "No regrets."

His fingers trail up my arm, his face nuzzling my neck.

"Are you sure it was a good idea to do this while Zoey's home? I kind of feel like this is breaking the rules a little bit…"

"A bomb could detonate, and Zoey would sleep through it. I hope you plan on staying the rest of the night... I like having you here. You're warm and you smell like the beach."

"I'll stay, only because I'm too happy to get up. But I'm trusting you to set alarms so I can get back to Annie's before Zoey wakes up."

He nods, stroking my hair. I close my eyes in bliss. Nobody has ever done this for me before. I hope he doesn't get tired of doing it because that would be a crappy end to my night.

"Derek?"

"Hmm?"

"Thank you."

He sighs.

"I'm not a prostitute, Ace. Don't thank me."

I giggle and hug the pillow closer to my chest.

"I know you're not a prostitute. I'm thanking you for making it easy to trust you. I wish I wouldn't, but I'm the dumbass in your bed right now."

"You're not dumb. And…I feel weird about saying 'you're welcome' to that. Kind of sounds braggy."

I giggle and breathe in the scent of our sex.

His bare skin warms me through. Derek is a cuddler, and I'm sure if I announced it to the world, he'd deny it. He doesn't seem like the kind of guy who likes hugging.

"What sort of…*things*...do you like?" I ask cautiously.

"How do you mean?"

"Like…in sex. Do you have a fetish? Is it okay if I ask you that?"

He chuckles.

"No, I don't have a fetish. But I like things rough. Passion blossoms out of a person when they completely let go, like they're doing this for the last time, and they want to make the most of it. I like raw. I like aggression."

I swallow nervously. How can I be like that? Where's the line? Am I supposed to choke him or something?

"Same question, and don't bullshit me."

I'm glad I'm facing away from him. This conversation is too embarrassing. I've never talked about *this* with anyone.

"I don't know."

"Close your eyes. When you see the two of us together like this, what do you see? Are we gentle? Am I selfish? Are you on top?"

I do as he says, my eyes grateful for the rest. So far, I've liked everything Derek has done to me. I like being on top. It gives me the control I crave. But I also like when he takes control. It isn't possessive or animalistic. It's…like it was meant for me. Like, he's thought about this for a long time, curated a list of my flaws and catered to them.

"What's your biggest fantasy, Ace? Don't be shy."

"I like being on top, though I don't think I'm all that good at it."

He kisses my back, taking one more giant piece of my heart I wasn't sure I was ready to give up yet.

"You're great at it. What else?"

"I don't like being in the same position. I like when we move around the room."

"And?"

"I…kind of like it rough. Just as long as you don't choke me or do knife play or use whips or something like that. I can handle you pulling my hair, but I won't take it well if you restrict my mouth or nose."

I feel him nod next to me, his breathing fanning on the back of my neck.

"Did you like going down? You kind of took control on that one. I know it restricts your breathing…"

"I liked that," I admit honestly. "You taste good. I like watching you be at my mercy."

He gently pats my ass in retaliation.

"Okay," he replies softly. "We'll move slow then. I don't want you to run."

That's the moment I know I've probably made a horrible mistake. But I'm warm. He's spent the time after he's thoroughly fucked me taking care of me, stroking my hair, talking softly to me.

It's nice.

And I don't remember what nice is like.

34

DEREK

A month later, I'm back to my regular routine now my brothers are here. Nate slaves away, looking for Charlie and coming up empty. All the vacant properties have been thoroughly searched, and still, he's a ghost. He threatens the safety of everyone who lives on the McKenzie property, and although there is no sign of him I still feel like I'm being watched.

Aria works at the old papermill during the day since the drywall has been put up. Sometimes if I'm lucky, she'll stop by and have lunch with Jackie and pretends I don't exist. But don't worry, she still sneaks over every night, cuddling in next to me.

I'm not a man who settles down. I've been there, done that and it didn't work out for me. Instead, it affected everyone around us. But when her long black hair tickles my nose, I'm reminded of how *right* it feels to be curled around her.

At four o'clock, Jackie leaves for the day while I sterilize the exam room. There's a timid knock on the front door, and when I peer out from the hallway, I find Aria waiting outside.

I quickly unlock the door and let her in, locking the door behind her.

"Hey, Ace. What's going on?"

She shrugs, rubbing soothing circles on her belly, and then finally turning to me. She wants to say something, but something's holding her back.

"We had our first meeting with the Live Oaks Foundation a little bit ago."

She lowers herself onto Jackie's chair and breathes a sigh of relief when she props her feet up on the desk.

"How'd that go?"

"We were granted twenty million dollars." It's like she can't believe it herself, she's still processing.

"That's a lot of cheddar."

She laughs and gazes at the ceiling.

"Yeah, it is. They truly believe in us."

Who wouldn't? Two women who lived a hell nobody else could ever properly explain, open a place for women and children like them to start over. Because Jo's right, essentially. There's life after abuse.

"What do you think about all of this?" I ask, dropping into the seat across from her.

"I…I don't know." She glances to me and gives a long suffering sigh. "The building will be finished in a few weeks. We'll be gathering volunteers, running background checks, thoroughly vetting them…but Charlie weighs on me."

Fucking asshole.

"You're worth it, Aria." She timidly gazes at me and frowns. "You've proven you can survive; you can start over. You're moving on and he's going to be behind bars."

She shifts uncomfortably. "Maybe," she murmurs. "But I can't stop thinking of what could happen. The FBI isn't going to let Olson stick around this long. Your brothers have their own lives. You…" She *almost* betrays herself.

"I'm here for you," I remind her.

"You have a daughter and are in the middle of a custody battle. What I'm trying to say is, Charlie's patient when he needs to be. He knows all he needs to do is to wait everyone out. And I'm afraid once this is all over, or if the baby comes, he'll make a move and I risk all of those women's lives." She blinks away tears.

"I know it feels like the weight of the world is on your shoulders, but I promise you we're going to catch him. Nobody is going anywhere until he's caught. He's a threat to national security."

"If that's the case, I should be staying home where he can't hurt anyone—"

But her.

This needs to stop. This martyr thing she has going on, it needs to stop.

"You can't let him win. He *wants* you to be cowering in fear over his next move. But Ace, that's not the answer. You're making major change with this shelter. You are going to change so many lives because of what happened to you." I pause for a beat while she soaks this all in.

"I wish you would stop giving me hope."

"Can you feel a change with us, Aria?"

She squeezes her eyes shut as a few traitorous tears escape her hazel eyes.

"Please don't do this, Derek. I'm not strong enough to fight you on this."

"Then don't fight it." I get out of my chair and cross the desk, crouching beside her, resting my chin on her thigh. "We've talked about reincarnation before, but I think every moment I spend with you, I start to believe it more and more every day."

She sniffles and shakes her head.

"Our hearts know each other, Aria McKenzie. I don't know how I know that, or how to explain it, but deep down, I think you know we are supposed to know each other."

She wipes the tears from her eyes and leans her head against the headrest. "Maybe that's the case," she admits. "Our hearts know each other from how many other lifetimes ago. But right now, I can't put a label on us. I can't be in a relationship with you because I'm not done healing. I'm not finished grieving who I was."

She gently rests her hand on my cheek, caressing the stubble of my five o'clock shadow.

"Okay," I tell her. Because in the end, I want her to be comfortable. I want her to be able to answer her phone without screening her calls and freezing when she wonders who it is. I want her to be able to leave the house without someone tailing her to make sure she's okay. "But I want you to know, you're not in this alone. I'm here for you."

A sob wracks her body and I pull her close.

In this reality, I'm a simple man who is actively falling for a broken woman. I believe in what I told her. Reincarnation is an odd phenomenon I haven't put a lot of thought into before I met her. But now, there's something so familiar about her. It's like I'm fully attuned to her thoughts, and I know how to act without her even having to tell me what she needs.

"What about Zoey?" She asks.

"I'm still going to fight for her."

"I don't want to distract you from that."

"My fight for Zoey doesn't end just because I care about you too." I reach for her hand and squeeze. "Nothing has to change right now."

We reach an impasse. So I finish cleaning up and then walk her to her car. I follow her home, making sure nothing happens on the drive home. But as I drive, I think about that last statement.

Please don't do this, Derek. I'm not strong enough to fight you on this.

She feels it too. I *know* she does. All I'd have to do is string together a few pretty sentences together and she'd melt into me and never let go.

But that's not who I am anymore.

I'm exactly where I thought I'd never be— in the position to care for someone–and I mean *truly* care for them. It's like falling into an anxious pit of love with stomach aches mixed in. When I look at her, or when she curls into me at night, I'm all in.

Even if it meant raising that baby with her. I'd do it.

When we reach the property, she pulls into Annie's driveway. I immediately disappear inside my house and change into my running gear. The sky is a dreadful gray, almost black. The heavens threaten to open up and rain it's frustration on the human race.

But whatever.

I need to run. I need to clear my head before I start spouting off forever's and babies.

Joey meets me outside, ready to run. We haven't spoken all day, so him reading my mind and not saying anything is welcome. I don't want to talk about it. I want to run.

We start down the cul-de-sac and off to the country road. I don't bother with my phone or music, but with our rhythmic thumping of our shoes slapping the pavement, I feel my stress melting away.

My heart thunders in my chest, and even as the first few raindrops fall, it doesn't bother me. The coolness of the rain is refreshing.

I didn't think I could ever give up the single life. It was nice, fresh, exciting. This woman, on the other hand, has some kind of magic spell over me—one that has me wanting to follow her around like she's a dog in heat but doesn't give a rat's ass about what I do.

That might be true, actually. She might not care.

But she came to you after work today. She warms your bed every night. She plays with your daughter when she doesn't have to.

Right.

Thunder rolls above us. Two miles off the property, Joey shoves me into a ditch just as thunder crashes and a bolt of lightning strikes too close to us.

"What the fuck was that for?" I bellow.

"That wasn't thunder," he says, his voice dropping.

We position ourselves so we can see ahead of us, from where the shot rang out.

"I'm not armed," says Joey.

Yeah, I'm not either. Fuck.

"If we move, we're done," I tell him. I can't see anyone around us. This mound of dirt and grass protects us for the time being. We have our hand to hand combat training should the guy get brave and come close to us, but we'll only have half a second to react.

"Somebody has to have heard that," he murmurs.

Aria's words come back to me. *Charlie's patient when he needs to be. All he has to do is wait everyone out.*

He *has* to know about us at this point. He's a sick fuck probably watching her like a hawk. Now he's here to take me out of the equation.

Joey glances around us while I keep watch, looking for anything to get his attention. Another shot gives up his location. And lucky for us, he doesn't have the same training as we do.

The rain pelts down on us, our clothes completely soaked through. And being this is a road nobody travels on unless it's to go to the McKenzies, we're stuck.

"I've got nothing," Joey says.

"My pockets are empty," I reply.

"Then we wait for him to come to us."

I shift my gaze to my brother, thankful he's here.

"She's pretty, Bubba."

I roll my eyes and agree. She's the most beautiful woman I've ever come to know.

"Yeah. She is."

"She's prickly too. I don't think I've ever seen any woman put you in your place like she has."

I swallow the lump in my throat, still scanning the pasture next to us.

"She's been through a lot," I reply.

Joey nods, and to my horror, he stands up and waits.

Another shot rings out, and I feel the bullet fly over my head, missing Joey completely. He crouches back down and smirks at me.

"He's a bad shot," he comments with a boyish grin.

"Dude, don't do that again. That was stupid!"

"Maybe, but I got a good look at where he fired from. About five hundred yards east."

He's on the mother fucking property and nobody knows.

"They don't know he's there," I tell him.

"He's not there for her. He's here for you, buddy. He's wiping out the competition."

For a moment, I'm relieved. If the pressure is off of her, then it's for the best. But then Zoey crosses my mind. If I leave her with Emily, she won't ever forgive me.

"Whose property is this?" he asks, pointing to the pasture behind us.

"Steve's."

"Any building we can find shelter in?"

"No, it's an empty pasture."

Joey curses.

"Okay. This ditch runs this deep for about a mile back to the main house. Stay low, stay out of sight."

It feels like Afghanistan all over again, only, it's raining. I stick close to Joey, stopping every few feet and listening to our surroundings.

We stop when a car stops a few yards ahead of us. I'm ready to pounce. I'm ready to end this fucker once and for all.

35

ARIA

33 weeks pregnant...

"THOSE WERE SHOTS," I say, pacing the dining room of *my* house. Logan stays with me while Nate and Tanner leave to find Joey and Derek. He watches outside the window, disregarding me completely. I wish he'd say something. I wish he'd tell me they're all right.

I need to know they're all right...

"Yeah," he replies.

That's it? That's all he has to say?

"Do you think they're okay?"

Finally, the sad man turns around to look me eye to eye.

"We're trained to notice everything around us. Even when we're running." He returns to the window. And while he *thinks* that should satisfy me, it doesn't to a god damned thing.

"He's been out of the Navy for a while now..."

"It's not something that leaves us. Trust me."

I stand next to him. If he can look out the window and be this calm, maybe it'll work out for me too.

My body vibrates. I can't stand the thought of losing them, Derek, more. If I got them killed, I'd give myself up to Charlie to end it all now.

There it is.

It's that thought that stops me in my tracks.

Would I sacrifice myself for Derek?

The black SUV makes its way down the driveway. I don't give it another thought as I race to the door and wrench it open. Logan's beefy hand wraps around my wrist and yanks me back.

"Don't go out there. Hold on."

We watch through the front window. Tanner and Nate hop out and open the passenger doors. Derek hops out, along with Joey. Relief washes over me and I feel Logan relax slightly next to me.

They're soaking wet from head to toe. Their clothes are muddy and clinging to their cut bodies. They talk for a moment outside and make their way inside. I launch myself into Derek's arms and squeeze the life out of him.

"I'm okay, Ace."

Tanner smirks and moves back over to the computer.

"What happened?" Logan asks.

Joey regards me for a moment, turning over if they want to tell him with me in the room.

"Sniper, two miles down the road. He's a terrible shot."

"I couldn't see *him*, but I saw where the shots are coming from."

He approaches the map that lies open on the table and points to the exact spot where they were ambushed.

"What's over there?" Nate asks.

When it registers, my blood runs cold.

"The treehouse," I murmur and meet Nate's eyes. "It was JJ's and Chris's when they were younger. It hasn't been used in years, but there is a roof on it and it's hidden in the woods."

Nate nods.

"Archer, Hawthorn, sit this one out. Shower. Barnes, Novak, you're with me. Novak, can you get any satellite images of that area?"

He nods, but I know they're not going to find him.

"He's going to change his location," I tell him. "If he saw you pick them up, he'll know he didn't kill them."

"He doesn't have time to move anywhere else," Derek pipes in. "There's literally nothing else around there. Unless he had a car, which I doubt since the only way in and out is by the main house. He would've been seen."

And there haven't been any helicopters.

"What else is around there?" Nate asks.

I wrack my brain, trying to think of the other hideouts I told him about.

"He could've slipped through the fencing and had a getaway car," Tanner offers.

"You're thinking one of the associates?" Nate asks.

"His people are loyal. It's possible he's been on the run with someone," I reply.

"Regardless, we need to search the treehouse." Nate turns to Logan and Tanner. "Suit up. Let's go."

While the flurry of men arm themselves and rush out the door, Joey and Derek stand quietly, dripping on the hardwood flooring in the middle of my dining room.

"I'm sorry," I tell them, looking them both in the eye.

"Ace..."

"Ms. McKenzie, the apologizing stops here."

I freeze at Joey's authoritative voice. For a moment, I'm transported back to the apartment, awaiting my punishment.

"You're ours now," Joey says, his voice softening.

"What?"

I shift my gaze to Derek who grins. "Just like Heidi was ours," he says. "Heidi was our sister. She was Logan's fiancé."

"Yeah. You're Bubba's, and we're not letting anything happen to you. We've already lost too many people we care about."

With a nod, he disappears up the stairs. Derek shivers in the cool air. He motions for me to follow him. He laces his fingers with mine and leads me outside, through the rain and into his house.

Locking the door behind him, we shuffle to the bathroom, leaving a trail of sopping wet clothes behind us. Derek turns the shower on, and while he leans over, my eyes follow the sharp contours of his back.

It's so picture perfect, like he was chiseled by an artist. Unlike me, his back is scar free, save for the one on his right arm…one I hadn't noticed before. We step inside the shower, and bask in the heat. He lowers himself in the tub, and I straddle his lap, wrapping my arms around his neck and breathing in his scent.

"I was worried about you," I admit while the water pelts my back. I feel his lips curl into a smile on my breasts.

"I live to see another day, Ace."

"If anything happened to you…I was ready to go back to Charlie—"

His head whips up and his hands cradle my face.

"Promise me, Aria, even if something happens to me, you *won't* go back to him." The look in his eyes is feral, urgent. I swallow the lump in my throat and nod. "No matter what happens, you can't go back to him. Your safety is what matters."

"And what about yours?" I ask softly, gently licking the pad of his thumb that's tracing my bottom lip.

He shakes his head. "Don't worry about me." He kisses me deeply, like he's trying to coax it out of me. That I won't do anything stupid that will make his sacrifice in vain.

"I know you're staying with Annie, but what do you think about sleeping over?"

"Tonight? Sure, I guess—"

"No, I mean…every night."

My heart stops in my chest.

"Derek…"

"It would give me peace of mind that you're safe. You don't have to sleep in my bed if you don't want to. Though, I hope you do…"

I giggle nervously.

"For a few nights," I agree. "But I don't want to leave Annie all alone." He nods.

"Okay."

A FEW HOURS LATER, when we're showered and in fresh, dry clothes, we meet back at my house. The boys who left to scout are in clean clothes and are deep in thought when we walk in. Nate nods to me and eyes Derek, speaking their own telepathic language I'm not privy to.

"Treehouse was empty, just like you thought."

"Did you find anything?" I ask.

"Other than the shells he left behind, no. The rain probably damaged fingerprints, but I'm sending them to the lab regardless."

"So...what do we do now?" I ask.

"Stay vigilant. We'll continue with property searches, and I'll start showing his picture around town to see if anyone recognizes him. You need to stay put. Maybe talk to Jo about working from home for a bit until we can catch him."

While the boys gather around the dining room table and talk their legal jargon about the case, I raid the fridge and pantry and start making dinner. The simplest thing I can make is spaghetti since I have everything for it. While my sauce is simmering, I make garlic butter for garlic bread.

After about an hour, a pair of strong arms wrap around my waist. "Smells good, Ace."

"Thank you."

"What are your plans tomorrow?" Nate calls to me from the dining room.

"I have my amniocentesis at Dr. Cash's office."

The room comes to an awkward silence as they silently figure out who will accompany me.

"What time?" Derek finally pipes up.

"Um, two o'clock. But it's okay. I can have my mom come with me."

"One of us needs to be with you too," Nate reminds me.

I timidly glance to Derek who turns the decision over in his head. He waits for my response, but I'm terrified to ask him. What if this is the straw that breaks the camel's back? What if this is moving too fast?

"I can come with you if you want me to," Derek offers softly, so only I can hear. "It doesn't have to be weird. I can wait in the waiting room."

"Um...okay."

Suddenly, the tension hangs in the air like ivy growing on the side of an abandoned house. I stay in the kitchen, avoiding Derek.

It's already weird. We're in this weird "not a relationship" relationship. It's not even his kid!

"So, what's there to do in town?" Tanner's voice sounds behind me, making me jump.

"Ah...not much. What are you looking to do? The nearest nightclub is an hour away, but if you're looking for a bar, Rico's is always good."

Tanner chuckles.

"Don't worry, I don't care. I came in here because you're acting weird and I didn't want Bubba to think I was bothering you."

I arch an eyebrow, Betty Lou McKenzie style, and smirk.

"So...what do you need, Tanner?"

He snickers and leans against the counter. "I want to hang. They tell me I'm a ladies man. I used to be best friends with Heidi and Eve, but..." his voice trails off. Heidi's dead and Eve was shunned due to Nate's job. "Anyway, I'm not trying to get in your pants, so you don't have to worry about that. I want to get to know you. Being friends with girls is a lot easier than being friends with those assholes."

He brings a smile to my face.

"Well, I'm afraid I've led a pretty boring life thus far."

Tanner shrugs. "I don't know about that. I don't think I've ever seen a woman lift one hundred pounds of *anything* as easily as you carry two feed bags."

Yeah, well, I'm not even supposed to be doing that either.

"Annie can lift more. But she's starting to lose her edge because she travels so much."

Her time working for the farm is dwindling. And my father's words echo in my head about keeping the farm in the family. I'd have to hire people, right? There's no way I can run this place by myself.

"And your brother?"

"He's a teacher. He doesn't want to run the family business. So I guess I'm the lucky winner." I stir and cover the sauce, slowly turning to him and pasting on my best fake smile.

"You may think you're slick, McKenzie, but I can tell when you're lying."

His phone vibrates in his back pocket, and I get a flash of Eve's name popping up on his caller ID. His face immediately falls. He wants to answer it, his thumb hovers over that big green button. With a sad sigh, he presses *'ignore'* and turns back to me, pasting on *his* best smile.

"You should answer it," I quietly encourage him.

"No…because if she asked, I'd tell her the truth." He sighs and hops up onto the counter. His chocolate eyes dart around the room, narrowing when they settle on Nate. Nate taps away on his computer, oblivious to his friend glaring a hole into his skull.

"Wouldn't it be better if she knew the truth?"

He shakes his head sadly.

"It would only put her in danger." He sighs. "And believe me, we've already lost too many people we care about." He glances over to me and grins. "I know it's not a *thing* with the two of you, but this is the first time I've ever seen him…"

What?

"Happy."

"Maybe it's gas," I quickly cut in, returning to the stove and placing the garlic bread into the oven to toast. I don't make him happy. We give each other a sexual outlet.

Even *that* is a joke to me.

Because…he makes me happy too.

"Probably that too, but…it's more than that."

I wish he'd shut up. I don't want everyone pointing out the fact I'm sort of dating the guy who lives two doors down from me when I just got out of an abusive relationship.

"Anyway, I know you've been through a lot. I heard you telling him you're going to be a spinster or whatever it was…but, he's a good one. He wouldn't let anything happen to you."

I know that. And *that's* what worries me.

"Isn't that a thing? Jumping from relationship to relationship? How am I ever supposed to love myself if I can't be alone for one second?"

"I think I might be the wrong person to ask about loving yourself." He gives me a half-hearted smile and leaps off the counter. "We all have our baggage. Some of us hide away, burying ourselves in work instead of facing the problem head on. Others go to therapy and talk to a shrink about all the reasons why they're unlovable…" he shrugs casually. "And then there are some who accept the baggage, unpack and chuck the suitcases away, and live their lives in peace."

"I wish I could be that third person."

"Maybe you can. Trauma isn't a one size fits all, and neither is therapy. You're doing the right thing. And while you're sitting here, thinking you're unlovable for whatever reason, I'm here to tell you you're not. Because that guy over there? The one with the stupid haircut and the piercing blue eyes, has always been closed off. And for the first time ever, when he smiles, it's because he means it. He's not saving face or trying to make us more comfortable."

I take his words in stride when Derek looks this way. Tanner flips him the bird and instead of charging over here, he laughs and shakes his head.

Derek Hawthorn isn't human. He is insanely beautiful with a perfect penis. And as much as I'm tamping my feelings for him down as far as they'll go, I'm falling for him too.

36

DEREK

Aria and I stroll into Dr. Cash's office the next day. Aria, though she won't ever admit it, is terrified out of her skin. She hardly spoke in the truck and picked at her breakfast. I asked if she wanted me to pick up her mother too, but she declined.

We sit next to each other in the waiting room. She stares at the pictures ahead of her, a sense of longing in her gaze. This isn't something she's openly talked about. In fact, this is a topic she refuses to bring up.

I reach for her hand and give it a reassuring squeeze. "It's going to be okay. These things are common and it's rare anything bad happens."

She swallows and glances away from the pictures but refuses to meet my gaze.

"I want to get this over with," she murmurs softly.

I get it. I'd be squirrely if someone was sticking a big ass needle into my stomach too. We're the only two people in the waiting room. And after about five minutes, Dr. Cash approaches us with a smile.

"You ready, Aria?"

She silently nods and stands up. When I make no moves to get up, her brows furrow.

"Derek…can you come with me?"

Shit.

"Sure."

I'm not sure if we're *there* yet. The last time I was in an ultrasound, I'll admit I cried seeing my daughter for the first time, even though it was a grainy image and you couldn't decipher what you were seeing.

I follow them back to the exam room where the ultrasound is set up. A nurse follows us in and takes Aria's vitals and then gets her comfortable on the table.

"Let's see this little person, huh?" Dr. Cash announces with a grin.

She squirts the jelly on Aria's stomach and starts moving the wand over her belly, searching for the baby. We find him, easily. Dr. Cash searches for a suitable spot to inject the needle, away from the placenta and the baby.

I catch it before she does, and I'm relieved when she finds it too. She has the nurse hold the wand still.

She pulls out a small needle and gives Aria a reassuring squeeze. "This isn't the needle we'll be using to collect the DNA. This is local anesthetic to help numb you up so it's not too uncomfortable."

My eyes are glued to the ultrasound screen, watching the needle. I pray the kid doesn't move. His heartbeat fills the air and Aria relaxes.

"Okay, local anesthetic administered. How are you doing Aria?"

"I'm okay," she answers, strained.

I glance down to her and smile. She weakly smiles back and then shifts her gaze to the ceiling tiles above her. It's almost like she's disassociating.

"Okay. You might feel a slight pinch and some discomfort. If you feel pain, please let me know. Just try your best to keep still." She nods to me, and I turn my attention back to the screen. I watch as the needle invades her amniotic sack, holding my breath as she pulls the plunger of the syringe up. As she pulls out, she immediately places a gauze patch on the injections site. I take over so she can get the sample ready to ship. The nurse keeps the wand in place as we all listen to the heartbeat, making sure the baby isn't distressed.

"You did good, Ace."

She sniffles.

"How long until we find out anything?" she asks.

"We won't see results for about two weeks. But, if we see it come through sooner, I'll personally give you a call. No overdoing it for the next twenty-four hours. No sexual activity either."

We stay like this for ten minutes, all of us watching the screen to make sure the heartbeat stays constant. When Dr. Cash is content, she cleans Aria up and sends us on our way.

She's quiet. I mean, that's Aria, always quiet. But this time...

Something isn't right.

I end up pulling into the parking lot to Rhonda's and wave Aria along. She trudges behind me, reluctantly walking into the restaurant and seating herself in the middle of the room. I sit across from her and order our drinks. When our waitress walks away, I finally open my mouth.

"Do you want to talk about it?"

She licks her lips nervously.

"What if I hurt him?"

"The ultrasound looked promising."

She frowns.

"And...what happens if everything is perfect?"

For the first time, I realize she's asking about our future. I'm not entirely sure where and how fast this is going.

"Then you'll finish out your pregnancy on a high."

She shrugs, and sips on her sweet tea.

"This is awkward, Derek."

She's right. It's awkward. And there's virtually nothing I could do about it without her freaking out off the deep end.

"Talk to me, then. What are you thinking?"

"I don't know. I honestly didn't think I'd make it this far." A wave of hard realization washes over her face. She briefly glances down at her growing belly, around the black and white checkered diner, and finally to me. She thought she would be dead by now.

I nod, wanting to hear more.

"If I made it this far, then maybe I'll get to see the baby before—"

"There isn't a pick your own adventure chapter where you die, Aria." Her watery eyes lock on mine, sad, mistrusting, and hopeful. "You get to have a future. You get to move on. You get to be a part of that great shelter you're building with Jo. You're allowed to be happy. Charlie will get what's coming to him."

She stares at the table for moment, contemplating her next words carefully.

"And if Charlie's caught and put away...what does that mean...?"

She trails off, but I know that *for us* is in there somewhere. It's been floating in my head for the past month.

"What do you want to happen?"

She sighs out of frustration and rolls her eyes. "I don't know," she snaps. "Why can't you just tell me what you want from me?"

She's squirming and uncomfortable. Aria McKenzie is like her father in the sense she doesn't like asking the deep questions. It isn't because they don't think about them, it's they're afraid of the wrong answer.

"Because for the last two years, you weren't allowed to have a choice." She stills at my words, tears leaking from her eyes. "And if you want this to happen, I want it to be *your* choice."

She's not used to being the one in power. She hates it. She's afraid of her choices because choosing Charlie was the *wrong* choice.

"I *hate* I've become attached to you," she snaps.

"I'm quite attached to you too. Trust me, I wasn't too happy about it either. I'm a guy who doesn't do commitment, Ace—"

"Yes, as you keep reminding me." She rolls her eyes and abruptly stands up. "I'm sure you must be *so* devastated by the lack of variety of women who come to your door at night. Don't worry, I'm going to the bathroom." She storms away without another word.

My stomach bubbles with anxiety and annoyance.

"Aw, where'd Aria go?" Nicole, our waitress asks.

"She ran to the bathroom. She should be back in a minute."

She nods and promises to be back when Aria comes back from the bathroom. I gaze out the window and stare at the small strip mall of boutique stores owned by a lot of the locals.

Bethany Hunt owns one of those shops—the floral shop to be exact. That's how she gets all her gossip. And you better believe she keeps a record of all the messages she's written to mistreated women.

Aria returns and drops down across from me, glowering. She's on the verge of a full blown panic attack.

"I know you're scared, but it's going to be okay."

Her bottom lip wobbles and she buries her face in her hands. I tell her to come sit with me, while the whole god damned restaurant is watching us now. She slides in next to me and rests her head on my chest while she cries.

"It's these stupid hormones. I'm not this person."

I know.

I gently kiss the crown of her head and breathe in her scent.

"Let's get a big, greasy burger and head home, okay? We can Netflix and Chill all day."

That earns me a giggle, but we both know nothing sexual can happen. It will be a literal day of binge watching shows and staying in bed.

Nicole returns and gets our orders. She calms down and her face returns to her natural paleness. It's almost laughable.

"Do you think we can go on a real date?"

I stare at her in surprise.

"Like, I'll get dressed up, put on some makeup and we go to dinner somewhere. Super low key because I'm a pretty cheap date…"

I tilt her chin so I'm gazing into those hazel pools of Aria and smile.

"You wanna go on a date with me, Ace? Just the two of us?"

She nods sheepishly, embarrassed she's the one who had to ask.

"Actually…I was going to ask you if Zoey could come on the date with us…"

My stomach jolts with…something I haven't felt before.

"What?"

"I mean, Emily would have to be okay with it, of course…but I thought it might be a good idea if the three of us spent some time together away from home." Her eyes widen. "Not that I want to get a hotel or anything, but like to a restaurant in Richmond or something."

I kiss her temple.

"Yeah, of course. I'll talk to Emily. And since you're thinking about this, I'm sure she's going to want to meet you in person."

Her face falls.

"Do you think she'd be okay with it?"

No.

"There's only one way to find out…"

COLOR ME FUCKING surprised when Emily agrees to come to dinner at my house tonight—on the same day Aria asks me out. Annie and Chris invite themselves, because they want to be there for Zoey, and then of course, you can't have a dinner with only *some* of the McKenzies. Betty Lou and Steve invite themselves too. And then…the guys overhear. So now it's a whole fucking family event.

Betty Lou helps me in the kitchen while Aria sets the table. When Emily arrives, Zoey ushers her in where she says hello to Chris, Annie, and Steve. She's totally overwhelmed, but the asshole part of me is glad she is. At least she knows how many people are on Zoey's side.

"Hey, Darlin'! It's so good to see you again!" Betty Lou exclaims, rushing out of the kitchen and pressing a kiss to Em's cheek. Emily flashes me a nervous look and pastes on a fake smile.

"Em," I greet cordially.

"This is quite the party," she says quietly.

"I know we talked over the phone about this, but do you want to step outside a minute?" She nods nervously, avoiding Steve's gaze. I usher her out the back door only to find my idiot brothers sitting around the fire pit, beers in hand A brief smile spreads across her face when she lands on familiar faces.

"Em!" Tanner greets the loudest. He's the only one who remains friendly with her, even though she's been nothing but rude to him. The others regard her politely and carry on with their conversation.

"This blossomed pretty quick, huh?" she asks nervously.

"Yeah. It did, but it's real." She purses her lips and gives me a knowing look.

"Real, as in rainbows and butterflies, or *real,* like how you and I were together?"

I consider her question as I try to put my feelings into words.

"Real as in she's the *one.*"

Emily raises her eyebrows in surprise.

"You don't do '*the one*', Derek. I've heard all about your flings since you moved here."

"I'm not saying I'm going to marry her tomorrow." It's too early for that. "But somewhere down the line…yeah. I could see myself doing that."

She watches me like she's waiting for me to pass it off as a big joke. It's not a big joke. It's the God's honest truth, a truth I wouldn't tell her right this moment, so I don't scare her away.

"Derek, sweetheart, I need your help cutting this ham," Betty Lou calls from the open kitchen window.

"Be right in," I call back. I give her one final glance and smile.

"This is going to be your life, Derek, you realize that, right? *She* doesn't have the best reputation around town. She's aloof, she's bitchy—"

"That's what Bethany Hunt says about her. And don't call her bitchy again."

She frowns and drops her gaze.

"Have you even spent any time with her outside of those stupid barbeques?" I ask her. She doesn't have to answer, because I already know she hasn't. "Just…have dinner with us. Give her a chance, okay? Because I have never met anyone who has become our daughter's best friend as quickly as Aria has."

She takes a reflexive step back like I slapped her across the face.

"I know about the guy you're seeing in California," I drop my voice.

Annoyance is written all over face. I'll have to give Zo the heads up for when she goes home on Monday.

"He hasn't even asked about her, has he?"

"No."

Great.

"One chance. That's all I'm asking."

She reluctantly agrees and follows me inside. I take the electric knife from Betty Lou and begin carving the ham. The boys come in, Nate staying close to Aria to deter Emily from saying anything too rude.

We get everything on the table, and everyone takes their seats. Zoey sits in between Aria and I; Emily sitting across from us, watching this all unfold with an uneasy eye. Steve says grace to pacify his wife where the rest of us aren't religious at all.

I haven't seen my table this full in a while. It brings a smile to my face seeing everyone I love, *and Emily,* in one place. It's like a pre-Thanksgiving, only with ham.

37

ARIA

33 weeks pregnant...

I'M on the verge of throwing up all over this fucking table. Everyone talks like they're best friends, and while I have my family, plus the new dysfunctional family I've come to create over the last month here to support me, I can't help but feel nauseous at the *one* woman I'm trying to impress.

She's been quiet, which I know isn't like her. From what Derek said, she used to be a party girl, the center of attention. She seems like she feels out of place too. Maybe she feels like I'm taking *her* family away from her. They were all friends at some point.

Zoey talks to me about the next few books in the *Heartland* series, and while I want to focus on every word coming out of her mouth, my stomach somersaults, threatening to send everything back up.

I politely excuse myself and move into the kitchen where I *know* there's a ginger ale with my name on it. Literally.

"Still sick in your third trimester?"

I freeze at Emily's voice and grab the bottle out of the fridge, timidly nodding at her. She reminds me of wife number five—the one and only time I ever met her. She wasn't unkind, but she wasn't warm either.

"Sort of. I find my anxiety still makes my stomach churn."

Emily nostalgically smiles and leans up against the counter.

"I was sick through the whole pregnancy. I carried two bags of plain Lay's potato chips with me wherever I went because it was the only thing I could keep down."

Nice to know I'm not alone.

"Do you know what you're having yet?"

Guilt swirls in my belly. I lean against the sink and weakly smile.

"No…I think I want to be surprised."

She considers this a moment and shrugs.

"I'm not going to pretend I don't listen to the gossip around town, but I've heard things…about this pregnancy."

"It's not Derek's," I quickly tell her. "That's what Nicole at Rhonda's thought when we ate there today."

"That's not the rumor I heard. You were with that socialite in Chicago, right? Charlie Dodge?"

Hearing his name makes me want to spew, so I gulp down my ginger ale and sigh.

"Yeah. I won't lie to you…this pregnancy was unplanned. Everything regarding it has been…traumatic."

"Don't worry, you're not the first to be crucified by a rumor Bethany Hunt has started. Her oldest daughter, Tracey, was in my graduating class. She's worse than her mother."

We both laugh at that.

"*But* I think this thing—whatever it is with you and Derek, it makes me uncomfortable. It's happening too fast and frankly, you don't have the best reputation around town."

"I love your daughter, Emily. She's bright, and bookish, and all around a great kid. I don't want to be a pain point. I'm sorry my family bombarded this…it's who they are. My mom can't pass up a dinner on the property and you bet she has to be the one to cook it."

Emily smiles.

"She's a good kid," she agrees. "Derek and I…we weren't good together. I'm not sure what he's told you, but we were kids when we got married. Zoey is the only good that came out of our marriage, so when *you* come along, and she talks about you non-stop, I get concerned.

I get that.

"Co-parenting is a bitch. Especially when our parenting styles are so completely different. But…I know he's a good dad and he'd destroy the world if it meant she was safe. Regardless of what the other boneheads out there say about me, they're looking out for her too."

I'm getting somewhere.

"I don't know if this *is* weird or anything, but would you be interested in getting lunch with me one day? The only person I know whose given birth is my momma and I don't need the nitty gritty from her…or Jo for that matter."

Emily laughs.

"Sure. I'd like that a lot."

Derek enters the kitchen and freezes when he sees us together. His eyes dart from me to her.

"Everything okay?"

"Yeah, we were talking about getting lunch together," Emily answers before I can. She winks and walks out of the kitchen, her heels announcing her exit.

"You don't have to get lunch with her," he assures me.

"*I* asked *her.*" I reassure him. He deflates a little, wondering if this dinner wasn't enough.

"We had a good talk. Anyway, I came in here to get my ginger ale."

He takes the bottle out of my hand and places it on the counter behind me and presses his lips to mine.

My cheeks flush in embarrassment, knowing my father could walk in on this at any point.

"Tomorrow night, we're going to Richmond. I'm taking you and Zoey to a fancy dinner, and we *all* will talk about our future."

Butterflies flutter in my stomach at his gentle threat.

I'm getting a future!

38

ARIA

33 weeks pregnant...

I STAND in Annie's bathroom while she brushes out my hair and uses her flat iron to make it super smooth and sleek. I hardly recognize myself in the mirror. My skin is clear and glowing for the first time since I've come home. My hair is healthy and strong. My eyes, clear and bright.

It's taken me some practice doing my makeup again. With Charlie, makeup was used only to cover up the evidence. When it was a special event outside of the apartment, he had a team to get me ready. Every bruise was covered. I looked like someone who sort of looked like me.

I feel like I'm getting ready for a wedding. My idiot brother has been on my ass all day, asking me if this is a good idea. It took Zoey telling him to get his head out of his ass to get him to lay off. Well, not in those words.

"You're beautiful, Peanut," Annie says gently.

"Thank you." She grins through the mirror.

Her phone rings and her Alexa picks it up.

"Hey baby. How was your day today?"

JJ's voice registers in my mind and we both stare in horror at each other in the mirror.

"JJ?"

"...Aria?"

Annie groans.

"Jay...I need to call you back." She swiftly hangs up, turns her Bluetooth off, and shoves the phone in her back pocket.

"He just called you 'baby'."

She flinches and continues to play with my hair. I see her pulse racing in her throat.

"Annabelle, why is Jay Parker, our extra brother, calling you 'baby'?"

She nervously bites her lips and looks everywhere else but me.

"I thought you were dating Tom?"

She groans again.

"Jay is Tom."

It suddenly starts to click into place. The reason why we haven't met Tom face to face, or the reason why she won't allow us to FaceTime.

"You can't tell anyone, okay? This is super secret. Nobody knows."

I raise my eyebrows.

"You're kidding."

"No, I'm not," she snaps. She takes a deep, cleansing breath and blinks tears away. "We were going to tell everyone when he gets out in a few months, okay? Daddy isn't going to take this well, and neither will Christopher. Just...keep it to yourself and don't mention anything to anyone, okay?"

I swallow nervously.

"You have to tell me everything."

The doorbell rings, and I see the relief in her face as the burden to spill the beans is temporarily taken off her shoulders.

"Sorry, can't now. Your dates are here." I scowl and sweep through the house, my black and white flowy sundress trailing behind me.

"This is not over, Annabelle. I'll keep your secret, I promise. But not until I know all of the dirty details."

Annie yanks open the front door and lets Derek and Zoey inside.

Derek wears a black button down dress shirt that hugs his bulky arms and chiseled chest like I would if we were naked. He pairs his dark jeans with black dress shoes and a mega-watt smile when he lays eyes on me.

Zoey wears a floral print halter dress that makes her look to be twelve years old.

"You are a sight for sore eyes," he greets, pressing a kiss to my cheek.

"You look handsome too." I shift my gaze to Zoey and pull her into a hug. "Look at you, Zo! Beautiful as ever."

Zoey beams and gives a twirl.

"It takes us about an hour and a half to get to Richmond. Are you ready? I already got some car snacks to tide us over."

"She's ready," Annie says hurriedly, shooing me out the door because she doesn't want to talk about what I overheard on the phone. I give her a warning glare, silently promising I'm going to interrogate her tomorrow.

Derek's truck shines brightly, like he got a carwash for tonight. We pile in together, with Zoey in the back, already doling out the iced tea and pizza flavored *Combos.*

When we reach the small Italian restaurant in Richmond, Derek helps both Zoey and me out of the truck and leads us inside. The cool air and garlic hit me like a tidal wave. I'm *starving.*

We're brought to a secluded booth near the back of the restaurant, away from the front door and hustle and bustle of people we don't know. It doesn't take me more than a minute to spot Tanner and Nate at a table nearby. Like the professionals they are, they don't look this way.

I sit across from Derek and Zoey and scan the menu for something cheesy and delicious. The waiter stops by, takes our drink orders and disappears shortly after.

"Zo, what did you think of dinner last night?"

"Oh, it was fun. Especially when Uncle Tanner was making fun of you to mom."

Derek scowls and rolls his eyes. Tanner's in for a roll in the yard later.

"What do you think of Miss Aria staying the night with us?"

She shrugs casually, still perusing her menu.

"It's nice. I like waking up to breakfast."

I stifle my giggle when Derek groans.

"Babe, I'm trying to be serious with you."

She places her menu on the table and glances up at Derek.

"What do you think of Miss Aria and I dating?"

Zoey's whole face lights up, her eyes as big as saucers.

"Seriously? I'd *love* that! I knew you like-liked her!"

Oh, boy. He has a good poker face; I'll give him that.

"Yeah, seriously," he replies with a grin.

"This is going to be great! You can move in with us and we'll help you with the baby!"

It's that mental douse of cold water that brings me back to reality. It's *that* reminder that makes me uneasy. In a few short weeks, this baby is going to come into the world. And this...? Who willingly enters a relationship with a baby that isn't his?

Am I wrong for bringing my shit to this little family unit? That one day, Charlie is going to demand his son and I'll never see him again?

"That's putting the cart before the horse a bit, Zo, but yeah. We'll help with the baby."

Fresh bread is placed in front of us, and I'm so grateful for the distraction.

I glance around the restaurant, locking eyes with Tanner who discreetly winks at me and gives me a silly grin.

"It'll be an adventure," Zoey adds.

"Yes, it sure will," I respond. I smile when she squeals with delight.

I try to picture my life with them. I picture myself in bed with Derek or cooking dinner together with Zoey making desert. I see weekends of going bargain book shopping and horseback riding lessons.

...But no where do I see the baby.

Does Derek's house even have a spare bedroom for a crib? Will we switch houses with Nate?

...Will Nate still be around?

"Get out of your head, Ace," Derek warns, covering my hand with his. His touch is electric, and I'm suddenly reminded when we're touching, whether we're fully clothed, or buck-ass naked as the day we were born, my thoughts stop racing. "This is just dinner."

Just dinner. Followed by a lifetime of being called Mrs. Hawthorn.

"Sorry. I'm nervous."

"You eat dinner with us every night. This is just a change of scenery." He winks.

Right.

It's just dinner.

"So I heard a rumor," Zoey starts with a sly grin.

Rumors aren't a fun time, especially when the small town of Sage Creek likes to put me in the center of them. I don't need Zoey hearing all the negative crap about me people love to peddle.

"I heard you're opening the shelter in two weeks."

I breathe a sigh of relief. I'd hate to have to explain to her why the people around town call me a slut.

"We are. I'm thrilled! On Monday the cable company is coming in and installing our internet and tv's. We're also vetting volunteers to help us around the place."

"What sort of volunteers would you need?"

"Well, maybe a doctor who can examine women who come in with injuries, a lawn company to keep the place looking nice, a few volunteer cooks that can help us with breakfast, lunch, and dinner…"

I suddenly realize Derek is watching me with a smile on his face. A dreamy one. Like he can picture this all with me.

I should be happy, but my stomach churns. Maybe I dove into this too fast. Maybe I should've ignored him and kept my legs closed.

"And what would you be doing?" Derek asks.

"My work would be behind the scenes. I'll be working closely with the Live Oaks Foundation—coordinating funds, working with the staff. Jo will be working exclusively with the women and children who come in."

Derek watches me cautiously, like he's wondering why I'm hiding behind my impenetrable walls.

"That cool," Zoey replies in awe.

The waiter comes back and takes our orders.

It's Derek and Zoey. It's a change of scenery. Stop projecting your bullshit!

For the rest of the meal, we engage in idle chit chat. Zoey goes on and on about school, Derek occasionally jumps in. But I sit there like a deer caught in the headlights. I'm so grateful when we step outside and I can feel my lungs expand. We walk back to the truck and Zoey hops in. Before I get in, Derek stops me.

"Where are you?" he asks quietly.

"I'm here," I reply, but we all know I'm not.

"Was this too much?"

Yes.

"No, not at all." I flash him a smile and get into the truck. We drive home, his fingers loosely tangled with mine. Zoey falls asleep on the way back and Styx plays softly in the background. From the side-view mirror, I see Tanner and Nate behind us. Tanner obnoxiously waves to me when he realizes I'm watching.

"You're not a good liar, Ace."

I gently recline my head to the headrest and sigh. He's right. I'm a horrible liar. I wear my heart on my sleeve.

"I'm sorry. I didn't mean to ruin the night."

He tightly squeezes my hand and smiles.

"You didn't ruin the night. Maybe we moved too fast. Maybe we should've found a place to eat in town."

Guilt knots my stomach. I don't want to be that stick in the mud. Why can't I be normal? Why can't I enjoy a nice dinner with a nice man?

"Charlie used me as a showpiece," I tell him quietly. "I used to have to stand tall, look pretty, laugh at everyone's stupid jokes. And the whole time, we were too far away from home." I shift my gaze to him, but he watches the road. "I didn't think longing for home would still affect me like it did when I was with him. So, I'm sorry. It's going to take me some time to adjust to a life without him."

"And that's okay," he assures me. "Not much has changed, Aria. We're still us. We still eat dinner together every night, we still do the horizontal tango in the wee hours of the morning—"

I snort at that last one, which brings a boyish grin to his face.

"There's no pressure, okay? Don't think you have to put on an act for me. Because even if we were sitting on the couch at home with the TV off, I'd still be happy spending time with you."

The kicker is, I would too. I enjoy Dr. Derek Hawthorn, the vet who lives two doors down from me. I enjoy the little girl curled up on the back seat with her sweater over her to keep her warm.

"We haven't talked about the baby," I tell him.

He doesn't flinch. But he does stiffen. It's the constant reminder Charlie will be in our lives whether he's dead or not. ...*And* this isn't Derek's child.

"I'm here to support you with whatever you need."

I fidget with his fingers as I try to find the right words.

"It's funny isn't it? Usually if you knocked someone up, you'd feel some sort of responsibility. But this one isn't yours..."

"Not biologically, no." He looks to me seriously. "Zoey isn't biologically yours, but you love her, don't you?"

"Without a shadow of a doubt," I say seriously. I briefly glance over my shoulder and weakly smile while she remains so peacefully still.

"I—it's weird talking about forever when we're just starting. I'm in, Aria. I'm all in. I'll help you raise the baby if you want me to. Whether it's as a father, or an uncle, or just the neighbor who lives down the street."

Realization dawns on me. He's willing to give me up if he thinks I'm not ready.

"What if you don't like who I am?"

He chuckles. "I like who you are, Ace. You called me a dumbass in front of the whole god damned town. If that's not cause for not liking you, I don't know what is."

I lick my lips nervously.

"Where do we live? My house is better suited for a family..."

He shrugs.

"We'll cross that bridge when we get there."

Yeah. Right.

When we get home, Derek carries Zoey inside and puts her to bed. I pad to his room, peeling off my dress and undergarments and turn on the shower. The heat against my skin is magic. I wish I didn't feel so heavy.

The shower curtain moves, and I feel Derek behind me. His strong, calloused hands wrap around my waist, his hands lay flat against the underside of my belly, gently lifting it up. Suddenly, it's like all the weight is taken off my shoulders. My tailbone doesn't ache, my skin doesn't stretch, and when I lay my head back on his chest, he kisses my forehead.

"Whatever happens, Ace, we're going to be okay."

39

DEREK

Two weeks later

WHEN ARIA SLEEPS, the whole world falls silent. It's a weird phenomenon. It's almost like the world is the way it is because she's awake and hyper-aware of everything around her. As she sleeps, the brick wall she insists on keeping intact, opens like in that *Harry Potter* movie. She looks peaceful. She looks…*happy.*

She even lets me hold her close to me. To hold her when she isn't so stiff, so reserved, is a gift. Part of me wishes she were awake so she could see herself like this. My lips find her shoulder blade, placing a gentle kiss to telepathically tell her subconscious I'm still here.

She stirs, gently moving, and then the thrashing begins. She kicks at the covers and scratches the mattress as if to crawl away to safety. The nightmares are the hardest. She doesn't like talking about it, but this one seems too vivid.

"Aria," I say her name, gently shaking her. "It's just a dream, baby. Wake up."

Her elbow strikes me in the sternum directly, taking my breath away, and sending me crashing to the floor. I wheeze as I try to catch my breath. She thrashes around on the mattress, her screams piercing through the night.

"No, Charlie—*please!*"

When I catch my breath, I get back in bed and grip her arms. Tears spill from her eyes and when her eyes finally fly open, she looks around the room until her eyes settle on me.

"Shit," she murmurs.

I kiss her forehead and get back behind her.

"Are you all right?"

She pinches the bridge of her nose and sighs.

"It was just a dream," she convinces herself.

We lie in bed, but it's obvious she's too worked up to fall back asleep.

"Come on. Let's take a walk."

She doesn't argue. And when I flip on the light and watch her rock herself out of bed and the sheet slips from her body, I can't help but stare. She's gorgeous. And she catches me staring at her. She bashfully turns her head away from me, instead, showing me her scarred back, and the full ass that fills her jeans out so nicely.

"Stop staring at me," she pleads.

"But you're so beautiful."

Her shoulders tense. I wish she could see herself the way everyone else around here sees her. She slips on the shirt I was wearing earlier, and her sleep shorts while I grab my sweatpants and a different shirt. I like when she wears my clothes. They look *so* much better on her.

I lead her outside to the fire pit that is a few steps away from the back of our houses. She makes herself comfortable on one of the benches, drawing her legs underneath her while I build the fire with only my phone's flashlight as my light source.

When everything is set, I sit next to her and pull her to my chest.

"Do you want to talk about it?"

She shrugs lazily and sighs.

"I wonder if I should be calling them dreams. They're more like flashbacks." I bury my nose in her hair, huffing her coconut scent, getting high on Aria McKenzie. "Nate says they went to the exact coordinates where he shoved me into the grave, and there wasn't anything there."

"Did Charlie ever take you back there?"

She sadly shakes her head.

"No. I learned my lesson that night. But I've been thinking they moved the bodies after he put me there."

Maybe he thought at some point Aria would rat him out. He doesn't sound like one to take chances.

Except to escape the FBI...

"Do you suffer from PTSD?" she asks cautiously.

"We all do," I reply. My eyes instinctually dart to Aria's house, where all of my brothers are staying. A few lights flick on and I know they're going to be coming this way to make sure everything's all right.

"Does is get better?"

"I don't think anything that includes trauma gets easier, or better. Some days are better than others. On those particularly bad days, when you remember *everything,* I tend to lock myself away."

"Did you see a therapist when you got out?"

"Not right away. But when the divorce started ramping up, I felt like I couldn't function. So, then yeah. I started seeing a therapist at the VA."

"How often do you get those bad days?"

"Not as much as I used to." The boys start down the hill, starting with Nate, ending with Logan. "But they still come. And I have a support system I'm not afraid to call on anymore."

The corners of her mouth twitch as they approach the benches. Tanner grabs the bench next to Aria and stretches out. Joey and Logan share a bench, and Nate moves Tanner's legs so he can sit.

"Everything okay?" Nate asks.

"I'm sorry for waking you. I had a nightmare," she replies shakily.

"This is a cool view," Logan says quietly, scanning the horizon where the barns stand proudly.

"We like it," I reply.

"I'd like to request a new room. Joey is a nightmare," Tanner whines.

It brings a giggle out of Aria, which only fuels Tanner's stupidity.

"*I'm* the nightmare? Dude, your shit is *everywhere*. The only thing I have is a hamper and you have the rest of the room. Not to mention you're an insomniac so your computer is on all fucking day!"

"I have a *job,* Archer. Unless one of you fucks want me to teach you what I know…"

Nobody says a word.

He rolls his eyes and stares into the fire.

"It could be worse. You could room with Nate and have Eve call you every five seconds," Logan quips.

Our eyes meet, and Nate swears under his breath.

"Dude," Tanner grumbles.

"You guys have no idea what it's like." He looks to me, and then to Aria. "You get it, right Bubba?"

Glancing down at the raven-haired beauty who is so fitting in the crook of my arm, absolutely. If I had a job that was forcing me to track down a maniac that could potentially put her in danger, I'd consider lying to her to make sure she's safe.

Her hazel eyes find mine, questioning me silently.

"I understand where you're coming from. But—" Nate growls angrily when I contradict him, "—I would think about telling her. She knows what your job entails, Olson. She knew what she was getting herself into. Be honest with her."

He doesn't like that.

"You want to know how I know you guys have never loved anyone before? Because Evangeline is the most important person in my life." He glares at all of us. "And if she were to get killed because of my line of work, I'd end my life."

That realization sits heavily on all of us. We knew it was bad, but not this bad.

"Would you have told Heidi?"

Logan shrugs. "I don't know. What we did overseas wasn't going to follow me home, Nate. My whole plan was to have my furniture shop and have a shit ton of kids."

Tanner snorts.

But Nate gapes at a loss.

"But…let's say you ended up doing what I did. You became an agent.

You had this dangerous asshole out there who could do one quick Google search on you and find your wife."

Logan ponders for a moment. "No. I don't think I would've told her. Because living a life constantly worried about me isn't a good life. I'd want her to be happy."

We all smile nostalgically. We miss Heidi. But there isn't a chance in hell she'd let him go that easily.

"What was she like?" Aria asks, reminding all of us she's still here and not a part of the hell we'd gone through before we landed in Sage Creek.

"Artsy," Tanner replies dreamily. "She liked to paint. And she was unbelievably kind."

"She was innocent," Joey replies quietly.

That's the sad truth, isn't it? She *was* innocent.

"She saw the best in everyone. Even when they didn't deserve it," Logan replies. A melancholy smile spreads across his lips. "She changed me for the better."

She changed all of us for the better.

"She held Em's hand when she was giving birth to Zoey," Joey chuckles.

We all snort.

"Yeah, Emily wasn't the nicest to any of us. *Especially* Heidi," Tanner laughs. "But she barged into the delivery room and held her hand when Bubba was about to faint."

"I wasn't going to faint," I counter.

I know that's a lie. I hadn't eaten a damn thing that entire day, and I was anxious about meeting my daughter.

"She was the kind of person who could get even the most miserable man to smile," says Joey. He briefly glances at me, and I nod. I know he's had his rough spots too.

We reach a comfortable silence, my mind flitting from Heidi to Aria. I miss Heidi. I *wish* she could be here to meet Aria, because I'd want to know what she thought. But I think I already know. She'd love her. She'd call her a diamond in the rough and love her until Aria reluctantly returned the love.

"What's your story, Joey? You're the quietest here. I only know you from your not-so-subtle glares across the barn."

The whole group bursts into chuckles, even serious Nate. Joey frowns and rolls his eyes.

"I'm the oldest one."

Yes. I'm sure she could tell.

She silently presses him for more.

"Why'd you join the Marine Corps?" She asks, finally, sick of his silence.

"It seemed like the right thing to do," he replies with a shrug. "I went to my brother's graduation when I was in high school, and I fell in love with it. I knew it's what I wanted to do."

Tanner guffaws.

"You wanted to do it because you got to boss everyone around." Tanner looks to Aria and grins. "We went to boot camp together. Even out of the older dudes who were there, Joey was the most serious. Gave the Drill Instructors a run for their money."

Joey rolls his eyes.

"My brother and I raised our sister. So I knew I needed to get a job that would guarantee me money. My brother was an officer, so he became her legal guardian, and between the two of us, we raised her all the way out of high school."

Another woman who likes to boss us around.

"I'm insulted you didn't ask me first," Tanner sneers.

Aria giggles underneath me.

"Let's hear it. Who is the great Tanner Novak?"

"Tanner Novak is a God among men." Every single one of us, including Joey, hoots uncontrollably. He looks on with disdain, giving us all the finger.

"Stop it," I say to him between laughs, "She wants the truth."

He rolls his eyes. "I got arrested as a teenager for hacking into the police database. They told me I could either join the Corps, or I could go to jail."

"How patriotic," Aria responds. Tanner's cheeks flush and rolls his eyes.

"What about you, McKenzie? Why'd you leave this place?" Joey asks.

I stiffen, because *I* know the answer. I'm not sure if she's ready to share this with people she doesn't know. But she surprises me by sitting up and smiling.

"My brother and sister went to college an hour away from here. I think it was inevitable that one of them was being groomed to take over all of this. I didn't want that for myself. I wanted to explore the rest of the country. I wanted to feel what it was like to live in a big city."

She glances up at me and shrugs.

"It was the wrong decision. I probably could've saved myself a lot of pain if I'd stayed put."

"I don't know about that," Logan says, a million miles away from here. "I've lived a lot of life in my short time on this planet. Life is short and unpredictable. Sometimes everything happens for a reason..." his voice trails off when I'm certain he's thinking of Heidi. "You're where you're supposed to be. And besides, if you would've stayed put, you two probably wouldn't have gotten together."

She sighs against me and I don't know if it's a good thing or a bad thing.

"I don't know about that. He still would've given the goods to the whole town. I probably would've ignored him."

Everyone snorts.

"I guarantee if I saw you first, I would've gone after you."

A smile spreads across her lips and she tries to hide it. She likes me. I know she does. She can hide her smile all she wants.

"What happens after all this?" Tanner asks. But he isn't asking Aria. He's directly asking Nate.

"I don't know. I'll probably return to DC and keep doing what I was doing."

Tanner shifts uncomfortably.

"So you're not going to try to get back with her?"

"I told her I cheated on her." The whole circle falls silent. "She won't come back to me and I'm not going to seek her out."

"Maybe you'll be in a better place to clear the air," I tell him. It goes in one ear and out the other. His mind is already set, and I can tell he's going to brood about it for the rest of eternity.

"And you?" Tanner asks Aria.

She stays silent for a minute, carefully pondering her words.

"I don't know. I guess I'll have to learn juggling working, farm work, and being a mom. It's going to hit me all at once."

It will. She'll be exhausted and emotional. But as long as she still wants to hang out with Zoey and me, I'll be happy.

"I was thinking about something," she says, looking at Nate.

"The Dodges have a property in Montana. It's bigger than our property, by like three hundred acres. But if they moved the bodies...they might take them there."

"Why Montana?"

"Do you honestly think that *they* think the FBI is going to waste days combing that entire property?"

Nate's gears are turning.

"What else is on the property?"

"A three bedroom house, one barn. I don't think there is much livestock there anymore. They pulled out of the farming game ages ago and are trying to sell the property piece by piece. It's the one thing that sticks out in my mind."

"I'll look into it," he promises. He excuses himself, probably to get on the phone and talk to his people about getting warrants signed.

"Ace?"

"Hmm?"

"You feeling tired?"

"Not yet," she murmurs. She grins up at me and then to Tanner who watches us with the smallest bit of admiration.

"What's your real job?" she asks him.

"I run a cyber security firm." Yeah, and our little group is his best client.

"Which is in...?"

"Brooklyn," he replies proudly.

"And you?" She refers to Joey.

"I go where I'm needed." Aria rolls her eyes, just like we all do.

"And when you're not needed?"

"Clinical psychologist," he replies darkly. We all snicker. How ironic. The quietest guy, the one that feels like you're pulling teeth to get a simple answer out of him is the one that listens to other people's trauma.

"How's the shelter going?" Logan asks.

"Pretty good. Tanner's helping with the vetting process for the volunteers so that will be a step in the right direction. As soon as we get everyone trained, we'll open the doors." She smiles proudly, and I am insanely proud of her.

"Is that what you want to do with your life?" Logan asks again.

Hesitating, she nods. "I think so." She takes a deep breath. "Lord knows this wasn't what I had in mind for myself when I was a kid, but I think this is the best course of action. My way of getting out is a little unconventional. Not everyone has the luxury of having the FBI involved. But if I can help someone start a new chapter, I want to do that."

For the first time since she's met Logan, he smiles. A genuine one.

"Yeah. I like that," he murmurs.

I glance at my watch, and when I see it's two o'clock in the morning, I coax her back into bed. Joey puts out the fire and we all trudge home. Aria's clothes are peeled off her body and when she's flush against me to the point I feel her want for me seeping onto my leg, I smile.

"Go to sleep, baby. You have to be up in two hours."

She pouts and reluctantly nods.

"Your brothers are cool," she says softly.

I *won't* be telling them she said that. But I agree. They are cool. And they'll make sure she's safe.

40

ARIA

Two weeks later

37 weeks pregnant…

I FIND myself in Dr. Nelson's office after not being here for ages. Nate sits next to me, albeit distracted on his phone, texting with his team. I'm anxious today, and I don't know why. Perhaps it's because I haven't heard from Charlie in a month, or maybe it's because I miss Derek when we're not together. It's not fair. I wasn't supposed to form any attachments and yet here I am.

"Good morning Aria, come on back." Dr. Nelson says in the hallway. I follow her into the office and take up my typical seat, this time lying down and staring at the ceiling. "How are you feeling today?"

"Like a whale," I reply honestly. My ankles ache, I'm exhausted even though I slept a full eight hours, and I'm sick to my stomach. Week thirty-seven of this pregnancy is a real bitch. I want it to stop.

"And outside the pregnancy aches and pains?"

"Anxious."

From the corner of my eye, I can see her putting the notepad down and getting comfortable.

"Why's that?"

"I haven't heard from Charlie in a month. You know, JJ always tells us that no news is good news. But in this case, his silence puts me on edge."

"Maybe he was caught."

"Nate would've known by now if that were the case."

"Maybe he gave up."

"He's too far into this to give up. He escaped the FBI and is a fugitive. There's no way he gave up. His reputation is on the line." *And probably worse off than it was.*

"What are you doing to cope?"

"I've been grooming horses, I guess. Derek is working with four of the rescue horses who need a little more love than the others do. So while he works on them, I distract them."

Dr. Nelson smiles.

"Giving them better lives makes you happy?"

"It makes me feel useful," I reply cautiously.

"You're doing a lot, Aria. Don't forget about that. You're building up the shelter for women like us. You're helping out at your farm..."

Yeah, I'm doing all that, but it doesn't change the fact I'm constantly looking over my shoulder.

"What's going on with Derek? Now that your second trimester is over, have you moved back into Annie's house?"

I inwardly cringe, because I know how this will look. Little Aria McKenzie can't *not* be in a relationship. She has to hitch her wagon to the first available mate in a ten step radius.

"No."

Dr. Nelson hums and writes in her legal pad.

"Talk to me about that."

"I don't know what you want me to say," I say exasperatedly. "I like him. He makes me feel safe. He makes me feel...*beautiful.*" I choke on that last word.

"What's wrong with that?"

"It's too soon. He has his own daughter to worry about. I'm not even done processing what's happened to me. This is...*wrong.*"

"But he makes you feel safe?"

I nod slowly.

It's different.

My dad and brother make me feel safe by existing.

Derek makes me feel safe because of what he's already done for me. He doesn't judge me for being prickly and mean. He accepts my cynicism and holds me tight at night even when my subconscious fights him.

"I don't know how to explain it. Before we were doing...*you know*...I felt this hollowness in my chest. I was perfectly fine with being alone for the rest of my life. I felt like I was living on borrowed time, Charlie would find me and end my life." *I still do.* "But being with Derek for the last few weeks, I feel like I can rest."

My eyes fill with tears. I'm angry I let him worm his way into my heart when that's what I was trying to avoid all this time. But now, I can't imagine going back to my scared self. I can't imagine not sharing a bed with him.

"Do you love him?"

"No." It comes out of my mouth so quickly I regret even forming my lips around the word. "I mean, I care about him. Very much."

"Do you want this relationship to continue?"

"I do. But I feel guilty for unloading my bullshit on him."

"That's how a relationship works, Aria. When you're with someone, you're sharing your life. Not just the good times. The bad times too. And whether you like it or not, it sounds like to me he wants you in his life.

"There's this woman I found on Facebook. She had gone through a rough divorce and was raising her two children. When she met her now husband, she kept saying to herself, he loves me *even though* I have kids. He loves me *even though* my life is a fucking wreck. He loves me *even though* I'm barely making ends meet. Do you see where I'm going with this?"

"That there are good men out there who will love me even though I'm carrying a murderer's baby and keeping it?"

She heaves an exasperated sigh.

"No. What I'm saying to you is the 'even though' has a negative connotation. You're so much more than 'even though,' Aria. He likes you because you're beautiful. He likes you because sometimes your cynicism can be passed off as a joke. He likes you because you make him happy. Period. End of story."

"But there are negatives in life," I counter. "Case in point, I had an inappropriate affair with my boss who then became my boyfriend. *Classy.* And if that wasn't enough, I ignored every single red flag and moved in with him so he could beat me within an inch of my life every single day."

"You're right. There *are* negatives in life. However, people tend to navigate towards the positive. We *want* to feel good. We *want* the positivity. And you, my dear, I know you want to feel better. I know you want to be happy. Is Derek Hawthorn the one who will help you find that happiness? I don't know. You're the only person who knows that."

Yeah, maybe. It doesn't help his gorgeous daughter is forever on the forefront of my mind. I want to make her happy too. I'd never forgive myself for pulling her into the middle of all this.

"What are you thinking about so hard over there?"

"What if it doesn't work out?"

"Then you move on."

My stomach churns at the thought.

"And if it does?"

"Then you can live your life and have the added bonus of having someone you truly care about on your side."

NATE and I drive to the clinic. Derek has a full waiting room, but I have a perfect opening with Jackie to hang out with her while I process the last hour. She's quiet at first, typing furiously on her computer, occasionally calling up dog parents and asking for money. But when she's done, she brews me my one and only cup of coffee for the day and grins.

"You seem chipper today," I tell her, wishing some of her cheer could rub off on me.

"I am. Derek is hiring another vet."

I raise my eyebrows in surprise.

"Really?"

"Mmmhm. It seems like your rescue barn is eating a lot of his workload, so we're hiring on someone to focus on dogs and cats and other small animals."

So he can spend more time babysitting me.

"Oh, that's great." It doesn't even sound enthusiastic coming from my mouth, and of course, she catches on to that.

"Babe, why the long face?"

"No, it's nothing. I'm coming out of a therapy session and I'm still stewing."

That's not a lie. It's not the full truth, either.

She reaches over and squeezes my hand.

"It's gonna be okay. Plus, I have something for you that might cheer you up. Mind the desk. I'll be right back."

As soon as she ducks behind the back door, the whispers start.

"Livin' in sin!"

"How inappropriate!"

"It's about time one of those girls got knocked up—"

"Ace, hey." Derek closes the distance between us and plants a kiss on my lips.

"Hey," I greet with a wicked grin now everyone is watching me and totally shocked Dr. Hawthorn has finally fallen for a woman. A McKenzie at that!

"What are you doing here?"

I wanted to be close to you because being home makes me antsy.

"I came to hang out with Jackie for a little bit."

"Oh, okay. Would you like to stick around and get lunch with me?"

"Sure." I don't mean it. I want to get out of these pants and into something shorter, something where my legs can breathe.

"Okay." He grins and turns to the waiting room. "All right, is Chuck

ready?" Betty Snyder and her dumb dog "Chuck" jump out of their seat and powerwalk the distance between them, disappearing behind the door.

"Got her hooks deep in him—"

"Actually, he made the first move."

Sort of.

The whole room falls in a dead silence as they all stare in horror at me.

"I'm not sure if you know this, but you ladies aren't whispering." I turn back around in my seat, grinning ear-to-ear. I embarrassed most of the rumor mill in one fair swoop.

Jackie returns with a gift bag with yellow tissue paper hanging out of it.

"I know you said you weren't having a baby shower, but I wanted to get you a little something. Maybe when the guys move out you can start making one of those guest rooms into a nursery..."

I gingerly peel the tissue paper away and reach inside the bag, pulling out a small frame. My eyes water when I pull it out. It's of all of us. Chris, Annie, JJ, Jackie, and me—all at the lake house my parents used to rent when we were kids. Chris is showing off his "muscles," JJ has his arm around Annie, giving her bunny ears, Annie's arm is around me, and mine is around Jackie. We all beam at the camera with wet hair and tanned skin.

"It's so the baby can see everyone who loves them."

My heart squeezes, staring into JJ's icy blues. I haven't seen him in years, and now when I miss him as much as I do and can't talk about what's going on with him and my sister, I'm emotional.

"This is so great," I say softly, my voice cracking with emotion. "I love it so much. Thank you."

I stand up and wrap my arms around her. Jackie O'Brien is my best friend in the whole entire world. She's the only person who can make me cry.

Though, these days, that isn't so hard anymore.

"So...?"

I glance up at her, wanting her to expand.

"You and Derek!" She hisses.

I roll my eyes.

"It's not serious."

She gives me a knowing look and rolls her eyes.

"Who are you trying to convince, Peanut? Don't forget, I've known you my whole life."

And vice versa.

"I'm waiting for the other shoe to drop. He'll eventually learn I'm not worth it."

"That's enough of that," Jackie snaps. "You're worth it, babe. He sees that. Don't think I wasn't watching him jump you when I left."

Oh god.

"And anyway, I've never seen Derek go steady with anyone. Ever. So if he's doing a full blown relationship with you, it seems pretty serious."

Panic surges through me.

Why would she say that? And why is this scaring me? We just had a giant family dinner together and a three person date!

"Um, do you think I can use the staff bathroom?"

She eyes me curiously but obliges. I disappear through the back door, but I don't go to the bathroom. Instead, I find his office and crash into his office chair. I'm breaking so many laws by being in here, but I doubt it will be Derek who rats me out.

Hercules, the horse Derek's been working with, has a thick file that sits on top of Derek's neat desk. I flip the cover open and find his intake pictures. He was so skinny. You could count every rib. His eyes were so sunken in and his coat was so dingy.

The preliminary report states they had to sedate him so he'd stop freaking out to get into the trailer. When they got him into the barn, he stood in the corner of his stall with his face hidden so he couldn't see anyone.

The gashes on his body were deep but were treated with ointment and monitored every day until they were gone. I flip the page and find his coggins, his horse birth certificate, essentially. He was bred for a little girl with the intention of barrel racing. But then one day, he was put in a stall and beaten within an inch of his life. I wonder what for…

"Breaking laws, Ace. Be careful. I happen to know a guy in the FBI."

He grins from the doorway. I quickly slam the folder closed and smile weakly.

"Sorry. I saw it was for Herc, otherwise I wouldn't have looked."

"What are you doing in here?" He crosses into the room and sits at the corner of his desk.

"There were so many voices out there. I felt…weird."

He cocks his head.

"Therapy went well, then?"

"Derek? Can I ask you a weird question?" He nods cautiously, waiting for me to ask it. "What about me made you throw caution to the wind?"

My question takes him by surprise. So much so that he gets up and closes the door.

"Fuck if I know, Aria." He sinks into the seat across from me and frowns. "You're beautiful—"

"But that can't be the only reason. Jackie's beautiful. Annie's beautiful."

"Do you believe in soulmates?"

No. Because God wouldn't tie somebody to my kind of crazy.

"No."

He smirks. "I don't know if I do either. Yeah, Jackie and Annie are beautiful—and that wasn't my only reason, Ace. You didn't let me finish. When I look at you, when I hold you close to me, you make me feel…*whole.*"

Fuck.

"You can't mean that. You barely know me."

"I *do* mean it." He stands up and offers his hand. I reluctantly take it in mine and allow him to help me up. He pulls me close to him, though I have to play Tetris with my belly. He smells like wet dog and cologne. But it's comforting. In fact, it's the first time my heart rate has lessened all day. "I know you well enough to know when we're around each other, the world seems to fall into place."

Again, fuck.

His words are so pretty, so soothing.

His calloused hands find my face and cradles it so I'm looking at him.

"You feel it too, don't you?"

I want to sew my lips shut.

Hope can be a good thing, or it can be a bad thing.

With the threat of Charlie looming over me with no strong leads on him ever being caught, having any hope is bad. Because if my future gets stolen from me, I'll grieve the life I never got to live.

"You don't have to say anything, Ace. I can see it in your eyes."

Damn it!

He kisses me deeply.

"I need to get back to work, but I wanted to come in here. Grope you a bit. Kiss you...that sort of thing."

I snicker and move in for one last hug before I face Jackie again. He kisses the crown of my head and gives me a heart stopping smile on the way out.

The waiting room has emptied out a bit, and before me is some guy in a lab coat I've never seen before, talking to Jackie. They wrap up their conversation and he sits in one of the waiting room chairs. He's cute.

"Doing okay?" She asks.

"I'm fine." I slink down into my chair, aware my cheeks are blazing because every time I close my eyes, Derek's lips are on mine.

"That's Dr. White. He's going in to meet Derek. If things go well, he'll start here next week." I quickly glance to my best friend and smirk.

"Do you have a crush?"

She rolls her eyes and puts her freezing hand over my mouth.

"You shut your dirty mouth, McKenzie," she hisses. Giggling, I glance out the front door to make sure Nate is still around. He meets my gaze through the windshield and motions for me to come over to him.

Excusing myself, I race outside and slide into the front seat.

"I have a lead. Do you think you can stay with Hawthorn today?"

I nod, though I want to ask him more. But...I also don't. I want one day where Charlie isn't the one to ruin my mood.

41

ARIA

One week later…

38 weeks pregnant…

ANNIE IS off to London for the week, so her house is empty. I clean out her fridge and take out all the ingredients I need to start preparing freezer meals for when the baby comes—hopefully, within the next few days. Annie is one of the sloppiest people I've ever met. Always living her life in the fast lane expecting everyone else to clean up her mess.

I don't mind. She has important work and I need something to do with my hands.

"So you're *dating* him now?" JJ's voice echoes through the kitchen from the speaker on my phone.

"Dating sounds so juvenile," I reply, taking out the produce and dumping it into the sink to get some soup going. "But, yes, we are together."

"He's dangerous."

I giggle and roll my eyes.

"I asked you if he was somebody I could be friends with, and you said he was the best person to be friends with. Don't go back on your word because you're feeling territorial. And while we're on the subject of dating people we shouldn't, when the hell were you going to tell me you and my sister are a thing?"

His end of the call goes silent, but I hear his heavy breaths.

"We're not talking about that."

"Yes we are. If my love life is on the table, so is yours. Spill."

"What do you want to know?"

"Why am I getting the skinny from you and not Annie?"

"Because we agreed we didn't want to be on your dad's shit list. We've been together for two years—"

"*Two years?*" I hiss. "That's a long time to keep a secret, JJ!"

"We wanted time to get used to…*us.*"

I laugh and start peeling the carrots. "When do you plan on breaking the secret?"

"We're talking about it." And that's all he has to say about that. "But getting back to you and Dr. I-Think-I'm-So-Pretty."

I roll my eyes.

"Is he nice to you?"

Don't worry. I won't be making *that* mistake again.

"Yes. Very."

"Ew!" he exclaims. "I don't want to hear about what you do in between the sheets!"

"I didn't even say anything about that! And if you're going to jump to conclusions, I'm ending the call."

He exasperatedly sighs.

"Fine. But you'd let us know if he wasn't good?"

Laughing, I nod, though he can't see me. "Yes. I'd tell you, but I don't think we have anything to worry about on that front. But…it sounds like he wants to raise the baby with me." My voice hitches with emotion.

"Peanut…"

"I wonder if he's thought this through. This isn't his child and I know his reputation. And with Charlie still on the loose…he could use Zoey as leverage."

"Do you want me to be brutally honest with you?"

"Always from you."

"I've known Derek since he's moved in, and I've seen him with Zoey. *Nothing* flies past him when it comes to her. Even with a past like yours," his voice trails off, waiting for the blowback he thinks he's going to get from me, "He's already calculated the risks. He wouldn't jump into anything half-assed, especially when it'll affect Zoey. I think he's thought this through, Peanut."

That's what I'm afraid of.

He'll mourn my death, and so will Zoey.

I'll be a fucking disappointment yet again, but to somebody else.

"I joke around, but I mean it when I say he'd take care of you."

Yeah. Maybe.

The front door bursts open and Derek strolls through and plops himself on the barstool.

"I have to get going JJ, but seriously, you and Annie need to talk about letting the cat out of the bag sooner rather than later."

"Yeah…I know. See you soon, Peanut. I love you."

"Love you too."

I hang up the phone and begin cutting up the vegetables while Derek ogles me.

"What are you doing here? I have a whole kitchen at your disposal, you know. Plenty of freezer space."

"Yes, but my sister's refrigerator desperately needed a cleaning and I'm taking advantage while she's gone for the week."

He gives me a halfhearted smile, like he has the weight of the world on his shoulders.

"Penny for your thoughts?"

"They're not worth that much, I'm afraid," he replies sadly.

I move the cutting board over to the stove and turn on the burner and put her biggest stock pot on the front burner.

"Come on. Talk to me."

"If I tell, you Ace, you have to promise not to react."

My stomach jolts.

"Okay. I promise."

Not really.

"Charles Dodge Senior was arrested today. And so was Charlotte. You were right. The Montana property held all the bodies."

When the oil is ready, I absentmindedly push the vegetables in to sauté as I process all of this.

"And the shelter was broken into. There are large holes in the walls, the wiring is all destroyed in your office...and there is graffiti everywhere."

It takes me a moment to realize he's telling me the shelter was vandalized. My stomach knots at the notion he was in my space—in a space that is supposed to help women from the likes of him.

"Aria?" He comes from behind me and wraps his arms around me, his hands flat on my belly. The baby kicks at the contact, and I feel his lips stretch into a smile in my hair. "It's going to be okay..."

"You keep saying that but still, he hasn't been caught."

"I know."

"How can you tell me it's going to be okay when he's *still* dismantling my life?" I turn around, wildly in his arms, my stupid, traitorous tears escape my eyes. "I *told* you he wouldn't stop until I was dead."

"But you're *not* dead. I'm telling you he's going to have to get through me to get to you."

"I didn't want to get anyone involved." I sound like a spoiled child. I should be grateful he's willing to put his life on the line for me, but I can't help but be angry at him for putting his life on the line when he has Zoey to worry about.

"Baby, we got involved because *we* wanted to." He kisses my forehead, even as I pull away from him. "We're trained for this—"

"Then why hasn't he been caught yet?" The words fly out of my mouth before I can stop them. I don't miss the fury raging in his eyes. He's trying. I know that. But I want to go to bed one time without worry that Charlie's watching me.

"These things take time," he says through gritted teeth.

"It's been months!"

God, why can't I shut up? This is an out of body experience. It's like I'm watching somebody else yell at him.

"We've torn the town apart, Aria. We've looked in abandoned buildings, we've scoured the property on *both* sides of the road. We've extended our search to surrounding towns. But you want to know what he hasn't done yet?" He spits poisonously, "He hasn't put his hands on you."

My heart stills in my chest.

"One of us is with you whether you like it or not, and let's not forget you *don't* like it, but he hasn't once approached you or tried to steal you away."

He's right. He hasn't. But…the pictures still get delivered. My office still receives visits from him when I'm not there…

"You're upset and I get it, but I'm doing everything I fucking can to keep you safe." He turns on his heel and storms towards the door. "Joey will be over in a minute. Stay put."

He slams the door behind him, leaving me with only the sound of sautéing vegetables over the otherwise deafening silence. I close my eyes in frustration and return to the stove, putting in the chicken until it's browned.

My phone rings with Annie's name emblazoned across my screen.

"I already talked to your boy toy," I tease darkly.

"Buttercup."

My blood runs cold. Fear holds me in a death grip, threatening to take me out once and for all.

"Where's Annie?"

"Funny thing about that. I've learned a thing or two from that techie you've got working for you. Novak. He's a bright one."

I swallow the screams.

"Anyway, I'm around. Not around Annie, of course, but you, I could never leave *you*."

"Charlie—"

"No, you're going to listen," he hisses. "I'm outside of Sage Creek Elementary watching a certain fifth grader playing outside on the monkey bars. So sweet. So perfect. What a *beautiful* smile—"

"Leave her alone! She has nothing to do with this!"

Charlie's dark chuckles make my insides cringe.

"She has *everything* to do with this. As does your doctor friend."

Shoot me now.

"This is what's going to happen, Buttercup. You're going to meet me at midnight, at that god forsaken shelter you've opened and then you and I are leaving."

"They found the bodies, Charlie. Even if I recant my statements, they've still got you on murder charges."

"I never said we were going home. No, see, I have a nice little dinner set up for us. You'll deliver the child, I'll give the Hawthorn girl back, and then you and I are going to find a nice little cabin in the middle of nowhere to pick up where we left off."

"And if I don't come with you?"

"Then, I will come into that house, steal the girl, and kill her in front of the both of you."

Derek doesn't deserve this.

"The games are over, Buttercup. You *are* mine. 'til death do us part."

We're not even married!

"You realize I'm being watched? More than Derek? I have a whole house of men looking after me."

"And I have contacts in the FBI jumping at the chance to arrest them for interfering with a criminal investigation. All of them will be arrested, including your precious Agent Olson. He's giving away company secrets."

I close my eyes in frustration.

"Fine."

He laughs, unhinged.

"Good. I'm glad you came to your senses. Father will be so happy to see you."

Little does he know he's arrested.

DINNER WAS PAINFULLY SILENT. Derek ate in the kitchen while Zoey and I ate at the table. I think she probably knows something is up, but I don't have the heart to tell her I'm leaving.

After Zoey showers, she begs me to listen to her read a few pages before bed. I agree, only because I know this is the last time I'll ever see her again. She cracks open the fifth *Heartland* book and reads flawlessly.

Her voice is so happy, and she reads with such wonder. She tells me all the techniques they use in the book on the horses that live here. I say let her. Let her be young and learn from my mistakes.

"You think you could help me with training?" she asks enthusiastically.

No. But Annie can.

I smile, giving her that encouragement. "Absolutely."

She grins and closes the book and sets it on her nightstand.

"I'm happy you and my dad are together. He needed happiness."

"You make him happy," I remind her.

She rolls her head and scoffs. "Yeah, but I'm his kid. You're his girlfriend. That type of love is different." She yawns and covers herself with the blanket.

I push her beautiful chestnut hair out of her eyes and smile. Such a beautiful girl, with a beautiful spirit. I'm going to miss her so much.

"Hey, Zo? Can you promise me something?"

"Sure..."

"Learn forgiveness, okay? It's one of those things that will set you free from everything in life."

She gives me a quizzical look and nods.

"I love you, kiddo." *So, so much.*

I kiss her forehead and reach for her light.

42

DEREK

She exits Zoey's room and wipes the tears from her eyes. She's going to fucking leave, because of a stupid misunderstanding from earlier. Well here's the deal. It's not going down like that.

"Don't do it, Ace."

She glances up at me in surprise and freezes.

"He isn't worth your life, I promise you that."

Her hand stays on the doorknob, ready to disappear and lock me out for good. "Derek…I *have* to."

"No, Aria, you don't!" My voice raises without meaning to. But I'm losing control on the situation and she's ready to bolt without even saying goodbye. "I love you."

There. I said it. And I'm not sorry for it either.

She stares at me in disbelief, like I shattered her world. Tears fill her eyes, and she buries her face in her hands.

"No, you don't. You can't!"

"Of course I do. I've been dying to tell you for weeks. I love you Aria McKenzie. I want to marry you one day and raise this dysfunctional family with you. But I can't do that if you leave!"

"We said no attachments," she whimpers.

I want this to be hard for her because she's not fucking leaving!

"I'm attached. I'm not sorry for it." She doesn't say anything, and it cuts me to my core. Did I misread the situation? Does she not love me back?

"Come to bed with me. Please. I'm begging you not to leave, Ace. I love you and I need you in my life." Bravely, I step closer to her, closing the distance between us. My hands find her belly. The baby kicks in reply and a smile spreads across my face. "This is *our* kid. I'm not going to let the both of you walk out of our life. Not when we're going to be the happiest fucking family that inhabits the earth."

She sobs against my chest.

"I love you," I whisper to her. Because the more I say it, the more she's inclined to stay. I love her. I love Aria McKenzie as much as I love my next breath.

"Okay. I'll stay," she whimpers.

I tilt her head up so we're staring eye to eye. Her watery hazel eyes are the most beautiful sight I've ever seen. I slam my lips into hers and she loops her arms around my neck, her fingers tangling into my hair.

I kiss her lips, her neck, her chest. Each kiss claiming her, forcing her to stay with us. I lead her to the bedroom and gently lie her down. I'm claiming every inch of her tonight and reminding her why she can't walk away.

43

ARIA

38 weeks pregnant...

IT'S when I hear Derek's deep and loud snores I know I'm in the clear. I'm up several times a night to use the bathroom, so getting out of bed to change in the bathroom isn't going to be a big deal. The bigger deal is sneaking out of the house and not having one of the guys find out.

Once I'm dressed, I tip toe to the door and briefly glace over my shoulder. He holds my pillow close to him. His tanned skin calls to me, begging me to come back to bed. I wish I could, but I'm bringing too much trouble here. I'm not worth it.

Please forgive me.

I turn off the alarm and cringe when the chimes are so fucking loud. I pray he doesn't wake up.

I sneak out the front door and watch my house for a beat while I figure out the best course of action. All the lights are out, save for the glow of Tanner's ten thousand computers. If he's watching, he'll sound the alarm faster than I can say "Albuquerque."

I walk slowly at first. My car is in Annie's driveway, and I know there's a key in the wheel well. If I run, the floodlights will catch me and give me away.

So, I shuffle.

When I get to the car, I keep the lights off until I hit the country road taking me to town. I take my sweet time, taking in every detail this dumb place has to offer me. I say a silent goodbye to my parents, my brother, the boys, Derek and Zoey, and the horses. I doubt I'll get another chance at the FBI saving my hide, but I did it before, and I can do it again.

Right on cue, my phone is blowing up. I turn it off for good measure, not wanting Tanner to be able to trace me. How fitting it is to be kidnapped by my abusive ex-boyfriend at the shelter I where I work to protect women coming out of abusive relationships?

Jo's going to be so upset.

Everyone will. But it's for their own good. They don't need the wrath of the Dodges.

When I reach the shelter, there isn't anyone in the parking lot. I quickly turn on my phone to get a glimpse of everyone who is trying to get a hold of me.

Daddy called and left four voicemails.

Derek *keeps* calling, leaving voicemails.

And Nate.

I shakily touch Nate's name and bring the phone to my ear.

"Holy shit, Aria! Where the fuck are you?" he shouts in my ear.

"Listen to me, okay? He was threatening to take Zoey, so I did what I had to do—"

"Aria, wherever you are, turn around. Come home. Zoey's here and she's—"

His voice cuts out when I hear Derek shouting Zoey's name.

"Nate? What's going on?"

Movement to my left catches my eye, and suddenly, I see Charlie grabbing Zoey by her hair and pushing her forward as Emily's car whips into the parking lot.

"She's here. With Charlie. Emily's here too. She just pulled in."

That son of a bitch! He lied to me!

I'm not even sure what Emily has to do with this. She looks too damn casual. That content, yet arrogant smirk she wears sends all my warning lights flashing.

"I'm sorry I got your family into this, Nate. Please tell them all I'm sorry. I'll fix this. I promise."

"No, Aria wait—"

It's too late. I end the call and race inside. I start searching the empty offices, the damage from his last visit is still proof he was here not that long ago. The auxiliary building is all lit up. The building is eerie this late at night. Tanner will be able to tap into the feeds to see where I am, and hopefully they can get the police, or any noncorrupted agents in the FBI to take him out. Maybe they'll find me in time to save my life. I'm not holding my breath.

I race in and find Zoey on the ground, crying hysterically. I sprint over to her and pull her into my lap, embracing her. Emily stands in the corner, stony; her judgmental eyes watching me like a hawk.

"I'm sorry Zo," I tell her quietly. "I'm so, so sorry."

Zoey cries hysterically and I barely can make out what she's saying.

"Up, Buttercup," he demands, pointing up with his index finger.

Protectively, I set Zoey down and stand up. This is the first time I've seen Charlie since the day I left. This is a man I don't recognize. Always so clean shaven and slick, now it's like I'm looking at a mountain man who hasn't showered in months. He's feral, and the wild look in his eyes tells me we've already passed dangerous. We're crossing the territory into lethal.

"You said if I came you'd leave her alone."

"I lied."

Fuck.

"I had to make sure you came one way or another. Your friend here tells me she's fighting for custody, is that right?" He asks, turning to Emily.

Emily nods and approaches me. I shield Zoey with my body, though it's no use. Charlie's hand fists my hair, yanking me out of the way. My scream is muffled and pained. My stomach twists painfully when Emily yanks Zoey's arm so she's standing.

"Don't do this, Emily. You'll break his heart," I plead. "You'll break *hers.*"

She shrugs nonchalantly.

"I'm not going through months of red tape when I already know what the outcome will be." She turns to Zoey and grins. "He's not a part of our life now, babe. It's just you and me from here on out."

"I don't want that!" Zoey screams through gritted teeth.

"All you had to do, Buttercup, was follow the rules. Now look who you've brought into all this. You sold my secrets like it didn't affect you."

"They don't affect me, Charlie. They affect *you.* I wanted to go home, and you wouldn't let me!"

"Do you honestly think that man loves you? Look at you!" he roars. "What man in his right mind would want you? Maybe you're a good lay, but that's about it. There's nothing remotely interesting about you!"

The last year slaps me in the face like a tsunami. All of his abuse, all of his negativity settles into the nooks and crannies of my brain, reminding me of all the anguish that settles deep in my bones. All the hard truths.

"All of those men in that house take out people like me," he spits. "Johnathan Rockwell, remember him?"

I do. The creep who cornered me in a bathroom and felt me up. The man who was later found to be a major player in a human trafficking ring. Good. I'm glad they took him out.

Zoey lets out a whimpers from Emily's tight grip. Charlie glares at her and shouts at her to shut up, spittle flying from his mouth.

"Charlie, she's a little girl. Look at her. She's terrified. She doesn't have to be here. I'll leave with you. I promise."

He chuckles and shakes his head.

"No, darling. Sweet Emily here is going to be taking Zoey away. Turns out it was easy getting your attention. Emily showed me how."

I close my eyes, tears leaking out. I pray to any god who has heart. I'd willingly give up my life it meant Zoey got to live hers with her father.

"Let me talk to her, please? She'll cry all night if I don't talk to her."

"Absolutely not. The time for games is over. Emily, kindly get your bitch and get the fuck out."

"I did what I had to do," she warns me. Zoey's tears are what do me in.

She's angry. She's passionate. And it's against her mother who leans heavily on her prejudices.

Derek's pained face flits in my watery vision. This will kill him. He'll lose both of us and it's all my fault.

I watch helplessly as she drags Zoey along and leaves through the back door. A pained sob escapes me when the realization comes along that paralyzes me and brings me to my knees. I'll never see her again. She shouts my name, begging me to help her. And I *want to.* I want to, so damn badly.

44

ZOEY

When I was little and my parents were still married, I used to stay up and listen to them fight. Sometimes they would fight about me, most of the time, they'd fight about absolutely nothing. But when I listen to Miss Aria and Dad fight, something is different.

Dad begs her to stay.

That never happened with mom. Most times, he'd beg her to leave and never come back.

He promises to protect her, to watch over and be a family with us. But *why* is she crying so hard? Why doesn't she want to stay with us?

On my nightstand, my phone lights up with mom's name. I don't want to talk to her. All she'll do is ask me to tell her about Miss Aria and I *don't* want to do that. I have no interest in being my mother's spy.

I flip the flashlight on my phone and pull out my tattered copy of *The Chronicles of Narnia* and pick up where I left off.

The loud voices have lessened, and moments ago, their bedroom door closed, and their bed creaked as I'm sure, sleep took them.

My hands and fingers tingle while I listen to the quiet air around me. This farm is the picture of peace. Nothing happens here. And when something *does,* it's taken care of immediately. I have nothing to worry about—not with my dad and uncles around.

My eyes start drooping two hours later. I dogear my page and set the book on my nightstand. The alarm is disabled, and the front door opens.

My dad is a smoker. He tries to hide it when I'm around, but he doesn't think I know he sneaks off to smoke behind the house.

The front door opens and shuts again, and different footsteps pad across the hardwood floors. The doorknob jiggles and the door swings open. The hairs on the back of my neck stick straight up. I draw the covers up to my chin, until the moonlight illuminates a face I've never seen before.

I open my mouth to scream, but his hand claps over my mouth.

"Keep your mouth shut," he hisses. "I will kill you and your father; do you understand me?"

I nod quickly.

The moon illuminates a sliver of his appearance. He has long, and greasy blonde hair. High cheekbones that boast of royalty, and blue eyes that promise pain if I don't listen.

And…he's *dirty.* Like he hasn't taken a shower in months. The stench of body odor and stale breath fills my room.

He yanks me out of bed and shoves me forward. It won't take long for my uncles to figure out what's going on. It's the only reason I'm not panicking. But my heart races in my chest as I try to come up with some sort of exit plan.

I'm thrown into the back seat of a four-door car. He jumps into the front seat and speeds off the property.

"Panicking is more dangerous than anything you'll ever encounter," Dad's voice rings in my ear.

My jaw tingles with pins and needles and tears blur my vision.

What are five things you can see?

It's my dad's voice in my head, helping me find my footing even though he's not here.

"The road, the headlights, the trees, the seats, the man in front."

"Shut up!" the man shouts loud enough to make my ears ring.

What are four things you can touch?

"The seats, my sweatpants, my face, the door handle..."

Suddenly, my eyes dart to the door handle. I move to grasp it, then the *thwump* of the locks shatter that illusion.

"You're not getting out of this," he snaps. "Stay quiet. Stop talking. Stop trying to escape."

I swallow the lump of tears and lean my head back.

What are three things you can hear?

"The gravel crunching underneath the tires, the man's breathing, the air conditioning."

The car comes to a screeching halt, launching me into the back of the passenger seat. My nose crunches and a little bit of blood trickles out.

"Last warning, kid. You say one more word and I will take you out of the car right now and end your life."

Tears once more fill my eyes, but I nod. If I listen, I might be able to get out of here alive.

What are two things you can smell?

I smell my blood, and the man.

I know I'm not really talking to my dad, but this is helping. When we get out of the car next, I can think of what I'll do.

What's one thing you can taste?

Blood trickling from my nose and into my mouth.

I rest my forehead against the cool glass of the window. Dad is coming for me. Uncle Nate will come for me.

Panicking is dangerous. Panicking gets us killed.

His phone rings and he answers it on speaker.

"Dodge," he answers harshly.

"What the *fuck* are you doing?" a woman shouts. "You had one job, and that was to take care of McKenzie."

"You have your prerogative, I have mine. The child is *mine* and I'm not leaving without it."

Does he mean me?

"Honestly, this is why you never give a man a job a woman can do better. How do you expect to get out of this, Dodge? Olson has already sounded the alarm with the FBI that she's missing."

"We had a deal," he hisses. "I'll take care of Aria, but I'm not leaving without my child. And *you're* going to ensure I get out of here alive."

The woman scoffs. "Don't fuck this up, Dodge. I don't need you as much as you need me. Kill Aria McKenzie and get out."

The line goes dead, and I meet his gaze through the rearview mirror.

"She wasn't going to be a good mother," he sneers.

He's wrong. Miss Aria may not be my *real* mom, but she's the best one I have.

We pull into the shelter and park. Aria's car is parked a few spots away. My door is yanked open, and Mr. Dodge grabs me by the hair at the crown of my head and pulls me out. I try to fight him off, but his grip is too tight.

Another set of headlights illuminate the parking lot and mom's car pulls in next to ours. He shoves me forward and punches in a password to the keypad on the wall next to the double doors. The doors demagnetize and he swings it open with mom following behind us.

The hallways are creepy this late at night. I've been here only once and that was with Dad and Miss Aria.

"Mom?" I ask shakily.

"Keep moving," he snaps.

"Listen to him, Zoey. We'll be out of this soon."

We head to the back of the building, where we'll find the annex building where the cafeteria is.

Mr. Dodge kicks open the doors to the cafeteria and forces me to the ground.

"Okay, I did what you asked. Give me my kid and let me go," Mom says shakily.

"Not yet. You did good. When Aria walks in here, you can leave."

"Mom, what are you doing?"

Mom's wild gaze focuses on me and she crosses her arms over her chest. "We're going to California."

"No!" I shout. "I'm not going with you!"

Mr. Dodge points his gun in my direction and smirks.

"Quiet! I've already told you too many times to shut the fuck up!"

I purse my lips shut and let the tears escape my eyes.

"Stop yelling at her!" Mom snaps.

"Listen here." His beefy hand wraps around mom's throat. She doesn't scream. She doesn't do anything except stare at him angrily. "I told you I'd get you custody of your kid and I did that. You let me live in your basement, and I'm grateful, but make no mistake, if you so much as defy me *one more time,* I will end your and your child's life right here right now. You're of no use to me anymore."

Mom swallows.

Is this her boyfriend? The one in California we were to move in with?

I keep my mouth shut. It's the only way I'm going to survive.

But when Miss Aria walks through the doors and rushes over to me, I can't stop crying.

She came for me.

"I'm sorry, Zo. I'm so, so sorry." She hugs me tight.

"Don't let her take me!" I plead, but it comes out a jumbled mess.

"Up, Buttercup," Mr. Dodge demands.

Miss Aria gets up with a purpose, standing in front of me for my own protection.

"You said if I came, you'd leave her alone."

He was watching me?

"I lied," he replies simply, his evil smirk making my stomach churn like I'm going to puke. "I had to make sure you came one way or another. Your friend here tells me she's fighting for sole custody, is that right?" he asks mom.

Mom approaches us, but Miss Aria stands her ground. She won't let me leave without a fight.

Mr. Dodge storms towards us and fists her hair in his hand, yanking her out of the way. Mom grasps my arm tightly and forces me to stand up. I wince in pain and cry for Miss Aria.

"Don't do this, Emily. You'll break his heart. You'll break *hers."*

"I'm not going through months of red tape when I already know what the outcome will be." Mom turns to me and smiles creepily. Evilly, like Mr. Dodge. "He's not a part of our life now, babe. It's just you and me from here on out."

"I don't want that!" When is she going to understand I don't want to be with her? Does she even care?

"All you had to do, Buttercup, was follow the rules. Now look who you've brought into this. You sold my secrets like they didn't affect you."

"They don't affect me, Charlie. They affect *you*. I wanted to go home, and you wouldn't let me!"

I fight mom's hold as they argue. Mom's hand smack's my butt and I whimper. Miss Aria begs to talk to me, but Mr. Dodge refuses.

This is it. I'm never going to see her again. I'm never going to see Dad or Uncle Nate ever again. My sob brings everyone's attention to me.

"Emily, kindly get your bitch and get the fuck out."

Mom pushes me forward. "I did what I had to do," she says softly to Miss Aria before we're leaving through the double doors.

When we get outside, I squirm until mom grabs me by the shoulders just outside our car. She crouches down so we're eye to eye.

"Zoey, that's enough."

"I don't *care!*" I scream.

She smacks me across the face and my cheek heats from the sting of her hand.

"Your name is Caitlyn now. Got it? We're going to be happy in California. We're going to live our life." She wrenches the back door open and pushes me inside.

She hops into the driver's seat and locks the doors. Dad's truck passes us, but they don't see us. I sob and pray he knows I love him. That I didn't do this on purpose.

Mom makes a phone call, and from the screen of the radio, I only see the name as Banks.

"Don't call me from your cell phone!" the female voice hisses.

I remember this voice. It's from Mr. Dodge's car!

"You owe me. He's unhinged, got it? I've held up my end of the deal. He has Aria."

With a sigh, the woman groans in frustration. "You are to meet me at the *Gas-n-Go* in Kingsport, Tennessee. I'll get you your cash and then you disappear forever. If you so much as call me again, I will sell your sorry self to my buyers."

Mom says something else that's too low for me to make out.

If we're meeting at a gas station, maybe I can sneak off. Maybe she'll be too distracted she won't even notice me get out of the car.

Panicking is more dangerous than anything you might encounter...

Keep quiet. Keep my head down. Get to safety.

That's always been the golden rule.

45

DEREK

I'm going to be fucking sick. My girlfriend and my daughter are gone in the same night while I slept in my bed. Why wasn't I alerted? Why didn't I stay up and make sure she wouldn't try to pull the wool over my eyes?

Nate calls in his other agents. It'll take forever for them to get here, and I'm not fucking risking it. I arm myself with a Glock and race to my truck, Tanner and Joey hot on my tail.

"Breathe, Bubba. You're no good to them dead," Joey instructs.

We're armed with our radios. Nate's voice comes over the airwaves, yelling at us to stay put. Absolutely fucking not. I'm getting my girls and I'm bringing them home.

"How the fuck did he get Zoey?" I demand.

"I don't know," Tanner mutters, working furiously on his laptop, trying to pull up the footage. "He got to Zoey after Aria left. How did the alarm not sound? Unless Aria didn't arm the system back up…"

I. Don't. Know!

I press the gas pedal all the way down. If I garner police attention, I don't fucking care. As long as we get as many people to surround the building so he can't escape. And then I'm going to kill him personally.

When we get into town, I can barely keep my cool. Tanner instructs she's at the Shelter. As long as she's in town, I can help her. I turn on to Western, and park like an asshole, taking at least three spots.

"Hawthorn!" Nate's voice screams over the radio.

"Bubba, you can't go after Emily. She's aided and abetted a known felon. We'll find her. Come back home," Logan pleads.

Police lights scream behind us and Joey takes the walkie out of my grasp.

"All hands on deck," Delgado announces quietly. "We're tracking the GPS on Emily's car. I'll personally go after her."

It's at this moment I realize I'm leaving the fate of my daughter in my brother's hands.

"Acknowledge," Delgado demands.

"Bubba," Joey says gently.

"Zoey's kidnapped and I'm not going after her."

"Emily's the FBI's problem right now. She kidnapped her while aiding Dodge. She's not getting out of that. You trust Henry. Henry will take care of her," Joey assures me.

My anger leeches through my fingers to the point where I feel my pulse pounding in my ears. I'm stuck in between a rock and a hard place. I can't be in two places at once. If I stay here for Aria, I risk losing Zoey forever. If I leave Aria, I'll sure as hell get Zoey back, but it'll be short lived because I would choke the life out of her mother.

"Listen to me," Logan's voice appears on the walkie. "I know what you're thinking. If you go after Zoey, you know you won't get her back." He knows me too well. He doesn't have to be in this truck with me to know my fists are clenching and murderous thoughts of my ex-wife are racing through my head.

In a fit of rage, I shout and bang the steering wheel repeatedly, and then the radio, cracking the LCD screen. Tanner and Joey watch on with hard exteriors. Gone are the brothers. Here are the Marines. Somebody has to be the tough one—and right now, it's not me.

"Henry," I bark hoarsely into the radio.

"I'm here, Bubba. Talk to me."

"You get my girl, okay? You make sure she's okay." I swallow the lump in my throat while tears escape my eyes. *I hope Zo will forgive me.* "You get Emily and lock her up for the rest of her life, you hear me?"

"I'll get our girl, Bubba. I promise. I'll keep you in the loop."

I'm grateful, truly I am. If it was anyone else, I don't know what I would've done.

The tap of the butt of a flashlight knocks on my window. Chief Parker glares at me and shouts to get out of the car.

As I do that, more vehicles with blue and red lights scream into the parking lot. Nate's the first one out, barking orders at everyone. Logan stays on his tail while the perimeter is set. When Nate's eyes settle on me, he races forward and glares intently at Chief Parker, showing his FBI ID.

"I need everyone you got, Chief. I need people on the roof. I need people at every window—"

"Agent Olson, I don't know what you think you're doing—"

"The man in that building is on the FBI's most wanted list. He escaped FBI custody and has my star witness hostage inside. Chief, you can have all the credit if that's what gets you off, but I'm *telling* you, if Aria McKenzie isn't brought out of that building alive, I will personally tear this town apart."

Chief Parker stares at Nate dumbfounded.

"So again," Nate seethes, "I need every exit of that godforsaken building covered. I need men at every window. I need men on the roof. And for fuck's sake, I need a laptop with internet connection and a way to get a hold of Dodge inside."

Chief Parker flounders for a moment, trying to decide which is his best option. He turns around and starts barking out orders to his men while Nate quietly sets up camp near my truck.

46

ARIA

Bright lights are shown in through the windows. A helicopter roars overhead and Charlie paces the length of the cafeteria as he figures out his next move. I'm not allowed to move. My stomach tightens and I try to breathe, just like I saw in the movies.

"Charlie," I plead with whatever energy I have left. "The whole place is surrounded. Am I worth risking your life for?"

He laughs maniacally. This is it. He's cracked.

"Do you honestly think it's you I'm here for?"

Please God, help me!

"No, Buttercup, I'm here for the child inside of you. *My* child."

"What are you going to do then? How do you think you're going to get out of this alive?"

"Not that you'll ever understand this, but when you're a man of my stature, you have friends in high places. I'll get out of here; I promise you that."

Fuck. Fuck. Fuck.

My breath hitches in my throat as the band of contractions start again. It feels like a rusty hook being dragged horizontally across my belly. So far, they're only five minutes apart. I know I don't have a ton of time.

Please don't come yet, baby.

The kitchen phone trills which grabs Charlie's attention.

"If you move, I will make sure you are wide fucking awake when I carve the child out of you."

I'm sorry, Derek. I'm so, so sorry.

"Agent Olson, what a pleasure to finally meet you," his slimy voice raises so I hear every word. I meet his gaze and nearly hurl when his lips curve into a smirk. He's enjoying every minute of my torture and knowing Nate is outside has me relieved and terrified all at the same time.

"No, you won't get to talk to her. She's perfectly fine. In fact, she was just telling me how excited she is to come back home."

I roll my eyes and lean back in the seat.

I wish I would've brought *anything* with me. A long line of shoestring, Annie's gun, a piece of string and a paperclip.

The rusty hook is back again, just a minute early. The groan escapes me before I can shut my mouth. Charlie hangs up the phone and storms over to me.

"Why are you making that god awful noise?" he demands.

"*Well,* labor isn't a walk in the park, Char—*oooohhhh!*"

I want to puke. I want to rip my uterus and throw it on the ground. Throat punching Charlie would make me feel a little better. But I can read the room.

He watches me dumbfounded. What I wouldn't give for a fucking epidural right now.

"I need to walk," I demand. I don't wait for permission. I hoist myself out of the seat, his hand clapping down on my shoulder.

"No. You're going to *sit.*" My ass sings when it meets the hardness of the chair. "Don't think I don't know what you're doing. This ends tonight, Buttercup. And the kid is coming with me."

Over. My. Dead. Body!

He walks away, pacing again.

"Hey, McKenzie," Tanner's voice echoes throughout the cafeteria. A watery laugh escapes me. I'm going to haunt him for doing this under my nose. But for now, I'm elated to hear his voice.

"Tanner?"

"Shut your god damned mouth!" Charlie shouts, barreling over to me and slapping me across the face. My head reels from the contact and my cheek sings in anger.

"Charlie, this is Agent Olson. You hung up on me before we could negotiate."

"Save it Olson. You don't have anything I want. I have everything I need," Charlie spits.

"Okay. You have everything you need. What about Aria? How is she doing?"

Horrible!

"Stop asking about my fiancé!"

The silence is deafening.

"Ace?" Derek's voice appears next.

The floodgates are open now. I'm in so much fucking pain and the only person I want right now is stuck on the other side of the building.

"Derek!" I cry.

"Talk to me, Ace. How are you doing?"

"I said *stop asking about my fiancé!"* Charlie bellows so close to my ears I'm sure I'm going deaf.

"Charlie, calm down please," I beg. Before he even has the chance to hit me again, I'm knocked to the ground from a contraction. This one is so painful my screams echo into the hallways.

"You fucking pissed yourself!" Charlie shouts.

Oh, *fuck!*

"My water broke. It's not piss." Tears prick my eyes. It's happening. The baby is coming, and Charlie is going to take him away.

47

DEREK

"Put me the fuck in, Olson," I demand, grabbing one of the bullet proof vests and throwing it over my head.

"You can't go in there, Hawthorn, you're a civilian." He looks over to Chief Parker. "Where are the paramedics?" Nate asks. I already know. Fucking Parker didn't call them.

"*Nate,*" I hiss when Parker flounders.

"Um...Tillerson!" Chief shouts. "Call the ambulance!"

"This isn't even a fucking conversation anymore, Olson! I'm the only one here who is qualified to deliver that baby!"

"You *can't,*" he shouts. "There are protocols—"

"That is my *life* in there!" I'm losing control, my edge. I feel like everyone is staring at me. But I don't care. I told her we would get him. I told her she wouldn't have to do this alone. I'm not letting fucking Charlie Dodge make me a liar. "That is *my* son, Olson! Give me a gun, or don't. I don't fucking care. I'm going in there to help her."

I storm off while Nate talks over the intercom to Charlie. The whole place is locked all the way down. But I have a feeling Tanner can disable the magnetic lock in Aria's office so I can slip in.

"Think about this, Bubba," Joey warns, following me all the way to the truck. I grab my vet bag from the passenger seat and grip it tight. I walk to the back of the truck and pull out a sterile, wrapped, surgical kit.

"I've never thought clearer in my life," I snap. I turn to Tanner who is already working his magic on the laptop. "Talk to me, Novak."

"I'm working on it. Hold on."

Nate storms over this way, hand on his gun. Fucking kill me, prick. I dare you.

"You're not going in alone." He narrows his eyes at me. We're still brothers. He'll still watch my six and be my ride or die.

"Who's going to stick around for negotiations?" Tanner asks.

"Parker's got it for now, not that it matters. Dodge isn't cooperating. He has something else up his sleeve, I don't know what it is or how he'll access it."

I nod. "Let's go."

We approach the side of the building and wait for Tanner's okay. The magnetic lock of the window clicks and I slide it up with no hesitation. *That's going to change.* When this is all over, I'll nail these windows shut myself.

I know exactly where I'm going, and I know he's going to fire a shot the second he sees movement. Nate takes the lead, gun at the ready and clearing the hallway. My Glock feels like a hundred pounds in my hand while we slink down the hallway. My whole life is being ripped at the seams and I swear, my head spins along with it.

We enter the hallway before the cafeteria slowly and quietly. The double doors are cracked. Aria lies on the floor, resting herself on her forearms while her heavy breathing echoes.

"Charlie, this is Agent Olson," Nate announces as we enter the cafeteria.

Charlie whirls around in surprise, aiming the gun at Aria. My heart catches in my throat and I pray to whoever's out there to spare her.

"Get out of here, Olson," Charlie growls.

"Don't hurt her," I plead. I hold up my bag, showing him I come in peace. *Sort of.* "She's in active labor, Charlie. If you want the child, she's going to need help. Let me help her."

"Drop the gun," he demands.

Fine. I'll do it as long as he'll let me be near her. I drop the gun and kick it towards him. He picks it up and motions for me to come closer.

"You too, Olson."

"Charlie, I can't do that. My job is to protect both of these people."

He shrugs carelessly and they argue as I crouch down to Aria. Her eyes swim with tears. Pain is etched into her rosy cheeks. Charlie and Nate argue. I tune it out so I can focus on Aria.

"I'm so sorry," she whispers.

"I know. It's okay, baby. I know what you were trying to do." *Even though I don't like it.* I push her night gown up and start pulling her panties down when she stops me.

"I love you too. I do and I'm sorry I didn't tell you sooner."

A laugh escapes me, and I yearn to smash my lips to hers, the situation doesn't allow me to.

"I need to look, Ace. Breathe."

I snap on gloves and reach into her, checking her cervix. She's fully dilated, but the thing that scares the shit out of me is I don't touch the baby's head.

"Shit," I curse, reaching for my radio. "Whoever's listening, I need you to get a hold of Dr. Erin Cash. Tell her Aria's baby is breech and I need her to walk me through it."

"What?" Aria whimpers.

"I touched his foot," I tell her. I glance back to Nate who is watching Dodge watch me. "This is serious. I need clean towels, linens, whatever you can get me."

Charlie scoffs.

"Do you honestly think I'm going to be the one who leaves for a second? Deliver the child and then you can be on your way. You're not a part of her life anymore."

I glance to Nate and grimace.

"The baby is going to need to be cleaned up. You want to transport the kid? He needs to be cleaned up."

"Deliver the child, Hawthorn. Then you can be on your way," he replies through gritted teeth.

Improvise.

It's Joey's voice in my head. I'm transported back to Afghanistan and I'm plugging up Delgado's bullet wound and I'm out of gauze.

Improvise. We want to get out of here alive, Hawthorn. You're capable.

I undo the Velcro on the vest and pull my shirt over my head and drape Aria's torso with it. Nate curses when the vest hits the ground.

"One of you come over here. I can't place my tools on the ground. They're sterile. Get gloves on because we need to do this as quickly as possible."

Aria sobs, and Nate crosses, reluctantly putting his gun down so he can assist.

"Hawthorn?" Dr. Cash's voice comes over the intercom.

"It's a breech baby, Cash. I need your guidance."

"How's she doing? Is she in distress?"

"Yes, but she's working through it. What am I doing first?"

"When she pushes on the next contraction, you're going to deliver whatever is presenting. Can you tell me if it's the bottom or the feet?"

I push her dress up and completely remove the panties. Two little feet poke out.

"Feet."

"Okay, it's important you don't pull on the baby. Guide it out while she pushes."

I glance up to Aria.

"You're doing great, baby. It's going to be okay. I need you to push, okay?"

"It hurts," she wails.

"I know. Once you get him out it'll be all over, okay?"

"Don't let him take my baby," she wails. "Derek, promise me you won't let him take my baby."

Charlie watches on with a twisted smirk.

Over my dead body, bitch.

"I promise. Deep breath. And push!"

The legs and feet are out and Nate finishes the count down, giving Aria a breather.

"Legs and feet are out," I announce.

"Okay, good. You want the baby's back facing up, okay? It'll make the birth easier."

"All right, babe. Give me a big push."

"Ten, nine, eight..."

The baby stops as does my heart. I glance up to Aria flat on the ground.

"Aria? Are you with me?"

"It hurts so bad," she sobs.

"I know, baby. But you're doing so great. He's almost out, I promise."

"Come on McKenzie, don't let the team down," Nate coaches, holding her hand.

She lifts herself onto her forearms, her eyes red and puffy.

"Push for me, Ace. Let's meet our son."

With one deep breath, she pushes. The tiny torso births, marking the floor with Aria's guts.

"When you get to the shoulder blades, you're going to need to sweep one arm out at a time. You're going to need to rotate the baby to sweep the other arm out." Cash's voice echoes into the cafeteria.

I have to tune everything out. Nate's coaching, Charlie's threats, Aria's pained screams.

You've birthed tons of horses. You've got this.

I stick my finger inside of her to sweep the arm out, and she screams in pain. I mutter a thousand apologies as I rotate the little guy and do the same for the other arm.

The pushing stops again. She's exhausted and spent. The pain is taking everything out of her to the point where screaming is too much energy.

"Baby, he's almost out. It's just his head that's left. One more push for me?"

"I can't," she whimpers. "I can't. He's going to take him away."

"Aria? It's Doctor Cash. You're doing great. You need to deliver the baby, sweetheart. You're almost done. This part is important."

Charlie crosses the room impatiently and crouches near her head, fisting her hair and yanking her head up so she's looking at him.

"Hey!" Nate shouts, but it goes ignored.

"Deliver the child, Buttercup. Or this will be the last you see of *anyone.*"

48

ARIA

Every part of my body is on fire. My hair, from Charlie yanking it. My lower half is like blinding pain. Derek watches me hopefully and Nate is ready to pounce and take Charlie out. Except Nate's service gun is lying on the floor close to me so he can assist Derek.

"This is the last bit, Ace. The pain will be over as soon as he's out."

Please God, be with them. Please don't let Charlie take my family.

"Hawthorn, you're going to flex the head down, got it?"

He mumbles a muffled yeah. I take a deep breath and push. I want him out. I don't want to be pregnant anymore. I want the baby to be okay.

Nate coaches while counting down, gripping my hand tight.

"Hi, buddy," Derek greets with an exasperated laugh. "I'm so happy to see you. Bulb suction," he directs to Nate as he places my baby on my stomach after wrapping him in his shirt.

He suctions out his nose and mouth. He gently taps his bottom and the glorious sounds of his high pitched cries are music to my ears.

"Okay, now you're going to deliver the placenta. Aria, this won't hurt as much, but you need to do another big push," Dr. Cash instructs.

I bear down as Nate and Derek watch on with hushed amazement.

This would be humiliating if I actually gave a damn. But I'm holding my baby in my arms and I don't give a shit who sees what.

"Charlie, we need to get Aria to the hospital," Dr. Cash's voice rings out. Derek's eyes squeeze shut in frustration. We know what's coming next. It doesn't matter my insides are outside of my body. My job is done. He'll be gunning for me next.

"She's not going anywhere," he shouts, cocking the gun and holding it to my temple. "You can leave, Hawthorn. Your work is done."

"I'm not leaving her, Dodge." Derek stands up and squares his shoulders.

"How do you plan on leaving, Charlie? The whole building is surrounded. The rest of my team are on their way. You're surrounded by SCPD and they're not going to let you go quietly for terrorizing one of their citizens."

"That's because you're going to get me out of here. *With* the child."

The baby's cries get louder. I should try to nurse, but I'm afraid I'm not going to get the chance.

We're going to make it out of here, I promise. I swear on my life you will live a good life.

"The paramedics are here," Tanner's voice comes over the intercom.

The guys look to Charlie.

"We need to get the paramedics in here so they can cut the cord and deliver the rest of the placenta," Nate reasons, but it doesn't matter. Charlie doesn't give a shit.

"Nobody is leaving!" He shouts wildly. He crouches on the ground and grabs me by the hair again. "Buttercup, tell them you're ready to come home."

"Charlie, please. This is over. There's no way you can walk out of here —" his fist comes into contact with my gut where I swear I'm being set on fire.

Derek bounds to his feet and runs at full speed towards Charlie. Charlie aims the gun at Derek and pulls the trigger.

The baby and I scream together as the shot rings and echoes through the cafeteria. My eyes squeeze shut when I feel Nate move away from me.

"If you get the shot, take it!" Nate shouts to anyone.

Please God, end this now.

Derek and Nate are out of my line of vision, but I hear the thuds and grunts, the closed fists hitting flesh. There's nothing I can do. I'm stuck in this one spot with a life I've sworn to protect.

He's calmed down a little. His gray eyes meet mine and he stares at me, almost like he's looking into my soul.

I'll do anything for you. I promise.

Silent promises. I suppose now I know what Derek was talking about when Zoey came around. My heart plummets at the thought.

Zoey.

Where is she? Is she okay?

A body hits the floor. I don't know whose it is, but a glint next to me from the floodlights outside catches my attention.

Nate's gun.

If this makes my baby deaf, it'll be worth it. I'll learn sign language. I'll spend all the money on hearing aids. But this ends now.

My body screams as I use my legs to turn me to face the action. The umbilical cord is still attached to the baby and the placenta. I'm reminded of that when it pulls.

Derek's on the ground, his hand clutching at his gut and blood pouring out of the wound. Nate has kicked the gun out of Charlie's hand. I ready the shot, especially since he's not looking my way. How fucking ironic. He instilled fear and panic into me. He burned me, beat me, and took the essence of who I am. So now, I'm going to take *him* away.

Nate drops to the ground, giving me the perfect shot. I pull the trigger. The baby screams. I scream. And so does everyone else.

49

DEREK

My eyes fly open, but it's not the cafeteria ceiling I'm looking at. I turn my head and find Aria sitting next to my bed, nursing the baby. Her eyelids are heavy and purple bags have taken residence under her eyes. Her dark hair is tied into a messy bun and her skin is the color of Elmer's glue.

"Ace." My voice comes out raspy, reminding me I need to quit smoking.

"Hey," she greets sadly, those beautiful hazel eyes filling up with tears. "God, I was so afraid I lost you." She leans over, wincing, and kissing me on the cheek.

"I thought I lost *you.*"

She weakly smiles.

"I'm sorry, Derek. For everything. I was trying to spare Zoey—"

"Where is she?" I demand.

"She's in the cafeteria with Tanner and Joey. Your friend, Agent Delgado arrived about an hour ago with her. Emily's been arrested. So...I think it's safe to say you have full custody. Logan's talking with CPS now..."

My lungs expand for the first time in months. My bitch of an ex-wife *finally* got what was coming to her.

"Aria," I rasp. With one arm, she strokes my cheek. "I love you, do you know that?"

"I know," she murmurs. "I meant it when I said it. I love you too, Derek. Truly."

"What happened to Dodge?"

"I shot him."

I vaguely remember. I remember her reaching for the gun and aiming, but I passed out before I could see what happened.

"Is he dead?"

She nods, her eyes filling up with tears. "Yeah. He's dead. The FBI has already came and collected the body. Nate was seeing to it personally that he's going to the right people." For the first time ever, a genuine smile spreads across her lips and *peace* sets in her eyes, her face, her posture. "You're going to be okay," she assures me. "They said a bullet grazed you. This is just a flesh wound—burn. But it'll heal. Otherwise, there's nothing else wrong with you."

My gaze shifts to the bundle in her arms. I delivered our son. I held him in my arms for barely a minute and he's okay. Zoey's okay. Aria's okay. I take a deep, shaky breath.

"What did you name him?"

She shrugs. "I haven't named him anything yet. I honestly didn't think of names while I was pregnant. I didn't think I'd get this far." Her melancholy smile breaks my heart. She truly thought she wouldn't get to live her life. "Do you want to hold him?"

I nod eagerly and she gingerly places him in my arms.

She puts her boob away and reaches for her phone, snapping a picture of the two of us.

"I'm proud of you, Ace. You birthed him like a champ."

Her cheeks flush and she avoids my gaze. I study the little man in my arms. His nose is pert like Aria's. It's too early to see whose eyes he'll get, though I'm hoping he gets Aria's. Her eyes are magnetic and kind. He snoozes in my arms, suckling on a pacifier. It's been years since I've held a baby in my arms. I've missed this.

"I was thinking about Troy," she says softly.

"Troy, huh?"

She nods and grins. "Troy Alexander Hawthorn."

My eyes snap to hers. *And she said she wasn't thinking about names!*

"Seriously?"

"I mean…unless you aren't comfortable with it. I could—"

"I'm honored you want to name him after me."

She stills, tears flooding her eyes. "I know what we said back when I was pregnant. If you don't want to be his father, I understand. Especially after all the shit I put you and Zoey through…"

"Aria. I love you so much. I was hoping you'd want to share this baby with me. If yesterday taught me anything, it's that I can't imagine my life without you, nor do I want to. I love you. I love Troy. We're *all* going to be a happy family. As soon as I make it out of here, I'll make it official. I promise."

Delgado and Logan enter the room with a timid Zoey in tow. She looks around helplessly, and when she bravely lays her eyes on me, she bursts into tears and rushes over to me.

"Hi, babe," I whisper into her hair, kissing the crown of her head. She sobs into my chest.

"I'm so sorry, Zoey," Aria whimpers, joining in our hug.

"Why are you sorry? Mom kidnapped me, not you."

"How are you doing, Bubba?" Logan asks, approaching us slowly.

"I'm fine. When can I break out of here?"

"They're keeping you for observation. You might be able to go home tomorrow, but we'll see." He playfully nudges Zoey with his elbow and grins. "But there's something we need to talk about. All of us."

Henry and Logan grab a seat while Zoey stays cuddled up under my arm.

"What's going on?" I ask hesitantly. Am I losing Zoey?

"So, Em's going away for a while. She's facing charges for abduction which is up to five years since she crossed state lines. She also harbored, aided, and abetted a known felon. That's another five plus years," Logan explains.

"What does that mean?" I ask.

"It means you have full custody of Zoey for good. Even if she gets out on good behavior, there won't be a judge around who would grant that arrangement. Being that she housed Charlie for the entirety of his time here in Sage Creek, they might be talking more than ten years." He grins widely as Zoey bursts into happy tears.

"How did they even meet?" Aria asks.

"He created a profile on a dating site. He claimed he lived in California. The rest is history," Logan replies.

"Nate and I will escort you to her house so you can get the rest of your stuff, Zo," Henry adds. "We'll make your room pretty fit for a *princesa* like you. I promise I'll make the bookshelves myself."

Zoey's megawatt grin has everybody's spirits up.

"Zo, you want to meet your brother?" I ask, propping Troy up so she can get a good look at him. Her wonder-filled eyes brim with more unshed tears. I glance over to Aria who watches on with anxiety. I kiss her forehead. "We're a family now."

50

ARIA

Since I got into this room last night, doctors, nurses, FBI agents have been filing in and out. I've given my statement at least eight times. My arms have been pricked with needles, my boobs have been milked, and my parents have been a permanent fixture in my room. I've been promised Derek will get moved into this room, but at this rate, he'll probably be released before I do.

When visiting hours are over, Momma and Daddy leave with longing glances towards Troy. It's a weird shift in the dynamic. Charlie is officially out of my life. At some point, I'll have to face off with his father, which I'm *not* looking forward to whatsoever.

"How are you doing?" Nate's voice filters in from the door.

"Oh, I'm fine. What are you still doing here? You should head home and get some rest."

He grins sleepily and occupies the chair next to my bed.

"You shot and killed him, Aria. Are you sure you're okay?"

It's the million dollar question, isn't it? I was the one with the upper hand and I won. I'm stronger than I ever gave myself credit for. Charlie's gone. My son is healthy, though they're worried about his hearing.

"For the last year and a half, I made myself into whatever he wanted me to be. I lost myself to him, Nate. For too long, I've let him be the monster who haunts and tortures me." I meet his steely gaze and smile. "I took back what I lost. It's not all pristine and fixed. He still broke me. But I also ended the horrors he bestowed on this Earth. *I* did that. So yeah. I'm okay."

"I'm proud of you."

My heart pangs. I'm going to miss him. He's become a big brother to me, a confidant who keeps my secrets.

"Anyway, the case isn't over. We're going to indict all of his associates. Senior isn't getting out of jail, ever. You can count on that. But *you* can live your life now." He glances over to Troy and a melancholy smile replaces his good mood. "You're going to be so happy, Aria. With Derek. With Zoey. With Troy. You're our sister now, whether you like it or not."

I giggle and lean back on the bed.

"Can I give you my two cents since we're family now?"

He nods warily.

"Go back to Eve. Say you're sorry. Pour your heart out to her and be happy. You deserve happiness, Nate. I'm forever grateful what you did for me. You're a hero."

He drops his gaze.

"This job you do is important. It's honorable and you've saved so many lives. But she makes you happy. Do something for *you*."

EPILOGUE

Six months later...

WITH THE SHELTER opening and me working full time with Troy on my hip, I'm exhausted. But the good kind of exhausted. My bouncing baby boy is full of positive energy. He has the sweetest smile and flirts with all the women around him. He's a cuddle bug of the highest caliber, *and* his hearing is fine.

We moved into my house. It's better suited for a family and mine felt more like a home. It's weird not having all the guys here, but we stay in touch. Tanner especially. He gives me new ideas to annoy the hell out of Derek.

It's something that's ours now. When Derek comes home from work, we cook together. Zoey's room is bigger than the one she had at Emily's house, but Henry made good on his word and built a wall length bookcase to house all of her new books.

We've fallen into a nice routine. One that ends with me and Derek naked every night.

It's Saturday, my day to lounge on the couch while I nap when Troy does. Annie was sweet enough to take him out to run errands with her while Zoey and I do a spa day, just the two of us.

"Mom?" she asks softly.

That's right. I've been Mom since I got out of the hospital. When she figured out what Emily was doing, she turned off any loyalty she had toward her. She ran away from Emily at a gas station and into a police station which was ironically across the street. That's how Delgado found her.

I love the new title she gave me. I love the girl time we get to spend together. Most weekends, we lounge around or make trips to the bookstore in town and load up on whatever new releases they have. And she *loves* Troy. She's the greatest helper and he adores her right back.

"Yeah, babe?"

"I was thinking about going to dinner tonight."

I arch my eyebrow in surprise. Being out in public has been a challenge. The whispers have been a constant nuisance in our new life together. Derek's even taken some time off to be with us and let Sam run the clinic so he doesn't have to constantly be bombarded by questions and snide comments about leaving me.

"Oh? Where to?"

"Alyssa Aldridge was talking about that new fancy place in town. It's French and they have macrons."

Sold.

"We'd have to get dressed up with makeup and everything, but I thought it would be a fun thing to do since Auntie Annie has Troy and Daddy's visiting Uncle Joey for the weekend."

"You know I can never say no to a date with you."

She giggles.

"Good. Can we go after we take off our masks?"

"Sure thing, Sweet Pea. I'm *starving.*"

My post baby body is weird. None of my dresses fit me anymore and I've been too lazy to work out and slim down. I birthed a baby, damn it! I survived my ex-boyfriend. I deserve a little leeway. But my *new* boyfriend is sweet and had a better fitting dress delivered when he heard we were going out tonight.

"FaceTime me. I want to see how beautiful you look in it," he says on speakerphone while I finish up my lipstick.

"Later. I'm exhausted. This is the first time I'm putting makeup on in a while. I forgot how tedious this was."

"I assure you, you're sexy without the makeup."

I stop in my tracks and smirk in the mirror.

"I thought you said 'sexy' was a word you used to build a barrier to women."

"It was. But you're everything, Ace. Beautiful. Stunning. *Sexy.* Delicious."

My cheeks heat, sending it down below. I wish he were here. I miss him so much. Once my lipstick is on, I slip on the dusty purple, wrap dress and some black heels. The skin on my arms are loose and flappy. I *hate* the way I look. I don't know what he sees.

"Get out of your head, Ace. You are the most beautiful and bad ass woman I've ever come to know. And, I love you."

"Don't make me cry. It took me forever to get this dressed up."

He chuckles.

"I'll see you tomorrow, baby. Don't forget to take a picture. I want to fall asleep to your face tonight."

"I love you. Talk to you soon."

I race out to the living room and find Zoey dressed in the pretty floral dress she wore on our first date with Derek. She holds a new book in her hands, one that we picked up earlier today.

"Ready to go, Zo?"

She dogears her page and sets the book down on the coffee table. Her eyes light up at the sight of my dress.

"Can I take a picture of you? You're so pretty."

Like father like daughter.

"Sure thing, babe." I hand her my phone and pose obnoxiously so I can send it to Derek later. He'll appreciate the ugly funny face I make.

"Let's go. I'm so excited!" She races over to the door and swings it open. I'm surprised when I find Chris waiting on my front porch.

"Hey, what are you doing here?"

Chris grins at my question and grins at Zoey.

"The first day you and Derek met, he thought you were some rando trying to mooch off of our security."

Oh. Cool.

"Um..."

"When he realized you were *the* Aria McKenzie, he felt bad for berating you. And then at the barbeque, when Charlotte, he thought you needed help. Turns out you're a bad ass and didn't need a damn thing from him."

"Well...you're damn right about that. But I don't understand what this has to do with anything. Can it wait 'til tomorrow? Zo and I are going out to dinner."

He holds my hand in his and squeezes.

"For so long I hoped you'd come back home. I wanted you to see that you belong here, even though our family is pushy, overprotective, and annoying."

I giggle. That's putting it mildly.

"But I'm happy you're home. I'm even happier you found a man who loves you. Truly, freely, and unconditionally loves you."

"Chris..."

"Come on. There's more."

I glance at Zoey who is vibrating with excitement. She follows on with a grin that goes from ear to ear.

Annie meets me in the middle of the paved road *without my baby.* She better not have forgotten him!

"Where's Troy?"

Annie gives me a shit eating grin as she rolls her eyes. "Don't worry about Troy."

How can I not!?

"Annie—"

"Derek knew you were the one when we went to Rico's."

My heart stops beating my chest.

"What?"

"He was testing the waters. He wanted to see if you liked him too. And you did. But he wanted to respect your healing. He wasn't going to push himself on you if you weren't ready. He was even more sure when you watched the International Space Station with him and Zoey. He thought it was cute when you cried."

Oh, god. That wasn't cute.

"Why are you telling me this? You guys said you liked him. He's been lovely to me. I'm not breaking up with him."

Annie laughs.

"Sorry for interrupting, Christopher. I want to see too."

Chris winks and waves us along.

My calves scream in my heels when we climb the hill to Momma and Daddy's house. I'm going to carjack one of their trucks so I don't have to walk all the way back. Jo grins from the porch and waves to us as we approach.

"Well don't the two of you look *gorgeous!*"

Zoey grins.

"She does, doesn't she? Dad picked a pretty dress."

My cheeks flush at Zoey's compliment.

"Baby, did you know when I opened the shelter, I *always* knew you were going to be my partner in it?"

"What is with everyone today? Did I do something wrong? Is Daddy pissed because I've been shirking my feed duties and you're all buttering me up so you don't have to hear me cry later?"

Annie giggles and shakes her head.

"You have done so much, sweetheart. You've made a great life for yourself outside of abuse. You've already helped hundreds of women create their new beginning. You've done nothing but put smiles on everyone's faces."

It hasn't always been like that.

"When you told Derek about the grant from the Live Oaks Foundation, he was so proud of you. But he didn't want to tell you because if he did, you'd run in the other direction. He was determined to keep you around."

And later that day, Charlie shot at him and Joey. I almost lost him. It was when I knew I was falling *hard* for him.

"He said when you jumped on him that day when he came back, he was going to sail to the ends of the Earth if it meant you were safe."

My bottom lip wobbles and I already feel my makeup smudging. "Come on, guys...please don't make me cry."

"Head inside, honey. Know I love you." She kisses my cheek.

What the fuck is happening? Am I in trouble?

I head inside the house and find Nate at the kitchen table. My heart soars. I wasn't even expecting him! He stands up with a wide grin, and suddenly, Tanner, Logan, and *Joey* walk out from the kitchen.

What. The. Actual. Fuck.

"Little sister!" Tanner exclaims. They all hug me tight. I marvel at the fact they're so dressed up. All of them. Suits with ties, cleaned up facial hair and sparkles in their eyes.

"When I met you, Aria, I knew you were special. And when Bubba saw that same spark, something inside me told me you were going to be perfectly fine," says Nate.

"You're the only woman who put Zoey before herself. We know why you left that night. It was to protect our girl." Joey grins at Zoey who holds tightly onto my hand.

"You tamed an untamable beast," Logan adds.

"You gave him his heart back," Tanner concludes.

"You guys...what's happening?"

"Come on, darlin'! Time's a-wastin'!" Momma singsongs at the back door. I reluctantly pass the boys, and they end up joining the party behind me. It reminds me of *Love Actually—Oh my god!*

Momma catches onto my realization and gently pats my hand as she leads me out to the back patio. Daddy sits at the table with Troy in his lap. Troy belly laughs when he takes Daddy's hat off. It's weird to see my dad smile so big—especially since this baby wasn't welcome a few months ago.

"Have a seat, Peanut."

I glance behind me and everyone is gone except Momma.

I sit down beside her. Troy immediately starts to reach for me when he sees me. My big baby is a total sweetheart which has given me relief. He's nothing like Charlie.

"I met Derek a few years ago. I knew Nate first, but then I found out

Derek married Emily and moved here, so I offered him a job. You were gone already, and he was always a hermit. There was no way the two of you would come together."

"But then I surprised you by coming home."

He chuckles and shrugs. "I always said you're unpredictable. You keep everyone on their toes."

That's one way to put it.

"He loves you, you know."

"Yeah? What makes you say that?"

"Look around, Aria."

He motions behind him, and it's then I realize the giant tent behind us. I move to stand up, but Daddy stops me.

"I'm sorry for not giving you enough credit. I'm sorry for constantly comparing the three of you. It's not fair to you. But I want you to know, Aria Louise, I love you. It's impossible to tell you how much. You deserve happiness. You deserve *life.*"

He gently kisses my forehead and helps me up.

"Come on. I think you know what's next."

Momma grabs my other hand and leads me up to the tent. The townspeople fill the tent, half of them staring at me with contempt, the other half smiling because they're too smart to listen to the busybodies around town. Jackie meets me at the edge of the tent wearing a beautiful, black, floor length gown.

"Hey, you."

"Jackie…"

"I didn't think he was in this for the right reasons. Not at first. But I know he's a good man. And he *loves* you fiercely." She wraps her long arms around me. Derek stands in the middle of the tent, his hair closely cropped, wearing a tux.

He's so handsome. *I'm* the lucky one.

"We all do, Peanut. Jay couldn't make it, but he knows this is happening. We love you so much. You deserve the world."

Daddy gently nudges me along, and when we're halfway to Derek, they drop my hands. I turn in confusion and they silently urge me on.

Derek reaches his hands out to me. I can't help it. I run the rest of the way and jump into his arms and sob.

"Did I do it right, Daddy?" Zoey asks, appearing beside me.

"Yeah, babe. You did great."

Zoey grins mischievously and stands beside Derek.

"I lied to you."

No, this is going so perfect. Don't ruin it.

He sets me down and pushes my flyaways behind my ear.

"I didn't leave to see Joey. *But,* I did bring them here for this. They're a part of our story just like this town is."

Tears stream down my face, my makeup is ruined for sure. I hope nobody is taking pictures.

"I didn't want to get married again, Ace. I thought marriage was a prison sentence. But then you came wandering into a barn wearing flip flops and walked right up to a psycho horse I was sure was going to break your toes. My life has been changed ever since then—for the better."

He wipes the tears from my eyes with his thumbs, his grin so wide and proud.

"You haven't had the easiest life. I wanted to remind you that you have people around you who love the *shit* out of you. You deserve someone who will tell you how much you're loved, valued, and appreciated every single day of your life."

He sinks to one knee.

God, I was expecting this! Why am I crying?

"Aria *Louise* McKenzie, yes, I asked Tanner ages ago to find out what your middle name is, will you make me the happiest and luckiest man in the world by being my wife?"

"And my mom?" Zoey adds.

"Yes. Absolutely I will."

EPILOGUE PART TWO

ANNIE

Derek slides the ring on Aria's finger and the sigh of relief amongst our family crushes the tent like a tidal wave. Aria is safe. She is with a man who loves her for exactly who she is. She's a *mom* and a great one at that!

A year ago, this was a pipe dream. The way she came home, battered and broken, I honestly thought she would never return to the land of the living. The sister I knew to be quiet, yet confident was a shell of her former self.

And now, she's the embodiment of pure happiness. I can't be happier for her.

My phone vibrates in the pocket of my dress. I don't need to look at the screen to know who it is. It's my own love of my life. The man I've kept close to my chest because my family won't understand. They'll stick their noses in where they don't belong, not to mention shame us for practically being family.

I was fourteen years old when I realized I had feelings for Jay Parker. He was my extra brother, the honorary McKenzie even though his real last name is the equivalent of cursing in front of your momma.

"Hey, handsome," I answer.

"Hello, beautiful. Did she say yes?"

I giggle. "Of course she said yes. She's got the fairy tale ending and she's the happiest I've ever seen her."

Jay sighs dreamily. "Good. I want her to be happy."

My stomach knots, because *I* want to be happy too. I don't want to keep our relationship in the dark much longer. I want to be able to shout my relationship to the world.

"You're going to get your fairy tale ending soon, baby. I promise you."

"I love you, Jay. It doesn't matter when I get it."

"But it's not enough," he counters, though the smile in his voice is contagious. "I'm getting out on VEERP."

My eyebrows raise and my heart soars to my throat. Voluntary Enlistment Early Release Program is what it's called. It means he's coming home.

"Are you serious?"

"What do you say, McKenzie? Is it time to come out of the closet?"

AUTHOR'S NOTE

-Phew!- I *never* thought I would be strong enough to get Aria's story out there. To say that it took every morsel of will power and strength I had, is an understatement. *But,* it's out there. It's *finally* out there!

We covered some heavy topics in this story. And with that, I wanted to include some resources if you ever feel that you need them. I know a lot of the time we feel alone, that there isn't a soul out there who understands what we're going through.

I can confidently tell you that is not the case. Someone understands. Someone has been through it. And someone will *always* be there to hold your hand.

I hope you were able to find comfort in Aria and Derek's story! As for me, I'm so glad they can finally stand in the sun!

National Suicide Prevention Hotline: 800-273-8255

The National Domestic Violence Hotline: 1-800-799-SAFE (7233)

Planned Parenthood: 1-800-230-PLAN (7526)

ACKNOWLEDGMENTS

There were so many times I wanted to quit this book. However, with every book, it isn't *just* written by an author. They lean on the people around them. They gain strength and encouragement from their friends, family, and colleagues. So, without further ado:

To my husband, Taylor - My dude! Thank you so much for being my rock through this book. I know this unearthed a lot of unprocessed trauma for me which made for some interesting conversation. You have no idea how much I love you, and how much I appreciate you being my constant. You're the bomb dot com!

Jessica - Jess, thank you so much for being my sounding board. You have read the early versions of this story and if it weren't for your kind and encouraging words, I probably wouldn't have finished this. Thank you for always being there for me, and especially holding my hand through all of this!

To my betas, Jessica, Scarlette, Andrea, and Lauren - You guys! Thank you so much for beta reading this beast! I was so nervous sending this to you and your feedback and suggestions are appreciated and loved!

Kimberly Steinke - Oh my gosh. Where do I even begin? I'm so happy I came across you in a Facebook group! Thank you so much for loving Aria and Derek, and reading this for me. I appreciate all you do and your feedback has made this book what it is!

To my editor, Amy Briggs - Amy! We did it again! Thank you so much for everything you do. Your expertise and (hilarious) comments on my manuscript has been life changing. Thank you for putting up with my 10,000 emails and holding my hand!

To Brieanne - Brieeeee! Thank you for proofreading this for me!

You're my bestie for the restie, and my confidant. Thank you for letting me lean on you this past year. I love and appreciate you!

To Janet - Janet! Thank you so much for working in tandem with Brie! Your notes were so helpful! Thank you so much for your feedback!

Laura Mowery - When I joined Instagram at the beginning of 2021, I was petrified of reaching out to other people. And when I found out you were also a Marine Wife, well, I felt like our stars aligned! Thank you so much for listening to me vent and distracting me from my own self doubt. So happy I get to call you a friend!

Last, but not least, my friends and family - Thank you all for supporting me through this new journey as an author. Writing was something I always kept under wraps in fear of being judged. But you guys have really rallied for me, and you have no idea how much that means to me. Thank you for the preorders, for sharing my work with your friends, and being there for me. I love you.

ABOUT THE AUTHOR

Dillon Bancroft is a Contemporary Romance Author based in Tampa, Florida. She was always considered a dreamer, and was constantly scolded as a student to get her head out of the clouds and pay attention.

She is a mother to two crazy girls and wife to a former Marine who has enhanced her vocabulary in the worst ways, but has supported her in *all* of her hair-brained ideas.

She is a sucker for second chance romances, puppies, and cheese Christmas movies. She watches entirely too much TV and quotes very obscure lines in popular TV shows.

LOOKING TO CONNECT?

Do you want to stay in the know and receive behind the scenes musings, deleted scenes, and upcoming project updates? Make sure to sign up for my newsletter and follow me on social media!

Email: dillon@dillonbancroft.com

LinkTree: https://linktr.ee/dillon.bancroft

Website: www.dillonbancroft.com

Bancroft Boulevard Facebook Group: https://www.facebook.com/groups/bancroftblvd

ALSO BY DILLON BANCROFT

Back and Forth

Made in the USA
Columbia, SC
29 April 2022